WARRIOR'S KNIFE

ERIC THOMSON

The Warrior's Knife

First printing 2017

Published in Canada
By Sanddiver Books
ISBN: 978-1-791811-85-3

— One —

I've always enjoyed the stunned silence triggered by my unannounced appearance, especially when accompanied by one of my most imposing and memorable detectives, Master Sergeant Destine Bonta. As we entered the offices of the Financial Crimes Division, two dozen gray-uniformed Constabulary investigators, many with long years of service, froze in place, their eyes wide with shock.

Though neither Bonta nor I wore a uniform, not even when making an arrest, they knew who we were. And they knew our arrival signaled the end of a cop's career.

I headed for the private corner office occupied by the division's commanding officer and entered without knocking. Behind me, Sergeant Bonta shouted, in her surprisingly deep voice, "Everyone stay where you are until Chief Superintendent Morrow is done. No one leaves, no one makes a call, and no one touches their terminal."

The inspector standing by Commissioner Haylian's desk, tablet in hand, immediately fell silent. Both he and Haylian stared at me with disbelieving eyes, too stunned for words. I pointed at the inspector and then jerked my thumb toward the door.

"Out."

When he didn't move, I glanced over my shoulder at Bonta and said, "Take the inspector to his desk, Sergeant."

"Now see here," Haylian cut in, his tone almost rising to a shout, "you'll not be giving orders in my division and definitely not in my office."

Bonta ignored the commissioner with the same stoic expression she wore every time we made an arrest and wrapped a long-fingered hand around the inspector's upper arm.

"Come with me, sir. I'm sure you don't want to witness this."

Once she'd hustled the younger man out and closed the door behind her, I turned my gaze back on Haylian, who was staring at me with incredulity rapidly metamorphosing into anger.

"Commissioner Joel Haylian, I am Chief Superintendent Caelin Morrow of the Professional Compliance Bureau, and I am placing you under arrest on charges of corruption, dereliction of duty and behavior unbecoming a member of the Commonwealth Constabulary. Please stand."

"I will most certainly not. Who the hell do you think you are, Morrow?"

A grim smile greeted his outburst. "I'm the one who invited you for an interview three floors up, in the PCB offices at oh-nine-hundred this morning, to discuss the professional compliance investigation into your conduct. Since you didn't present yourself as requested and it is now ten-hundred hours, I have no choice but to carry out your arrest in full view of the Financial Crimes Division."

His face twisted into an unattractive sneer. "This is bullshit."

Haylian wasn't wrong. I didn't need to arrest him. I could just as well have conducted the interview here or used a less drastic method of persuasion. But I've found that the higher the rank, the harsher I had to be when they didn't cooperate.

"You are nevertheless under arrest. You do not have to say anything. But, it may harm your defense if you do not mention when questioned something which you later rely on in court. Anything you do say may be given in evidence. You have the right to ask that an advisor from the Commonwealth Constabulary Senior Officers' Association be present during the interview."

I paused to let my words sink in, then said, "Now that I've cautioned you, your choice is to come with me voluntarily or be cuffed and hauled away by Sergeant Bonta. Your call."

Haylian climbed to his feet, his face turning a lovely shade of red. "This is entirely inappropriate. Someone of my rank or senior to me should be handling this, not a damned chief superintendent with personality issues. I'm a flag officer, for crying out loud."

"Shall I call Sergeant Bonta in with the restraints, sir?" I asked in a deadpan tone, ignoring his insult. "I've cautioned you, and will charge you with resisting arrest if you do not follow my orders. And I'm sure you're aware the courtesy of being interviewed by an investigator of equal or superior rank doesn't apply to professional compliance issues. I am the senior PCB officer for the Rim Sector and have full authority to charge anyone, whatever his or her rank may be. The sole courtesy I'll extend is to let you walk up to the PCB interview room unrestrained and under your own power. Unless you'd rather do the perp walk in front of your staff."

If eyes spat plasma, I'd be a charred, smoking heap of incinerated protoplasm at that moment, and it took some effort to restrain any show of emotion, such as a mocking smile. Haylian wasn't the first senior officer I'd charged with corruption, but so far, he was proving to be the most graceless.

"Very well," he finally said through gritted teeth as he reached for the jacket draped over a side chair. "Let's sort this out, so I can return to my duties."

"A wise choice, sir," I replied. I caught Bonta's eye through the glass wall separating Haylian's office from the rest of the division's desks and nodded once, the signal our suspect would come voluntarily.

We crossed the bullpen in silence, under the incredulous eyes of Haylian's entire staff. All, that is, except for a chief inspector trying hard to keep a pleased smile from tugging at her lips.

Bonta tossed an "As you were," over her shoulder before following us out to the seventh floor's central corridor. A burst of puzzled conversation chased us to the lifts until the closing door cut it off.

The Professional Compliance Bureau owned most of the tenth floor, sharing it only with the Rim Sector HQ building's environmental systems. Being summoned to the tenth had become a byword for career-ending trouble long before my arrival here. Our isolation from the rest of the staff and the aura of dread it gave us suited me. We might live under the same roof as the other Rim Sector divisions, but we weren't part of their family. On the contrary.

Bonta took Haylian to an interview room and left him there to wait, alone and without the offer of coffee or juice, while I visited the office kitchen for a quick cup. Letting suspects stew made them easier to crack, and Haylian, with his highly developed sense of flag officer entitlement, should be thoroughly annoyed by the time I started the interview. Irritated, if not downright angry people talked more than they should, even cops. Especially cops.

"That's one unhappy puppy in there," Bonta said, joining me by the dispenser. "You should have seen the stare he just gave me when I said you'd join him in a few minutes."

"Good. If Haylian was putting on a show of confidence, I'd be worried we missed something during the investigation."

Bonta snorted. "Not a chance, Chief. Do you intend to wait for Inspector Galdi before tackling him?"

I shook my head. "No. It'll be just you and me. Inspector Galdi needs to secure Haylian's data files and case repository now we have him in custody. I'd rather not see a repeat of the Grint case."

"Roger that, sir. I remember Inspector Galdi telling me how someone did a real number on the evidence while Superintendent Rowan tried to bring Grint in." Bonta raised her cup in salute. "Here's to another scumbag sitting in your parlor."

"Try to avoid feeling excessive joy at the sight of a one-star finally getting his comeuppance."

"The higher they are..." she replied, grinning with bloodthirsty delight.

We sipped the bland brew in companionable silence for nearly ten minutes.

I allowed myself one piece of the morning's sticky bun offering and then watched Bonta devour the rest with gusto. Granted, she wasn't a small woman, but with the office almost empty thanks to cases taking my investigators all over the sector, it was still a healthy heaping of sugared dough.

I glanced at my timepiece and emptied my mug. “Shall we?”

— Two —

Perps always tried to brazen it out when facing me during the interview that marked the end of their careers. Some blustered, a few threatened, many sat there, smiling as if I had just made the most significant blunder of my life. Now that he had recovered a measure of composure, Commissioner Joel Haylian turned out to be one of the latter.

He ran the Constabulary's Financial Crimes Division for the Commonwealth Rim Sector, where dirty money ruled, and figured he could reach out to friends in every corner of the Service including mine.

Apparently, over three decades as a cop hadn't been long enough to teach him that Professional Compliance Bureau officers had no friends. Anywhere. There's a reason they called us the Firing Squad, and it wasn't because of our winning personalities, but because of our ability to end the most promising careers, including those of flag officers.

The day they moved me to the PCB without warning, let alone asking my opinion, I thought at first my career had ended. I initially took the transfer as a message from on high that said, Caelin Morrow, it was time to find yourself a new job. But I've been in the Constabulary since my late teens, and with no family, friends, or a life outside the Service, I accepted my new responsibilities and soon came to enjoy the work.

Since we investigate other cops, the military, and politicians, we have to be the incorruptibles. That means we're the ones with nothing left to lose, the ones who aren't afraid to get on anyone's wrong side and don't care about consequences.

We're the ones who have no qualms about moving from planet to planet and system to system, dispensing justice to those who should have known better than to cross the law.

The bureau won't transfer me from the Rim to one of the more comfortable core systems anytime soon. I had become highly proficient at finding those who sullied the uniform and was particularly skilled when it came to corrupt senior officers like Commissioner Haylian, who knew all the tricks, something my commanding officer appreciated.

But he also preferred me where I was, dealing with the dirty cops and politicos who took advantage of the Rim Sector's gray zone to amass enough riches for whatever perversions drove them.

Dirty military? Well, by the time they called us in, it meant they figured their guy or gal wasn't in the frame but someone in the chain of command or the political establishment wanted to hang them anyway. The Fleet had a more direct way of dealing with those who pled guilty when caught.

The military used us because we were the impartial investigators. When we exonerated them, it meant there was never a doubt about innocence in the first place. While the Firing Squad rarely shot anyone, we've left plenty of dead careers in our wake.

That's why no one ever left Professional Compliance. Once you were in, you retired from it, either on a pension or in a coffin.

I still had a few decades before I could afford to quit. And once I did, then what? No one in the policing business would hire a Firing Squad 'rat' as many liked to call us. Rent-a-cop outfits weren't choosy, but who wanted that after a life spent kicking ass while holding some of the sleekest handguns ever designed. So I took the cases they gave me and worked them through to the bitter end.

Commissioner Haylian might have believed he had enough connections to squirm out of my grasp, but he'd soon realize that even though I'm his junior by two ranks, I held his future in my hands. That feeling of power was one of the few compensations of a job where everyone else looked at me with suspicion if not outright hostility. Seeing the realization I had them dead to rights dawn on their smug faces came in a close second.

The man who sat across the table from us with an infuriating smirk on his lips, faced charges of corruption and a career ending in disgrace. And for no better reason than his inability to keep it in his pants.

It was a familiar story. A cop in a sensitive position forgot discretion and found himself trapped by the wrong people who then used creative blackmail.

He might have been a decent officer, a good investigator once, but now, he was merely another uniformed politician who believed in his ability to write his own exemption from the law.

Considering the amount of wealth that flowed across the Commonwealth's porous borders, it took someone with a strong sense of morality to investigate financial crimes on the Rim. The morals that kept one from bedding the wives of influential planetary politicians with mob connections.

"Commissioner Joel Haylian," Sergeant Bonta said, "do you wish to have an advisor from the Senior Officers' Association present?"

"I do not," he replied in a brusque tone without looking at her. Instead, he examined me as if I were a piece of roadkill before saying, "Ask your damn questions, Morrow."

"Tell me, Commissioner Haylian, why did you risk your career for an ordinary piece of ass?"

— Three —

My opener was deliberately crude. I hoped it would further infuriate a man who professed to believe in esthetic refinement — not for its own sake, to be sure, but as a way to enter the more rarefied strata of society.

"I don't know what you mean, Chief Superintendent," he replied in a calm tone that belied the anger I could sense like a physical presence in the room. My ten-minute coffee break had been perfectly timed. "But I deplore your lack of manners."

"And I deplore senior officers who sell their souls for sordid liaisons. I hope she was worth it. By the time the indictment comes through, you'll be looking at ten years in a penal colony. The liaisons in prison are equally sordid but a lot less consensual."

Former cops found life in jail especially hard. Their long-term survival rate wasn't anything the Correctional Service bragged about, and it wasn't only because of inmate on inmate violence. After a few years of protective custody — really no better than solitary confinement — many hastened their own demise hoping to make better choices in their next incarnations.

Haylian's attempt to climb on his high horse was unimpressive. But then, he wasn't an impressive man to begin with, merely one who'd risen through the ranks by sucking up to the right people and making himself useful to those with power. Digging into his life as we had done over the course of many weeks left little to the imagination and had shattered any remaining illusions I might have held about merit rising to the top.

"My dear Chief Superintendent, you and I know there's nothing on which to base a supposed indictment. Insulting me won't make that fact vanish; though once you're done, I'll make sure you enjoy the fruits of your discourtesy. And arresting me in my own office? That'll cost."

I pulled a tablet from my pocket and placed it on the table. These were the moments I lived for, when a perp stared down his nose at me as if I was a cockroach, seconds before I showed him my evidence. And it was always enough evidence for an early and involuntary retirement to a nice cold cell on the far end of frozen fuck all.

"Those three investigations into Louis Sorne's business dealings quashed at your orders in the last year are a sound basis for charges of corruption, don't you think? How did it go? Sorne offered you his wife for fun and games in return for consideration, was that it?"

Haylian eyed my tablet for a few heartbeats, but remained silent.

"Or did he catch you between her legs," I continued, "and offered a choice between a gelding without anesthesia and closing an eye to his more questionable financial arrangements? Or better yet, did you fall into a honey trap with Hannah Sorne as bait? Even though she's the cheap kind, I bet she knew how to make your toes curl."

I touched my tablet and called up summaries of the investigations he'd buried and tilted it so he could see the screen. For the first time, I noted genuine worry in his eyes as he realized someone in his division must have squealed to the PCB. Commissioners, even here where the law was sometimes elastic, didn't always command the respect they wanted.

Haylian had made the mistake of pissing off one of his chief inspectors over a minor disagreement on an unrelated investigation. The words arrogant asshole were used to describe Haylian's general attitude toward his staff.

Unfortunately for him, the chief inspector in question already suspected Haylian's good friend, Louis Sorne, one of Cimmeria's top politicians, of extensive money laundering. When she discovered the commissioner's sexual relationship with Hannah Sorne through some after-hours sleuthing, I received the call.

Even if Haylian wasn't dirty, his job as commanding officer of the Rim's Financial Crimes Division meant he had to make a confidential declaration to my office whenever he began an extramarital relationship. It would have covered his ass in case someone took strong objection to the liaison.

He had violated a dozen regulations; enough to see him relieved of command at the very least and encouraged to take early retirement. Interfering in ongoing investigations because he screwed a rich, criminally connected prick's oversexed wife was about to earn him a uniform very different from Constabulary gray.

"Who accused me of having an inappropriate relationship with Hannah Sorne? Louis Sorne? Certainly not. We're social acquaintances and move in the same circles."

"So he offered Hannah up, did he?" I smirked at him. "Like a common prostitute? Can't say I'm surprised. Politicians are natural pimps although Hannah doesn't strike me as having the assets of a successful whore. She's neither young enough, pretty enough or pleasant enough. But I suppose with the lights out, technique is what counts, right?"

I had the satisfaction of seeing Haylian's nostrils flare with barely suppressed fury. He glanced at Sergeant Bonta, who sat silently beside me like a bronze statue, her eyes locked on the suspect, doing an excellent job of making him feel uncomfortable with her scrutiny. Then he turned to me again.

"Do you realize you're talking about one of the wealthiest and most powerful men on Cimmeria and his spouse, Chief Superintendent? Words have consequences where he and his like are concerned, even for Firing Squad rodents such as you."

I ignored the deliberate insult because I'd heard every variation on the theme. A self-satisfied smirk briefly twisted Haylian's thin lips. I ignored that as well.

"Actions also produce consequences, Commissioner, and Sorne's as dirty as they come. We'll eventually nab him, once HQ appoints a new commanding officer for your division, one more interested in doing his job than plumbing the depths of perversion with another man's life partner."

"Oh?" His confident smile returned. "And where am I heading? As far as I know, my tenure here isn't coming to an end until next year."

"Do you think we would be talking if I didn't have enough evidence to see you relieved of command?"

That sublime moment of truth was nearing. Even after years in this job, I could still feel the thrill of cornering my prey. Screwing every Hannah Sorne in the galaxy couldn't offer a tenth of the pleasure.

"Please don't take me for a cretin," he replied, putting on that self-important air the less personable flag officers reserved for browbeating those they considered village idiots. "Your so-called evidence is nothing but unrelated facts, Chief Superintendent."

The man knew how to bluster, but on a scale of one to ten, he barely broke a seven. I had seen bent cops hit a solid ten, which didn't do them much good, but watching the dirty bastards try was part of the entertainment.

"So you deny having a sexual relationship with Hannah Sorne."

"Of course I do." The aura of self-righteousness he tried to use as a cloak was a nice touch.

I reached for my tablet again and made sure Haylian could clearly see its screen. These were the moments I lived for, considering I found little to entertain me beyond my job.

Haylian's choleric face turned from puce to a deathly white so quickly that I almost missed the transformation.

"If you had declared your relationship, Commissioner, then this little video of you and Hannah Sorne getting it off would mean nothing. But you didn't do so and placed yourself in a vulnerable position, thereby violating paragraphs three hundred and forty to three hundred and fifty-two of the Constabulary Code of Conduct. A mere patrol sergeant might escape serious consequences.

The head of the Rim Sector Financial Crimes Division can't."

"How?" He seemed to have difficulty finding his words. I was always amazed at how quickly they fell off their high horse once I placed the evidence before them.

"An anonymous source contacted the PCB and told us that a commissioner might have put himself in a compromising position, thereby threatening the integrity of the Constabulary. I obtained a warrant and put a recording device in the premises you used for your trysts with Hannah Sorne. We have several recordings, each as damning as the others. They're great when it comes to unimpeachable evidence, but the entertainment factor is rather low, even for amateur stuff. I doubt either you or Hannah Sorne has much of a future in the erotica business. And with that, your tenure as commanding officer is over, no matter what a disciplinary board may find once it reviews your case."

Haylian stared at me in disbelief, unable to utter a single word.

"Orders relieving you of command and appointing your deputy on an interim basis should come from Wyvern within a day or two. But in the meantime, I'm suspending you from duty without pay, under paragraph four-hundred ten of the Constabulary Code of Conduct. Of course, we will pursue criminal charges as well. Conspiring with Louis Sorne to pervert the course of justice isn't something the Chief Constable will overlook for the good of the Service."

The truth concerning his situation dawned on him, and that look of incredulity turned to one of understanding. A warrant to record his activities would have required at least an assistant chief constable's sign-off, maybe even the Rim Sector's deputy chief constable. He no longer had friends in high places. If they had ever existed other than in his imagination.

I sat back and waited. Nine out of ten inevitably came to the same conclusion. Haylian looked up at me after less than a minute.

"I can give you Louis Sorne," he said, "in return for letting me retire without indictment."

And just like that, I owned his soul.

— Four —

My position as head of the Professional Compliance Bureau's Rim Sector detachment placed me in a strange situation. I reported directly to Deputy Chief Constable Hammett, the PCB's commanding officer, through a chain of command hermetically sealed off from every other.

But he was back on Wyvern, several dozen light years away. Here, on Cimmeria, the most senior Constabulary officer was Deputy Chief Constable Maras, commander of the entire Rim Sector Group, and emphatically not in my chain of command.

Since we both reported separately to Constabulary HQ, it made us, in a few respects, quasi-equals even if the size of our respective units varied by a few orders of magnitude, mine being vanishingly small compared to hers. But because a deputy chief constable was a three-star appointment, several levels above a chief superintendent, I found treating Maras with as much deference as I did my real boss was prudent.

Unlike Commissioner Haylian, Maras actually had powerful allies who could make my life a misery. Besides, she and Hammett saw eye-to-eye on many matters, meaning any complaints Maras made against me would find my boss lending a sympathetic ear.

That's why her office was my first stop after listening to Haylian spill his story. To the annoyance of many officers more senior in rank, I had almost automatic access to the deputy chief constable. But it was mainly because she wanted to hear about dirty cops in her group as soon as I found them and not because she liked me.

I think she tolerated my unit as a necessary evil, and that made her more agreeable than most in her command. She was no rank conscious stuffed shirt either and acknowledged the reality of our relationship.

I could live with that and took pains to keep her happy. Fortunately, I knew her public image didn't mask the sort of peccadilloes that would make her the target of a future PCB investigation. As a result, I had no qualms about sharing details of my cases. It helped keep her supportive of my work.

Her adjutant looked up from a cluttered desk when I walked in, and a grimace of annoyance briefly crossed his face. I saw that reaction a lot when I showed up, whether or not they had a guilty conscience. You learned to accept the suspicion, dislike, and fear as part of the job. Some PCB officers relished the unspoken power we exercised, but I hadn't sunk that low — yet.

"If the DCC's available, I have an update on the Haylian matter."

"One moment," he replied, tapping his console screen. We waited in silence for Maras to answer, neither of us interested in small talk, until he received an all-clear from his boss. "You may enter."

DCC Maras' office could have easily held the annual garrison ball, an event I did my best to avoid. Not that I didn't look fetching in my formal mess uniform, but I was about as socially inclined as a Sister of the Void. Besides, who wanted to be seen partying with the local Firing Squad CO? Just walking up to her desk at the far end of the sprawling room gave me my daily dose of physical training.

Our HQ building had been the previous government house, the seat of the colonial administration before Cimmeria gained its independence. When the Cimmerian bureaucracy moved into newer accommodations, the Constabulary had inherited a ten-story structure with offices designed to impress the hoi polloi back in the old days. Fittingly, the sector commander ended up in the former colonial governor's reception room.

A dense stand of flags backed Maras' desk, while various awards, commendations, and paramilitary scenes decorated the walls. There were days when I thought we remembered our origins as a branch of the Armed Services with an unseemly amount of reverence.

The infantry training we still underwent as part of our recruit course didn't help sever the link. But more than a few colonies had nothing other than a Constabulary regiment as its sole police and defense force so that connection to our past wasn't about to evaporate.

Since I seldom wore a uniform, I rarely bothered with the military-inspired drill when reporting to a senior officer. However, I made an exception for Maras and executed a credible halt three paces from her desk before standing rigidly at attention while reciting the age-old words the Constabulary shared with its Fleet cousins. "Chief Superintendent Morrow reporting to the DCC on the Haylian investigation as ordered, sir."

"I gather you're here because he's spilling his guts," she said by way of greeting after she waved me to a chair. "Well done."

"His former division will soon have a significant amount of evidence to support Louis Sorne's indictment."

"And I'm sure they'll do it right this time so we can finally extinguish his destructive influence on Cimmerian affairs. Did you make a deal?"

"Early retirement, effective the moment he's told us everything. He avoids jail, but it wouldn't surprise me if Sorne's friends caught up with him one day. At the very least, Haylian will spend the rest of his life looking over his shoulder. As punishments go, it fits the crime, especially since he came clean in the end."

Maras nodded. "Agreed. Why did he go bad?"

"He claims they trapped him with a honeypot scheme. I think he simply lost control of his senses one evening. Hannah Sorne is known for her appetites and he's her type — the successful, arrogant asshole with influence. Plus, he's thirty years younger than her husband. Either way, Haylian will see a massive idiot stare back at him every time he shaves. There's no sugarcoating what he did."

The DCC shook her head and sighed.

"He would have received his second star and a plum assistant chief constable post at HQ next year without this complaint."

"The Service dodged a bullet there. Owning a mole at the heart of the Constabulary would have delighted Sorne. Might I suggest the chief inspector who lodged the complaint receive a reward commensurate to the harm she prevented by speaking up?"

"Hard to do without people wondering. You know what the regular members think of rats, even though Haylian was an egotistical, vain, and corrupt sonofabitch, hated by most of his officers. But I will make sure her name is at the head of the list for the next promotion board. She should be a superintendent this time next year, which will put her well ahead of her peers."

That was one thing I liked about Maras. She gave a damn about her people, which wasn't as prevalent among the high and mighty as it should be. The Constabulary had a full complement of fools with stars on their shoulders who paid nothing more than lip service to the principles of leadership, and then only when necessary to help in their own advancement.

"I'm sure she'll be happy with early promotion, sir. Especially if she gets to stay with Financial Crimes in a supervisory role."

"Indeed." Maras nodded. Then she touched her display and turned it so I could read a new case summary.

"Your next job," she said, signaling our discussion of the Haylian case was over. Once I signed the investigation report, our soon to be former commissioner would no longer be my problem.

"The Cimmerian Gendarmerie has arrested a Navy commander on suspicion of murdering a Shrehari trade envoy on Aquilonia. Vice Admiral Kingsley, the flag officer commanding Sixth Fleet, kicked the case over to us the moment word reached him. Since it involves both a high-ranking officer and has a diplomatic angle, I'd say this is a Professional Compliance investigation and not one for the Major

Crimes Division. The details are on their way to Wyvern via a special subspace transmission, but it's a given DCC Hammett will want you to take the job. I suggest you book a seat on the next shuttle to Valerys Station and catch today's ferry to Aquilonia. The Fleet thinks this one is a high priority, and considering the circumstances, I can understand them wanting you on the case as quickly as possible, before it becomes an interstellar crisis."

— Five —

Cases involving senior Fleet officers were often more convoluted than those implicating high-level politicians caught with one hand in the till and the other one deep inside official secrets. But the military knew when to cover up, and when to open the kimono. And an open kimono became a job for someone like me or in this instance, a job for me, and me only.

Even if my teams weren't scattered to the four corners of the Rim Sector, I had to deal with the Fleet's problem personally, just as I had to lead the investigation of a senior officer like Joel Haylian. Because that's what the PCB detachment's commanding officer did.

I was one of the rare chief superintendents who didn't spend her life armpit-deep in administrivia, and that suited me just fine. The less time I spent in the corridors of Sector HQ being ignored by most of my colleagues from the other divisions, the better.

I left Inspector Arno Galdi, my senior wingman on the Haylian case, to finish the report and to answer any questions Maras or Hammett might have, with orders to join me as soon as possible. Master Sergeant Bonta already had two cases lined up, and I couldn't let those languish even further. A bit of corruption here and there became a lot of corruption everywhere if we allowed it to fester. That meant I would be alone for a time. Not ideal, but I didn't have enough people to handle everything.

After settling matters with my staff, I headed to the spaceport, hoping to make Valerys Station in time for the daily run to Aquilonia, the sector's primary free port on an airless moon orbiting Cimmeria's sister planet, Thule. I booked a first class berth on the ferry since the military would cover my bills while I solved their problem. If one of the Navy's bean counters objected, she could take it up with PCB HQ on Wyvern. It was an eighteen-hour trip, and I was damned if I would spend it in economy class.

As I crossed Valerys from the shuttle hangar to the central docking ring, an unremarkable man in a sober business suit stepped across my path. His eye movements were those of someone checking an image projected directly onto his retina from some unseen source hiding in the brim of his hat. I knew instantly he was comparing my face to something, and the smile on his lips proved that something was a picture of me.

When I swerved to pass him he said, "Louis Sorne sends his regards, Chief Superintendent Morrow, and wishes you a safe trip to Aquilonia."

Before his words registered, the man melted into the crowd and vanished. I saw no point in trying to catch him — he would be nothing more than a paid messenger. Besides, the ferry was leaving soon, and the encounter left me more puzzled than concerned.

Either Haylian got word of his detention out to his patron, or Sorne had a second mole inside HQ. I was betting on the latter. Haylian's arrest occurred less than eight hours ago. That meant the Financial Crimes Division might have another corrupt officer in its midst, and I faced a fresh investigation after dealing with the Aquilonia situation.

If this was Sorne's way of warning me off, he didn't grasp two essential things. First, I was no longer involved with the matter. Haylian's former division had taken over from the PCB. And second, I wasn't intimidated easily. High-ranking cops, politicians, and Navy officers have threatened me with all manner of retribution. None ever followed through once they realized retaliation only strengthened the case against them. Besides, Sorne was about to face more significant problems than me putting his second mole out of business.

Nevertheless, I called Arno before boarding the ferry and swore out an incident report. He would pass it on to the Financial Crimes team tasked with the Sorne investigation. Every contact with a suspect, even if it was through a third party, became part of the case file. Then, I did my best to forget the incident and focused on my next job. I had plenty of reading to do, most of it about the Shrehari Empire and Aquilonia Station itself.

The free port began life as a mining operation during humanity's first stab at colonizing Thule a century earlier. Like so many grandiose plans, the attempt to end the planet's ten million year slumber beneath a thick crust of ice failed miserably.

When the Thule Corporation went bankrupt, a mercantile syndicate bought Aquilonia for a song and convinced the Cimmerian government to grant them a free port charter. Although they made many enhancements over the decades, it remained a rough sort of place. The free porters neither liked nor trusted law enforcement, mainly thanks to Cimmeria imposing its planetary police force, the Gendarmerie on them. They liked Feds such as me even less.

After reasonably decent dining and a not so restful night's sleep, I took advantage of the first class lounge and admired the scenery through a large porthole.

Thule was once a brilliantly white orb, but the planet I saw as we maneuvered to land on Aquilonia was liberally dotted with black smudges. The second terraforming effort, started by the Shrehari during their long occupation of the Cimmeria system, had taken a more forceful approach and triggered massive volcanic eruptions via kinetic strikes from orbit.

I remembered reading somewhere that the Imperial Deep Space Fleet also used Thule as a planet-sized firing range for its starships. Although decried by the Commonwealth as a war crime back then, the results of their bombardment had turned into a planetologist's dream. Where else could you watch an entire ecosystem undergo such radical and rapid changes?

I took a good look at Aquilonia Station itself while we landed, and it didn't appear that much had changed on the surface since my last visit, years earlier. Set near the edge of an ancient crater on the tidally locked moon, the hexagonal facets of the free port's surface dome glittered in the sunlight reflected by Thule's icy surface.

To my eyes, it still seemed cold and desolate, no more hospitable than any artificial habitat on the Rim, but I knew the goods that passed through the port kept many a bank account warm. The Cimmeria system sat on the main shipping route between the Empire and the Commonwealth, and a large part of the two-way trade filtered through Aquilonia. Naturally, a portion of the profits stuck to both official and unofficial fingers.

We settled on a pad connected to one of two dozen docking arms radiating from a large hub that encircled the dome. The arm extruded a short gangway that latched onto the ferry's main airlock. A few minutes later, I stepped ashore along with my fellow passengers and walked down the long, bare passageway.

When I passed through the arrivals control gate, a lean, dark-complexioned man in his thirties, wearing Cimmerian Gendarmerie blue with a lieutenant's stripes on the collar, made a beeline for me.

"Chief Superintendent Morrow?" He seemed to hesitate, wondering whether a formal salute was in order. My rumpled civilian wardrobe must have stayed his hand. Not that I could manage a more martial air when in uniform, even though various Constabulary schools had made heroic attempts in the past, mostly in vain.

"Yes."

"I'm Lieutenant Thalman, sir. Major Pullar sends his regrets. He's unavoidably detained but will join you the moment he can."

Pullar — the guy in charge of law and order on Aquilonia. He wasn't around the last time I visited, but if he ran true to type, Pullar would be long in the tooth, disillusioned, and close to retirement. This place wasn't a prime career-enhancing assignment.

Judging by his relative youth, Thalman could be an exception to the rule. Maybe he played hide the salami with a Gendarmerie colonel's partner to end up here for all I knew. In my experience, cops everywhere shared the same problems with self-restraint when it came to sex and booze. Those two weaknesses alone shone brightly in a surprising number of my investigations.

"A pleasure, Lieutenant. How about you take me to the crime scene straightaway? I've retained a suite in the VIP section so we can drop off my luggage at the same time."

I wasn't about to deprive myself of what little luxury Aquilonia offered, not when I was on the military's expense account.

— Six —

Lieutenant Thalman guided me through passages burned into the moon's mantle by mining lasers until we walked up a shallow ramp to the promenade level. This was Aquilonia's commercial, recreational, and touristic heart, basking in the rays of a distant sun beneath the thick, meteorite-proof dome.

From there, we took a lift down several levels to the station's segregated VIP section where wealthy and powerful visitors enjoyed Aquilonia's amenities away from commoners and watchful eyes.

A pair of troopers wearing Cimmerian Gendarmerie uniforms let us into the suite that had become a crime scene. I could honestly say that in my years as a cop, I'd never seen so much dried blood, not even when I infiltrated a particularly vicious rebel gang as a young and naïve constable.

A homicidal maniac bent on redecorating couldn't have made a bigger mess. The blood spatters on the walls made me remember hyperspace jump nausea with fondness. But I couldn't mistake it for anything other than alien. The Shrehari envoy's dried blood was a dark purple that almost appeared to be midnight black.

No one expected me to search for clues or carry out my own crime scene analysis — the locals had already done the legwork. They only wanted someone to let them turn it back into moneymaking luxury accommodations. As far as station management and the Gendarmerie were concerned, my job wasn't to find the killer. The local cops had already taken care of that.

Our Navy cousins had called in the Constabulary because the suspect was one of their senior officers, an intelligence analyst to boot. They wanted me to tell them why she was proclaiming her innocence after being found with the murder weapon in her hands and the envoy's blood on her clothes.

I suppose they might have figured it out by themselves, but if the evidence showed she was guilty, the Constabulary had to lay the charges anyway, since it was a federal crime, not a military one.

On the other hand, I had to wonder whether, considering the diplomatic angle and the old grudges between the Empire and us, they gave me the case because I was politically expendable. I had no idea what evidence a Shrehari would consider enough to determine guilt or exonerate a suspect.

As a matter of fact, I didn't know much about their justice system. However, I understood they had a huge fetish for honor, something we might learn from if guys like Commissioner Haylian reached flag rank without knowing when to keep his pants up.

I didn't spend much time in the suite. Anything relevant would be in the case file, which I had read on the ferry. If the locals had overlooked something, I wasn't about to find it. And if the Navy thought the Gendarmerie might miss clues, they could bloody well send a forensics team, or ask DCC Maras for one. I certainly wouldn't waste my time with a sensor.

My escort took me to the police station on one of Aquilonia's lower levels, where visitors didn't go. Unless, of course, it was in shackles and between a pair of unsmiling guards, something that happened regularly from what I recalled. Free ports attracted sentient beings eager to avoid government interference, and some forgot that the lack of oversight applied only to customs and excise matters.

This place was far from lawless, and station management had a direct interest in keeping things quiet. Otherwise, the Cimmerian government might revoke the Syndicate's charter and impose direct rule.

After signing in, he took me to the cellblock and parked me in front of a console with multiple screens, each showing the inside of a cell.

Talyn wasn't much to look at. Middle-aged, slender, with graying black hair swept behind the ears. A face that was neither beautiful nor ugly, nor very memorable, which I suppose was an asset when you spent your life rifling through other peoples' underwear drawers.

She sat on the bunk, legs crossed, eyes closed as if meditating on the enormity of her crime. Her features seemed relaxed, almost those of someone in a deep coma. The one thing she didn't look like was a suspect drowning in guilt and the fear of retribution.

Mind you, I've come across plenty of hardened criminals over the years who appeared entirely at peace with the universe. It was easy when you didn't have a soul.

"Was Talyn alone? Or does she have a partner roaming the station, looking for ways to spring her?"

Thalman shrugged with the disinterest of someone who had a high-profile investigation taken away from him. If he was sore at me for that, he apparently had no idea how crappy a Fleet case might become, especially when it involved nonhumans.

"We weren't able to find anyone or any sign she hadn't stepped off the ferry from Valerys by her lonesome," he replied. "She didn't even bother to hide her identity when she passed through arrivals. It was above board, just as if she was on a holiday or a business trip. Then she murders a bonehead trade representative. Go figure."

When I said there was no love lost between the Shrehari and us, I meant it both ways, though I hoped my escort didn't go calling them boneheads within earshot. He might not live long enough to appreciate the lesson in defending one's honor that would ensue. But the pejorative name was apt. Who knew what they called us behind our backs? Probably something involving the Shrehari word for weak.

"Has Talyn said anything since she gave her statement?"

"Not a word. She didn't make a call to her superiors, a lawyer, or the local betting shop."

Thalman had no idea she was more than just another Fleet officer. As far as everyone knew, the PCB taking an interest in the case was purely due to the identity of the victim and the diplomatic storm brewing between Earth and Shrehari Prime.

"The Navy didn't get in touch after you alerted Sixth Fleet HQ of the situation?"

He shook his head. "No. Unless someone spoke to Major Pullar, and he didn't share it with me. Pardon me for saying this, sir, but I'm surprised they sent a PCB officer to investigate a murder."

"You know how it is." I shrugged off the comment, my eyes never leaving the screen. "Senior Navy officer goes loco on the Rim and kills an alien envoy. It means we catch the call."

"Cut and dry case, the way we see it."

"Sure, but once the imperial government screams at the SecGen, it won't be so dry anymore. In fact, it might become so wet you'll wish you were running security on Andoth, or Kilia, where things are a lot quieter."

"Then it's a good thing you're in charge of the investigation, sir."

And it would be my ass on the line if things fell sideways. "How about you let me in to speak with our suspect? I have just about everything I can get from watching."

Which wasn't much. Talyn merely sat there, looking like she'd sent her spirit on an astral journey, and showed none of the behavior I usually saw from a suspect in custody. Then again, some perps had that particular emotional emptiness resulting from a deep-seated streak of sociopathy and appeared unconcerned until I started squeezing them. Thankfully, we didn't see many of those in the Constabulary ranks, even among the worst of the bent cops. Politicians, on the other hand...

"I'm sure the major wouldn't object. Have fun." He touched a screen by the door, and it opened with a hiss.

Even if his boss wanted to voice an objection, it wouldn't matter. This might be his brig, but Talyn was now my suspect. As to having fun? I'd see about that soon enough.

— Seven —

When I entered the cell, she snapped out of her trance and stared up at me with cold, dark eyes, the kind that saw everything and forgave nothing. It made me feel like a suspect, and that proved to be a strange and unusual sensation.

I already knew what she saw: a washed-out, middle-aged blond, all hard angles, the proud owner of a face that looked like nature had sculpted it with a hatchet. In other words, except for the hair and eye color, she must have thought she was looking in a mirror, right down to mussed civilian clothes that had come from a cheap fabricator rather than a talented tailor.

"Commander Talyn, I'm Chief Superintendent Caelin Morrow from the Constabulary's Professional Compliance Bureau."

Her right eyebrow twitched. It was the first sign of emotion I'd seen on her face so far.

"The Firing Squad. I'm honored."

"Kill an alien trade representative, and you earn first class treatment." I sat on the steel chair bolted to the granite floor, facing her. "Do I need to describe the storm that's brewing? Can you figure out why the

Navy asked us to take over the investigation, I mean other than because we're looking at a federal crime?"

"Indulge me, Chief Superintendent. Why are you here?" A vaguely sardonic aura seemed to envelop her. Was she mocking me?

"The Gendarmerie said they caught you red-handed — or to be precise, purple-handed; the Empire is short one trade representative, and the Navy wants no one to accuse it of a cover-up. If you're guilty, the Constabulary lays the charges, and everyone else can step back. If you're innocent, well, when the Firing Squad lets you go, there's no doubt, right?"

"I'm innocent."

"Sure." I nodded. It was a refrain I heard at the start of every damn case. Every one of them. "You'd be amazed at how often I get that, even when I lay out enough evidence to convince the dumbest jury monkey. I had one recently. He's spilling out his whole life story right now. It's his final act before premature retirement, and a life spent looking over his shoulder for an assassin sent by the folks he betrayed. Why are you innocent?"

"Do juries know you call them monkeys? I'm pretty sure they would resent the comparison."

Great, I'd caught a comedian who liked to ask questions instead of answering them. This case was already turning into a laugh a minute.

"I toss them a bunch of bananas before taking the stand. It keeps them sweet during my testimony. Why are you innocent?"

"Because I didn't do it." She gave me a stare that placed my intelligence at the level of a tree-dwelling primate. "Doesn't the Firing Squad always come in twos or threes?"

"I pissed off my DCC, so no partners on this one. It's my punishment for bringing fruit to murder trials."

Talyn laughed. To my surprise, it seemed genuine, or at least more so than the rest of her demeanor.

"And where's your partner? I thought you spooks always spied in twos."

She waved her hand at the laser-polished stone ceiling. "Out there somewhere. He had a lot of leave coming and took it in one go. I figure he's plowing through his bucket list of exotic brothels and breweries."

"In other words, none of my business."

She gave me a mocking smile. "None of mine either, Chief Superintendent, so you don't have to feel special. I'm a solo act these days, just like you."

"Tell me why you're innocent."

"Because I didn't do it."

She sounded like someone dealing with an unusually slow child, and I had to repress a sudden urge to backhand her across that smug face. The gendarmes wouldn't have been impressed. Neither would DCC Maras once she saw the recording.

Talyn must have read the thought in my eyes because her thin lips twitched with a barely suppressed amusement I was probably supposed to notice. Great. She was trying to provoke me. This was why I hated investigating the military. They always seemed to behave like arrogant pricks.

"Why are you putting on a smartass act, Commander? I'm here because the Navy tapped us on the shoulder and said pretty please. Perhaps they'd like you to cooperate. Why not take me through that day, from the moment you climbed out of bed to the time they found you standing over

Envoy Shovak's corpse, wearing half of his bodily fluids?"

"I'm sure you've read the statement I gave the Cimmerian Gendarmerie. There's nothing I can add."

She unfolded her legs and stretched without leaving the cot, then extinguished that annoying smile.

"I don't want to tell you how to do your job, Chief Superintendent," she continued before I had a chance to reply, "but I'll do it anyway. Start with the Shrehari delegation. If I'm not guilty, then one of them is. They had even better access to the knife that killed Shovak than me. After all, that was a real warrior's blade. They don't export those as trinkets for hairless apes. Or maybe you should look at whoever he came to meet as part of his duties. I'll bet Envoy Shovak was more than he seemed. The Shrehari are always up to something."

"Is that an intelligence analyst's evaluation?"

"It's the gut instinct of someone with excellent bullshit detectors."

"Okay." I stood and tugged my jacket into place. Forcing the issue right now wouldn't help matters. "Have it your way. I'll be back to speak with you once I have a better sense for the lay of the land."

My native guide still waited on the other side of the glass, so I told him no one was to interview Talyn or move her from this cell without my say-so. I could see from his face he wasn't overjoyed at the Gendarmerie losing control of the suspect, but life's tough.

A dead Shrehari trade representative and a naval officer as prime suspect made me the lady with the most law enforcement clout on Aquilonia. At least where it concerned this particular case. And I could reliably bully my way into other matters merely by behaving in the manner most people expected from the Firing Squad. Having a reputation, no matter how checkered, was an advantage at times.

After making sure he understood I could sink his commanding officer's career with a single sneeze, I headed for the lift that would take me up to where VIPs breathed fragrant if recycled air. It was time to grab the Shrehari by the skull ridges.

— Eight —

"Your investigation is a waste of time," a man's voice said when I stepped out of the cop shop and into the bare, harshly lit corridor.

I turned and gave him a standard-issue senior officer's stare and waited for that bit of courtesy I expected from a man wearing the silver badges of a Cimmerian Gendarmerie major. Perhaps, as with his lieutenant, my lack of rank insignia, a uniform, or even a reasonably sober business suit threw him off his game.

"Pullar, Jon Pullar, Chief Superintendent Morrow. I run the Gendarmerie on Aquilonia."

He almost came to attention and then decided against it. On the far end of fifty-something, with thinning gray hair, his solemn expression struck me as that of a man ready for retirement.

"And why am I wasting my time?"

"Talyn's guilty. Envoy Shovak's aide found her standing over his body, a bloody knife in her hand. One of those big, brutal bonehead blades they like to wear."

Since the Cimmerian Gendarmerie couldn't boast of a better success rate than anyone else for solving murders, his casual, almost dismissive manner seemed misplaced. However, he didn't seem as truculent as the officer who had met me at the docks.

Perhaps a lifetime of policing had given him enough experience to smell a nasty case when he came across one and give thanks to the deity of his choice for a smooth hand-off to the Feds.

"Commander Talyn insists on her innocence, Major, and my superiors have ordered me to find out not just what happened but why it happened. You are familiar with the remit of the Constabulary's Professional Compliance Bureau, aren't you?"

"Sure." He nodded. "You ferret out misconduct in the Commonwealth uniformed services and arrest the occasional politician with a tendency for sticking his or her fingers where they don't belong."

"Then you understand why telling me I'm wasting my time is a waste of your breath, and based on the aroma around here, Aquilonia's dealing with more waste than it can handle. Was that everything you wanted to share? I plan on speaking to the aide who found Talyn and his dead boss."

Pullar gave me a heartfelt grimace. It matched his forlorn appearance. "That would be Thopok. Nasty bugger. Seems to think the war ended last week, not seven decades ago."

Considering a fair number of veterans from both sides of that long-running conflict still roamed the galaxy, I wasn't surprised.

"Shrehari have long memories and hold grudges forever, Major. I understand they pass them from generation to generation as an inheritance. The fact they had to return this system to us without a fight still makes some of them want to slit throats. That's probably why they insist on wearing those big brutal bonehead blades, to use your unfortunate turn of phrase. I suggest you and your people scrub that nasty insult from your vocabulary, by the way. They're very touchy, and we don't need another diplomatic incident."

He nodded once without showing a shred of emotion at my rebuke. "So noted, Chief Superintendent."

"I hope this Thopok speaks Anglic. My Shrehari is pretty rudimentary, meaning I speak next to none."

Pullar fell into step beside me as if he'd decided to sit in on the interview. I may have taken over the case, but Aquilonia was still his patch of ground, and so, in the interests of maintaining good inter-agency relations, I didn't protest.

Besides, he could be useful as a second pair of eyes and ears until Arno Galdi joined me, and that could take a few days. Fortunately, he wasn't signaling that faint distaste for the PCB I sensed from so many members of my Service. It made for a welcome change.

"Thopok has a reasonable command of Anglic, as a matter of fact," Pullar replied after a moment. "He just gives the impression he doesn't like using it."

We stopped by the lift and Pullar touched the call screen. "And he might get annoyed at being interviewed again, seeing as how we already have what he considers the perpetrator in custody. Remember, he walked in on her. So for him, it's a foregone conclusion. The way Thopok sees matters, we need only charge Talyn, try her, and execute her according to Shrehari tradition."

"So Thopok found her in Shovak's suite, with Shovak's blood on her, the murder weapon in her hand. But he didn't actually see her do the deed, and you've found no evidence proving that she killed the envoy. I mean, it's merely circumstantial, right?"

"I suppose so, Chief Superintendent. But it's solid circumstantial evidence."

"Solid? I'm not convinced. You've seen Talyn. She's no bigger than I am. In a straight knife fight, no power weapons involved, my money's on the Shrehari, not the scrawny woman with the personality dysfunction. Heck, everyone's money would be on the Shrehari."

He thought about it for a moment, and then gave me a grudging, "Perhaps."

"If Talyn's guilty, we need answers. One of them is how can a woman my size, armed with a knife taken from its very reluctant owner, kill a Shrehari? And redecorate the suite in a spray of dark purple. I suppose Thopok hasn't been able to answer that little conundrum."

Pullar hiked his shoulders. It was an amusingly indecisive gesture from a man who'd proclaimed certainty moments earlier.

"He figures Talyn surprised him somehow but wasn't inclined to elaborate. Who knows what fighting techniques they teach in the Fleet? Maybe she slipped Shovak a drug to knock him out. Although we'll never know. The Shrehari aren't allowing an autopsy. They won't even go for a noninvasive sensor scan. Shovak's body is in a stasis pod awaiting repatriation, guarded night and day by his own guards. I understand there's a ship on the way from the nearest imperial outpost, or there will be soon."

"I hope you told the delegation that no one and nothing, not even Shovak's body, is leaving Aquilonia until I say so, or until they whip out full diplomatic credentials, which I know they don't carry. Yet."

He nodded. "I did. Thopok snarled something at me in Shrehari that was probably the equivalent of fuck off and die, if you'll pardon my crudeness."

"Perhaps, though from what I've read, they're pretty inventive when it comes to insults and put-downs. More so than we are."

The lift door opened with a sigh and Pullar ushered me into the waiting cab. He stepped in beside me and touched the control screen. "There. A straight run to the VIP section. Commandeering transport is one of the few privileges we have around here, for what it's worth."

Moments later, the cab came to a smooth halt, and the doors opened onto the same plush corridor I'd entered earlier. The two Gendarmerie troopers still stood at the entrance to Shovak's suite, which meant they were waiting for my formal permission to release the crime scene, and not just assuming that my brief visit had been enough. Smart.

We stopped one door down, and Pullar touched the call panel. After a lengthy wait, a deep, rough voice roared something in an alien tongue. Pullar was about to speak, but I raised my hand and pointed back at myself. He nodded.

Forcing my voice to imitate that of an enraged sergeant major I remembered from basic training, I said, "My name is Chief Superintendent Caelin Morrow of the Commonwealth Constabulary. My government has ordered me to investigate the death of Envoy Shovak and I would speak with you."

Another growl in Shrehari erupted from the hidden speaker, no doubt choice words insulting my ancestry, cooking skills, and general hygiene. By the way, my lineage is unremarkable, my cooking skills are nonexistent, and my cleanliness is excellent, in spite of looking like I'd just fallen out of bed. But Thopok didn't need to know. He must have purged the insults from his system because his next words were in rough, but understandable Anglic.

"You hold Envoy Shovak's assassin, and I would see her executed as soon as possible. I know about the duplicity of your species. Don't waste my time with words. Summon me for the execution. And now be gone."

Textbook Shrehari posturing. Thopok was behaving exactly as I'd read in the species briefing on my way here. Bluster, aggression, and arrogance were standard, especially since I was not only human but also female.

However, he'd never met a PCB chief superintendent before now. I eat power packs for breakfast and spit out plasma all day. Or at least that's what they say about me behind my back when they think I can't hear.

"You will speak with me, or you won't see the Empire again. I have the power to deny your departure or forbid any imperial ship from landing on Aquilonia, and that means you will stay here, living on my sufferance."

Okay, so I was laying it on a bit thick. I couldn't actually prevent an imperial ship from landing, but yeah, I could keep the entire Shrehari delegation here until someone up my chain of command said otherwise. Unfortunately, if the boneheads made enough of a stink, I knew word would come across the light years from Wyvern telling me to stop blowing smoke.

That would take a few days, however. They still hadn't found a way to make subspace radio waves travel instantaneously between star systems, and I hoped they never did. The last thing I wanted was for DCC Hammett to micromanage my investigations.

Another long string of Shrehari assaulted my ears, and for a moment, I felt relief at not understanding their tongue. This time, I was sure he wasn't merely denigrating my personal hygiene, but offering to improve it using various torture implements.

Then, after a few moments of dead silence, during which I wondered whether Thopok had given himself the Shrehari equivalent of a rage-induced stroke, the door opened.

— Nine —

Pullar and I stepped into the suite's lobby and the outer door closed behind us. We came face-to-face with a tall, massive being almost twice my width. Thopok had the skull ridges, leathery olive skin, and crest of hair I expected from a pure race member of the warrior caste. His deep-set, black within black eyes reflected no discernable emotions, the soul behind them utterly alien. It wasn't my first sighting of a Shrehari. The species was hard to avoid in this sector, but it was my first close-up encounter.

Thopok towered over me, and if I had to stand any closer to him, I'd develop a crick in my neck before the end of the interview. Our proximity allowed me a whiff of his scent, but it would be hard to describe in human words.

Not exactly unpleasant, but outlandish, with odd feral undertones. I didn't know if it was the odor, or Thopok's size, or both, but the small hairs on the back of my neck stood to attention while a sinking feeling tugged at my gut. For a moment, I wondered how we had convinced them to sign an armistice and vacate every star system they'd taken from us.

Shovak had undoubtedly been just as massive and, to a human's fight-or-flight reflex, just as threatening. Now that I stood before another of his species, I couldn't imagine Talyn killing him with a mere knife, especially his own, twin to the one Thopok wore on his hip.

Naval Intelligence might well breed skilled assassins, and if Talyn was among them, I didn't doubt she could dispose of me in a matter of seconds. But when it came to Shrehari, I could not see ability outfight sheer muscle mass and ferocity. Not without power weapons.

Thopok fixed me with a blank stare I couldn't interpret to save my life. "Speak, Caelin Morrow."

His voice rumbled up from deep within his massive chest, a sound akin to one of Andoth's more spectacular volcanic eruptions. He was clearly disinclined to invite us in whether to sit down or even for a cup of tea. Perhaps the lack of hospitality denoted a subtle insult in his culture. Such behavior showed reticence if not outright disdain in ours.

With humans, I always knew how to bully my way into their inner sanctums, but Thopok had me at a loss. Crossing the fine line between forcefulness and mortal offense might happen without realization, thanks to my rudimentary knowledge of his species' customs and taboos. And by an inability to divine his thoughts and moods through facial expressions or body language. None of the psychological tools, so vital to an investigator, would be of the slightest use.

"My questions may take time."

The Shrehari made a gesture with his thick, shovel-sized hands that I interpreted as their version of a dismissive shrug and his mouth opened to show cracked, yellowing teeth.

"They will take the time they must. Speak."

So we would do this standing in his suite's lobby? Fine with me. As long as I got answers.

"What was the purpose of your visit to Aquilonia?"

Thopok pointed at Pullar. "This one already knows."

"Perhaps," I replied, "but I will hear the answers again from your mouth, not from that one's report. My duty demands it, and if I am to keep my honor, I must do that duty. I'm sure you understand."

I thought I saw a flash of something in Thopok's deeply sunken eyes and hoped it wasn't wishful thinking. My review of everything Shrehari on the way here might pay off handsomely.

"Envoy Shovak was to meet with negotiators from your Honorable Commonwealth Trading Corporation to discuss establishing direct links between it and the merchant consortium Shovak represented, called *Quch Mech*."

Which would explain why the Shrehari weren't traveling on diplomatic documents. The fact they were merchants made my job easier. Dealing with diplomats always added a uselessly complicated layer of weapons-grade bullshit to any investigation.

"Did meetings occur before Envoy Shovak's death?"

"Yes, we met once, in the hours preceding his murder, but it was merely to become acquainted."

"I'll need the names of everyone involved."

Thopok pointed at Pullar again. "He has the list."

This time, I didn't insist. Human names might be confusing for Shrehari tongues.

"The accused killer, was she invited to meet with Envoy Shovak?"

"No. She must have entered Shovak's quarters through trickery."

"Shovak shared everything with you, correct?"

"Yes. My duty was to arrange every meeting on Shovak's behalf. The assassin did not request a meeting."

I nodded, then realized the gesture might be lost on Thopok. "Understood. You found her standing over Envoy Shovak's body, a knife in her hand."

"I did. And it was not just a knife. It was the envoy's own consecrated blade. I would have killed her right there, but she had already called station security, and they entered at that moment."

I glanced at Pullar, who nodded.

"And the female was unfamiliar to you?"

"She was."

"Thank you for your cooperation. I will have further questions for you at another time."

The Shrehari tilted his head to one side, eyes still on me. "Do not take too long. I leave once our ship lands."

"You leave when I say so."

Thopok's eyes widened, and he reared back as if to protest, but I turned to the outer door and touched its control panel. When it slid open, I nudged Pullar, and we left an angry Thopok behind, still struggling to spit out a meaty protest in Anglic.

These chest-thumping games would turn wearisome fast, but I had little choice. My sole option was to meet the Shrehari based on their social and cultural norms, not ours.

Back in the corridor, I glanced at Shovak's suite and said, "I don't think we need your gendarmes to keep guarding the crime scene, but please make sure the compartment is secure, and don't have it cleaned just yet."

Pullar replied with a grave nod. "Certainly."

We left the VIP sector and took the lift to the Gendarmerie station's level again.

"I'll want the names of the Commonwealth Trading Corporation representatives. Whether Talyn murdered Shovak or someone else did it, I need to find a motive for his death. His meeting with ComCorp could be involved in some way."

"Of course."

"Then, I'd like a download of the security sensors in and around Shovak's suite."

Pullar hesitated. "The pickups in that half of the VIP section seem to have malfunctioned, and there aren't any in the suites themselves. We dare not invade the privacy of our visitors." His voice had taken on a sarcastic edge. "They might object, and that could harm trade."

"Undoubtedly, though that malfunction seems incredibly convenient for the killer."

Pullar gave me an apologetic grimace. "Things break. Station management isn't inclined toward preventive maintenance on non-vital systems. The attitude here is profits over everything else. Those pickups aren't the only ones needing repair."

"So the sole evidence we have is her standing over the body, knife in hand. Talyn might be telling the truth about walking in after Shovak's death. Without sensor evidence or an autopsy, we can't link her directly to the crime."

And without a direct connection, no federal prosecutor would take the case. When it came to interspecies relations, prejudice in favor of the home team still ran as high as it did at the end of the war.

"Yet she had his blood on her clothing and her prints were on the knife. I still say it's enough to charge her."

"Perhaps, but I don't think it's enough to secure a conviction. And if we're to satisfy the imperial government as well as ours, we need to present them with evidence establishing guilt beyond a reasonable doubt."

The lift stopped, and we stepped out into the now familiar bleak corridor leading to Pullar's domain.

"If you know anything about the Professional Compliance Bureau, you'll know our cases are always airtight. When we charge someone, we make sure that the evidence stands up to the best defense attorneys in the Commonwealth. Because that is what we often face. Equally, if we exonerate someone it will be because of irrefutable evidence they're innocent."

That wasn't always true, but our effectiveness depended on an aura of ruthless competence. Sometimes, we had just enough facts to convince a corrupt bugger that confession followed by resignation was good for the soul. But it did the job. As DCC Hammett told me when I reported for duty with the PCB, justice didn't always come through the legal system.

"The famous incorruptibles, eh?" Pullar asked. A corner of his mouth lifted in a half smile, half smirk.

"When your job is to investigate your own Service, the military, or the high and mighty of the Commonwealth, you can't afford mistakes, and you don't charge people based on a balance of probabilities. Right now there's a likelihood that Talyn appeared on the crime scene after the fact. Not to mention the *im*probability of her murdering a Shrehari with his own knife unaided."

And that was the single most significant argument any competent barrister would use to raise the specter of reasonable doubt. From there on, acquittal became almost inevitable.

He nodded. "Fair enough."

"If we could examine Shovak's body, we might find something that ties Talyn directly to his death, but I can't violate a deeply held Shrehari taboo. *That* would turn this into a diplomatic crisis and transform my investigation into an interstellar circus, so we need to find our evidence elsewhere. I'll send a request, through official channels, asking the Shrehari to conduct an autopsy when the body gets back to the Empire, but I'm afraid it won't do us a damn bit of good. We'd have no chain of custody at that point."

"What will you do?"

My grim smile probably dropped the temperature by a few degrees. I certainly didn't feel warm and fuzzy about my prospects right then.

"Nibble around the edges until I reach the center. Along the way, I'll likely annoy enough people to trigger a few useful reactions that could point us at the truth, starting with Thopok. I want him watched at all times, including when he's in his quarters, and to hell with privacy. He's a suspect."

"As I said, Chief Superintendent, we don't invade the privacy of our visitors." A mulish look crept over his tired features.

"This time, you will. I know you have pickups in his quarters. If not, your security setup needs a complete overhaul."

Pullar seemed about to argue, but then he nodded. "Very well. I will log the activation of surveillance in Thopok's suite as under your orders."

"Please do. If it helps overcome your scruples, consider this. Who would you rather bet on as being able to kill a healthy Shrehari male in the prime of life with his own knife? Thopok or someone Talyn's size?"

— Ten —

We passed by the brig and checked in on our prisoner from the guard station before going over the list of Honorable Commonwealth Trading Corporation representatives who met with Shovak a few hours before his death. Talyn was back in the lotus position, eyes closed. Perhaps she had sent her mind soaring across the galaxy.

It wasn't what you'd expect from someone guilty of murdering a Shrehari envoy. Then again, she was with Naval Intelligence, and one heard stories about their black ops specialists. Two of my senior investigators, Ange Rowan, and her partner Leoni Crava were sure they'd crossed paths with a pair of them as they tried to track the late, unlamented, and very bent Inspector Grint.

Pullar waved me to an unoccupied desk in the security bullpen and called up the names. Only one of them rang a bell.

Of all the bad luck, it had to be her. Dealing with a herd of well-nourished, smarmy diplomats suddenly seemed a lot more congenial. My native guide must have seen something in my face.

"Anyone familiar?" He asked.

"Unfortunately, yes." I pointed at the screen. "Gerri Kazan, ComCorp's director of security for their Rim Division. We worked together before she resigned and took up a private sector job."

"Can I assume you didn't part on friendly terms?" Pullar cocked a questioning eyebrow, inviting me to expand. It wasn't something I wanted to discuss, but as my instructors were fond of repeating, nothing remained private in a murder case, not even the investigator's past. Besides, I preferred to have Pullar's ungrudging support. It meant being open with him on matters that might be germane to the case.

"We didn't." I repressed a sigh and shook my head instead. "Gerri and I were a team for many years and cleared a lot of cases when we worked for the Rim Sector's Major Crimes Division in what we used to call the Flying Squad. The nickname was on account of our spending so much time traveling between star systems. We handled crimes that didn't come under planetary jurisdiction and were beyond the capacity of local Constabulary units."

"I've heard of them."

"At first, she was a top-notch investigator. Then, as time went by, she took shortcuts that jeopardized our ability to secure indictments — an irregular interrogation here, an incomplete chain of evidence there. Things that happen when a detective has done it for too long and gets lazy. Finally, a fraud case fell apart because she'd skipped a few steps, and that proved to be her undoing. They kicked her off the Flying Squad, and she resigned soon afterward. We had harsh words for each other; especially when she found out I had come clean with our commanding officer. Shortly after quitting, she was hired by

ComCorp, which coincidentally owned the company involved in the fraud case that collapsed. The ownership was through the subsidiary of a subsidiary, but it was still part of the same conglomerate or zaibatsu as we call them in the Service. We didn't think much of it, but after years chasing dirty cops, I've had cause to reconsider."

"Flukes happen, Chief Superintendent."

"Perhaps." There would be no getting around it. I'd have to interview Gerri along with the rest of the ComCorp delegation. "We've not spoken since the day she walked out. I presume the ComCorp lot took up residence in the VIP suites as well?"

"No. They're in the Aquilonia Excelsior. No doubt squatting in deluxe suites with a full view of the surface."

"Of course. One of ComCorp's subsidiaries owns the Excelsior chain." I tapped the name at the head of the list, a guy called Yan Houko, who had the impressive title of Vice President, Rim Sector Trade Development. "Let's start with the top man. Since you're plugged into everything around here, I'd take it as a favor if you could find his whereabouts and let him know I'd like half an hour of his time today. He can choose the location."

Pullar nodded. "Will do, Chief Superintendent."

The Cimmerian disappeared into his office while I kept staring at the list, trying to determine the nature of these trade negotiations with the Shrehari.

Gerri's place in the delegation hinted at a security component. It would be something other than the military kind, which dealt with keeping star lanes safe from marauders.

The others seemed innocuous. Consultants or executives for this and that mostly, titles which didn't help me form a clear picture. I was adding Thopok's statement and the ComCorp names to the case file when Pullar stuck his head out into the bullpen.

"Ser Houko has neither the time nor the inclination to speak with you. He considers the matter of Envoy Shovak's murder none of his concern."

I should have expected a ComCorp vice president to act like a high and mighty corporate pasha. Over the years, I'd come across his kind before, so I wasn't surprised.

Houko was about to learn you didn't decline an invitation to meet with a senior Constabulary officer investigating a high-profile murder. At least not without reaching high up my chain of command for someone willing to wave me off.

Since DCC Hammett wouldn't do so without a damned good reason, it would likely take the Chief Constable himself. And he was too busy fending off political interference from Earth to take much notice of a zaibatsu nabob with ego problems.

"You talked to him directly?" I asked, knowing what his answer would be. The Houkos of the galaxy didn't speak with mere mortals, not even the most senior Gendarmerie officer on the station.

"No, with Houko's aide. His attitude makes Thopok's seem like that of a kitten."

I stood. "Mind if I use your office?"

"Sure." He stepped aside and waved me in. "Do you want me to get Houko's aide back on the comm?"

"Please."

Pullar motioned me to take a seat by his untidy desk while he reestablished the link. After a few moments, the three-dimensional, holographic projection of a man's head materialized.

"This is Major Pullar again," he said, then pointed at me. "Chief Superintendent Morrow would like to speak with you."

The disembodied head turned to face me, and I immediately pegged him as someone who wore his superior's authority like a cloak.

His sort might wield unofficial power in a corporate environment, where venomous aides could ruin a career with a single word placed in the right ears, but not here, and not with me.

"I'm Chief Superintendent Morrow. I need to speak with Ser Houko sometime today on the matter of Envoy Shovak's murder."

"As I told the gendarme," he replied in a condescending tone, "Ser Houko sees no reason to speak with you on an issue that doesn't concern him. I trust you'll not harass him any further. Otherwise, he will file a formal complaint with your superiors."

Harass? He had a strange idea of what actually constituted police harassment in the legal sense. I knew how far I could go and still stay within bounds, and we weren't even close yet. And filing a complaint? For merely requesting an interview? Good luck. DCC Hammett's first reaction would be to wonder what Houko, and by extension ComCorp had to hide, meaning he'd expect me to dig a little deeper than I otherwise would. And I would do so with pleasure.

"Your boss seems to believe speaking with me is optional. It isn't." I stuck to a polite, emotionless tone. It made my next words resonate that much more. "Unless he consents to speak with me today, I will order his arrest. Is that clear enough? He's a potential witness in a capital crime that may have serious diplomatic consequences. Either you arrange a meeting, or Ser Houko will find a pair of

Major Pullar's finest at his door. Your call. I don't care either way."

His eyes widened in shock as if no one had ever dared speak to him like that. "I must protest."

"You can protest as much as you want, but get me thirty minutes with Ser Houko before the end of the day, or he'll be spending quality time in one of Major Pullar's interview rooms."

The aide gave me what he believed was his iciest stare, but once he realized I was serious, he nodded with apparent reluctance at having to back down. "I'll contact you shortly."

The hologram vanished, and I slumped back in Pullar's office chair.

"How much do you want to bet that someone from the ComCorp delegation is even now pestering Deputy Chief Constable Maras about me?"

"You don't sound concerned."

"Why should I be? My boss is on Wyvern, dozens of light years from here. By the time a subspace message makes the round trip, I'll have solved this one." I gave him a confident grin. "Besides, DCC Maras and I have an understanding. I tell her everything, and she doesn't interfere with my job unless I go completely off script. Annoying a corporate big shot is nothing."

"In that case, I envy you. Our subspace link with Cimmeria makes transmissions next to instantaneous and the number of times my bosses have attempted to micromanage the way I police Aquilonia defies belief."

"I'm sure the good DCC will reach out and let me know the ComCorp folks have complained. Then she'll suggest I don't take too much pleasure from stepping on their toes and that'll be it. Maras is one of the good senior officers. I dread the day they promote her to a job on Wyvern or she cashes in her pension. With my luck, the next DCC won't be as tolerant or understanding."

"I hear you, Chief Superintendent."

The comm system chimed and Houko's aide, or at least his head, rematerialized over Pullar's desk. He seemed even less happy with the universe at large than before.

"Ser Houko will meet you in the lobby of the Aquilonia Excelsior at sixteen hundred hours, station time. Don't be late."

"Thank you."

The hologram faded away, leaving nothing, not even a smile. Then, the system chimed again, this time announcing a subspace transmission from Cimmeria. Pullar touched the controls, and a holographic DCC Maras appeared in the spot Houko's aide had just vacated.

"You may have set a record, sir," I said before she could open her mouth. My flippant tone earned me a brief frown.

"I've had the senior aide of a very irate ComCorp vice president on the link," she replied, ignoring my remark, "complaining about Constabulary harassment. He wants you reprimanded and off Aquilonia. I'm astonished you made friends there so rapidly. The record's yours, not mine."

"It's both a talent and a curse, sir. I requested thirty minutes of his boss' time today to discuss the Shovak murder, and he brushed me off in a less than cooperative fashion. I then indicated Ser Houko didn't exactly have a choice. That's about the gist of this harassment, sir."

"It figures," Maras said in a resigned tone. "He made it sound like this Houko character was thoroughly imbued with his own importance. I would suggest you tread cautiously, but I'm afraid my warning would fall on deaf ears."

"It's a murder investigation, sir. Rattling cages and annoying people comes with the territory."

"Indeed it does. Well, I've done what I promised Ser Houko's aide. I've spoken with you. Now do me a favor and try to make sure I don't receive regular calls from halfway across the system. I still have a sector to run, and you're not in my chain of command."

"I'll do my best, sir. Thank you."

"Just settle this case, Caelin. Maras, out."

Pullar gave me an admiring look. "You called that one."

"I've been doing this for a while, Major." I glanced at the ship's clock that held pride of place in Pullar's office. "Time to head out. Do you want to sit in on my conversation? Since I don't have a wingman, I could use another set of eyes and ears, and another brain. Besides, it might be entertaining."

A faint smile briefly crossed his lips, wiping away some of his ever-present wariness. "Sure. I wouldn't mind seeing how you handle a fellow thoroughly imbued by his own importance, to quote your DCC."

Jon Pullar had a sense of humor after all. The universe never ceased to surprise me with unexpected discoveries.

— Eleven —

Sculpted into the moon's solid mantle, the Excelsior boasted a grand entrance on a prime stretch of the promenade beneath Aquilonia's dome. It promised luxury that no other off-world hotel in this system could deliver. One of a chain with branches across the Commonwealth, each called Excelsior something or other, it catered to those who wanted to live large. Budget-conscious travelers avoided the entire brand like the plague.

This particular hotel seemed out of place in a former mining operation turned free port on an overgrown asteroid. But who was I to judge? If Aquilonia didn't have VIP accommodations on offer, I'd have reserved a room at the Excelsior on the Navy's expense account.

The station's other hotels weren't the sort where a senior police officer might feel safe, considering they catered to a distinctly cosmopolitan crowd that lived more often than not in the shadows of the law.

It was the nature of free ports. They attracted those interested in a quick cred alongside legitimate traders looking to save a few percent in taxes and excise payments. Neither type enjoyed the idea of a

Constabulary officer glancing over their shoulders out of sheer curiosity.

If the hotel hadn't belonged to ComCorp, I didn't doubt the delegation would have chosen the VIP suites, even without the magnificent view of Thule's smudged brilliance overhead. But it would have looked bad if a vice president scorned accommodations offered by his own conglomerate.

We were about ten minutes early, which suited me. I wanted to scout out the lobby before Houko showed up. It was the closest to ComCorp home turf on Aquilonia.

Translucent doors opened silently, welcoming us into a vista of pseudo-marble, gilt metal, and tastefully scripted signage in Anglic, Mandarin and, to my amusement, Shrehari. I wasn't sure what the latter would think about the fake opulence though I figured they'd use choice words.

As I expected, the lobby sported several chair groupings scattered on either side of the reception counter. When I walked up to one, I felt the soft tingling of a sound barrier on my skin and smiled. Of course.

The Excelsior chain would make sure to give its guests privacy even out in the open, though I wouldn't put it beyond management to snoop inside the electronic cone of silence. Thankfully, I had my own little gizmo to disrupt any listening devices. If Houko intended to record our conversation, he'd find nothing but disappointment and a lot of white noise.

We took seats that gave us a view of both the front door and the lifts and waited in silence. At sixteen hundred hours Aquilonia time, one of the gilded elevator doors slid aside, and a short, middle-aged man with salt and pepper hair stepped out. He wore a suit I couldn't pay for in a decade of Fridays and a cold, almost reptilian expression. The sour-faced aide I'd spoken to earlier followed on his heels. He was shorter than his boss and a lot wider. Pullar and I stood to attract their attention.

Houko said something to his assistant then walked toward us. He stopped just short of the small coffee table and, dismissing Pullar after a brief glance at his Gendarmerie badge, fixed a pair of emotionless eyes on me.

"Chief Superintendent Morrow, I presume."

"Indeed. Thank you for consenting to speak with us." I gestured toward an empty chair, inviting him to sit. He accepted with a curt nod.

"You've been most insistent," he said after settling in and crossing one perfectly clad leg over the other, "something my aide has mentioned to your deputy chief constable, by the way. I'm not used to anyone approaching me in such a rude manner. I trust Maras took up the matter with you?"

"She did, but you should know my commanding officer is at Constabulary HQ on Wyvern. I'm in charge of the Professional Compliance Bureau's Rim Sector detachment and report to Deputy Chief Constable Hammett, not DCC Maras."

Houko's eyebrows crept up by a few millimeters.

"Oh. I wasn't aware of such peculiar arrangements."

"Since, among others, Professional Compliance investigates members of the Constabulary accused of malfeasance, no matter what their rank, we have a separate chain of command. My boss reports directly to the Chief Constable. We also investigate members of the Armed Services when asked to do so and of course, we handle the more delicate cases involving government officials. In the matter at hand, the Navy has requested we take charge. And since it involves an alien visitor, even if he didn't enjoy full diplomatic status, the Constabulary would eventually have taken over anyway."

"I see," he replied with an air of cold disinterest. "Well, you asked for thirty minutes of my time, and DCC Maras recommended to my aide that I cooperate, lest you set up camp in front of my door, so please go ahead."

"Thank you, Ser Houko. You met with Envoy Shovak exactly once, the day of his death. Correct?"

"Yes, it was only that one time, a meet and greet to open the negotiations on a festive note."

"Who was in attendance?"

"On the Shrehari side, Shovak, and his man Thopok. I had Gerri Kazan and Almas Mostrom with me."

"Kazan being your security director and Mostrom the head of opportunity development for the Rim Sector."

He nodded. "Correct."

"Yet your delegation has several more members. Why didn't they attend?"

"Shovak wished to keep the meet and greet small. He only brought Thopok and a pair of bodyguards with him to Aquilonia. The Shrehari don't believe in ostentation and apply the same moderation to the size of an envoy's retinue."

"But you brought two of yours to his one."

"It was expedient, considering the shape of the negotiations. Both Gerri and Almas were to be deeply involved. Shovak understood."

"And what shape would that have been?"

Houko didn't immediately reply, but his stony gaze never left my face. Then he said, "On the advice of ComCorp's legal division, I cannot answer questions relating directly to the substance of the negotiations between ComCorp and representatives of the Shrehari mercantile consortium known as *Quch Mech*. However, you may rest assured that Envoy Shovak's unfortunate demise was in no way related to our discussions."

I held his stare for a few seconds, just to show that I understood the game he was playing. We weren't yet at the point of demanding the release of commercial secrets.

"How can you be sure, Ser Houko? Few murders are random, especially in an enclosed habitat. And on Aquilonia in particular, they're remarkably infrequent thanks to the Cimmerian Gendarmerie."

Granted. I was laying it on a bit thick. Pullar was probably doing a sterling job keeping the worst of the riffraff in line. But I knew the place had a violent crime rate not too different from any other environmentally sealed habitat in this part of the Commonwealth. A station that attracted crooks looking for illicit gains inevitably found itself with regular shootings or stabbings. Just not of VIPs.

"Envoy Shovak was here to meet with you," I continued, "so it stands to reason his death could be linked to ComCorp's outreach efforts. Don't you think?"

"Doubtful," he replied in a skeptical tone. "But I suppose you must consider every possibility, no matter how outlandish."

"What can you tell me concerning Shovak and his employers?"

"Very little about Shovak. None of us had ever met him before, nor had we been in communication with him before his arrival. Our first contact with *Quch Mech* occurred via subspace radio perhaps eight or nine months ago. Then we set up a low-key meeting between a ComCorp representative and one of theirs in a neutral place, which I'd rather not name at this point. These talks culminated in an agreement to meet here on Aquilonia for substantive negotiations. That's when Shovak's name first surfaced. And before you ask, I have no idea how or why his employer selected him, but since the Shrehari are very status conscious, he would have been roughly my equivalent, which means quite senior."

"And *Quch Mech*?"

"One of the mercantile groupings allowed to trade with private Commonwealth businesses through the personal approval of the Shrehari *Kho'sahra*, their military dictator. They deal in a wide variety of goods and are more akin to an import-export broker by our standards. I gather the imperial government doesn't want direct business-to-business contacts between their people and us. If you want more details on the Shrehari side of these negotiations, you must ask them. As I said, I'm not in a position to discuss our end of things without authorization from our legal department."

"Did Shovak seem to feel threatened in any way?"

Houko's humorless laugh raised the hairs on the back of my neck.

"How," he asked, "would I be able to interpret anything other than his words? Picking up Shrehari behavioral cues isn't my forte. He seemed in good spirits."

"And Thopok?"

"He acted with more discretion than his boss did and seemed rather subdued. But considering the nature of their societal taboos, at least the ones I know about, I wasn't surprised to see an underling behave with reserve in the presence of his betters."

Something told me Houko knew more about our nonhuman guests than he was willing to admit, perhaps even more than I did, but that wouldn't be unnatural, all things considered. ComCorp didn't become one of the most influential zaibatsus in human history by appointing cretins to senior positions.

"Will Shovak's employers be sending another envoy to pick up where he left off?"

Houko gave me a noncommittal shrug. "That remains to be seen, and it may likely rest on the results of your investigation. If our potential Shrehari partners don't feel proper justice is served, they may decide we're not honorable enough to become business associates."

"In spite of your conglomerate's formal title?" I had to repress an ironic smirk.

"Indeed. Trust is hard to gain in Shrehari society, more difficult than among humans, but much easier to lose. Seeing their envoy murdered on a human station will have damaged what little we've built up so far. And second chances are uncommon."

"I'm sure you'll find other opportunities. The Empire is large."

His dark gaze harden. "Perhaps, but if we're forced to abandon these particular negotiations, we stand to lose a great deal, Chief Superintendent, and would need to find another partner who might be less trusting from the start. Imperial trade with the Commonwealth requires *Kho'sahra* backing, and I doubt he'd look kindly on allowing *Quch Mech* to continue working with us. Our chief executive officer would undoubtedly voice his displeasure. An incalculable amount of money is riding on our success, as are a lot of jobs."

I didn't need to ask to whom the ComCorp brass would complain, and it wouldn't be DCC Maras. If it involved enough money, the Secretary General's office would have a quiet word with our Chief Constable, although using the term incalculable seemed overwrought.

Zaibatsus of ComCorp's size amassed their wealth and power by tracking every bit of income and every expense to the last cred. They knew the value of each deal. Either he was trying to impress me, or they really were contemplating a more significant trade arrangement than I could fathom.

"Rest assured that I have as much interest in bringing this case to a suitable conclusion as you do," I replied, knowing I sounded terribly trite. But what else was there to say?

"Of course, Chief Superintendent." He inclined his head. "I didn't mean to imply that you weren't fully invested in resolving this deplorable matter to everyone's satisfaction. The Constabulary has a well-deserved reputation. What is it they say? You always get your suspect?"

"Only in bad fiction, Ser Houko. Can you think of any reasons why someone wanted Shovak dead?"

"Perhaps you're dealing with a murderer who hasn't accepted that the war is long over. But I understand you already have someone in custody. You might ask her."

"We have a person of interest, Ser Houko, nothing more."

"I see." But his tone made it clear he didn't. "I thought Major Pullar's people had caught the individual in question red-handed, so to speak."

I gave him my coldest smile. "Just as you have commercial matters you cannot discuss with outsiders, we in the law enforcement community can't discuss ongoing investigations with members of the public. Not even if they've graciously accepted to answer our questions."

Houko nodded, as if to acknowledge the point, then said, "And yet Thopok told us about his finding a human female at the scene of the crime, with the murder weapon in hand. Frankly, I fail to see why you're investigating at all."

"Our person of interest denies doing the deed. And if she's guilty, the imperial and Commonwealth governments will want to know why. Relations with the Empire can be rocky at times. Therefore, it would be best if we made a full report back to Envoy Shovak's superiors. After the meet and greet, did you and your two subordinates return straight to the Excelsior?"

"We did. None of us had contact with the Shrehari delegation afterward until Thopok notified us of the unfortunate incident the next morning."

"Is there anything about the meeting itself, or about the negotiations, in general, you can tell me that might shed light on Shovak's death?"

He shook his head. "I'm sorry, Chief Superintendent, but nothing comes to mind. None of us is in any way connected to this deplorable matter. I'm sure Major Pullar has already consulted the Excelsior's records and those of the station's surveillance network and confirmed that we were here when the murder occurred."

I glanced at Pullar who nodded. It could mean nothing, of course. Aquilonia seemed to have an alarming number of maintenance issues, especially when it came to sensors. And as for the hotel's records? Who would gainsay a VP of the conglomerate that owned the Excelsior's parent company?

"Thank you, Ser Houko. I'd like to speak with Gerri Kazan and Almas Mostrom at their earliest convenience."

The ComCorp VP gave me another dose of his emotionless stare, then said, "I'll tell them to contact Major Pullar's office. If that is everything?"

"It is. For now. In this kind of investigation, it's normal for us to interview witnesses several times as further information becomes known."

Houko stood and, with nothing more than a curt nod, he rejoined his aide, then both vanished into a waiting elevator cab.

Pullar gazed at me with a quizzical expression. "I'm not sure we obtained much by way of fresh evidence from this conversation, Chief Superintendent. We didn't even use up a full half hour of his time."

"It wasn't about gathering new evidence but getting a feel for the man. The negotiations between ComCorp and the Shrehari could be at the heart of this case. Otherwise, why kill a minor commercial envoy from that friendly Empire next door? You know, the one whose ass we kicked seventy years ago? Shovak isn't the first Shrehari to visit on a peaceful mission. I'll bet he isn't even the first one this month, and as far as I know, none of the others ended up lying in a puddle of their own blood."

Before he could reply, Pullar's communicator vibrated for attention. He held it up to his ear and then nodded. "Thank you." Tucking it away again, he said, "Ser Houko's aide just advised me that Almas Mostrom is on his way down."

"That was quick. I guess Houko wants us out of his hair as soon as possible."

— Twelve —

Mostrom proved to be a younger and suaver copy of the ComCorp vice president, and just as unhelpful. But he was a real bullshit artist if I'd ever seen one. His story matched Houko's almost word for word, but at least he tried to sound as if he wanted me to believe there was substance to his statement.

When we finished with him, he said, "I understand you wish to speak with Gerri Kazan next. Shall I send her up, or were you planning on seeing her at another time and in another place?"

His tone and the way he worded that last sentence led me to believe he knew Gerri and I had a past. I caught just a brief spark of amusement in his eyes.

"If Sera Kazan is available, please ask her to join us."

"I shall. Enjoy your day."

As we watched him enter the lift, Pullar said, "Would you prefer I not sit in on the next conversation? My presence might be a hindrance."

The offer surprised me, but it shouldn't have. Pullar had hidden depths he worked hard to conceal for some reason.

"Perhaps it would be best."

"In that case, I'll return to my office. If you join me there once you're done, I can show you one of the better eateries on Aquilonia."

"I'd like that, thank you."

"Until later."

And then I was alone but pregnant with a growing sensation of both trepidation and dread as my memories of Gerri and our acrimonious split bubbled to the surface. I tried to imagine what our reunion would be like, but when she stepped out of the lift, I realized nothing could have prepared me for the new Gerri.

With her pixie haircut, carefully sculpted face, and an expensive suit that seemed to be the corporate uniform, she looked a far cry from the hard-edged Flying Squad inspector I remembered. Even her gait had changed from a cop's deliberate pace to an elegant stride that screamed 'I own this place.'

When I stood, and our eyes met, I expected a spark of electricity at the renewed contact with someone who used to be my closest friend and confidante. But instead, I felt a piercing cold that sank my heart. Why I half-expected this to be a friendly reunion, I didn't know. Gerri stopped once she'd passed the sound screen and examined me without showing a shred of feeling.

"I heard you went from the Flying Squad to the Firing Squad," she said by way of greeting. "Congratulations. It's a good place for a rat, though I should thank you for making me look outside the Service. I've done so much better for myself with ComCorp. If I had stuck around, I'd be a washed-up chief inspector by now, with about as much advancement possibilities as you. Instead, I enjoy a gratifying and lucrative private sector career. You have no idea how lucrative. And I need not put up with bureaucratic garbage or your brand of hypocrisy."

"Hello, Gerri." I had to clamp down hard on my sudden urge to babble and somehow break through her icy demeanor. "I've been fine, thanks for asking. Please take a seat."

A mocking eyebrow slowly crept up her smooth forehead, and her full lips twitched as if she knew about my discomfiture and found it amusing.

"As you wish, Chief Superintendent."

So that's how it would be. The urge to reach out passed with breathtaking suddenness.

"Has Ser Houko informed you of what I'm after, Sera Kazan?"

"He has. And I'm sure he's informed you we cannot answer questions relating directly to the substance of the negotiations between ComCorp and representatives of the Shrehari mercantile group known as *Quch Mech*."

"Without your legal department's authorization. Yes, I understand." The same words used by her boss and also parroted by Mostrom before he answered my questions. "Were you involved in the talks between ComCorp and the Shrehari that culminated in Shovak and his entourage coming to Aquilonia?"

"Not the original discussions, but I had a hand in preparing for their visit, as part of my normal duties."

"What do you remember of your meeting with Envoy Shovak?"

"He was hospitable, jovial, and relaxed. We spoke of trivial matters. Shrehari don't mix business with ethanol."

"And Thopok?"

"Watchful, withdrawn but utterly correct. His job as an aide was not to take part in the festivities. But I'm sure Yan and Almas already told you that."

I nodded. "They did, but you used to be an investigator so you know I'm required to crosscheck. Did you sense anything amiss, with either Shovak, Thopok, or their surroundings? And I'm asking the former investigator now, not the potential witness."

She seemed to give my question serious thought, and then slowly shook her head. "Nothing. It was a standard meet and greet between a Shrehari commercial envoy and a ComCorp delegation."

"You've experienced many such meetings?"

"A few. The Shrehari are very security conscious. More so than we are, and I attend initial talks with new business partners regularly. Having me there gives them a measure of confidence that we take things seriously."

"Even though you're female?" I tried not to sound too skeptical. After dealing with the taciturn Thopok, I had a hard time seeing how Gerri would reassure his sort. Though more muscular and taller than I was, she didn't have the size and strength to earn a Shrehari's respect.

"I'm always introduced as a former Constabulary officer. Their equivalent is the much-feared *Tai Kan* so you can imagine how they see me the moment their brains make the connection."

"Ah." That certainly made sense. And it might explain Thopok's reluctance to speak with me. "Since you can't discuss the details of your relationship with the victim and his employer without permission from ComCorp's legal department, is there anything you can think of that might help my investigation. You used to be a good cop, so I'm sure that if you came across something of interest, you'd have noted it, even if it wasn't consciously."

Her cold eyes seemed to say, not bloody likely as she shook her head. "Nothing, although I question the PCB's involvement. According to Thopok, the Gendarmerie already holds the culprit, with enough evidence to convince any jury."

"Circumstantial evidence," I replied without thinking. A flash of amusement momentarily warmed her icy demeanor as if she'd caught me in a mistake.

"Being found with the murder weapon in hand and covered with the victim's bodily fluids is hardly circumstantial. Has the PCB addled your instincts? I suppose hounding good officers out of the Service doesn't need a nose for clues."

The cold blade of her contempt sliced through me. It hurt. Gerri's smile returned, showing pleasure at an insult striking home. I barely managed to smile back, although mine probably showed more teeth than it should.

"The degree of difficulty involved in catching a bent cop who knows all the dodges might surprise you," I replied. "It takes a special nose to ferret out the stench of corruption hidden beneath layers of well-constructed camouflage. But we're not here to discuss my personal or professional failings, Sera Kazan, nor yours." Retaliation was childish, but I couldn't help myself. "We're here to talk about a violent murder currently under investigation by the Commonwealth Constabulary."

I held her eyes long enough to force a restrained nod, then added, "Your knowledge of the Shrehari is better than mine, much better, so let me ask you a question. How do they view murder?"

She shrugged in a gesture of disinterest. "How does any advanced species view it? As a legal and social taboo. Although the Shrehari have a category of lawful killing that includes dueling on a matter of honor, summary execution for capital crimes like treason, and of course self-defense. Having an outlet means that the taboo against murder is much stronger in the Empire and the penalties much harsher. If you're wondering whether Thopok or either of the bodyguards could have killed Shovak, then the answer is a qualified yes. But I can't see them as likely suspects."

"Why qualified?"

"If Thopok or one of the guards clashed with Shovak on a matter of honor, then a mental switch might have flipped from trusted retainer to implacable enemy at the drop of an insult. Though I use the term retainer lightly since he wasn't a member of their nobility but a commoner with a high-level job. And that means the others are bound to him by employment, not oath of fealty. Now, the fact that Shovak was killed with his own knife..."

"Actually, we only have Thopok's word that it belonged to his boss."

Gerri nodded. "Fair enough. Let's say he was killed with a ritual knife, ownership unproven. Seeing as how the Shrehari fight duels with a bladed weapon, the notion isn't impossible. What leads me to qualify the answer is that unless Shovak uttered a deadly insult demanding immediate reparation, any notion of revenge would have waited until the delegation's return home. Resolving matters of honor in front of another species is dishonorable in itself."

"But if it is murder and not the result of a duel to the death, wouldn't its commission in human space be less dangerous than doing it back home?"

Her perfectly shaped lips twisted in a dismissive moue. "Not really. Our government would have no qualms about repatriating a Shrehari guilty of killing another of his species."

I was unexpectedly pleased to hear Gerri speak like the investigator she'd been years earlier before she turned blasé and sloppy.

"Are there any other tidbits of Shrehari sociology you think might help me shed light on the matter?"

"No. But if I can pass along a piece of advice, for old times' sake, sort this one out fast. Yan Houko is already annoyed at the Constabulary sticking its fingers into this mess. That you're PCB only makes it worse, especially with a suspect in custody. You call the evidence circumstantial, and perhaps you're right, but he doesn't see it that way. Unfortunately for you, he has the ear of the CEO who, in turn, has the ear of several prominent government members on Earth. If this proposed partnership falls through, it'll inflict a significant opportunity cost on ComCorp, and you know how we greedy, grasping private sector vampires are. Was there anything else, Chief Superintendent, or can I go?"

"That was it. If you think of anything more, you can reach me through Major Pullar's office." We both stood, and I held out my hand. "Thank you, Sera Kazan — Gerri."

As soon as I spoke her first name, I knew it was a mistake. Her eyes turned to ice again, breaking the tenuous rapport between us.

She spun around and walked away, leaving me standing alone, feeling like an idiot. Even reminding myself that Gerri had brought it on herself, ignoring my warnings, advice and near the end, indulging in temper tantrums, didn't help ease the deep pain.

Had I known she'd be on the witness list, I would have brought Arno Galdi with me right away and assigned him the job of interviewing the ComCorp folks. It might have given Sergeant Bonta a good dose of professional development if I'd left her to wrap up the loose ends on the Haylian matter. This was my reward for rushing in without a full background briefing.

The sheepish part of me glanced around to see if anyone had noticed. But other than the invisible surveillance sensors, no one cared about a middle-aged frump wearing the last decade's fashion and not doing it that well either. Now what?

Interview Shovak's bodyguards? I doubted they had half a word of Anglic between them, and my Shrehari wasn't much better. Gerri could probably spit out a few coherent sentences, but there was no way I'd ask her now.

Maybe Pullar had someone. It was a damn shame we never could build a translation AI able to cross species boundaries. Go figure why.

Since I had no way of speaking with the rest of the Shrehari, I wouldn't get much more by way of background. That meant interviewing Talyn again and going through her movements from the time she arrived on Aquilonia. And more importantly, hearing about her motives in entering Shovak's quarters from her own lips.

Just then, my stomach reminded me I'd skipped the midday meal, and it was already well past seventeen hundred hours, station time. Pullar had said something about showing me one of the better restaurants on the station.

With a last glance at the fake opulence of the Aquilonia Excelsior's lobby, I rejoined the stream of humanity on the promenade. But after taking no more than a dozen steps, I felt an itch between my shoulder blades — my instinct's unmistakable signal someone was taking more than a passing interest in me.

— Thirteen —

I kept walking at the same pace, but now my eyes searched every reflective surface within visual range, trying to spot a tail.

The itch had been wrong before, but for some reason, I knew it wasn't a false positive this time. Fortunately Aquilonia's promenade, in keeping with those of almost every station in human space, tried to replicate a commercial boulevard no different from those on any developed planet. It teemed with small shops, bars, and restaurants, creating an artificial impression of size thanks to the sheer number of them.

Within minutes, I spotted an ordinary-looking, if muscular man in black trousers and a high-collared blue shirt following me without trying very hard to hide. He slowed and sped up whenever I did, and he stopped and pretended to window shop in tandem with me.

After I passed the lift bank twice without heading for the Gendarmerie offices, our eyes finally met in the reflection of a gadget shop's mirrored display. Instead of hastily looking away, like any inept tail would do, he held my gaze, and a small, mocking smile twisted his bloodless lips.

I spun around and, dodging other pedestrians, I headed for the man intending to extract answers. But instead of fleeing, he waited until I was within earshot and said, "Louis Sorne welcomes you to Aquilonia and hopes you'll enjoy a long and happy stay."

An unaccustomed chill ran up my spine. "Who are you?"

"Merely a messenger, Chief Superintendent Morrow," he replied backing away until he cleared the nearest corner. Then he vanished. I only realized afterward the man had been speaking without moving his lips so that his words couldn't be deciphered without audio. With the noise level on the promenade, any sensor more than a few meters distant wouldn't pick up much. I had the distinct feeling the messenger chose his spot carefully so that no one could record him speaking Sorne's name.

On my way to Pullar's office, I hosted an internal debate on whether to tell him about this latest incident, knowing it would mean my discussing sensitive parts of the Haylian case. But if I wanted to track down the so-called messenger and question him, I would need the Gendarmerie's help. At the very least, I had to send another report to my folks back on Cimmeria, for the Sorne file.

What the hell was Sorne thinking? Was he merely messing with me, or was there a more sinister motive behind his false solicitude. A long and happy stay?

When Pullar, talking to the desk sergeant, spotted me walking through the door he frowned. "Are you okay, Chief Superintendent? You seem a little disconcerted. Did the interview go well?"

I nodded toward his office. "Could we speak in private?"

"Certainly."

He settled in behind his desk and watched me with an expectant air while I closed the door and took one of the facing chairs.

"The interview went pretty much as I had expected. We didn't have a tearful reunion, but that's not what concerns me right now. It's something related to the investigation I wrapped up before coming to Aquilonia. Technically, I shouldn't be sharing anything with you, since it's a case where the perp turned state's evidence in exchange for a walk. But someone involved with my perp, someone who's about to become a suspect as well, reached out to me after I left the Excelsior. It was the second time that happened since I arrested our guy. The first time was on Valerys."

Pullar winced. "That doesn't sound reassuring. What can I do to help?"

"Retrieve the video surveillance record of the promenade near the Shimmering Stash electronics store for the last fifteen minutes. A man tailed me from the hotel until I confronted him. Then he gave me a verbal message similar to the one I got on Valerys. You should find a ten-second stretch where we're facing each other. I want to know his name and his employer. And I need a secure comm link to Cimmeria so I can report the incident."

"We can do that for you. Would it be overstepping my bounds if I asked who reached out to you twice, and why?"

It was a legitimate question from a cop concerned about criminal activity on his patch.

"I can't figure out the why, Major. Things are already in motion against the individual, and I can no longer influence them, so intimidation would serve no purpose. Even if I wanted to stop inquiries resulting from the arrest I made, the matter is now entirely out of PCB hands. Revenge, perhaps? Or a warning to steer clear of further forays into a sensitive area? We're talking about corrupt buggers with enough hubris to believe themselves untouchable. As my perp found out that's not necessarily the case."

He studied me in silence for a moment before saying, "And you'd rather not reveal the person's identity right now. Understood. Let me have my folks call up the relevant recording."

Definitely more perceptive than he cared to show. "Thank you."

"Did you plan on waiting for the results, or should we eat and come back?" He asked after putting through my request.

"Why don't we take our meal first? I'd rather send my report home with a name attached."

"Done."

Pullar led me to a quiet spot off the main drag where the locals ate. It bore the unimaginative moniker Aquilonia Arms. Its emblem was an overdone piece of heraldry that combined mining equipment with elaborate starships and fanciful animals. The Commonwealth Master Herald, on faraway Earth, would have suffered a spurt of nausea at its sight and demanded its erasure by nuclear fire forthwith.

Tucked in a corner of carved stone polished to a dull shine, the pub was away from the usual tourist and transient haunts, which suited me. The dining room seemed like a reproduction of a pre-spaceflight country inn, something that struck me as odd here, on a moon orbiting a planet far from the cradle of humanity.

But the atmosphere seemed cozy and inviting, and the chairs weren't nearly as hard as they appeared, proving that even reproductions could be updated to the most modern comforts while losing none of the charms.

Once we had our drinks, beer for him, and what would probably be no better than a red Chateau Sewage for me, he raised his glass.

"Here's to you wrapping this case up quickly."

I took a sip of my wine and mentally apologized to its makers. It was slightly above a Chateau Sewage, but not quite up to the standards of the ubiquitous red shipped out from Dordogne aboard FTL starships.

"Wrapping it up fast seems to be a common refrain today," I replied. "I know why Thopok's impatient. He wants to go home with Shovak's remains. I know why the ComCorp folks want me done and gone. They face a sticky business situation. But why are you keen on speed?"

Pullar grimaced. "Half a dozen people with political weight are riding my ass right now, from the station's chief administrator to my boss on Cimmeria, to the Cimmeria Trade Department and more. The sooner you haul off the guilty party, the sooner my life goes back to collaring drunks, pickpockets, and corrupt dockworkers. My tour here has only six months to go, and then it'll be one last posting before retirement, hopefully in my hometown."

I couldn't entirely repress a snort. "Political pressure, eh? The story of my life, except I can shrug it off more easily than most unless it comes from very high. Our friend Yan Houko seems to be the kind to try calling down a shit storm on my head, and good luck to him. That said, you have my sympathies, but it'll take as long as it takes. Between the Navy and the Shrehari Empire, if they don't see an airtight case or at least one they can live with, I'll be stuck here, and I prefer breathing fresh air."

He took another sip of his beer before flashing a sad smile at me. "I guess we all have someone leaning on us, even in the Firing Squad. Speaking of which, what did you glean from your interview with Sera Kazan, or should I not ask?"

"She gave me pretty much the same story we heard from Houko and Mostrom." After I related the discussion, if not verbatim then damn near, he nodded.

"Strange beings, those Shrehari, with notions of honor that our species might do well to relearn, at least a little. Do you think one of them might be our real culprit if Talyn's telling the truth about being innocent?"

"Not a clue. I'd like to question the two bodyguards, but I would need a decent Shrehari translator. Hired guns usually aren't multilingual, and I wouldn't trust Thopok to translate, even if he volunteered."

"How about your former partner?"

My brief burst of laughter must have sounded bleaker than sunrise on Andoth. "There's no chance in hell she would volunteer to do me a favor. Gerri still hasn't forgiven me. Besides, I don't know if her Shrehari is good enough. Unless you know someone, I'll call for help from Cimmeria, and that'll take time."

Pullar shook his head. "Sorry. I can't offhand think of anyone on Aquilonia who speaks fluent Shrehari and can be trusted, but I'll check with a few of the less venal merchants willing to entertain helping the Gendarmerie."

"I'll ask DCC Maras' staff to rustle one up for me." Although if her folks gave me the usual cold shoulder, I'd have to call on Maras directly for help and that wasn't something I could afford to do often. "What about the Shrehari guards? Letting the killer slip past them would have been dishonorable, no?"

"We severely restrict armed private security on the station and don't allow any in the VIP section. You and I accessed that level with ease, but anyone without the necessary authorization wouldn't be able to do so, be it via the lifts or the stairs. So, there's no reason for guards standing outside the door. Shovak's people are quartered in a section one level lower reserved for VIP hangers-on. It's where we found them after securing the envoy's body. My men had to pull their weapons to keep them under control after they heard the news. Neither had a trace of blood on them, and both were outraged at our lax, dishonorable security measures — or so Thopok told us."

"You'd count them out as suspects?"

Pullar grimaced again. "Yes and no. One of them was seen leaving their room about an hour before Talyn called us to say she'd found Shovak's body. He went up to the VIP level and spent a few minutes with Thopok before returning. He would have had enough time to kill his boss. With the video pickups inoperative, there's no way of determining who entered the envoy's suite."

I caught my fingers tapping the tabletop and wrapped them around the stem of the wine glass instead. "I can't believe how timely this little maintenance issue was for the killer. Did anyone other than the guard enter the VIP section during the hours before Shovak death?"

"Several people, humans only. Trade representatives, high-profile travelers, guests of the station." Pullar chuckled. "A high-level member of the Star Wolves, even. Aquilonia's administrator has a relatively liberal definition of VIP. Enough money or political power, preferably both, will give you that status."

"And the Confederacy of the Howling Stars has enough wealth to buy its way into the best Aquilonia offers, I suppose. Did you interview everyone present that evening?"

"No. With Talyn in custody, it didn't seem worth the effort to bother people we could trace from the lift directly to their rooms. The security sensor net is out of order only on the Shrehari side, and the administration left a good buffer of unoccupied suites between them and the other guests. We had enough evidence, even on the Star Wolf, to leave them out of our inquiries."

I wasn't sure I blamed him. If you could eliminate witnesses or suspects through electronic means, it was a time saver. And it avoided a lot of potential unpleasantness. Just because people had VIP status didn't make them love law enforcement representatives.

But the sensor net failure near Shovak's rooms was unlikely to be a coincidence. Isolating the Shrehari, banishing the guards to the servant's quarters, and removing the possibility of surveillance placed Shovak in a trap. An assassin couldn't have set it up any better. I said as much to Pullar and his face puckered into a sour expression.

"I hope you're wrong. A conspiracy of that sort could play into the chief administrator's hands when it comes to the politics surrounding security and policing on Aquilonia."

"How so?"

"Donul Darrien, the man who runs this place, hates the fact I don't report to him, but to Gendarmerie HQ on Cimmeria. He's itching to create his own private force, accountable only to him. But for that to happen, the Aquilonia Syndicate's board of directors would have to convince various government ministers it would be in everyone's interest to withdraw the Gendarmerie and hand policing duties to Darrien. But once they have enough ammo to lobby the government, what with the amount of money they can wave around as political donations..."

"Do you think he might have organized it?"

A bitter laugh escaped Pullar's throat. "Donul Darrien? Sure. I wouldn't put anything past him. He recently brought in a private security company, with government approval, to increase safety in and around the docks, warehouses, and other parts of Aquilonia directly connected with the flow of trade goods. They have no policing powers, can only carry non-lethal weapons, and have to call us in for any arrests. But I figure it's his way of laying the groundwork for a future Aquilonia-run law enforcement unit. Darrien knows all the bureaucratic dodges and can play nasty political games with the best of them. Fancies himself the King of Aquilonia. If only he knew what we call him behind his back."

"And what do you call him?"

"Darrien insists on being called D.D. as if that gives him a formal-informal cachet. What he doesn't know is that a lot of his own staff decided D.D. stands for Dangerous Don, and it's not meant to be flattering." Pullar sighed. "I can't leave this place soon enough."

"I can think of several other word games you can play with those two letters, but I hear you." At my touch, a holographic menu appeared in the center of the table. "Shall we order? My last meal is a distant memory."

When our food arrived, we ate with relish, our conversation turning to the inconsequential, which meant mostly Pullar's more or less funny stories about arresting the clueless, the stupid, and the downright unsafe.

His daily routine seemed much more interesting if not quite as intellectually stimulating than mine. But it gave me fresh insight into the follies and foibles of our species and did nothing to dissuade me from the belief most people were idiots.

"I never asked," he said after swallowing his last bite, "but where are you staying while you're on Aquilonia?"

"On the VIP level."

His eyes widened in surprise, and I laughed. "I'm here at the Navy's behest. They're paying the freight, which means I won't deprive myself. Don't worry, my suite is about as far as you can get from the Shrehari, but if you're wondering whether I'll use my special access to that area for investigative purposes, the answer is yes."

Pullar chuckled. "I should have known. Did you plan on any other interviews for today or are you calling it quits?"

"My circadian rhythm is a few hours ahead of station time, so yeah. I'm done for the day, other than finding out the identity of Sorne's messenger.

I'd like to put Talyn through a proper interview tomorrow, not just a lightweight chat like I had today since I now know more about the context."

Pullar suddenly froze, then produced his communicator and held it to his ear. After a few moments, he tucked it away again and puckered his brow.

"We know who your man is."

— Fourteen —

"My desk sergeant recognized him the moment he called up the video," Pullar said.

"You don't seem happy about it."

"Remember me mentioning the private security firm Darrien brought in recently? The guy is one of theirs. Ward Loriot. He was even wearing their uniform when he approached you, minus the badges and superhero belt, meaning he didn't care if we linked him to CimmerTek."

"That would be the company in question? CimmerTek Security Solutions?"

"Yes. I see you've heard of them."

I nodded. "CimmerTek likes to maintain a low profile, but the Constabulary keeps an eye on all private security firms. Organized crime has infiltrated several of them in the last few years."

"If someone is openly using Loriot to pass on a message, does that mean the company came up in your last case?"

"Not CimmerTek as such, but one of its largest shareholders and silent partners, who will shortly face criminal charges because of my investigation."

Sorne had his fingers in so many pockets I might have missed the private security firm during my investigation. But Haylian had been helpful in covering up several occurrences of Sorne laundering his money through CimmerTek's coffers to evade taxes, and those formed part of the indictment I built against him.

"Thanks to your perp who turned state's evidence." Pullar nodded. "Dare I ask who the shareholder might be?" When he saw me hesitate, he quickly said, "I withdraw the question with my apologies. I realize this is neither the time nor the place. Now that you have the information, what are your intentions?"

What were my intentions? Have Loriot or his superiors give Sorne a message of my own? And what would it say? On further reflection, I decided it would be best to let the team charged with the Sorne investigation handle the matter at their end.

"Let my colleagues know about the message, Loriot, and CimmerTek. I have my own case to pursue."

"Aren't you worried they might graduate from words to deeds?" Pullar asked with an air of genuine concern.

"These clowns aren't the first to try their hand at scaring me, and the few who've gone beyond threats are now either in a penal colony or dead."

Pullar examined me with thoughtful eyes. "I see. Are you armed?"

I shook my head. "No. My suspects are rarely of the violent sort. I only carry when needed."

"If a presumed criminal is sending you hate messages, perhaps you might want to reconsider. Did you at least bring something?"

Again, he noticed my hesitation and quickly said, "I have no issues with you carrying a concealed weapon on Aquilonia, even of the lethal variety. Our restrictions don't apply to visiting law enforcement or military personnel."

"I brought a needler, but only non-lethal loads."

"Then please carry it, Chief Superintendent, and if you want something more deadly, I can help. I assume your gun takes standard clips?"

"It does. And thank you, Major."

"I can also lean on Loriot's boss, the CimmerTek general manager for the Aquilonia contract — a gorilla by the name Javan Burrard."

The vitriol in his tone and his choice of words made me smile. "Why do I think you and this Burrard person might have a rocky past?"

"Probably my calling him a gorilla," Pullar replied with a rueful grin. "Javan Burrard is a former Gendarmerie master sergeant. We served together years ago when I was still a noncommissioned gendarme. Javan outranked me for a while, but soon after I became a master sergeant myself, I passed the commissioning exams and earned a promotion to lieutenant. He either never achieved a passing mark, or his commanding officer told him he'd never be promoted. Or possibly both. Long story short, Javan retired as soon as he became eligible for a pension and bounced around the private sector. I lost track of him until he showed up here as the CimmerTek GM a few months ago."

"Why would he not have been able to earn promotion beyond senior noncommissioned rank?"

Pullar snorted. "For pretty much the same reasons your former partner, Gerri Kazan, found herself in trouble. He had a propensity for cutting corners, except he did it in an aggressive pursuit of results, sometimes to the detriment of suspects and fellow gendarmes alike. It was never enough to attract the attention of our own internal affairs branch, but no one could see Javan with a commission."

"And now he's running private security on your patch. That must be interesting."

Pullar sighed. "The bastard knows exactly where the line is drawn and dances as close to it as he can. His superiors wouldn't thank him if he got CimmerTek in the Gendarmerie's bad books and so he cooperates, but with as little enthusiasm as possible. That he's buddies with Donul Darrien makes it worse."

"Let me guess — your old colleague thinks he might have a shot at running Aquilonia's police force if you and your troopers leave."

"Probably. It would be a form of vindication for Burrard." He pushed his chair back. "I suggest we go send your report and then I'll let you turn in."

As if on cue, I yawned. "Good idea." I pulled out a data wafer and tapped the menu screen. "Supper was the Navy's treat."

"In that case," he replied, climbing to his feet, "please pass my thanks to the Grand Admiral."

A short stroll took us back to his station, where I quickly composed another incident report, with the notation that it be forwarded to the team investigating Sorne.

I yawned again after sending the message and smiled at Pullar. "It's been a long day. Can we pick this up again at oh-eight-hundred?"

He dipped his head once in an oddly formal gesture of acknowledgment. "Certainly. If you'll excuse me, I must do my rounds before clocking off for the day. Until tomorrow, Chief Superintendent."

"Until tomorrow."

I wish I could say sleep came easy that night, considering the expense of the luxurious suite with its form-fitting bed, gently scented air cycler, and absolute silence. But seeing Gerri again had thrown me for an endless loop that didn't appear to be slowing.

The brief burst of cooperation when she shared her insight into Shrehari culture had somehow amplified my pain at her cold rejection. For a moment, I'd felt as if we were still a team of hotshot investigators making a name for ourselves.

They said you should never become emotionally involved with your partner. They didn't say what you should do if, against common sense, you did, and it turned to radioactive dust.

— Fifteen —

Talyn still sat on her bunk in the lotus position, eyes closed, when I looked at her cell's video feed the next morning. If it weren't for faint signs of breathing, I might have thought her dead. I lingered around the guard station for a few minutes, trying to decide on an approach.

Here was presumably a trained interrogator, a woman who made her living by hunting for the most innocuous bits of data and building a coherent picture. She was probably better at it than I would ever be and I wondered whether somewhere, deep inside, I felt intimidated by Talyn.

She had shown more amusement than concern during our first meeting, as if she knew I couldn't pin Shovak's death on her. When I entered the cell, her eyes snapped open, and a faint smile played on her lips as if she had been expecting me.

"Good morning, Chief Superintendent."

"Commander." I took the only chair and sat facing her. "You seem blissfully unconcerned."

"That's because I didn't kill Shovak, something you'll confirm soon enough."

"I'm touched by your vote of confidence."

"The Professional Compliance Bureau has a reputation for closing cases with irrefutable evidence." A brief twinkle lit up her dark eyes. "Did you speak with Thopok and the folks Shovak was meeting?"

I caught myself before automatically answering yes, annoyed that she had thrown out the first question. Trained interrogator indeed.

"Never mind what I did, Commander." I held her eyes for a few heartbeats. "I've read the case file and your statement, and this morning I expect more useful answers than the ones you gave me yesterday. Why did you come to Aquilonia Station? You're attached to Naval Intelligence at the Armed Services HQ on Caledonia, in a system that's not even remotely nearby. Was it on duty or personal?"

"On duty. You didn't think I'd be able to book myself a VIP suite without serious Fleet leverage, let alone pay for it on a commander's salary? And no, I can't tell you what my mission orders were, other than highly classified. You'll need to ask the relevant Fleet authorities if you need more details. I can't reveal anything without explicit permission. Suffice to say they didn't concern the Shrehari. I don't work for the section dealing with the Empire."

"Were your orders related to ComCorp?"

The faint, knowing smile returned. "So that's who was meeting with Shovak. Interesting. I spotted a group of corporate warriors in the ferry's first class section. It must have been them. No, my orders did not involve ComCorp."

"You arrived at Valerys Station on a civilian ship, the *Xenophon*, and then took the regular run from Valerys to Aquilonia. Why not take a naval transport?"

"It was a matter of timeliness, and *Xenophon*'s routing fit my needs. Besides, naval vessels rarely visit Aquilonia so I would have been forced to take the ferry from Valerys anyway."

Her answers were quick and smooth, and her tone mercifully devoid of anything that might irritate me.

"You stepped off the ferry approximately thirty-six hours before the gendarmes found you standing over Shovak's body. What did you do during that time?"

She shrugged. "Enjoyed the amenities. My cabins aboard both *Xenophon* and the ferry weren't exactly luxurious. I wandered around the station and took in the sights. I didn't hide. While wandering, I conducted business related to my orders, that kind of thing. If you're expecting me to say I stalked the Shrehari, plotting vile murder, you'll be disappointed. I saw the delegates in passing the day before Shovak's death but didn't pay them much attention. If they're on a human station, in VIP quarters at that, my colleagues will know. As I said, my orders didn't involve Shrehari."

"And that evening?"

"Let me see." She turned her eyes upward, in a show of searching her memory, though we both knew she had the details readily at hand. "I ate my evening meal on the promenade, a little place called Cam's Bistro, then took a stroll around the station, for a bit of people watching. I stopped in at one of the bars for a nightcap, listened to live music, and then, at around oh-one-hundred hours, I headed to the VIP section. When I came out of the stairwell, I realized something was amiss in the area assigned to the Shrehari delegation. I went to investigate and found him on the floor, blood pumping from a stab wound in the neck. Of course, I tried to staunch the flow."

Her face took on a rueful expression. "That's how Shovak's blood ended up on me, but he died seconds after I arrived. I immediately summoned the Gendarmerie. They'll have noted it in their incident log. Then, another Shrehari, whom I now know to be Thopok, burst into the suite, knife drawn, ready to kill me. I picked up the bloody blade the murderer used so I might defend myself. Major Pullar's men arrived moments later and arrested me. They probably saved my life too. An angry Shrehari is a frightening thing to behold, especially one almost twice my size. The rest you know."

Talyn told her story without hesitation, showing none of the signs that usually warned me a suspect was embellishing, or outright lying. She either was telling the truth or had an impressive mastery of her unconscious gestures and expressions.

"Yet conveniently, there's no sensor record of you entering the secure VIP area, let alone Shovak's suite. We already know the sensors in that zone malfunctioned."

"That's because I took the stairs to help me metabolize the evening's alcohol intake. I wish I had taken the lift. Then I wouldn't have noticed the open door. The sight angles are wrong. It would have spared me this." She waved a hand to indicate the cell and its spartan furnishings.

Often, when suspects tried to bullshit me, they would examine my reactions to see if I believed them. I saw none of that in Talyn's face. She had the assured expression of someone convinced she was telling the truth.

Still, a few things bothered me. The sensor failures in that wing, and in the controlled-access staircase, for one. They were convenient, enough so to call for an in-depth verification. Also, why did the killer leave Shovak's door open? If you wanted to hide a crime for as long as possible, you kept it hidden. Finally, there was something about the way it unfolded that didn't quite work with Talyn's statement.

"Commander, your testimony doesn't mention seeing anyone in the minutes before finding Shovak's body, either in the VIP section or in the staircase. Yet if you aren't the killer, then someone should have either registered on the working sensors around the time of your arrival or crossed your path. The nature of Shovak's injuries and the way you say he was pumping out blood means the stabbing occurred moments before your arrival. Any comments?"

"I didn't see or hear anyone between when I entered the staircase from the promenade until I found Shovak. Maybe you'll find other dead sensors in the VIP section. Better yet, if Thopok is the guilty party, he did not need to leave the Shrehari's assigned area and expose himself to working sensors around the lift." She paused for a moment. "The guilty party could also have used the stairs going downward. Someone taking care to make no noise would have escaped my attention. Perhaps Major Pullar could check the sensor logs for the lower levels. The killer had to leave the staircase at some point and step into range of a working pickup."

Looking at Talyn, I had to remind myself that her guileless expression could easily come from years of careful training as a spook and not necessarily from innocence. But she was plausible.

"A hypothetical question, Commander. If you personally had to kill a Shrehari male in the prime of his life, how would you go about it?"

She chuckled humorlessly. "With a large-bore blaster, preferably. I'm not strong enough for hand-to-hand combat. Even my partner, who's much closer to their size, would have a hard time of it. Every Shrehari male undergoes military training during adolescence, and they learn how to use those knives they carry."

"Did you see anything on Thopok at the time that might show he came in contact with Shovak's blood?"

"No." She shook her head. "My eyes were on his blade more than anything else. When the gendarmes showed up, they hustled me out with commendable speed. I suppose he could have had traces on him that weren't immediately apparent. Shrehari blood is dark, and they do like to wear dark clothes. Did Pullar's folks not examine him on the spot?"

"Not quickly enough. After the gendarmes took you aside, Thopok knelt to gather Shovak up in his arms before anyone had the presence of mind to scan him. Once that happened, identifying any transference related to the murder became impossible."

Talyn let out a low whistle. "Nicely done, Thopok."

"You think it's him?"

"He certainly had the means, more so than pretty much anyone else other than Shovak's bodyguards. Ordinary humans don't stand a chance once they're within arm's reach. He had the opportunity, seeing as how his suite is adjacent and the space between both was a sensor dead zone that night, thanks to the station's crappy maintenance. The only thing you're missing is the motive. But when it comes to the Shrehari, you never know what will trigger their ticklish sense of honor. I'd focus my attention on the rest of the delegation if I were you."

Oh, joy. That's what I really wanted. Have I mentioned I thoroughly loathed cases involving the military? Talyn must have sensed my unease, and she smiled again.

"I'd help you out since my Shrehari is better than most people's but..." She raised her hands, palms up and shrugged. "I'm afraid I can't unless you'd like to exonerate me on the spot and swear me in as a special constable."

At that moment, I discovered something I hated even more than military cases — cases where the primary suspect was a smart ass.

"I think it's still early for you to cross over from suspect to crime hunter. The optics wouldn't work, would they?" I stood and tugged my jacket into place. She remained in the lotus position and studied me with the same detached expression she had shown when I first met her. "Thank you, Commander. I'm sure we'll be talking again soon."

"Until you release me, I'll be here, ready to answer questions at your convenience, Chief Superintendent."

As I turned to leave, I could have sworn I saw a glint of amusement in those dark, watchful eyes.

— Sixteen —

Pullar waved at a vacant chair when I stuck my head into his office.

"Please take a seat, Chief Superintendent. How's our guest this morning?" He dismissed the holographic display hovering over his desk with a wave of the hand.

"Unchanged. Talyn's the calmest suspect I've met in years. It's as if she's certain we'll let her go in the end. Normally, once I have them in a cell, they're in various states of agitation wondering how they'll slip out of my grasp. *If* they'll slip out of my grasp."

"I'm not sure I'd trust a spook's body language," Pullar replied with the puckered brow of a lifelong skeptic. "And since she's our only suspect, releasing her anytime soon doesn't seem likely."

"But we still only have circumstantial evidence and spook or not, she's plausible. There are too many questionable bits in this case still needing answers, including the cause of the sensor failures in the VIP section and the staircase. If you were preparing to assassinate Shovak, you'd have made sure those were out of order. And if it was that thoroughly planned, getting caught at the scene of the crime with the murder weapon in your hand just doesn't fit."

"The failures could have been random. If I were to plan something nasty in that part of the station, I'd sabotage the sensors in and around the lift as well," Pullar countered.

"Too obvious. I'm sure the lifts are higher on the engineering section's maintenance list since they're inspected annually by the Cimmeria Department of Transport."

Pullar nodded. "True."

I related my conversation with Talyn. When I fell silent, he sprang up, went out into the bullpen, and issued orders to the desk sergeant. Once back in his chair, he leaned forward on his elbows and tapped his fingertips together.

"We'll ask engineering to extract the broken sensors, but I can't guarantee they'll make it a priority. Analyzing them for tampering might be even more challenging. I don't have a forensics team. It means I have to rely on people who work for Dangerous Don."

"What are the chances of sweet-talking the station's chief engineer into giving this a rush job?"

"About as much as Darrien giving up his dream of owning the station's police force."

The disgust in Pullar's tone sounded so sincere I almost smiled in sympathy. Aquilonia's lord and master must be a piece of work.

"I really have to meet this paragon of virtue."

Pullar made a face. "You probably will sooner than you'd like. Darrien's been hounding me again this morning to make sure we wrap things up quickly, so as not to annoy our esteemed guests. I assume he means the ComCorp folks although he didn't name them. Don't be surprised if you receive a summons to appear in his throne room on command."

"That should be fun."

"You mean you'll go?" Pullar asked, not bothering to hide his astonishment. "I thought you PCB folks were above us common mortals when faced with petty bureaucrats. The one time I dared not obey him with enough alacrity, I heard from my HQ on Cimmeria within twelve hours, never mind Darrien's not in my chain of command."

"We are immune from jumped-up donkeys to a certain extent, but meeting Darrien might prove instructive. Wanting you and your gendarmes gone from Aquilonia means he has a motive to foment a scandal involving the Feds. And this Fed wants to know if the motive is enough to trigger a search for the means and opportunity. Seeing as he's in control of Aquilonia's engineering and maintenance, who better to orchestrate the sabotage of your sensor net?"

Pullar cracked a smile, showing glee for the first time since I met him. "I think I'd pay to see you and D.D. spar. Though it'll probably be more like watching you play chess while he plays three card monte. Was there anything else you'd like me to do?"

"I'd still like to find a competent Shrehari translator."

"Actually, I might be able to accommodate you in that respect. There's a guy who runs an import-export business with trading partners in the Empire. It's small-time compared to the likes of ComCorp, and some of it is dodgy, but apparently still profitable. He owes me a favor or two for squinting at his cargo manifest in the past. I'll reach out to him."

Now that was better. I knew buttering up my friend the major by keeping him fully informed of my investigation would pay off. Cooperation by the locals was rare. Pullar must really be pleased I took this case off his hands.

I wondered whether he thought it one of those instances where the results would satisfy no one, especially not the folks who could make your life miserable. He was an old cop looking for one last assignment where he could gently slip into retirement. Incentive enough to take a step back and let me handle it.

"If you would," I said, "provided we can trust him."

Pullar's laugh sounded like a bark. "We can't, but I can make it worth his while, and I'm sure you can think of something to sweeten him. Colin Fiers is only about profit and not letting any slip through his fingers. Given the assurance that the latter won't happen, I'm sure he'll wish to cooperate. I doubt he's keen on seeing ComCorp eat up even more of the cross-border trade, so there's that."

"I'm sold. Set up a meeting with this Colin Fiers. If I must, I'll even pay for drinks."

"Oh, trust me." Pullar grinned again. "You'll pay for something."

Just then, the office comm chimed for attention, and he glanced at the caller ID.

"Crap. It's the office of his Grand Worship the Ruler of Aquilonia. Want to bet it's a summons for the rogue Fed to present herself at court?"

"No bets. Gambling has led more than a few senior officers to my interview room with the knowledge I was about to end their careers in disgrace."

Pullar touched the controls, and I heard a querulous female voice demanding to know the whereabouts of one Chief Inspector Moran of the Constabulary. I had the distinct pleasure of watching my newest best friend Jon Pullar struggle to keep a straight face when he told D.D.'s assistant he knew no one of that name and rank.

"What do you mean?" She asked with the outrage of someone wearing her superior's title vicariously.

"I mean what I said. There is no Constabulary officer of that rank and name on Aquilonia. You can check with arrivals control."

Silence. Then, the same voice, with a touch less venom, "Is there a newly arrived Constabulary officer charged with the Shovak investigation on Aquilonia?"

"If you're referring to Chief Superintendent Morrow, then yes. She's here, and she'll probably be a little put out at having been mistaken for an officer two ranks lower."

Yep. Jon Pullar had definitely become my best if only friend on this station. He glanced up at me with questioning eyes. I shook my head.

"Unfortunately," he continued, "I have no way of contacting her right now. May I relay a message?"

"You may," the disembodied voice replied. "D.D. wishes to confer with Chief Superintendent Morrow at ten-hundred hours precisely."

"I'll try to let her know, but I can neither guarantee I'll catch up with her or that she'll be free at ten-hundred hours. Morrow is investigating under federal auspices."

"Make sure she presents herself on time, Pullar. You know D.D. doesn't like tardiness."

By his expression, the venomous aide had abruptly cut the connection.

"She seems nice." I gave him an ironic smile.

"Lisbeth is Darrien's partner as well as his aide." He sighed. "She sometimes suffers from the delusion she runs Aquilonia on her own, and it's no improvement on him. The staff calls her B.B. for Bitchy Betty. B.B. and D.D. make a beautiful pair. As you saw, she won't even do me the courtesy of a visual link."

"I think maybe I'll show up at ten-thirty. Would that work?" I tried to look impish.

Pullar's laugh, although restrained, conveyed a degree of pleasure I hadn't expected.

"Oh, it'll work all right. Bitchy Betty will pester me at one minute after ten and every five minutes after that, and I'll be able to say truthfully that you're on your way to his office. The King of Aquilonia will be livid by the time you appear. Your casual manner will give him and his beloved a fit of apoplexy." He raised a clenched fist and said, in an ironic tone, "Go get 'em, Chief Superintendent."

— Seventeen —

At ten twenty-five, I strolled into the station's executive suite after passing through a security checkpoint manned by a serious, but somewhat seedy looking man wearing CimmerTek insignia on his blue shirt.

A human sitting there throughout the day, checking people in and out seemed wasteful, especially in an artificial habitat where everything, even the breathable air, had a cost. But an AI controlling access wouldn't make visitors feel they were being admitted into somewhere special. In other words, the setup was to flatter Darrien's vanity, nothing more.

A middle-aged, plump, and over-dressed woman rose from behind a large desk. She might have been pretty years ago, but a scowl of disapproval had permanently etched her face. It transformed what had once been finely traced features into those of an aging scold. I could see how B.B. earned her unflattering nickname. She suffered from one of the worst cases of resting bitch face I had ever seen.

"Chief Superintendent Morrow. At last. D.D. has been waiting for you, and he is getting rather impatient." Her scowl deepened. "You're terribly late, you know. D.D. is a busy man and can't afford to waste a single minute. You simply cannot understand what it takes to run the Commonwealth's largest free port."

I wanted to shrug with the sort of naked indifference that led to charges of insubordination if done in front of a senior officer. It would convey just how much I cared about Dangerous Don's patience issues. And after doing so, I also wanted to point out Aquilonia was hardly the most significant, or even the most successful free port in all of human space. But I exercised restraint instead. Best I save my powers of aggravation for a more appropriate moment.

Instead, I answered, "The exigencies of a high-profile investigation sometimes take precedence over timeliness. I'm sure a worldly man of Ser Darrien's caliber understands."

Lisbeth's sour expression showed she thought Ser Darrien took precedence over everything, but she merely nodded. "Well, at least you're here now, though I'll spend my day re-jigging D.D.'s schedule."

If she was waiting for an apology before letting me enter the holy of holies, good old Dangerous Don's daily program would go even further out of whack.

"If you'll follow me." She gestured toward a door marked 'Chief Administrator.'

Darrien's office beat DCC Maras' by a parsec when it came to the sheer quantity of wall hangings and other adornments, but Maras still showed better taste. The view, however, made up for the questionable decor. Thule looked rather lovely from here, its uneven surface filling the large, rectangular porthole.

A tall, pale, raven-haired man with dark, hooded eyes sunk in a pinched face stood with his hands clasped in the small of his back by a desk broad enough to serve as a gravball court. The cut of his suit would have made senior ComCorp executives proud, and the cold expression with which he watched me enter matched Houko's reptilian stare.

"Chief Superintendent Caelin Morrow of the Commonwealth Constabulary," Lisbeth announced as if this were the governor general's levee, or so I fancied. I've never attended those. My tacit understanding with DCC Maras didn't extend to the command performances at social events she enforced on her own senior officers. She had enough of those to wave the Constabulary flag convincingly and didn't need me as another cheerleader.

Darrien made a great show of glancing at the grandfather clock ticking away in a corner.

"Thank you for taking the time to see me," he said without the slightest trace of irony in a tone that would suit an undertaker. He waved toward a settee group just beyond my immediate field of view. "I believe you know Sera Gerri Kazan, of the Honorable Commonwealth Trading Corporation. Beside her is Javan Burrard, the CimmerTek Security Solutions General Manager for Aquilonia operations."

I turned my head just in time to see my ex-partner look up from the tablet in her lap. Malice sparkled in her eyes although her expression gave nothing away.

"How are you, Sera Kazan?" When she didn't reply I gave Darrien a deliberately hard glare. "I thought you wished to discuss the investigation."

He nodded. "Indeed. I want to hear what you've done so far, and when you expect to charge the suspect held by Major Pullar."

"In that case," I replied, waving a hand toward Gerri and the dark-complexioned, bald man wearing a CimmerTek uniform, "I'm afraid I must ask Sera Kazan and Ser Burrard to leave. She is a potential witness, and he is a member of the public. Neither can be present for a case briefing."

"Sera Kazan is here as a ComCorp representative. Her employer has a significant stake in the outcome of your investigation and must be kept up to date."

In other words, Yan Houko either leaned on him or used his vanity to slip Gerri into his inner sanctum. A not unexpected development.

"And Javan," Darrien continued, "is hardly a member of the public. I use his company to police those areas the Gendarmerie can't or won't cover. As such, he and his people carry out law enforcement duties and need to know of your investigation's progress."

Pullar would love that last bit — if he didn't have an aneurysm instead.

"Nevertheless, Ser Darrien, I cannot discuss the case with Sera Kazan or Ser Burrard present."

His eyes darted between Gerri and me. He was a man with a dilemma. ComCorp likely had tendrils up the rear end of Aquilonia's managing syndicate, meaning Houko's displeasure could affect Darrien's continued employment.

"I'm sure we're able to talk this through as the reasonable people we are," he said after a moment's indecision. "And please call me D.D. I don't like to stand on formality, Caelin, is it?"

"It's chief superintendent. And to repeat myself, I can't discuss the details of an ongoing case in the presence of a potential witness, as Sera Kazan knows, since she might have to testify in court. And even though you state Ser Burrard is carrying out law enforcement duties, he is not a sworn officer, and that makes him a member of the public. In fact, just to be entirely clear, whatever I discuss with you, Ser Darrien, cannot be shared with anyone else, including your assistant, nor can I allow you to record anything."

And if he tried, the scrambler I carried in my pocket would turn my words into gibberish. He stared at me with an air of exasperation before finally coming to the rational conclusion I would win this battle of wills. He gave Gerri an apologetic grimace.

"My apologies, but you'll have to go back empty-handed, for now. Please convey my regrets to Yan."

Gerri rose in a fluid motion and nodded pleasantly at Darrien. "Of course."

"Have a good day, Sera Kazan," I said as she headed for the door where Lisbeth still stood, mouth wide open in astonishment and outrage that I wasn't giving D.D. the respect he deserved.

"Prepare to get your knuckles rapped by HQ, honey," Gerri murmured in reply.

If I had a cred for every time someone threatened me with thunder from on high, I'd have retired by now, but coming from a veteran of Constabulary politics the threat held more menace than usual. Perhaps ComCorp actually had enough political influence to obstruct a professional compliance investigation. Or Gerri thought they did.

Burrard remained seated until Darrien gave him a significant look and nodded toward the door. When he climbed to his feet, I realized he was much taller and broader than I thought. He might even measure up to Thopok in height. Judging by the spark of irritation in his eyes, my choice of words hadn't gone over well.

"A pleasure to meet you, I'm sure," he said as he passed me. His tone proved it was anything but.

With Gerri, Burrard, and Lisbeth gone, Darrien invited me to sit by his desk, no doubt intending to glower down at me from the throne-like chair behind it. Instead, I took Gerri's place on the sofa and gestured at him to take a seat.

"I must say, Chief Superintendent, I find your lack of cooperative spirit dismaying," he announced after reluctantly sitting across from me. "ComCorp is an important business entity and deeply concerned by this lamentable case."

"That's precisely the reason I must treat the ComCorp folks as potential witnesses and not interested parties. Gerri Kazan knew damn well how I would react, considering she spent almost twenty years in the Constabulary. So ask yourself why she played this little charade. It certainly wasn't to help you or me. If I may offer a bit of advice, treat Yan Houko and his folks as VIPs if you like, but avoid discussing anything related to Envoy Shovak's murder. Until I've completed my investigation, they are part of the case. So far, you're not."

That last line always worked like a charm when folks refused to back off after I asked them politely. Darrien gave me a stunned fish gaze, but his expression quickly morphed into something more calculating. I was willing to bet no one on Aquilonia dared speak to him as I just did.

"When do you expect to charge this naval officer Pullar holds in his cells? The sooner, the better, I'd say. I'll eventually hear from imperial authorities, and I'd like to present them with a guilty party."

I debated whether to tell him he had no official standing in this case, other than as someone who might have a very distant motive.

When the Empire finally complained, it would go to someone a lot higher up the food chain than he was. The governor general of Cimmeria would be a good candidate, since he was the senior Commonwealth representative in this sector, and thus nominally, the SecGen's voice.

"Our evidence linking the suspect to the killing is still merely circumstantial, Ser Darrien. We have nothing concrete that proves she stabbed Shovak to death. You've met Shrehari before — picture a woman my size and age murdering one of them with a blade. It doesn't hold up. Since the Shrehari won't let us scan Shovak's body, let alone do an autopsy, I can't even begin to check for evidence that might prove how a much weaker human could have overcome the envoy. So I can't just charge her and walk away. No prosecutor would take the case based on the evidence collected to date, and if she didn't do it, I'd have allowed the real killer to escape. I need more proof, whether it points to the suspect in custody or someone else, and I will take the time required to find it. But your help could speed things."

"Oh?" He cocked an eyebrow in question. "And how would I do that? You didn't want Javan to stay and take part in this discussion."

I bit back a choice comment on the usefulness of his rent-a-cop in a murder investigation. "The sensor net near Shovak's suite and in the nearby staircase failing on the night of the murder is very convenient, almost too much so. Major Pullar will ask your engineering people, if he hasn't already done so, to remove the affected modules and analyze them. We need to know why they stopped working. If you could hasten his request, it'll help us find the truth that much faster."

He thought about it and then gave me a dubious nod, eyes narrowed. "I'll see what I can do. Engineering can only handle a given amount of work at the best of times. But I will point out that Major Pullar and his gendarmes do not belong to me, so I'm not required to offer them technical services."

"Not even if it might speed up my investigation? Am I to deduce that you're not a fan of the good major? Or is the fact security doesn't come under your control an irritant?"

"I beg your pardon?" He glared down his nose at me with an air of indignation. "My staff and I are most scrupulous in collaborating with Major Pullar and the Cimmerian Gendarmerie. You could learn something from us on the matter of cooperation."

I turned a cold smile on him, hoping it would shrivel his false defiance, along with other things.

"Then I'm sure you'll see your way to helping us analyze the sensor net failures. But since we're on the subject, am I correct in thinking you'd rather have a private police force answerable to you instead of a Cimmerian Gendarmerie detachment, accountable only to the Minister of Public Safety? Perhaps a force under the command of your friend Javan Burrard?"

He scowled at me for picking at what was a long-standing and sensitive scab. "Not being in control of my station's security force is a significant inconvenience, I'll admit. There are points of contention I'd like to resolve, for Aquilonia's welfare."

"So a law enforcement scandal wouldn't exactly be unwelcome from your point of view, seeing as how the responsibility is out of your hands."

"What do you mean?" This time, there was genuine surprise and even a dash of outrage in his tone, but whether it was at the mere idea or because I'd hit the bulls-eye, I couldn't tell.

"A murder happens on Major Pullar's watch, so everyone looks bad, especially if ComCorp raises a stink. The Feds arrive and you get extra ammunition for your board of directors. Perhaps enough to convince the Cimmerian authorities that station security has to come under your full authority. Sounds just as plausible as a woman of my size killing a Shrehari in hand-to-hand combat, no?" I paused and put on a thoughtful air as if a fresh idea had struck me. "Speaking of size, wouldn't you say Javan Burrard makes a better suspect than the one Pullar holds? He's almost as large as Thopok, the late Shovak's aide."

Darrien's eyes widened in dismay. "What a ridiculous notion, Chief Superintendent. I resent the insinuation. Javan Burrard is a loyal, upstanding man, one with a bright future on Aquilonia."

"We still enjoy freedom of thought in the Commonwealth, Ser Darrien. You may resent every word I speak, but be honest. You considered how this case might help you eject the Gendarmerie from Aquilonia, didn't you?"

"Damn Pullar flapping his lips to everyone he thinks might listen." Darrien's eyes slid to one side while he fumed. "So what if I did? Surely you don't think Javan or I, or anyone else employed by the Aquilonia Syndicate had anything to do with Shovak's murder?"

"Your people are best placed to kill the sensor net in exactly the right spot to let the killer in and out without being seen, better than anyone else on the station."

His face lost what little color it had, and he looked at me, aghast. “Surely you’re not...”

“If the naval officer Major Pullar is holding didn’t do it, then I must follow up with anyone who might have had the means, motive, and opportunity.” I suddenly needed a cup of coffee, something that wouldn’t be on offer here and I climbed to my feet. “On that note, Ser Darrien, I’ll leave you to consider what I said, and to decide whether you’ll help us by having your engineers analyze the defective sensor modules.”

Without waiting for a reply, I left D.D. staring at the floor, lost in thought, and let myself out. The ever-charming Lisbeth, puzzled by my sudden departure, and no doubt irritated that she couldn’t overhear our conversation, watched me leave in silence. I could almost feel her eyes slicing through my vertebrae.

— Eighteen —

Making new friends was never my forte. But, since landing in the PCB, I'd developed an uncanny ability to make new enemies, a talent that followed me to Aquilonia, judging by the dirty look the CimmerTek man at the security desk gave me. He must have already heard I disrespected his boss by tossing him out of Darrien's office. At least he didn't offer me greetings from Louis Sorne.

Stepping out of the lift and into the press of humanity on the promenade gave me a curious feeling of relief. But it was one tempered by the knowledge I didn't have a viable suspect, in spite of the evidence against Talyn. And that meant returning to the Shrehari who were still more likely killers, as was Javan Burrard, although I figured him for a long shot.

It might have been worse. A kindly soul might have invited a *Tai Kan* officer to join my investigation, in the spirit of interspecies cooperation. I skidded to an abrupt stop. What were the chances one of those three Shrehari was an undercover *Tai Kan* agent?

The *Kho'sahra* kept a close eye on any of his subjects involved with outsiders, meaning species not under the Empire's thumb. Why not stick a secret police burr to Shovak's backside? Talyn probably knew plenty about their practices and could tell me whether I should worry, but did I dare ask her?

I was beginning to loathe the joker who thought my only job would be to find a motive so the Fleet could prove its people understood the war ended over seven decades ago. Although to be fair, the Navy didn't always speak with enough clarity to the Constabulary. A favor we returned out of general principle.

Pullar gave me a questioning look when I entered his office. "How was D.D.?"

"Pretty much as you described him. He must have good friends high in the Cimmeria government because he didn't earn his job thanks to a winning personality."

"Probably. This place generates its share of trickle up funding in the form of political donations and no-show contracts for favored family or party members."

It was a statement loaded with cynicism. Maybe that's why Pullar and I got along. We hardened cynics preferred our own kind. I took the empty chair and gave myself a breather before continuing.

"Darrien had Gerri Kazan and Javan Burrard there with him and expected me to discuss the case in front of a potential witness and a rent-a-cop."

"Really? D.D. isn't *that* stupid."

"Neither is Gerri. The ComCorp folks are playing games. I'll wager she engineered the situation to ensure my first meeting with Darrien started off on a bad note. It certainly worked. She and Javan eventually left, but Gerri warned me of reprisals from my chain of command. Darrien, like everyone else, wants this case wrapped up last week, but he didn't much like my intimation he had a motive to foment a scandal discrediting you and the Gendarmerie."

"You raised that with him?" Pullar emitted a semi-comical sigh. "They'll hear about it on Cimmeria before the day is out. I predict your words will wend their way through the halls of government, then Gendarmerie HQ, and finally come back here with a request to avoid airing out Cimmerian laundry in front of the Feds."

"I had no choice, Major, and if my intervention causes you grief, I ask for forgiveness in advance."

He brushed away my apology with a wave of the hand. "I understand. It's a valid motive."

"Valid, yes. But a little unlikely even if Burrard strikes me as the first human I've met on Aquilonia large and strong enough to face a Shrehari. But I wanted to see Darrien's reaction. He reacted all right though I suspect it's more because he's hoping the situation will give his board of directors leverage with the minister than because he had a hand in the murder. I can't see a man like D.D. involved in something so brutal, fraught with so many consequences, especially on his station. The downsides outweigh the sole upside of seeing you gone. And he can achieve that through legal means, given enough time, money and political lobbying."

"He has a mean streak, Chief Superintendent, one that Javan would be glad to exploit for his own ambitions. But whatever you told him, it seems to have shaken his engineering section loose. They'll be extracting the dead sensor modules later today, with analysis to follow. No promised date for results, however."

"I figured he might want to seem more cooperative, lest I pursue him as a suspect." Glancing around his office for a dispenser and finding none, I gave Pullar a pleading smile. "I could murder a dozen Shrehari Marines for coffee right now. Any good cop shop has to have an urn somewhere. Care to point me at it?"

"I can do even better. How do you take it?"

"Black. Apparently, it matches my soul, or so I hear."

"One black coffee coming up." He left me sitting alone by his overloaded desk for a minute or so and then returned with two steaming mugs. "Tell me what you think. It's a homemade blend of Cimmerian and Earth-grown beans."

I took a tentative sip and had to smile with pleasure. Whoever developed this one had hit the jackpot, and I said so. The satisfied expression on Pullar's face told me my ability to make friends hadn't completely vanished.

"I experienced a disturbing thought on my way back. What if one of the other Shrehari is a secret police agent working undercover, to keep an eye on Shovak while he was beyond the Empire's sphere of control?"

Pullar cocked his head to one side like a curious bird or the little dog I had as a child.

"*Tai Kan*? I suppose it's possible. That puts a different slant on the case."

"I want to ask Talyn about them. She'll probably know a lot more than either of us."

"Mind if I join you for that? Even if I have one eye on retirement, I'm always up for a little professional development."

"Sure. But first, we finish this dark nectar of the gods."

Twenty minutes later, we found Talyn still sitting in the lotus position on her cot, eyes closed, as if she hadn't moved. She remained as expressionless as before, although once I'd told her about my idea that one of the other Shrehari might be *Tai Kan*, I thought I saw a fleeting spark of something in her eyes.

"Possibly, Chief Superintendent. If Shovak wasn't one of those favored few who either enjoys the regime's full confidence or is of noble enough birth not to care, then he might have had a minder with him. The current *Kho'sahra* supposedly has a wider paranoid streak than his predecessors did. That's not surprising since his appointment didn't exactly follow the rules of succession laid down by the first *Kho'sahra* at the end of the war. This one made plenty of enemies who'd like to see a career naval officer seize power. Considering the current emperor has a vast and loyal following inside the military, even though he has no real power other than as an influential figurehead, the *Kho'sahra*'s worries are founded."

"Who might be the best candidate? One of the bodyguards or the aide?"

"Hard to say. I've only met the aide over the blade of his knife. But it's more likely a bodyguard if there is indeed a *Tai Kan* operative."

"Why?"

"My limited understanding of the situation tells me Shovak was probably a minor player when it comes to imperial politics — those in the merchant caste usually are. In which case, giving him a minder for the trip would have been routine. That means it'll be an under-officer. They wouldn't waste an officer on him, and Thopok, by being an envoy's aide, albeit not one with full diplomatic accreditation, occupies a higher status. But, I could be wrong."

"Will the minder understand Anglic?"

"Perhaps, but I doubt it. The *Tai Kan* isn't enlightened enough to teach its under-officers alien languages. As an internal security service, it generally deals only with imperial subjects."

Talyn paused as if to gather her thoughts before continuing.

"But it wouldn't surprise me if a hypothetical non-Anglic speaking *Tai Kan* flatfoot among the bodyguards made himself known to the aide, especially now Shovak's dead. Remember, the job is to ensure Shovak's loyalty to the regime, not to spy on us. The first *Kho'sahra* established another agency, the *Tai Zolh,* to gather intelligence, and we're always aware of their agents operating in Commonwealth space."

I wasn't about to ask her how they were aware – the answer was obvious. None of my business.

Instead, I asked. "What if our hypothetical *Tai Kan* officer had orders to eliminate Shovak if he seemed about to do something the regime wouldn't like?"

"An interesting thought," Talyn said, nodding slowly. "I suppose it's possible, though they don't like to air their internal conflicts in front of humans. The *Tai Kan* sometimes carry out assassinations openly as a public warning. But here in the Commonwealth? It would take an egregious misstep on Shovak's part, one that wouldn't let them wait for the return home. Still, another Shrehari remains your best bet, for obvious reasons."

Great. The more I dug into this, the murkier it became. "Would a *Tai Kan* agent bother disguising his status if I confronted the bodyguards with the question?"

Talyn's half shrug was as controlled as the rest of her expressions. "There's nothing illegal about *Tai Kan* minders accompanying Shrehari traders and diplomats into the Commonwealth, as long as they break none of our laws. Within the Empire, most of them don't bother hiding who they are except in particular circumstances. Much of the organization's power lies in its reputation. You can't run a true centralized, authoritarian state if it spans multiple star systems, not without instantaneous communications. So they rely on bluster backed by surgical strikes."

"What could be egregious enough to warrant summary execution?"

"For me to make even a half-educated guess, I'd need to understand the nature of Shovak's business on Aquilonia."

You and me both, I thought. "Thopok told me very little other than Shovak was meeting with ComCorp to set up a new trade relationship on behalf of the mercantile house he represented, called *Quch Mech*. The ComCorp folks were no more forthcoming."

"ComCorp." The corners of Talyn's lips twitched. "Massive political clout, plenty of enemies, a long list of questionable business practices and even more questionable subsidiaries, partners, and associations. But they're one of the biggest players around, what you call a zaibatsu in the Constabulary, and yes I'm aware the term isn't one of respect, Chief Superintendent. I can see where a Shrehari with more extreme notions of honor might be conflicted about a business deal."

"Why?" Pullar asked. It was the first word he'd spoken since entering the cell.

Talyn turned her emotionless gaze on him. "The Empire might be an interstellar dictatorship barely kept in check by its noble and warrior castes, but they have notions we humans would find antiquated.

Deals, business, or otherwise, with entities that offend the average Shrehari's sense of honor can sometimes provoke extreme reactions, and ComCorp can be offensive in so many ways."

"You're remarkably well-versed, Commander," Pullar said.

"As the saying goes, know thine enemy."

"Do you consider the Shrehari Empire our enemy?" He asked. "Even after seven decades of more or less peaceful coexistence?"

She gave us a sibylline smile. "No, I don't."

— Nineteen —

"Major," one of Pullar's men waved at him when we reentered the bullpen, "our friendly neighborhood merchant of all things dubious called back. He claims to have a solution for the problem you mentioned."

"Ah!" Pullar rubbed his hands together. "Colin Fiers came through. Let's pay him a visit."

"Your man who can rustle up a Shrehari speaker?"

"The very same."

Colin Fiers didn't work out of a storefront on the promenade as I anticipated, but from a cramped office suite near one of the freighter docks, on Aquilonia's periphery. A small sign on the door advertised the Fiers Import-Export LLC with nary a corporate logo or motto in sight.

It wouldn't have surprised me if the limited liability designation meant he could evade customs and import regulations with impunity rather than indicate more prosaic terms of incorporation. His front office seemed to bathe in that sort of dodgy aura, something I could sense before we even stepped inside. A good cop developed a nose for such things after years chasing crooks infesting the Commonwealth's frontier sectors.

Pullar hadn't explained why he felt comfortable calling on the goodwill of a man involved in questionable commercial activities and I wasn't about to ask. Every cop needs sources on the wrong side of the law.

I still had a few scattered around the Rim from my days in the Flying Squad. So did Gerri for that matter, and she'd have even less ethical problems using them now than she had back in the day. It was something I'd do well to remember.

The front office seemed like a mismatched hybrid of warehouse and showroom. Half a dozen display cases holding everything from replica Shrehari cutlery to low-grade Andothian pseudo-opals were interspersed with stacked boxes covered in two dozen human and alien scripts.

I recognized Shrehari runes, but other markings were as foreign to me as the contents of a case showing implements whose provenance, let alone uses were impenetrably obscure.

"Arkanna animal traps," an ancient voice said from a door hidden by a stack of Dordogne brandy crates.

I looked into the wizened face of a short, smiling man clad in extravagant robes that appeared vaguely incongruous on such a small person. He seemed like a little wizard from a long-forgotten fairy tale.

"They resemble nothing you've ever seen. But a few of my clients swear by them and will pay a premium price for the real thing which I'm pleased to charge for my services in procuring the items."

"Colin, I'd like you to meet Chief Superintendent Caelin Morrow of the Constabulary." Pullar gestured toward me with his hand, then flipped it at the old man. "Chief Superintendent, meet Colin Fiers, trader, raconteur, and station gossip. He's also an occasional scofflaw when it comes to declaring imports."

"Merely the forgetfulness of old age." Fiers inclined his head in a polite bow. "A pleasure to meet you. I've rarely had dealings with the Constabulary, but your reputation precedes you."

"Oh?" I had to smile at the wicked twinkle in his eyes.

"Tales of your meeting with our esteemed station administrator, Donul Darrien, and his charming partner Lisbeth have made the rounds, Chief Superintendent. Aquilonia is a village lost in space, and like most villages, news, especially when it concerns those who believe themselves to be our betters, flows at light speed. And if the stories are correct, you banished Javan Burrard from Dangerous Don's office, an act that will gain you many admirers around here. Believe it or not, most of us prefer the Gendarmerie to CimmerTek's bully boys."

"The accounts of my meeting were no doubt embellished in the retelling, Ser Fiers."

His head bobbed. "No doubt. And now I've met you, I shall take care to add a little more juicy gossip to the tale. It's the way of these things and our sole homegrown entertainment. Fear not, I won't fabricate anything libelous. Your status as the local Firing Squad's commanding officer prevents me from doing so." He waved toward the door. "If you'll follow me. We should be more comfortable in my chambers."

He ushered us into a salon filled with an eccentric collection of alien furnishings and artifacts, and I wondered whether Aquilonia's chief administrator knew Fiers' office beat his for splendor. The merchant must have read something in my expression because he chuckled.

"I'll bet I know what you're thinking, Chief Superintendent, and it concerns that nasty snake Darrien. He considers me a tasteless bounder and parvenu. No man of his standing would surround himself with the leavings of a dozen cultures, or so he says, but I like the eclectic charm. It feels more genuine than his artificial formality."

"Your office certainly has a unique atmosphere," I replied, eyes jumping from one item to the other.

"My clientele seems to enjoy it."

He led us to a set of comfortable chairs surrounding a small table topped by an intricate mosaic. It depicted something undefinable but distinctly not human. After a moment, I realized what it was and hoped my blush didn't show. A few humanoid species produced somewhat shocking erotica.

"Can I offer you tea or coffee?" Fiers asked once we were seated. "Or perhaps a juice?"

Pullar shook his head. "Nothing for me. If I drink one more coffee this morning, I'll bounce off the bulkheads."

"How about you, Chief Superintendent?" He examined me with a quizzical expression. "I can offer a delicate herbal tea you might enjoy."

"Perhaps another time, Ser Fiers."

"Please, call me Colin." He adjusted his robes and took a seat across from us, looking like a smallish emperor on his throne. "I understand you need someone fluent in Shrehari, no doubt because of the matter that brought you here."

"That is correct. I don't speak or understand the language and would like to interview every member of the Shrehari trade delegation, but only one knows Anglic."

"Surely the Constabulary has people with the proper skills on Cimmeria."

"Probably, but I don't have the luxury of time. As so many people are fond of telling me, it would be best if I wrapped this case up quickly."

A sly smile tugged at Fiers' thin lips. "And you might not find one willing to work for the Firing Squad, which makes it even more challenging."

"There is that, yes." The man's casual comment should have annoyed me. But his benevolent expression seemed primarily designed to let him make even the most outrageous declarations with impunity.

"You're willing to trust a civilian? One recommended by such as I, even after Major Pullar no doubt qualified me as a scoundrel living on the outer edges of legality?"

"We often hire consultants, and I can assure you that I trust but I verify. Here, expediency forces my hand."

The smile returned. "With ComCorp breathing down Dangerous Don's neck and yours, I can understand. You're fortunate, because one of my suppliers and occasional contractor, fluent in Shrehari, is on Aquilonia right now. He's between jobs and would likely accept a brief stint as your interpreter, for a reasonable honorarium of course."

"Of course. And you'll be expecting a finder's fee, no doubt?"

Fiers made a dismissive gesture with his bejeweled hand. "A mere percentage of the honorarium, I assure you."

A derisive snort escaped Pullar's lips. "I know what you consider a mere percentage, you old fraud."

Fiers took on an aggrieved expression. "I have to make a living in this cold and cruel galaxy. Besides, since it comes out of the pockets of our benevolent Commonwealth government, I consider it a fair return for the extortionate taxes I'm made to pay."

"In that case, you should give Chief Superintendent Morrow a fee, since you forget to declare half of your profits."

"Scurrilous accusations. Besides, this *is* a free port." Fiers winked at me. "Ignore the sad man in the rumpled uniform. I've tried to bribe him many times without success. You can't find that sort of integrity everywhere these days. Now, back to the reason for your visit."

He was about to continue when a faint chime floated through the air. "I do believe that's him."

Fiers jumped to his feet and scurried toward the entrance, glancing at a small holographic representation of the front office floating above his desk. He nodded once and touched the controls, sending the door panel into the bulkhead with a soft sigh.

The man who stepped in looked like everyone's mental image of a roguish smuggler operating beyond the Rim, right down to the earring and fashionably casual Navy surplus clothes. Tall, dark, powerfully built, with silver-shot black hair in a ponytail and a square jaw outlined by a thin beard, he moved with the assurance and watchfulness of a born fighter. His eyes met mine without embarrassment or fear though I thought I saw a spark of devil may care amusement in their chestnut depths.

"Chief Superintendent Morrow, Major Pullar, may I present Captain Montague Hobart of the free trader

Harpy. Monty, these fine law enforcement officials would like to hire you."

Hobart bowed at the waist in a comically overdone gesture and said, in a rich tenor voice, "A distinct pleasure. As the saying goes, your reputation precedes you, Chief Superintendent."

Fiers chuckled. "Like I said, Aquilonia is a small village with a highly refined grapevine and little by way of live entertainment. Take a seat, Monty."

"The offers I usually receive from law enforcement," Hobart replied, dropping into a chair across from me, "are because of jobs they don't want me to do. They also generally involve an all-expenses paid stay in a detention cell, so this could be a novel experience."

"They need your Shrehari language skills," Fiers said.

"Ah." Hobart nodded with a knowing air. "I should have guessed. The unfortunate Shovak murder. You want to interview the delegation, but don't have enough Shrehari to do it yourself if they don't speak Anglic."

"And she can't get an official interpreter over to Aquilonia in a timely manner," Fiers added.

"Understood." The smuggler dipped his head. "I suppose the pressure to resolve this case quickly must be enormous. No one in the Cimmeria system wants to antagonize imperial authorities. Or annoy ComCorp for that matter. I'm at your disposal, Chief Superintendent, and will gladly take satisfying my curiosity as payment."

Fiers raised both hands in protest. "Don't work for free, Monty. Particularly not for the Feds."

"You're just worried you won't receive a finder's fee, Colin." The man grinned at me. "Very well, I'll take the Constabulary's standard hourly rates, Chief Superintendent. Annoying Colin might make him seek vengeance by shutting me out of his more lucrative contracts."

"Standard rates?" Fiers sputtered. "You can name your price, Monty, and I wish you'd do so."

"You would prefer that I gouge our charming chief superintendent? Never. Besides, doing the law a favor always pays dividends."

"Be that way," the merchant grumbled. "This is why you'll never make it big. You're not ruthless enough."

"Don't mind Colin," Hobart said. "He has a deep and abiding attachment to profit. When would you like to start, Chief Superintendent?"

"As soon as possible, but I'd like to ask a question first."

He spread out his arms in an expansive gesture of openness. "Ask me anything."

"If I dig into the Constabulary database, what will I find on you?"

"That I've been stopped for inspection at regular intervals, detained a dozen times in the last few years on suspicion of carrying contraband, but never formally arrested or charged. At least not by Commonwealth authorities."

"And non-Commonwealth authorities?"

"Nothing was ever proved, although I'm persona non grata in a few Protectorate Zone systems these days. Mind you they're places where the laws are whatever the ruling warlords want. What was legal yesterday becomes a capital offense based on a whim, a bad hangover, or a losing poker hand."

I gave him a skeptical look, one pale eyebrow cocked. "You know I'll check, right?"

"I wouldn't want it any other way, Chief Superintendent. Shall we?"

Hobart rose to his feet with effortless grace and held out his hand to help me up. I ignored it and stood under my own power. When I glimpsed Pullar's face, he seemed pained. Whether that stemmed from Montague Hobart's obvious attempts to be charming or from what he suspected were lies about his criminal record, I couldn't tell.

But there was something about the man's smooth, confident manner that intrigued me. Most smugglers I came across during my time with the Flying Squad were truculent, shifty, or downright hostile the moment I flashed my warrant card. This one seemed to be enjoying himself, or at least he gave the impression of being amused by the notion of helping me with my inquiries.

— Twenty —

“Shall I inform Thopok you wish to interview the guards?” Pullar asked as he led us back through the labyrinth of corridors connecting Aquilonia’s warehouse district to the promenade.

I glanced at Hobart to assess his reaction. If he knew the Shrehari well enough to be fluent in their tongue, he likely had a more informed opinion than either Pullar or I. He shook his head, so I said, “No. Let’s surprise them by showing up unannounced.”

“Are you sure?” Pullar’s tone wasn’t precisely one of disapproval, but I heard his hesitation.

“If you’ll allow me,” Hobart replied, intervening with practiced smoothness, “the Shrehari don’t like being taken unawares, and they’ll be off-balance if we merely appear without warning. I think we might get more useful information if they don’t have time to compose themselves for our visit.”

“Considering Shrehari temperament and their incredibly touchy sense of honor, it sounds dangerous,” Pullar said.

Hobart grinned at him. “What’s life without risk, Major?”

The Cimmerian made a face. “Long and uneventful?”

My temporary interpreter laughed with delight. "I prefer to live hard even if it means I die young. Leaving a beautiful corpse behind is optional."

"That last bit wouldn't be a problem in my case," Pullar replied in a dry tone. "I'd still rather we collar Thopok first and have him take us to where his men are guarding Shovak's remains. From what I recall about their customs, they would perceive it as a gross violation of protocol if we barge in on lower caste troops without their nominal superior present. They might refuse to cooperate. Let's find out if Thopok is in his quarters, shall we?"

He stopped and pulled out his communicator. "Control, this is Pullar."

"Control here. What can we do for you, sir?"

"I need a location report on the Shrehari called Thopok."

"Wait."

We resumed walking toward the shallow ramp leading back to the land of tourists. A few moments later, the major took his communicator out again, summoned by an unheard signal.

"Pullar."

"This is Control. Thopok is in the Aquilonia Excelsior."

"Thank you. Advise when he leaves. The chief superintendent and I wish to speak with him in private."

"Will do."

"Pullar, out." He gave me a quizzical glance. "I suppose Thopok's meeting with the ComCorp folks. Do you think he's replacing his late boss?"

I shrugged. "Why wouldn't he? *Quch Mech* could have empowered Thopok to negotiate the deal himself if Shovak became unable to do so."

Though it made sense, I felt a strange unease at the idea. If Shovak's death wasn't a Shrehari honor killing, then it was related to his trade mission — there could be no other explanation. Might Thopok have put himself in jeopardy by taking on his late superior's task?

The last thing I needed was a second dead alien representative although it would help Talyn's case. While there was a possibility, no matter how remote, that she might be skilled enough to kill a Shrehari with a blade, there was no chance of her killing a second one from inside the station's brig.

We had barely made it to the promenade when the Gendarmerie station called Pullar about a minor emergency involving a newly landed starship. He peeled off and headed down again after telling us we might as well wait for Thopok to emerge from the Excelsior. As a result, Hobart and I took seats in the hotel's lobby, facing the lifts.

"So tell me, how does a nice lady like you end up running the sector Firing Squad?" His smile was genuine if mischievous.

"How did you know I'm in charge of the Rim's PCB detachment?"

He chortled with delight. "A real investigator — answering a question with a question. As I said, your reputation precedes you. The only folks on Aquilonia who haven't heard about Chief Superintendent Morrow yet are transients and the odd drunk living in a disused warehouse cavern."

"I somehow doubt that. Most folks outside law enforcement or criminal milieus wouldn't care. But I shouldn't be surprised at you knowing. Your kind has a very efficient grapevine."

"My kind?" He raised a hand to his heart in mock hurt. I had to repress a smile of amusement.

"People who dabble in tax and duty-free import-export schemes."

This time he laughed openly. "I'm beginning to like you, Chief Superintendent. There's a sense of humor hidden behind that stern expression, and I know from painful experience that most of you gray-legs can't scrape up a smile to save your lives, let alone crack a joke."

"We rarely have a sense of humor when we're dealing with scofflaws, but catch us off-duty with a glass of ethanol in hand, and we can party with the best of them."

Although that applied mostly to my people. I wasn't the sociable sort to begin with, and I'd seen enough cops crawl inside a bottle to keep my intake low and slow.

"No doubt." He winked at me. "I might just try that on you, say tonight?"

"I'll be on duty for as long as I'm here, so no dice."

"Then at least answer my question. How does one end up doing the Constabulary's dirty jobs?"

"There's not much to tell. I joined at seventeen and made my way up through the noncom ranks before they selected me as a candidate for a commission. My marks at the Academy were high enough I could choose my career path as a commissioned officer, and that turned out to be criminal investigations. After a dozen years, culminating in a tour with the Rim Sector's Major Crimes Division, HQ tapped me for a shift to Professional Compliance along with a promotion. I've been there ever since, taking another step up the ranks and eventually obtained command of the detachment."

A wry smile twisted Hobart's lips. "That little thirty-second bio openly hints at a much more interesting story, Chief Superintendent. Few people join the Armed Services or the Constabulary at seventeen, and I doubt you ended up in the Firing Squad because your superiors wanted to grease a career path into the very senior ranks. Once an investigator joins Professional Compliance, she never leaves."

"That's because we're so good at making friends in high places." I felt a pang of regret at telling him anything. He seemed to know more about Constabulary internal politics than I expected and saw scars I tried to keep hidden. "And how did you become a smuggler?"

He shrugged. "I was never great at following regulations, so that ruled out most respectable jobs. Besides, I developed a keen sense of adventure at a young age and wanted to see the galaxy from something other than the observation deck of an FTL liner. You might say I almost came by my career naturally. Falling in with the right crowd in my late teens sealed the deal. I guess we both chose our paths in life early on. Seventeen is mighty young for a recruit. Do you come from a Constabulary family background?"

Irritation at his casual question flared up unexpectedly though I should have anticipated my reaction. For a moment, the urge to end the conversation fought with hard-won stoicism. It must have been visible in my eyes because he raised both hands, palms outward, in surrender.

"Fair enough, Chief Superintendent. I see that it's a touchy subject."

Lift doors opening to disgorge the massive shape of a Shrehari saved me from a reply. The crest of hair on his ridged skull brushed against the top of the frame.

Seeing him again made me realize that he was tall even for one of his species, something I couldn't appreciate up close in the tiny lobby of his suite. If the gendarmes hadn't shown up on time the night of Shovak's murder, he'd have snapped Talyn in two without breaking a sweat.

Hobart and I rose in unison, and before I could utter a single syllable, the smuggler barked out something halfway between a snarl and the howl of a Cimmerian velociraptor dying in agony. Whatever he said checked Thopok's arrogant stride with an effectiveness I envied. His massive head turned toward us.

Judging by the way his cracked black lips peeled back to reveal yellowed fangs, he recognized me as the impertinent human female who barged into his suite yesterday. The only words in Hobart's guttural diatribe I recognized sounded suspiciously like *Tai Kan*.

I dearly hoped he was equating me to a member of the much-feared imperial secret police and not asking whether anyone in the Shrehari delegation worked for that little-loved organization.

Thopok stared at the smuggler with an eerie stillness. It might have been an ordinary Shrehari countenance for all I knew, but something was unnerving about the lack of visible sclera or even a clearly defined iris in a pair of eyes set deep beneath bony brows.

He barked out a few syllables I interpreted as both a question and a challenge, though it could have been a 'hail fellow, well met' in his tongue. But I doubted it.

Time to take control, old girl, I thought, before my interpreter said something to provoke a member of a notoriously touchy species into doing something rash. Such as filleting us with the oversized knife stuck in his sash. If it was sharp enough to kill a member of his thick-skinned species, I could only imagine how quickly it might take off my head with a single swipe.

"I would speak with you," I said in my deepest voice, staring up at him over the tip of my nose in the way I imagined a *Tai Kan* officer might. "Envoy Shovak is dead, and my honor demands that I find the true culprit."

There, a little posturing never hurt, whether I was dealing with humans or a nonhuman species.

"You have your culprit," Thopok growled back.

"If you actually believe a small, weak human female killed a Shrehari male of Shovak's size, you're a bigger fool than I thought, or Shovak was a weakling of the worst sort."

"She must have bewitched him, or used an underhanded stratagem." His dismissive sneer crossed the inter-species boundary losing nothing in translation.

"If that's what you believe, let us examine his body. Thus we may determine how she did it and prove her guilt. Otherwise, I shall continue to investigate more likely suspects, such as other Shrehari who would have both the strength and the access to the envoy's rooms. And I will begin with the guards. You will take us to them now."

He eyed me in silence for a long time with those black in black eyes. If he meant it to be intimidating, I had news for him. Since I couldn't read his emotions, he came across as a living statue rather than an irritated, two meters tall alien with the skull ridges of an antediluvian creature and the strength to tear off my arms.

"You may not examine Envoy Shovak's remains," Thopok finally said in a low growl. "You are not of the Imperial race. Your own government will insist you respect our customs. If you try by force, the guards have orders to resist and fight until death, something that will not bode well for future relations between the Empire and your Commonwealth."

Thopok had suddenly become talkative. How interesting.

"Then I will interrogate the guards. Take us to them."

The Shrehari muttered something in his tongue that made Hobart chuckle. He snarled back an equally incomprehensible declamation, but whatever he said made Thopok rear backward in what was either astonishment or anger.

"Our imperial friend has just impugned your gender and family tree. I reminded him you were the most senior Commonwealth government official on Aquilonia, with the power to arrest him at will, just as a high-ranking *Tai Kan* officer might do after being insulted."

Thopok's leathery upper lip curled back again again to expose a chipped incisor, but he said, "Very well. You may speak with the guards. Follow me."

As a concession to diplomacy, I inclined my head in thanks, but I knew this wasn't over. Far from it.

— Twenty-One —

Darrien's people had given the Shrehari delegation a room next to the guards' quarters for Shovak's stasis pod. It allowed them to carry out their ceremonial duties without interruption and hidden from prying human eyes.

The guard on duty snapped to attention when Thopok entered, but I fancied that his face twisted into the Shrehari version of astonishment as Hobart and I followed him in. He said something to Thopok and Hobart leaned over to whisper in my ear.

"Another customer unhappy at the sight of a human female. Though it might have something to do with the fact that this compartment is, at least temporarily, a consecrated space under their religious and social beliefs."

Thopok barked out something that included the words *Tai Kan* and the guard's face seemed to harden even more.

"He's ordered the guard to answer your questions and refrain from insulting remarks, lest he attracts the wrath of the human police."

"This," Thopok said, "is Aktuh. You may begin."

I suppressed an unexpected rush of hilarity at the name — it sounded so much like a human sneeze — and nudged my translator.

"Please ask him to account for his movements two evenings ago, in the hours before and after Envoy Shovak's death."

"He says," Hobart began, after an exchange in Shrehari that meant nothing to me, "after he and his colleague Rorg helped Aide Thopok prepare the envoy's quarters for the reception, Shovak dismissed both of them to their room. He stayed there until roused by Thopok after the envoy's cowardly murder was discovered."

"Did he return to the VIP level earlier that evening?"

Another short back-and-forth in Shrehari, then Hobart shook his head.

"He says it was Rorg."

"Does he know why Rorg returned to the VIP section after being dismissed for the evening?"

"No."

The interview was proving to be particularly short on useful information, in part because of my inability to read Shrehari facial expressions, let alone body language. It was like interrogating a large and menacing sentient brick wall.

"Ask Aktuh whether he's the delegation's *Tai Kan* or *Tai Zolh* operative or whether it's Rorg."

Upon hearing me utter the names for the imperial police and intelligence services, Aktuh turned his black eyes on Thopok for a fraction of a second. Perhaps he expected the aide to protest at my delving into Shrehari secrets. Or did he glance at Thopok because the aide was the government agent? Then the guard spoke.

"He is not aware of any *Tai Kan* or *Tai Zolh* officers," Hobart said.

"Of course he isn't."

What did I expect? For Aktuh to say, sure, I'm your opposite number from the Empire. How about you and I grab a drink and talk shop? Mind you, Shrehari ale was an acquired taste I had never found quite to my liking.

On the other hand, I'd seen him react, but whether it meant anything, I couldn't tell. Perhaps Talyn might know, but I couldn't base part of my investigation on help from the only suspect in custody — at least not overtly.

I turned to Thopok and said, "I would speak with the other guard now."

"He is in his rest cycle."

"Then wake him."

The aide grunted, but stalked over to a side door and touched its controls, sending the panel into the bulkhead. He shouted something in Shrehari, then stood aside and waited, heavy hands joined in the small of his back.

Only ninety seconds elapsed before the other guard, hewn from the same granite as his colleague, appeared, fully dressed. He skidded to a halt when he saw me and asked Thopok a question, probably the same one Aktuh had asked, and no doubt got the same answer.

"Ser Hobart," I said when Rorg's emotionless eyes settled on me, "Please have him account for his movements in the hours before and after Envoy Shovak's death."

I could have sworn we heard the same answer, word for word, with no mention of his return visit shortly before Shovak's death.

"Ask him why he attended Thopok later in the evening. Make sure he understands that we have a video of him leaving his room."

"Rorg says he went to confirm orders for the following day since they might have changed after the first meeting with the humans."

Plausible. It's what any decent bodyguard would do.

"Now ask him whether he's a government agent."

I kept my eyes on Rorg, and sure enough, the moment Hobart spoke those magic words starting with *Tai*, the guard's eyes turned toward Thopok for a heartbeat.

Were they not conscious of doing it, or did they think we contemptible humans wouldn't notice? The aide, however, hadn't reacted on either occasion which, considering the amount of ill will he'd shown me, was perhaps another sign.

Or maybe he had better self-control than the guards. Have I mentioned I hated investigations involving nonhumans? Most if not all the cues I relied on to assess a suspect or a witness didn't show, or when they did, they often indicated something completely different. But in this case, my instinct told me I was correctly interpreting the reason for the guards' involuntary reaction.

"Have you any more questions for Rorg?" Thopok asked.

"No. Please thank both of them for their cooperation."

Thopok barked out something in Shrehari and then stalked toward the exit, intent on getting us out of the room. I barely had time to see Rorg vanish into the next compartment and Aktuh resume his solitary watch over Shovak's body before Thopok swept us back into the corridor.

"I hope this is the last I will see of you," he said over his shoulder, heading for the stairwell that led up to the VIP level, the shaft with the broken video pickups.

I still had questions for Thopok and raised my hand to stop him. Hobart saw the gesture and shouted something that sounded suspiciously like an order to halt, followed by a string of harsh sounds which I took to be dressing down for his disrespect toward a high official of the Commonwealth.

The Shrehari stopped, then slowly turned back to face us. Even I could read the intense anger in his posture, mostly thanks to a hand reaching for his sheathed knife. Whatever my personal translator had said, it seemed to have put him on the verge of committing a very undiplomatic act.

I felt a tremor of fear at the realization that this alien, who had the strength to crush my skull with his bare hands, was furious at me. But, happily, I didn't let it show. At least not so a nonhuman might notice.

"*You* still have to speak with me, Thopok," I said. "I know you have not told me everything there is to tell, and I still say a small human female is a less likely candidate for Shovak's killer than a Shrehari male. Not to mention that you and the guards had easier access to the envoy's quarters than anyone else on Aquilonia."

"Your government will receive a formal complaint," Thopok growled. "This harassment is unseemly and verges on the dishonorable."

Crap. Dishonorable was one of the strongest pejoratives a Shrehari could fling. Thopok *was* unhappy with me.

"It is your prerogative to complain, but I must question you about the death of your superior. I will do my duty, and then you will be free to exercise your prerogative. We will continue this discussion in Envoy Shovak's quarters now." I pointed at the stairwell door. "Please lead the way."

I'd have paid good money to hear Thopok's thoughts when we entered the suite's blood-spattered main room. Fortunately, the environmental systems were keeping the smell of decay a few notches below nauseating.

I pointed a settee group that had escaped the spray of bodily fluids and said, "Please sit."

Thopok complied wordlessly, and we sat across from him. The smuggler had taken in the crime scene with clear interest but knew better than to gawk. Since the aide spoke Anglic, I didn't need a translator anymore, yet part of me felt better for having a partner, be he ever so unofficial and temporary while facing an irritated Shrehari. I took a deep breath.

— Twenty-Two —

“Let’s cut through the lies and obfuscations, Ser Thopok, shall we? For which agency do you work? *Tai Kan* or *Tai Zolh*? Are you a secret police officer charged with ensuring Shovak’s loyalty to the *Kho’sahra*? Or are you an intelligence operative here to collect information unrelated to Shovak’s trade mission? You’re one or the other. Which is it?”

Thopok’s posture was so stiff that I couldn’t even detect his breathing.

“Keep in mind,” I continued when he didn’t reply, “that as long as you commit no crimes, your membership in either organization is irrelevant. There are no laws forbidding someone who belongs to a *Tai* from visiting the Commonwealth.”

“Who I may or may not belong to is none of your concern,” Thopok finally replied in his usual flat tone. “My status is only that of an aide to Envoy Shovak who, I can assure you, was a most loyal supporter and confidant of the venerated *Kho’sahra* and a respected emissary of the *Quch Mech*. The *Tai Kan* has no reason to believe otherwise and would not waste resources on a subject whose reliability was beyond doubt.”

"Meaning you're *Tai Zolh.*" I shrugged dismissively. Though whether my body language was intelligible to the Shrehari would remain a mystery. "It has to be one or the other and if Envoy Shovak enjoyed the confidence of your *Kho'sahra...*"

I could have sworn his facial features stiffened even more at my words. Whether I had touched a raw nerve or not, it was enough to engender a new line of thought. Why would a Shrehari intelligence agent be talking to the ComCorp people? And what about Talyn's assurances that Naval Intelligence knew of *Tai Zolh* agents entering the Commonwealth? Did Shovak die because the Empire and our own Fleet were playing spy games? Did I mention I hated cases involving Naval Intelligence?

"What interest does the *Tai Zolh* have in trade agreements between private commercial entities?" I wasn't really expecting an answer, but I was hoping for more unconscious signals that might show I was knocking on the right door.

"Truth is," Hobart said, "the imperial regime exercises tight control over private commercial entities, Chief Superintendent. Over the legitimate ones at least. This trade delegation likely operates under the close direction of Ser Thopok's government, especially since it involves ComCorp, one of the major players in our part of the galaxy."

This time, Thopok's reaction was unmistakable. A string of angry words in Shrehari filled the air, taking even Hobart aback. The smuggler turned toward me with a mixture of amusement and surprise on his face.

"I must have touched a raw nerve. If you want my opinion, our friend here is indeed an officer in their intelligence service."

Another tirade in Shrehari elicited a chuckle from my interpreter.

"He just warned me I'll never find another willing business contact in the Empire again. Make of that what you will."

I pointedly ignored Hobart and kept my eyes on Thopok. "Account for your movements on the night Shovak died, starting with the preparations for the meeting with the ComCorp representatives."

The aide gave me another long stare I couldn't interpret but then spoke in his thickly accented Anglic. "I oversaw Aktuh and Rorg while they prepared the envoy's rooms to receive the humans. Then, I ordered the appropriate food and drink items from the station's administration. These were delivered shortly before the reception. Once everything was in place, I dismissed Aktuh and Rorg. The humans arrived, three of them, Houko, Mostrom, and Kazan."

Thopok massacred the names, but I had to give him props for trying.

"We shared a welcome drink, ate, and discussed various matters unrelated to business. This lasted for approximately two of your hours. Then, the humans left. I proposed recalling the guards to clean up, but Shovak preferred to leave it until morning. After confirming our schedule for the following day, I retired to my quarters. Rorg visited me later that evening to ask if there were any changes to the morning's itinerary. Following his visit, I composed myself for sleep."

Now that I sat in Shovak's former quarters, something that had been bugging me since the beginning finally swam into focus. I asked him, "How did you know to enter Shovak's quarters while the human female was there, standing over his body?

You wouldn't have heard anything. These bulkheads are soundproof."

"I am a light sleeper. Something roused me, so I looked out into the corridor. The entry to the envoy's suite stood open even though Shovak should be abed and thus I did what any aide must do. I investigated. It was then I saw the human female holding Shovak's consecrated knife, standing above him amid this carnage." He waved at the spattered walls and floor. "I was about to kill her for assaulting the envoy when station security arrived. They took the female into custody, making it abundantly clear with their weapons they would not tolerate any retribution on my part. I examined Shovak for signs of life, but the killer had done a thorough job. He was quite dead."

"And you cannot say what woke you."

"No."

I let my eyes roam over the suite again and examined the dried bloodstains. It took very little to turn a crime scene into an abattoir. But even accounting for a Shrehari's larger size and a heart to match, one capable of pumping great gushes through a severed artery, the killer could have escaped unseen before Shovak bled out. Without examining the body, it was impossible to tell.

"Describe his injuries."

Thopok made a gesture that might be his species' version of a shrug, then pointed at the side of his neck. "The murderer stabbed him once here."

"And this," I indicated the stained walls, "came from a single wound?"

"Yes. The main blood vessel was severed."

"Had the blood stopped flowing when you examined him?"

"It had," he replied.

"How long before a Shrehari bleeds out when a major blood vessel is severed?"

"Why do you assume I know this? Every death takes the time it must."

"Does your species bleed to death quickly from the type of wound you saw on Shovak?"

This time, he seemed to give it thought before replying. "Yes. Perhaps two of your minutes. Shovak was strong. His body would have tried to repair itself but in vain. If the assassin had not fully severed the blood vessel with such precision, Shovak might have survived long enough for me to provide aid."

"It makes me wonder why our sole suspect, after delivering the death blow, would bother to watch him die," I said. "A murderer would strike and flee, no? I mean if Shovak had stopped bleeding by the time you examined him, which was what? Less than a minute after you entered this room?"

His black within black eyes seemed to bore right through me, but I refused to look away. "You seek an explanation to support the female's innocence when I saw the truth that night?"

I could have sworn he sounded incredulous, but I suspected my subconscious was trying to match the right emotions to his words, emotions that weren't present, or at least detectable by a human. It was something I'd have to watch. Anthropomorphizing an alien species could lead me to inaccurate conclusions even if they were bilateral bipeds like us humans.

"I seek the guilty being, whoever that might be. Let me ask you this. The female you saw is approximately my size. Would someone so much smaller than a Shrehari be able to shove a knife through Shovak's neck?"

"If the killer incapacitated him beforehand? With ease."

"But what if he wasn't incapacitated?"

"Then no."

"And did you see anything on his body that might show his killer had somehow rendered him unable to resist?"

"I did not, but I am unskilled in these matters. Who knows what sleight of hand or treachery she used?"

Fair point. But the incident report prepared by Pullar's troopers didn't mention finding any sort of weapon in Talyn's possession or at the scene of the crime, other than Shovak's knife.

"What happens to your mission now?"

"I await orders from my superiors on that matter."

"Then why were you meeting with the ComCorp representatives earlier today?"

"To inform them I'm awaiting instructions, and to tell them that should my superiors decide so, I might take Shovak's place."

"How did they react?"

"They reacted cautiously, as I would expect." He paused for a few heartbeats, then climbed to his feet with ponderous deliberation and stared down at me. "I believe I have answered all of your questions."

I sensed that Hobart was about to berate him for his curtness toward me and placed a restraining hand on his arm.

"You were most cooperative, Thopok. My thanks. Keep in mind I may wish to speak with you again."

He subjected me to that expressionless stare for another few seconds and then left without a further word.

"That's what I hate most about the boneheads," Hobart murmured.

"What is?"

"Their damned inscrutability. Never play poker with them, Chief Superintendent. It's a losing proposition."

— Twenty-Three —

“Do you really think Thopok could be a *Tai Zolh* officer?” I asked Hobart once we’d entered the lift.

His expression turned thoughtful. “It’s possible. How much do you know about the Shrehari Empire’s inner workings, Chief Superintendent?”

“About as much as most Constabulary officers. It’s a dictatorship under a figurehead emperor, with the *Kho’sahra* held in check only by the Empire’s hereditary nobility. The nobles and the *Kho’sahra* play constant power games by setting their loyalists within the military and security services against each other. It creates a political balance of sorts, but one that verges on societal stasis.”

“Would you believe there was a time when the *Tai Kan* had political officers aboard each naval vessel and in each ground unit?”

“Sounds like it was a laugh a minute. I recall reading somewhere that when various human polities tried imposing commissars on the armed forces back in the days before spaceflight, it never ended well.”

Hobart nodded. “It didn’t end well for the Shrehari either. The first *Kho’sahra* abolished the practice. When he founded the *Tai Zolh*, after witnessing the failure of the Shrehari military's intelligence-gathering apparatus during the war, he also reined in the *Tai Kan* by carefully circumscribing its role. Though it remains a secretive police force, which by the way differs significantly from your Constabulary, it no longer holds sway over matters beyond the Empire's sphere of control as it once did. And it holds none over their Deep Space Fleet."

"What you're saying is that if their government placed an agent in Shovak's trade delegation, he would more likely be *Tai Zolh* than *Tai Kan*."

Hobart nodded. "Precisely. The current *Kho'sahra* wouldn't have allowed someone with dubious loyalties to leave the Empire in the first place. Thus no secret police minder needed."

Which begged the question why Shrehari intelligence was discussing cross-border trade with ComCorp? This sounded like something more up Talyn's alley. At that moment, my traitorous stomach made its opinion known, reminding me that the hour for the midday meal had come and gone. Hobart gave me a knowing smile.

"There's a place nearby where we can solve your little appetite problem, Chief Superintendent."

We stepped out onto the promenade beneath Aquilonia's faceted dome and made our way to a small bistro tucked into a side corridor not far from the Excelsior. The smuggler was proving to be a fascinating man, and yes he was easy on the eyes, in a tall, dark, and handsome way, but his knowledge of everything Shrehari had caught my interest.

"You must have intriguing stories to tell, Ser Hobart," I said once we sat in a booth far from the door and its passing parade of sentient beings. "Considering how well-acquainted you seem with the Empire and its dark corners."

"No more fascinating than the ones you could tell, I'm sure, Chief Superintendent, and please call me Monty. Ser Hobart sounds too formal for a light lunch after facing Shrehari poker faces."

"I suppose," I replied with a smile, "that since you're not a suspect, another cop, or a witness, there's no harm in your calling me Caelin while we're breaking bread."

Hobart dipped his head in an abbreviated bow. "Honored, Caelin. You're the first law enforcement officer to treat me like something other than the scrapings off the bottom of her shoes."

"Surely it isn't so bad."

He gave me grin meant to be sheepish, but the amused twinkle in his eyes ruined the effect. "I enjoy exaggerating every now and then. My dealings with the Constabulary have always been correct. I wish I could say the same about the *Tai Kan* or various planetary police forces."

"Glad to hear my brethren show restraint in your presence. Otherwise, I'd be overrun by complaints. Although no one likes the PCB on general principle, they like us even less when we're investigating alleged mistreatment of suspects already deemed to be lowlifes."

Hobart put a hand on his heart. "Speaking as someone who dislikes lowlifes just as much, since they're bad for business, I agree."

A human waiter appeared by our booth and took our orders.

"Based on what you heard this morning, what are your thoughts about this case?" I asked once we were alone again. "Considering your extensive experience with our boneheaded friends."

"There's more than meets the eye, to overuse a cliché."

"Really?" I cocked an eyebrow at him. "What a splendid deduction, Monty. It also happens to be true of almost every case I investigate."

"Which means you should be right in your element. My instincts tell me Thopok works for the Empire, not whatever commercial corporation ostensibly sent this trade delegation. But then you have to ask yourself why an organization like the *Tai Zolh* is in contact with a conglomerate as powerful as ComCorp. Once you slip into that rabbit hole, things turn weird. Too weird for the likes of me. In fact, I'll be avoiding the Empire for a while, just in case Thopok makes good on his threat."

"Sorry to have sabotaged your business."

Hobart made a dismissive gesture. "I can find plenty of profit on the Commonwealth Rim and in the Protectorate Zone. I don't need the Shrehari. Besides, the Constabulary now owes me a favor."

"We owe you an honorarium, Monty, not a get out of jail card if you're ever caught doing things that would make your mother blush."

"Too late for that. My mother blushes with embarrassment every time she thinks of where I went wrong."

Just then, the food showed up, and we ate in companionable silence. I figured he would move on to other subjects once he'd cleaned his bowl, but Hobart sat back with a thoughtful expression on his face.

"Returning to your question," he said, "my gut tells me your murder case revolves around whatever has the imperial government reaching out to ComCorp under the guise of a trade agreement."

"That's a heck of a leap, don't you think? The Honorable Commonwealth Trading Corporation in cahoots with the Shrehari?"

"Not really. ComCorp has deep pockets, a broad reach, and no morals. If its executives smell profit and power, they'll do whatever they think necessary. With the sole stipulation that neither your lot nor the Fleet sees something that screams for intervention."

"ComCorp is hardly alone among the major mercantile conglomerates when it comes to the single-minded pursuit of money and power. Every single one of them does things that wouldn't withstand intense scrutiny. And they escape the consequences because we can't do everything, even if our political masters let us slip the leash from time to time. Apparently, humanity's future hinges on unfettered interstellar trade, or that's what they'd have us believe. But sleeping with the Shrehari? I know the war ended long ago, yet it's still within living memory for many people, in and out of the Commonwealth government."

Hobart gave me a noncommittal shrug. "I call things the way I see them. Figure out what the Shrehari are doing with ComCorp, and you'll find your answer. What is it you cops say? Means, motive, and opportunity? The means are clear, and the opportunity shouldn't be hard to pin down, leaving only the motive. Find your motive, and you'll find your killer."

"Are you sure you're merely a merchant who skirts import-export laws and pockets the difference?"

His roguish smile returned. "You'd be surprised what one picks up in my line of business. I've dealt with enough shady characters and organizations to fill a book. ComCorp and its multiple subsidiaries are high on the list as is anything even remotely connected to the Shrehari."

I had already come to that conclusion independently, if only because of one Commander Hera Talyn, Commonwealth Navy, but it was interesting to hear my hired translator voice the same thoughts. There was more behind those dark eyes than he let on.

"What will you do now?" He asked in a conversational tone even though I could sense his interest was more than merely superficial.

"My job."

His delighted chuckle told me he had expected that answer. "Well, if ever you need more Shrehari translated, or added insights into the shadier side of cross-border commerce, I'm at your disposal – at least for a few days while I sort out my next contract. I'd also be delighted to show you my ship. She's not particularly big, but I can outrun pretty much anything."

"I'll keep that in mind. And now back to work." I pulled out a payment card.

Hobart raised his hand to stop me and said, "My treat, Caelin."

This time it was my turn to laugh. "Thanks, but no thanks. A well-traveled man like you should know accepting a freebie from a known scofflaw is an absolute taboo for a cop."

"Fair enough. I wouldn't want to sully your reputation."

"How generous of you. It's all I have left. Working Professional Compliance isn't conducive to keeping friendships alive."

"Ah, but I'm no cop, which means being seen as your friend won't cause me grief." That aura of mischief surrounded him again. "My peers would consider it an asset."

"But among my peers, making friends with a smuggler would be an issue. I'd have to report myself to my own superiors, and who wants to do that?" I climbed to my feet. "Thank you for the lunch recommendation and for your services. I'll have your honorarium transmitted by the end of the day."

"There's no hurry. Hang on to it in case you need my services again."

— Twenty-Four —

I left the bistro without looking back, knowing his eyes would track me until I turned the corner. It's just as well I escaped before he amped up the charm. I'm a sucker for smart, slightly mischievous men with bedroom eyes, and Hobart was the first in years who didn't shy away because of my job description.

When I finally checked the time, I realized that my afternoon was more than halfway over, and I was no further ahead than I was this morning. On the contrary. The possibility of espionage being involved would make a quick resolution even less likely.

Lost in thought, I didn't notice Javan Burrard standing across my path until I almost bumped into him. Was I about to hear another greeting from Louis Sorne? After a quick glance at the fully loaded equipment belt he now wore, shockstick included, I looked up at his square face and decided he definitely came close to Thopok in both bulk and height.

"Chief Superintendent Morrow," he said in his gravelly voice, "might I take a few moments of your precious time? We got off on the wrong foot this morning, and I'd like to fix that."

We didn't actually get off at all, but since saying so might sound out of place, I merely held his gaze and nodded.

"Go ahead."

"I was a Gendarmerie noncom for twenty years, and I'm aware cops don't think much of private security outfits like CimmerTek. I didn't back in the day, but then I learned they have their place if you train and use them properly."

Burrard eyed me for a reaction, and when I didn't even blink, he continued. "When you think about it, you, Jon Pullar, and me, we're concerned about the same thing. Keeping Aquilonia safe and finding Envoy Shovak's assassin. Dead visitors aren't good for business and murders give this place a bad rap. I figure Jon told you about my folks and me. He also must have mentioned we worked together years ago. But I know Jon doesn't let personal opinions influence his way of policing, and neither do I. So I figure it would be in everyone's interest if we cooperate in solving the murder as quickly as possible. That's why I'm putting the resources of CimmerTek Security Solutions at your disposal."

"Are you now," I murmured to myself. Was Burrard acting on his own, or did Darrien prompt him? And why? In a louder voice, I replied, "Thank you for the offer, Ser Burrard. I'll gladly speak with anyone who has information pertinent to the case."

"I've canvassed my staff. If they saw or heard anything, I'll let you know. And if you need people to help with the legwork, they're yours."

It would be a warm day on Thule before I enlisted a company partially owned by a notoriously corrupt politician facing indictment. But since Burrard might find himself on my list of suspects at some point, it was best to stay on neutral, if not friendly terms. Therefore, I merely said, "Of course."

Then, a devil may care moment overcame me, and I asked, "I believe you employ a man by the name of Ward Loriot, don't you?"

He gave me a cautious nod. "I do. He's a long-time employee and a former military police noncom."

"Are you aware one of CimmerTek's owners uses him as a messenger?"

A frown briefly creased Burrard's shiny forehead. "I'm not sure I understand what you're getting at, Chief Superintendent, or what this has to do with the Shovak case."

I let a sly smile tug at the corners of my mouth. "Could you ask Loriot to give Louis Sorne my best wishes and my thanks for his kindness?"

The fleeting look of confusion in Burrard's eyes made me wonder whether he was unaware of Sorne's message. Or perhaps my brazenness took him by surprise.

But he recovered swiftly and replied in a noncommittal tone, "I'll talk to Loriot."

"Thank you. If there was nothing else on your mind, Ser Burrard, enjoy the rest of your day."

I stepped around him and left without a backward glance. Burrard's attempt to ingratiate himself with me could stem from many reasons — Darrien, professional pride, curiosity, or orders from his head office. Or it could be a perp's desire to monitor my progress. I would have to ask Pullar for a trace on Burrard's activities at the time of the murder.

When I entered the Gendarmerie station, Major Pullar's head immediately popped through his open office door, and he waved me over.

"Your Sector HQ has notified us that an Inspector Arno Galdi is on the ferry and will arrive in approximately eighteen hours."

News to brighten my day at last. It meant he'd wrapped up the final details of the Haylian investigation.

"Arno's one of my officers and for this case, my wingman. I'll be happier when he joins me."

Pullar pointed at the coffee urn and raised his eyebrows in question. When I nodded, he walked over and drew two mugs, then indicated I should take a seat by his desk.

"Any progress?" He asked.

I took a sip before replying. "One step forward, five steps back, or so it seems."

"Oh?"

"Shovak's guards had nothing useful to add, but Thopok did. He gave me a description of Shovak's stab wound and confirmed that it had stopped bleeding when he entered the room, or at least when he examined his boss a few seconds later. Our victim was fatally injured minutes earlier, giving the assassin ample time to escape down the stairwell."

"And that begs the question why Talyn stuck around. She could have left without even alerting my people, yet she rang the alarm and stayed there. Perhaps she wanted to make sure Shovak was dead."

"Doubtful. According to Thopok that type of injury ensured death. Anyone conversant with Shrehari physiology would have seen no need to loiter."

"A step forward, at least."

I shrugged. "The only step forward, but it serves to reinforce the hypothesis Talyn might be telling the truth, that she's not the killer. Unless we accept she had a way to incapacitate Shovak before using his own knife to finish him off. And if she did, what is it? Where is it? And why create a mess of blood? Someone with access to a weapon that can put a Shrehari out of action could have killed him outright. And why deliberately let herself be arrested? It makes no sense."

"And the steps back?"

"Neither of the guards struck Hobart or me as being government agents. By the way, Hobart's an interesting fellow. If the Gendarmerie has any records on him, I wouldn't mind taking a peek. He's well-versed in Shrehari affairs."

"I doubt we have much. He hasn't come to our notice before now, but you were saying?"

"Thopok might well be an imperial officer. Both Hobart and I picked up a few clues that could indicate he's *Tai Zolh.*" I gave him a rundown of the guards' reaction and our conversation with the aide.

Pullar made a face. "Ugh. I don't envy you, Chief Superintendent. No one likes cases involving espionage." He paused, as if a light had come on, and then asked, "Why in God's vast universe would Shrehari intelligence be reaching out to ComCorp?"

"That's exactly what I wonder. And now, always assuming that my, and Hobart's gut instincts are right about Thopok, I'm also wondering whether Shovak was *Tai Zolh*. Or whether he was a genuine negotiator used as a front by the *Tai Zolh*. Considering the tight grip their *Kho'sahra* keeps on interstellar trade, either is possible. Besides, we don't even know if this *Quch Mech* Corporation is a real mercantile organization or an arm of the Shrehari government. We've seen enough examples throughout human history of intelligence agencies hiding behind seemingly genuine private sector companies. Why wouldn't the Empire?"

"Where does that leave your investigation?"

"Once I finish your excellent coffee, I'll pay Commander Talyn yet another visit. Since she works for Naval Intelligence, even if it's only as the desk analyst she claims to be, I'm hoping she can shed light on these new developments."

Pullar chuckled and said, "At this rate, I might as well turn custody over to you so you can take her along for your interviews."

"Don't tempt me. Corrupt cops, military officers, or politicos, I can handle. In fact, I can handle pretty much any criminal case, but this is becoming just a little odd. I'll be happy when Arno shows up. He has a greater tolerance for the bizarre than I do. And speaking of bizarre..."

I told Pullar of my encounter with Burrard on the promenade. When I finished, he gave me a look halfway between exasperation and disgust.

"Javan should know better than that. The top brass might not have selected him for a commission, but dummies don't become master sergeants either. I'll put a trace on his movements, but he's no killer. At least he wasn't back then."

"Burrard could have changed since you last worked with him, or latent tendencies might have surfaced. Besides, everyone has a price. Perhaps someone met his."

"A paid hit?" Pullar sounded dubious. "No one can change *that* much. We didn't always agree on methods, but Javan was an honest man. Even a viper like Dangerous Don wouldn't be able to make him cross the line into criminality."

"Nonetheless, he remains a potential suspect until we've found an unquestionable alibi. Between him and Talyn, who would you see as the more likely killer?"

Pullar hesitated, and then replied in a grudging tone, "Javan."

I drained my mug. "And on that thought, time to revisit the sphinx of Aquilonia."

Talyn graced me with a cold smile when I entered her cell.

"We must stop meeting like this, Chief Superintendent, otherwise people will talk."

"I think that ship has sailed. Major Pullar suggested I ask you to tag along and offer running advice on matters more in your area of expertise than mine."

She laughed with genuine delight. "I didn't know our dour Cimmerian gendarme had a sense of humor. It goes to show that people will never cease to surprise you."

"True. When we spoke this morning, you told me you doubted anyone in the Shrehari trade delegation would be *Tai Zolh*. What if I told you that Thopok, Shovak's aide, might be an intelligence officer?"

"How did you come to that conclusion?"

"Clues unwittingly dropped by Thopok and the guards. I don't think their concept of body language resembles ours, or perhaps they believe we're too stupid to interpret theirs. Thopok also sinned by protesting too much. Perhaps I'm completely off my rocker because they're an alien species, but my investigator's instinct has rarely led me astray."

"It led you into the PCB. I'm sure a vast swath of the Constabulary would call that seriously astray."

"Amusing." Was Talyn trying to irritate me again? "Let's play a little game, Commander, where I'm the cop, and you're the suspect who has proclaimed her innocence and is willing to cooperate fully, without making editorial comments. Deal?"

She nodded, but her eyes remained as hard and cold as ever beneath a thin veneer of amusement. "Deal. I offer you my complete and wholehearted cooperation, so long as national security matters aren't involved."

Somehow, I doubted that. For a woman who claimed to be falsely accused, she seemed very nonchalant about her precarious position. "Would the *Tai Zolh* use trade delegations to conduct intelligence work?"

"I don't see why not? It's a time-honored practice used by virtually every human society since governments began to spy on each other. I suppose they might slip an agent into the Commonwealth that way without us knowing. As much as we'd like, we're not omniscient."

"Do we send agents into the Empire under cover of commerce?"

"You don't expect me to answer that, do you, Chief Superintendent?"

I didn't, but I had to ask. "Why would the *Tai Zolh* want to contact ComCorp?"

"What makes you think ComCorp is in any way involved?" She replied. "If the trade mission is a cover, then our Shrehari friends might be reaching out to anyone."

"But it's possible?"

"Sure. None of the large mercantile conglomerates are paragons of patriotism and virtue. They favor their shareholders' interests over any others, which is also a time-honored practice. Isn't that why you Constabulary folks call them zaibatsus?"

I ignored her question and asked, "So Shovak's assassination could stem from whatever ComCorp was up to with the *Tai Zolh*?"

"Only if you're correct about Thopok being an imperial operative."

"But even if I'm not, his death might still stem from something related to ComCorp."

"Sure." She nodded. "But the probability that another Shrehari killed him remains your best bet. Few humans can wrest a warrior's knife from its Shrehari owner and shove it through his neck, severing a major blood vessel so completely that he dies within minutes. I don't know of anyone. Besides, I can't see ComCorp sponsoring the assassination. Not if your culprit is another Shrehari. No human can convince a member of the imperial race to murder another of his kind. They simply don't think the way we do."

"Is that why you're here, Commander? Because the trade mission is a cover for imperial intelligence, your counterparts?"

"No. If the Fleet had any inkling the *Tai Zolh* was coming for a visit, someone from counterintelligence will watch them. I'm from a different division, so I wouldn't know. We deal with matters that don't involve the Empire."

"Meaning you wouldn't know if Shovak and company are under surveillance?"

"Exactly. The various branches of Naval Intelligence keep their activities compartmentalized in the same way your PCB does when it comes to investigations. My visit coinciding with that of the Shrehari is a fluke. Allowing my curiosity free rein led me into this mess. If I had left well enough alone and not checked when I saw the door to Shovak's suite standing wide open..."

"And picked up his knife."

"Pure reflex, Chief Superintendent, sadly for me. I'm confident you'll find that my involvement in this matter is entirely innocent. Besides," she added, with a faint smile, "contrary to popular fiction, spies don't go around assassinating each other unless they're on opposing sides of a war. It would quickly become a tit-for-tat that leaves everyone weaker."

"And you're merely an intelligence analyst, not a field operative, right?"

"Correct."

"Then tell me, Commander Analyst, what should I do with this *Tai Zolh* matter?"

"Be very careful. If you've uncovered something involving it, and their agents know you know, things might turn dicey. Perhaps not because of the Shrehari themselves, but their human partners. The latter would have more to lose than a fake trade delegation we would expel as a matter of course on suspicion of espionage."

Great. I had accused Thopok of being a spy. The thought must have shown in my eyes because Talyn grimaced, shaking her head.

"Oh dear, you've said something. May I suggest that you carry a weapon and find a partner who can watch your back?"

"You think someone might try to terminate me and not merely my investigation?"

"Anything is possible once you enter the wild and wacky universe of undercover operations, Chief Superintendent."

"That may be so; but this is still a criminal case, a matter for the police. My interest is in finding the culprit. Spy games belong to your lot."

"Agreed, but not everyone can distinguish the line between the two."

— Twenty-Five —

Exhaustion overtook me without warning even though long days and I were no strangers to each other. Had Talyn's warning rattled me?

"Get anything interesting?" Pullar asked when I rejoined him in his office.

I dropped into my usual chair and sighed. "A warning that if Shrehari intelligence is involved, I could be at risk. Not from the boneheads directly but the humans doing business with them."

He grimaced. "Then it's a good thing your Inspector Galdi is on his way. Are you carrying your service weapon?"

"Yes." I lifted the left side of my jacket to show him a needler in a soft-shell shoulder holster tucked into my armpit. "It hasn't left me since this morning, except when I was in Talyn's cell. Your duty sergeant wouldn't let me in otherwise."

"Good. I'd rather not end up with two dead bodies in one week, Chief Superintendent. Just remember to duck before you return fire, discretion being the better part of valor."

"I won't argue with you on that point. Any progress with the sensor pickups engineering was supposed to retrieve and analyze?"

My Cimmerian friend shook his head. "Nothing yet, but I've launched a trace on Javan Burrard's movements."

"Perhaps I should send a missile up Dangerous Don's posterior."

"Please feel free to do so. If you record the event for posterity, it will boost morale, not only among my people but throughout Aquilonia." He hesitated, then asked, "Do you have plans for the evening meal?"

"Considering I had a late midday soup less than two hours ago, I haven't given it much thought, but I'm open to suggestions."

"The Aquilonia Excelsior has a highly rated restaurant. If you'd like, I'll make reservations. Perhaps dining at the heart of ComCorp's business interests on the station might prove educational while we boldly show the banner of law and order."

The exaggerated and obviously fake solemnity of his last few words broke through my semi-funk, and I laughed. As Talyn said, people never ceased to surprise you.

"I accept. How about two hours from now?" A little alone time wouldn't come amiss, perhaps augmented by a hot shower to kick my neurons back into high gear.

"So it shall be done." He turned to his terminal and tapped the screen. After a few moments, he nodded. "There we go. It's under my name."

I excused myself and returned to the VIP level. Stepping out of the lift, my eyes inevitably turned toward the Shrehari quarters on my left, near the stairwell door. Without quite knowing why I went over to stand halfway between their suites and the stairs, then slowly turned around in a full circle.

Even I could cover the distance between the rooms and the assassin's likely escape route in two or three steps. In other words quickly enough to escape notice unless someone was nearby.

Since Aquilonia was dug out of a mining operation's remains, little within its confines ran in perfectly straight lines, including this corridor. The digs would have followed ore seams rather than a rigid grid. For instance, I couldn't see the door to my quarters from where I stood.

Station management had left a buffer of half a dozen empty suites between the Shrehari and the other guests. I counted off the doors I saw from where I stood and came up with six, not counting Thopok and Shovak's quarters. Convenient.

Unless someone stepped out of the lift at the exact moment when the killer entered or exited the victim's room, he would be invisible. My suspicion that someone sabotaged the video pickups in this area and in the stairwell seemed more like a certainty. Once station engineering checked them, we would know for sure.

As I turned toward my room, the door to Thopok's quarters hissed open, and he stepped into the corridor. Those chilling black within black eyes examined my face for a few seconds, then he detoured around me to take the stairs. The brief encounter sent my heart racing, and my right hand almost reached for the weapon under my left arm out of sheer reflex.

Two hours later, feeling not much fresher than when we last spoke, I joined Pullar at a corner table in the grandiosely named and richly decorated Excelsior Court restaurant.

A smattering of patrons dotted a space cunningly designed to appear much more substantial than its actual and rather narrow footprint. A transparent ceiling giving diners an unobstructed view of Aquilonia's dome helped to complete the illusion.

Human attendants in formal dark jackets such as the one who had greeted me at the door and guided me to Pullar's table, took care of the guests. Even the menus were printed and bound in a material imitating soft leather. No holograms here, not even a discreet screen on the wall listing the daily specials.

"I trust your time out was adequate," the Cimmerian said, half rising out of his chair while I sat. The gesture struck me as charmingly quaint.

"Adequate might be pushing things, but I'm sure a good meal on the military's expense account will brighten both our evenings."

A smile softened his severe features. "You might experience push-back if you try to claim reimbursement for dinner in this place."

"They either pay up, or they won't have us to rely on the next time one of their senior officers steps on a live wire."

"You can refuse a case?" He seemed surprised.

"If I believe taking it might cause harm to the Constabulary, the Armed Services, or the Commonwealth, sure. But my superiors might disagree, in which case I suck it up and investigate, no matter what I might think. Of course, there's always early retirement, although I probably wouldn't know what to do with the free time. The only organizations who hire former PCB officers are the kind I wouldn't care to work for."

"No family?"

I shook my head. "None within light years. I might still have a few distant relatives scattered across the

Commonwealth, perhaps even on Pacifica, but I'm one of those wedded to the job, more so since I joined the PCB."

One of the attendants approached our table to inquire about drinks. Pullar ordered a beer, and I wine, hoping that the Excelsior Court served a better quality house plonk. My taste buds hadn't fully recovered from the previous day's serving of almost *Chateau Sewage*.

"Is that where you're from, Pacifica?" He asked after the attendant left.

Strangely, Pullar asking about my past didn't irritate me as much as Hobart's attempt. Perhaps it was due to his being a fellow law enforcement officer. The great interstellar police family. So I nodded.

"I was born in Hadley and lived there until I joined the Constabulary at seventeen, when I left Pacifica for good."

"You haven't been back since then?"

"There's no reason for me to return. My family is gone."

Surprising me yet again, Pullar examined me with a knowing look on his face. "Would it be prying if I asked whether you joined up at such a young age to escape the authorities? Pacifica isn't exactly known for having a liberal government and enlisting in the Armed Services or the Constabulary is one of the better ways to escape if the Pacifican State Security Police is on your tail."

He must have seen something in my eyes because he raised a hand, palm outward and said, "My apologies, I withdraw the question."

Our drinks showed up at that moment and when the waiter had left again, I said, "No need to apologize. You seem remarkably knowledgeable."

"I did a hitch in the Corps before returning to Cimmeria and a job in the Gendarmerie. During that time, I came across more than a few Pacificans who joined the Marines to avoid arrest on political charges. The way a few of them tell it, they literally hit the recruiting office one step ahead of the State Security Police and had to be sworn in on the spot, so Pacifican authorities no longer had jurisdiction."

I took a sip of the wine — a tolerable vintage this time — then nodded.

"That's how it was for me. My father was a university professor. They eventually fired him for his political views because he had become an increasingly vocal thorn in the ruling Progressive Party's hide. One day, just before the evening meal, my mother sent me out to buy fresh bread. When I returned to the street where we lived, I saw my parents and younger siblings dragged out of our apartment building by State Security assholes and bundled into black skimmers. Dad feared it might eventually happen after watching so many of his friends in the opposition movement disappear when the Proggies tired of them. The day I turned seventeen, he told me that if ever the cops came for him, I was to head for the Commonwealth recruiting office and enlist on the spot."

"And here you are, a career cop."

"Pure chance. The Constabulary recruiting sergeant had the early duty that day. He took me off the street, knowing right away that I was another kid on the run from the State Security Police. In the space of a few hours, he processed me, had his CO swear me in, and then smuggled me through Hadley to the Fleet base in the back of a staff car. By then the police goons had issued a notice for my arrest. Once on the base, they kitted me out in a

Constabulary uniform and issued me official ID. Two days later, I left Pacifica behind aboard one of the Fleet's transports, headed for basic training on Wyvern."

I took another sip of my wine before continuing. "Any of the four services would have done, but the kindness shown to a terrified girl by the Constabulary recruiter made me choose the same uniform as his. If the Marine recruiting sergeant had been the first, we wouldn't be having this conversation, and I'd be humping a plasma rifle on some frontier world. The rest, as they say, is history. I never saw my family again. There's no trace of them in any official police records. They simply became nonpersons after their arrest, which is pretty much proof they've been moldering in an unmarked grave for the last thirty years. I haven't checked recently, but there's probably still an old warrant out for me on charges of undermining the Pacifican government."

"Wow," Pullar whistled softly. "I always figured the guys who took the enlistment route to escape were embellishing their tale."

"It's depressingly true and still happening nowadays. The Progressive Party hasn't lost a single election in the last half-century because it keeps eliminating dissenters who become too vocal. Of course, officially, nothing of the sort ever happens on Pacifica. Otherwise the Commonwealth Senate would have to take notice."

"As a wise man said, it's not the people who vote that count, but the people who count the votes."

"My father used that line a lot. If the Proggies could end elections altogether, they would, but that's the one thing our otherwise ineffectual Supreme Court will never allow. After all, we must preserve the illusion that every human world is an enlightened democracy, even though it's a sham in places like Pacifica. And on that depressing note, I won't even apologize for changing the subject. What's your story?"

He made a dismissive gesture with his shoulders. "Nothing quite as riveting as yours. To use a well-worn cliché, I'm Cimmerian born and bred. I had the usual wanderlust after school and did a hitch in the Corps, as a grunt, before coming home and joining the Gendarmerie. I started at patrolman and climbed through the ranks. Decades later, I'm a major looking forward to retirement after enforcing the law in every corner of the Cimmeria system. I've always served in uniform and never felt the inclination to become a detective, something for which I likely don't have the aptitude anyway."

Our food's arrival saved him from further interrogation and, so as not to spoil the excellent and costly meal, we talked about inconsequential matters. He even regaled me with a few funny stories involving Aquilonia's chief administrator and his partner.

We were enjoying an after-dinner coffee when Pullar glanced over my shoulder and grimaced. "It looks like our friend Thopok, escorted by his ComCorp hosts, has decided to sample the menu, though I saw nothing that might tempt a Shrehari."

Resisting the urge to turn and gawk, I replied, "The restaurant offers ale imported directly from the Empire if he's happy with a liquid meal. And since both humans and boneheads can drink it with similar effects, they probably find our food digestible, if not necessarily palatable."

"Your former colleague doesn't seem pleased to see you."

"She must have heard I accused Thopok of being *Tai Zolh*. It's the sort of faux pas that could mess with delicate negotiations — if they're telling the truth."

"And if they're not?"

"I'm sure I need not draw you a picture, Major."

"Of course. My apologies." Then, "She's coming over."

Damn. Facing Gerri was the last thing I wanted tonight. I turned in my chair and watched her approach, still feeling the sting of her earlier rejection. She stopped a pace away and looked down at me with an expression oozing contempt.

"I understand you've resorted to flinging unfounded accusations at our honored Shrehari guests," she said in a low voice only Pullar and I could hear. "Perhaps the PCB has made you paranoid, but try to keep your delusions under control. Now charge the suspect held by Major Pullar and go harass the guilty party instead of wasting the taxpayer's money which, as you might remember, also flows from ComCorp profits."

I forced myself to meet her cold eyes with an impassive stare. "Your complaint has been noted, Sera Kazan. But until otherwise ordered by my superiors, I will pursue any and every line of inquiry, so both the Commonwealth government and the Empire are satisfied I've charged the right being with Envoy Shovak's murder. Now if there's nothing else, I wish you and your companions a pleasant evening, like the one Major Pullar and I enjoyed until you interrupted us."

She leaned over and murmured, "You always were a sanctimonious, self-righteous bitch. Take care that this case doesn't become your last."

"Is that a threat?"

"Merely a statement of fact. Yan Houko has dispatched a complaint that will land on your Chief Constable's desk soon enough." With that, she rejoined the others.

"How long do you expect before your boss sends new orders?" Pullar asked

"A few days, perhaps a week if he feels like dragging his heels. Longer, if Houko uses ComCorp's government connections to apply pressure. Deputy Chief Constable Hammett doesn't respond well to politicking. It makes him rather uncooperative."

"You don't sound particularly concerned."

"What happens, happens, Major. One thing I've learned since joining the PCB is to never invest myself emotionally in a case. Expediency can pull the rug out from under an investigation without warning."

"Does that happen often?"

"More than I'd like. But it's mostly for the good of the Service."

"Not for justice?"

"Justice?" My laugh sounded bitter enough to make Pullar wince in sympathy. "Provided I rid the Constabulary, and when necessary the Armed Services and Commonwealth government of the corrupt, venal, and criminal, I've fulfilled my responsibilities. If the brass lets a culprit walk because prosecuting him or her might cause even worse damage, then who am I to complain? We're constrained by a legal system that might, occasionally, dispense justice."

"How do you withstand it and not turn into a virulent cynic?"

I gave him a crooked smile. "What makes you think I'm not a virulent cynic already?"

"Touché." He raised his cup in salute and drained it. "That was excellent. I rarely come here. A major's pay goes only so far, and the Excelsior Court is a few steps beyond my means. Please thank the Navy on my behalf."

— Twenty-Six —

Pullar and I parted ways by the central lift bank. He was heading to his office for a final check with the duty watch before turning in and I was returning to my room. With any luck, he'd find something from station engineering about the faulty sensors so I could pick up that particular thread in the morning.

I watched the door to his lift close, then glanced at the nearby stairwell, trying to decide whether it was better to work off the substantial meal or succumb to postprandial laziness. In the end, I gave in and touched the call screen. The AI accepted my identity and indicated it would send me a private cab since my destination was a restricted area. Funny how the security measures hadn't kept Shovak's killer out unless it had been another VIP or someone with special access. Someone like Talyn, for example. Or Burrard.

The security system's log had shown no unauthorized persons attempting to enter the section, something that weakened Talyn's claims to innocence. But as with the stairwell sensors, it wouldn't surprise me to find access control had been equally spotty if not outright defective that evening.

A lift car arrived, and I stepped in, alone. The doors closed behind me and, with an unexpected lurch, it descended with such speed that my meal almost came back for an encore. Within seconds, the display showed we had left the habitable area.

Despite a mounting sense of panic, I remembered Aquilonia obtained water, oxygen, and hydrogen for its fusion reactor from gigantic sheets of underground ice. That meant it operated what was effectively an automated ice mining operation deep beneath the station.

Somehow, the lift I had boarded was one of the few that descended to those depths. Except a tourist shouldn't go beyond the artificial gravity envelope, let alone that of breathable air.

A few seconds later and with equal abruptness, the lift came to a halt. I fell to my knees, bruising them on the hard, plasticized surface before the moon's micro-gravity kicked in and my meal made a second stab at resurrection. I gasped at the sudden pain, but found myself unable to breathe. One look at the instrument panel told me why. The cab was depressurizing. With an unprotected, air-breathing human, namely me, inside.

Half-panicked, my eyes darted around for the emergency switch while I fought the atavistic instinct to hold my breath. Instead, I forced myself to exhale slowly so the expanding air in my lungs didn't send deadly bubbles into my bloodstream.

A cloak of pain enveloped me as my skin swelled thanks to the water in my tissues trying to vaporize. At the same time, my open mouth and eyes flared with an intense burning sensation when the surface moisture boiled away.

The voice of a long gone lecturer, culled from a thirty-year-old memory, cut through the buzzing in my brain. It told me that without air, I had fifteen seconds, give or take, before my body used up the oxygen still in my system. Unconsciousness and a quick demise would follow.

Dark spots began to dance before my eyes while the last of the air in my lungs escaped, and I knew my fifteen seconds was up.

The cab shuddered and then, even though the black veil of death was descending on me, I realized I was in motion once more.

With astonishing quickness, I felt pressure return, and the pain from my swelling body subsided. My first few breaths of recycled air seemed as sweet as anything I'd ever tasted.

Artificial gravity returned, dragging me back to one gee, and the cab stopped. Its doors opened onto the VIP section, and I scrambled out, still half-blind with panic.

Malfunctioning lifts with kilometer-long shafts had been a staple of my nightmares for decades, though I never knew why. That this one's lower end led to airless underground caverns, where the ambient temperature was close to absolute zero, made it even more frightening.

I hauled myself up against the bulkhead and stared back at the closing lift doors. Aquilonia had more than just sensors suffering from upkeep issues.

With one hand on the wall to keep myself steady, I made my way down the deserted corridor on shaky legs. Every step sent a fresh throb of pain through my nerves and I had to stop several times so I could wipe away the tears without stumbling. Once in the privacy of my suite delayed shock took hold. It was the closest I'd come to dying in years. I slipped to the floor, back against the wall and sobbed.

Eventually, the shock subsided and a spark of rage flared to life, warming innards chilled by the imminence of death. Anger was something I could harness and use, as Donul Darrien was about to discover. But Pullar first. He answered almost at once.

"Chief Super..." His voice faded away once my haggard expression registered. "What happened?"

"I was taken on an unscheduled lift ride down into Aquilonia's bowels, beyond the artificial gravity envelope."

"What?" Pullar's voice rose by almost a full octave. "Someone's going to get a rocket up his ass for this. Lifts aren't supposed to leave the station proper without authorization from the operations center."

"It gets better. When the lift stopped, and by the way I have no idea where that might have been, it began to depressurize."

A string of highly imaginative curse words erupted from his lips, then he said, "Forget the rocket. An antimatter torpedo will do a better job. Lift cabs shouldn't depressurize without human intervention. Either we have a massive failure here, or this was attempted murder."

"I think we can discount attempted murder, Major. Just as I was about to pass out, atmospheric pressure returned and I was taken to the VIP section, bruised, scared out of my wits, but alive."

"Then I'll take great pleasure in telling Dangerous Don that his damned station is falling apart — after I have them take that entire shaft out of service."

"How about you quarantine it, and I call Darrien? It might help kick his engineers' analysis of the failed sensors into high gear, assuming he's still dragging his feet."

"Yes he still is dragging his feet, and may I say you're a cruel woman, Chief Superintendent, depriving me of the pleasure. But somehow, I think it'll be even more entertaining, coming from you. Please be so kind as to describe how he reacted the next time we speak."

"Of course. I assume that you'll impound the operational logs for that particular car, so we can independently look for the reason this happened."

Pullar frowned. "Even though it might not have been a botched attempt on your life, are you thinking it wasn't necessarily an accident?"

"At this point, I'm just about ready to believe anything. Someone mentioned falling down a rabbit hole a few hours ago. This might have been a contrived incident warning me to climb back out. The lift cab regained pressure at just the right time to prevent any permanent harm."

"Perhaps, though it seems like an overly complicated way to warn you, considering the safeguards that are supposed to prevent such an accident. And speaking of harm, did you want me to arrange for a medical examination, to make sure you've suffered no lingering effects from decompression? The Gendarmerie has a contract with the local clinic, and I'm sure they'll see you if I ask."

"I doubt that will be necessary. I'm feeling bruised but otherwise unharmed. If I was fated to suffer an embolism, it would have happened by now."

"Very well. If you change your mind, just say the word. In the meantime, enjoy ruining Darrien's evening. I'll investigate your mishap. Until later."

The screen went dark, and I immediately called the station administrator's office, surprised to find a human instead of an AI on the other end of the link. An AI generally wouldn't have that 'I wish I were somewhere else' expression on its face. Unless whoever installed it wanted to add as much verisimilitude as possible to something in Dangerous Don's service.

"Can I help you, Chief Superintendent?" He asked.

"Put me through to Ser Darrien, please."

"D.D. cannot be disturbed at this time. Call back in nine hours."

"One of your systems malfunctioned, almost killing me. In nine hours, I'll have this station crawling with federal inspectors. They'll probably have Aquilonia evacuated and shuttered. I'm sure Ser Darrien will wish to know. Don't you think it's worth disturbing him under these circumstances?"

Butter couldn't melt in my mouth. The flunky's world-weary expression turned into a semi-comical mask of alarm.

"I'll put him on," he stammered. "One moment please."

Aquilonia's logo replaced the man's face. I mentally counted the seconds until Darrien came on, wishing Arno were here so we could bet on how long he'd take. It was one of the small things we did for entertainment in my outfit.

When Darrien finally appeared, he reminded me of a dyspeptic toad, with bulging eyes and quivering cheeks.

"I understand you threatened my receptionist so he would disturb me during my few hours of peace and tranquility," he said, dispensing with the usual courtesies, such as a polite greeting. I often have that effect on people. "It's most unprofessional of you, Chief Superintendent. I wonder whether another complaint is warranted."

"Good thing I work for Professional Compliance. I'll investigate myself at the appropriate time. But I wasn't joking. Your station had a systems malfunction that almost cost me my life."

"Oh?" He didn't bother to hide his skepticism. "Please describe this so-called glitch."

"One of your lifts took me down into this moon's bowels, beyond the artificial gravity envelope, instead of to the VIP section. Then, it began to depressurize. The only reason we're talking is because pressure returned just before I passed out. The cab then took me to my destination as if nothing had happened. I'd say that was more than a mere glitch."

Darrien stared at me in appalled silence, eyebrows raised, mouth open, unable to speak.

"Major Pullar," I continued, "has already quarantined the shaft in question, pending investigation — a police investigation to be precise. Add this latest unfortunate occurrence to the surveillance sensor malfunctions that prevent us from identifying an assassin, and I think Aquilonia is ripe for a federally mandated safety inspection. I wouldn't doubt the inspectors will recommend a thorough overhaul that includes new management."

I couldn't actually order any of it, merely make recommendations to DCC Maras, who upon consideration would either pass them on to the proper authorities or tell me to stop making empty threats. But Darrien didn't know that, and wouldn't have caught on to my wording, which merely expressed an opinion, not intent. A review of the conversation by a complaint adjudicating committee would note as much.

I've learned to equivocate with the best of them, a professional hazard thanks to a life spent chasing savvy crooks who knew every dirty trick. But the PCB aura, for those who've heard of us, could appear somewhat more substantial than our actual powers.

He kept staring at me and I wondered what thoughts lurked behind those calculating eyes, then he shook himself.

"I'm sure there's no call to make these minor incidents seem worse than they are," he finally said in the smooth tone of a career bureaucrat experienced in dodging responsibility.

"A lift going haywire in a kilometer-long shaft while a human is on board would hardly qualify as minor, Ser Darrien. Not when it was about to disgorge me into an airless cavern beneath Aquilonia's surface. These things should stop the moment their programming senses something is wrong instead of moving at speeds sufficient to cause injury. They should definitely not depressurize without confirming the humans on board are properly equipped to survive a vacuum. I suggest you have every lift inspected forthwith. I also expect a full analysis of the failed sensor components near Envoy Shovak's quarters and in the adjacent stairwell. Please have a report on Major Pullar's desk by oh-eight-hundred Aquilonia time tomorrow. When Pullar's people have completed their investigation of this latest incident, I'm sure we'll talk again. Strange things are happening on your watch, Ser Darrien, and I'd rather there be no recurrences, least of all involving me."

"Maintenance failures happen from time to time," he replied, full of oiliness and insincerity now that his initial surprise had passed, "even though we might wish they don't. Thankfully, you came out of this incident unhurt."

"The sensor analysis, Ser Darrien, in nine hours if you please, and full cooperation with Major Pullar regarding the lift."

I cut the comlink, no doubt leaving him to fume at my rudeness. What did that conversation tell me? Maybe a lot, maybe nothing. The lift controls could have failed due to sloppy maintenance, but I was with the guy who said don't piss on my back and tell me it's raining.

Hopefully, Pullar's gendarmes would find something that explained it either way. But after Talyn's warning, I could well believe someone just sent me a message, and there was no shortage of potential senders.

Had someone just told me to climb out of the rabbit hole and forget about Shrehari agents? To accept Talyn's guilt, charge her, and leave. Or had Louis Sorne, via his CimmerTek goons, graduated from verbal intimidation to physical threats, or even attempted murder?

— Twenty-Seven —

I was half-asleep in my suite's sinfully comfortable easy chair after a hot shower, my nerves no longer raw from the incident, when the comlink chimed for attention. My hand scrabbled for the controls in the chair's arm and a holographic rendition of Pullar's solemn face materialized in the middle of the room.

He noticed my drowsy expression and said, "Chief Superintendent, I hope I'm not catching you at a bad moment?"

"No worse a moment than any other I've had tonight. What's up?"

"We've completed our preliminary examination of the lift in question and found that the mechanical aspects functioned as designed, though I've requested a full verification of every component. God knows how fast the station staff will do that."

"Perhaps sooner than you might expect." I recounted my conversation with Darrien.

"Dangerous Don must feel confident if he's treating it as a minor incident," Pullar replied, scowling. "Does he know something we don't?"

"Perhaps he's counting on ComCorp pressuring my superiors. Or he had a momentary brain malfunction."

"It wouldn't be the first time." My Cimmerian friend shrugged dismissively. "After tentatively ruling out mechanical failure, we checked the controller and found nothing wrong with the programming. But, my expert says introducing a self-erasing virus into the code wouldn't be particularly difficult, provided the culprit had access to station engineering's segregated networks. We'll need someone with more experience to determine that. I've been told an expert might detect something."

"How difficult would it be to penetrate the network?"

A frown. "It depends. The security measures to prevent unauthorized access are fairly robust — I inspect them myself at intervals, as part of Aquilonia's ongoing certification with various government entities. But nothing can prevent someone with authorized access from either enabling a saboteur or turning rogue."

"Or acting on orders."

Pullar nodded. "That too. But I've kept the most interesting part for last. The log shows no malfunctions. You entered the lift on the promenade level and left it on the VIP level. According to the records, your car made no unexplained movements, it did not leave the artificial gravity envelope, nor did it lose pressure."

Wonderful. Now I'd be accused of fabricating stories to impugn Darrien and his precious Aquilonia, which wouldn't help my investigation in the least. I should have waited for Pullar's preliminary report before poking Dangerous Don in his den.

"And that means I'll have the chief administrator on the comlink momentarily to ask me whether I had too much wine with my evening meal. Perhaps I should take that medical exam after all. It'll show evidence of decompression."

A grim smile broke through Pullar's solemn demeanor. "That won't be necessary, Chief Superintendent. Whoever falsified the log made one little mistake. As it must, the record shows the precise time you entered the cab and then left it. Yet there is a discrepancy of almost thirty seconds between what it would be if the car had taken you directly to the VIP level and what it actually was. That discrepancy is enough to account for an unexplained trip to the ice mine. This is unmistakable evidence of sabotage."

"It sure is. You can plant something well in advance to cause a malfunction under a given set of conditions and take your time doing so. Cleaning up the log afterward, when someone's sounded the alarm, not so much."

"Perhaps the error was deliberate, and the saboteur meant us to find it," he replied. "If they sabotaged the programming and then erased every trace, surely they'd be smart and skilled enough to clear the time discrepancy. That's probably easier to do, even under pressure."

"Meaning they might have left a deliberate mistake for us to find so I would understand my near accident was a warning. Nicely deduced, Major."

An unexpected spark of pleasure lit up his usually guarded expression. "What do you intend now?"

"As it happens, my inspector, Arno Galdi, is an AI systems wizard. I'll have him retrace your steps the moment he arrives in the morning. Perhaps he can find a digital fingerprint or two that'll lead us to the culprits. Whoever believed they could push me into wrapping up the case quickly with Talyn as the accused made a grave tactical error. Officers who can't shrug off intimidation attempts don't work for the PCB."

"Do you think Dangerous Don's involved?" Pullar asked.

"Hard to say. Darrien doesn't strike me as reckless enough to take part in this sort of stunt unless under duress or offered an inducement he would find irresistible."

"Meaning power or money, or preferably both. Our chief administrator has turned venality into a virtue."

"Lucky Aquilonia." I paused, wondering whether the time had come to mention Louis Sorne and decided it had. His henchmen figured high on the list of possible suspects. "This incident could also stem from my earlier case, Major. Our bent officer fingered Louis Sorne, who will shortly face ten to fifteen years in a penal colony for a long list of financial crimes. My colleagues are building an airtight case against him."

Pullar winced. "That'll cause a major stir back home. Am I right to think the message Ward Loriot relayed to you came from Sorne?"

I nodded. "As did the one I received on Valerys. Since Sorne is one of CimmerTek's owners, he has the means to reach out via Burrard and company. And if he's decided to escalate matters..."

"It gets worse, Chief Superintendent. I've heard rumors that Sorne is one of Aquilonia's backers, a silent partner of sorts, meaning he can exert pressure on Dangerous Don as well as Javan Burrard."

I didn't remember seeing Aquilonia among Sorne's many interests, but if he was backing the free port via one of his holding companies, I might easily have missed it. Haylian was my target, not Sorne. But by now, the Financial Crimes Division should have started peeling back the many layers of Sorne's political and business interests and could confirm Pullar's rumor.

"If it's Sorne, why come after me now? My role in the matter was over once our bent cop finished confessing. Another team, from another division is building the case against him."

"Revenge?"

"Possibly, or as a warning to others. It's only been a few days since I wrapped my part up, so I doubt Sorne has anything more than an inkling of how bad his future looks. If he knew things were bleak, he might think twice about adding to his indictment. Federal judges have a habit of handing out the maximum penalty to crooks who intimidate, harass, or assault law enforcement officers."

"Considering his connections at the highest levels of the Cimmerian government," Pullar replied, "he may still think he's untouchable."

"Then he had better think twice, because his arrest is imminent, and he'll be facing the federal justice system." I thought of warning Pullar that everything I'd just discussed was highly classified, then decided against it. He was an old pro, and I might offend him. Moments later, he proved the wisdom of my choice.

"Too bad this has to stay a secret until your bunch lays charges, Chief Superintendent," he said with an ironic grin. "I could have made a killing on the stock market by shorting Sorne's various companies. In any case, I'll add the CimmerTek staff to the list of suspects without explaining why, other than their access to various parts of Aquilonia, courtesy of Dangerous Don."

"Thank you."

"And in other news, I've ordered that the lift stay quarantined until further notice, which didn't please the Aquilonia operations officer one bit. But for these sorts of incidents, I can usually overrule anyone. That is until Darrien convinces his cronies back home to put pressure on my superiors. But even so, I'll only be able to hold it for perhaps another twenty-four hours, provided they install added safeguards to prevent a recurrence."

"Understood. If Arno finds nothing, we'll put the incident aside and deal with what will hopefully land on your desk before morning — the analysis of the malfunctioning surveillance gear."

Pullar gave me a sardonic look. "If D.D. cooperates, that is."

"I'm sure he will. The vision of a hundred federal inspectors tearing the place apart after shutting everything down should be incentive enough. A free port can't generate profits if it ceases to be a port. The Aquilonia Syndicate might feel enough displeasure to replace him."

"You can make that happen?" He sounded genuinely impressed, and not in the least skeptical.

"No, but if an experienced cop like you didn't see the bluff right away, Darrien won't catch on until it's too late."

Pullar chuckled. "And here I thought PCB investigators were the most honest and upstanding police officers in history."

"We are, but we don't deny ourselves the right instruments for the job. And if that means exaggerating the reach of my powers, so be it. I'll send Arno an update, then turn in."

— Twenty-Eight —

Still feeling like I'd been run over by an out-of-control skimmer, I met the ferry from Valerys Station the next morning and felt relief when I saw Arno Galdi's beard emerge from the docking arm. Framing a round, grandfatherly face, it was still mostly black except for a broad white streak over the chin.

Although we teased him mercilessly about it, the beard added just the right touch to an unassuming demeanor that put witnesses and suspects at ease in a way I never could, often to their own detriment.

Older and more experienced than most in my unit, me included, Arno was nonetheless happy to stay at the rank of inspector until he retired. He was one of those contented people who loved their lot in life even if it meant spending decades investigating the worst that the uniformed services could cough up.

After updating my case notes and sending an encrypted copy to Arno as well as one to the PCB office on Cimmeria, the night had been uneventful, thanks to a sold dose of analgesics. I hadn't heard from Darrien or Pullar yet, but my day was young.

As soon as he spied me waiting on the other side of the arrivals control gate, his hand shot up, and he waved, smiling, but kept walking at the same sedate pace. That was another of Arno's characteristics, one which he always said would let him live to be two hundred. He never showed a shred of impatience, a virtue when interviewing suspects who hadn't yet figured out we'd already put a noose around their necks.

"Quite the investigation we took on, Chief," he said by way of greeting. "I read your notes on the way over. Cases involving the Navy aren't among my favorites, especially when spooks are lurking in the bushes, but a cop's gotta do what a cop's gotta do."

"Undeniably." His breezy manner invariably made me smile.

"By the way, I took the liberty of asking Financial Crimes to find out whether Sorne is an Aquilonia backer. We should find out within the next few hours."

And that was yet another of Arno's endearing characteristics — his ability to anticipate my orders.

"Excellent. Let's go drop your bag off. I've arranged for a room next to mine. We're in the same section as the murder scene. We'll give that a look before visiting the police station where you'll meet my newest friend, Major Jon Pullar, Cimmerian Gendarmerie. He's one of those unusual cops who doesn't seem worried by a visit from the Firing Squad. On the contrary, he's been very helpful, and he's no dummy either."

"Glad to hear it. He's probably happy we took the case off his hands, but still, the man's a rare find."

We made our way from the docks to the promenade and thence to the VIP area while talking about inconsequential matters though I knew Arno was brimming with questions. He'd ask them when we were in a more private setting, away from civilian ears.

"Nice digs." He dropped his bag on the bed and examined the suite's amenities. "You have the same type of room?"

"Mirror image. Mind you, they gave us the low end of Aquilonia's high-end accommodations. The victim had enough space to hold a plenary session of the Commonwealth Science Academy."

"Figures. Still, this is better than our usual. But enough about our life of luxury. You were pretty coy about yesterday's lift incident in your notes, Chief. What's the story?"

"We don't know much yet. Pullar and his folks have found no trace of what may have caused the lift to drop, depressurize, and then shoot up, damn near breaking both my legs and giving me an embolism. The operational log says it took me from the promenade to the VIP level directly without a side trip to the ice mine. There's no trace of it running through a decompression cycle either, but there's one discrepancy that may or may not be intentional. The log shows a difference between the time I entered the cab and the time I left it that is far greater by several multiples than it should be. Either the hacker was sloppy, or deliberately left a clue for us to find."

"So you'd understand the malfunction was sabotage, meaning, cross us again, and the next time, we'll finish depressurizing and let you take a moonwalk without a suit." Arno nodded. "Once a hack reaches a certain level of sophistication, I always start with the assumption the culprit planned and executed every step with care. Considering the safeguards built around systems that could kill a human, I'll put my marker on intentional rather than sloppiness."

"That's what Major Pullar figures as well."

"Smart man. But is it related to the current investigation, or the previous one?"

I couldn't help but shrug. "Or is it related to something else altogether?"

"Doubtful." Arno shook his head. "If it has to do with Shovak's murder and was a warning of sorts, then I'd say accusing the victim's aide of working for Shrehari intelligence might have hit the mark dead center. But since Shrehari AI is radically different from ours, I doubt they have the wherewithal to carry out such intricate sabotage and leave no trace other than a subtle clue. That means humans are involved. And I don't mean this Commander Talyn although I'm not as prepared to remove her from the suspects list, as you seem to be. I've known women of your size capable of overpowering much bigger men through guile and a well-placed jab with something incapacitating."

"Men, not Shrehari, Arno. There's a big difference. Wait until you meet Thopok."

"Understood, Chief. It's a shame we can't arrange for an autopsy, but the Shrehari have incredibly severe proscriptions surrounding the treatment of mortal remains. I guess there's not much call for forensic science in the Empire anyway, not when the law is whatever the *Kho'sahra* wants."

"And the nobility allows. If you don't need the facilities, how about we visit the scene?"

Arno rubbed his hands together and grinned. "Take me to where you discovered murder most foul. Or at least the bloody traces thereof."

"And then, I'd like you to examine what Pullar's lot found in the lift car programming and the operational log. You might see traces of sabotage where they didn't, and if you do, that'll give us another thread to pull."

"Provided it's related to this case and not Sorne escalating matters, pun intended."

"Perhaps, but humor me, Arno."

"I always humor you, Chief. Having seen the sharp side of your tongue when someone steps on his you-know-what, I'm not inclined to welcome learning through personal experience. I always prefer to learn from that of others."

"Which makes you smarter than most." I nodded at the door. "Shall we?"

Once in Shovak's quarters, Arno looked around and pulled a face. "Aquilonia needs a better interior decorator. This is simply too bloody."

"Shrehari have major arteries that can gush just as much as ours. Try to picture me with a knife that has a thirty-centimeter blade, something much heavier than what humans might carry. Then, picture me stabbing a being approximately two meters tall and almost twice my width in the neck. Of course, I'd have to wrest the knife away from him first, an almost impossible task."

"A needler with a fast-acting incapacitant and your sacrificial victim is on his back, ready for the slaughter."

"The Gendarmerie found nothing on Talyn or at the scene. Other than the knife, I mean. And as you may recall, Talyn alerted the Gendarmerie, then waited for them to arrive. Her only proven connection to the killing was being at the scene and touching the murder weapon."

"She wouldn't be the first assassin to claim she merely found the body. Besides, she was covered in bloodstains."

"Stains are easy to get when you're checking injuries gushing blood like geysers."

Arno raised his hands in surrender and grinned. "All right, Chief. Your instincts are rarely wrong, and I'm willing to go along with the idea that someone other than Talyn was responsible. For now. Once we've ruled out the impossible, we'll take a greater look at the implausible, and the sole suspect in custody surely belongs to the latter, not the former."

"I wouldn't want it any other way. Have you had enough? Or do you want to absorb the crime scene's aura a bit more?"

He shook his head.

"I've had enough. Let's visit your Cimmerian major and see if we can figure who turned a lift car into an amusement ride to oblivion."

"I was aboard, buddy. It wasn't amusing."

— Twenty-Nine —

"Major Jon Pullar, meet Inspector Arno Galdi."

The Cimmerian thrust out his hand. "Welcome to Aquilonia, Inspector. Your boss tells me you're an expert with AI systems."

Arno gave him a self-deprecating shrug. "I know my way around them, but the chief likes to think I'm some sort of wizard, on account of the beard, you understand. She probably wouldn't mind my wearing long robes and a pointy hat, chanting incantations, and telling evil beings they may not pass."

Pullar looked puzzled. "I'm not sure I understand the reference."

His air of incomprehension made me smile. "Arno has a fascination for ancient literature involving fantastic things, such as magical rings, dragons, uncomfortable thrones, and twisted, mythical creatures."

"Sorry, still not following." Pullar gave us a self-deprecating smile. "But never mind. You'll be glad to know engineering has retrieved the faulty sensor modules and is analyzing them as we speak. They've promised preliminary results within the next few hours. Your bluff is paying off."

"Or so we hope." I nodded toward the bullpen. "Do you think we could sample your extraordinary coffee?"

"Certainly." Pullar nodded. "How do you take yours, Inspector?"

"As black as an orc's soul."

"I thought you said orcs were soulless," I replied without missing a beat. By now, my Cimmerian friend was looking at us as if we were slowly losing our minds. He seemed to shake himself mentally and then headed for the urn.

"Black results from the absence of light and everything else, including souls, thus my statement stands."

Arno might look like a kindly grandfather, but he had a magical ability of his own, and that was to twist everything into logical pretzels until you couldn't figure out who was arguing for what. I had learned early on about the futility of discussing politics or religion with him, and no, he's had no qualms about using that particular power on his commanding officer. What could I do? Exile him to the PCB's Rim detachment? Someone else had done that when I was still a callow young constable.

Arno pronounced himself delighted by Pullar's coffee and attacked it with gusto. After making half of his serving vanish in a matter of seconds, he proclaimed himself ready for work.

"Let's see what you folks dug up on the chief's unplanned excursion to Aquilonia's netherworld. I understand that hell around here has indeed frozen over?"

Pullar indicated a vacant workstation in the bullpen. "If you'll sit there, Inspector, I'll connect you to the evidence. What would you like to see first?"

Arno dropped into the proffered chair and said, "How about the lift's code and operational log? I understand there's a noticeable time discrepancy which may or may not have been introduced by accident. This could take a while. Have a coffee, take a tour of the catacombs or whatever sounds fun. I'd rather you didn't hover."

That placed me at loose ends, something I should have expected. I saw no point in another round of interviews without Arno. And absent any results from the surveillance sensor analysis, my investigation was marking time.

Pullar proposed a stroll through parts of Aquilonia off-limits to visitors, assuring me that his desk sergeant would call us the moment Arno had anything to report. With no better offers available, I accepted.

"Tell me, Chief Superintendent," Pullar asked as we left the Gendarmerie station, "assuming last night's incident is connected to the Shovak murder, does it change your views on Talyn's guilt or innocence?"

"She's hardly in a position to fiddle with the lift from her cell."

"But she might have a partner on Aquilonia we know nothing about, one able to give you a little push in another direction. Perhaps one who took part in Shovak's assassination?"

The concept was a bit too paranoid for my tastes, but then again, maybe he was on to something. "A false flag operation, Major? Give the PCB rat a scare that points away from Talyn and at someone else?"

"It's not impossible. Implausible, perhaps, but not entirely out of the question. And once you rule out the impossible..."

Great. He and Arno should compare notes. They would probably get along like a Shrehari and his favorite vintage ale.

"Perhaps we *should* take a harder look at whatever our alien guests are doing with ComCorp."

"Did you need more convincing?" Pullar asked.

"Not really. Once Arno has done his magic, I intend to give the ComCorp folks another, more thorough grilling, starting with my former partner this time, and see how they react to the *Tai Zolh* angle. I assume you now have eyes, human or AI on Thopok at all times, including in his quarters?"

He nodded. "Yes. So far he's done nothing of note, other than sending a further message to his superiors in the Empire. Encrypted, though I'm sure you could ask the Navy if they're able to read Shrehari code."

"If Naval Intelligence can decipher the boneheads' mail, I doubt it'll share with a mere Constabulary flatfoot, in spite of the fact I'm here at the Navy's request."

Pullar waved me into a lift reserved for maintenance staff. "I'll show you the engineering level, the last pressurized space within the artificial gravity envelope. It's where lift shafts end, except for the three oldest ones that go all the way to the ice mining operation, including the one you rode. They date back to the original mine and should have been physically blocked from leaving the artificial envelope. But someone seems to have forgotten about it. There are enough controlled-access lifts between the engineering level and the mine to serve any possible purpose. If you'd like, we can pick up pressure suits there and visit the catacombs as well. The ice cavern is worth seeing."

"Why not? Travel broadens the mind, provided it's done safely." The doors closed, and we dropped at a more sedate speed than last night. "Those three shafts going below Aquilonia's artificial gravity envelope, wouldn't they be individually monitored, since they're such a weak spot?"

"They are. But apparently, whoever sabotaged the controls ensured the operations center didn't receive warning of an unscheduled trip. Descents into the mine must be pre-approved. Had the system worked correctly, the cab wouldn't have gone any lower than the engineering level without a release by operations. If it did so anyway, an alarm should have sounded. Yet operations were unaware of the incident until I told them about it."

"Do you experience many lift malfunctions?"

"The last one predates my time here, but it was relatively minor, immobilizing the cars in one shaft due to a power coupling breakdown. The Cimmeria Transport Department mandates annual inspections by independent experts to keep the technical certification valid. Whatever else Darrien does, he keeps anyone with power over him happy, and the Transport Minister has power over major parts of Aquilonia's infrastructure."

We came to a gentle stop, and the doors opened on a utilitarian corridor redolent of ozone and lubricants.

"We've arrived," my guide said, ushering me out of the cab. "The last bit of livable habitat. There's nothing more than uninhabitable micro-gravity beneath our feet."

Pullar took me on a stroll around the level, nodding politely at the few technicians we met. They apparently knew him well enough to ask no questions. We stopped at one of several large, vertical tube clusters and he pointed at a single cylinder on the far end, with red caution markings on it.

"You traveled in that shaft last night. The others in this group end here, on a light antigrav bed that keeps any wayward cars from smashing into solid rock. Its generation module is a meter beneath the shafts, which is why you might feel a little light on your feet right now, due to residual effect bleeding through the baffles. Aquilonia's artificial gravity generator sits a meter below that."

I stared at the rounded shape of the shaft, my eyes following it from floor to ceiling, and an oppressive sensation briefly washed over me. It was triggered by my mind's eye view of where we stood, beneath ninety percent of Aquilonia's massive bulk, with nothing but a few meters of airtight rock between our feet and the moon's sterile, freezing mantle.

"Are you okay, Chief Superintendent?"

I turned my head and smiled at his expression of concern. "Merely a small human, big station moment. There's something both awe-inspiring and terrifying about how much is above our heads. And how close we are to the primitive heart of a moon incapable of supporting human life."

"The imagination runs wild every so often, doesn't it? Occupational hazard for a cop, I'd say."

"Yes, but my misadventure wasn't a flight of fancy. I'm now more convinced than ever it was a warning. That points the finger either at Louis Sorne or at the ComCorp-Thopok axis. Especially the ComCorp half which made nice with Darrien, but it still doesn't tell me why Shovak died, or who killed him. The two matters could be entirely unrelated. In any case, I've seen enough, Major."

"Would you like to visit the ice mine?"

"Why not?"

My guide went to one of the consoles embedded in the walls at regular intervals and touched its screen. "I'm asking for clearance."

His communicator vibrated just then. He tapped it and said, "Pullar."

"Inspector Galdi needs to speak with the chief superintendent, sir."

Pullar handed me the unit.

"Morrow here."

After a few seconds, Arno's familiar voice came on. "Chief, someone definitely tampered with the lift's operational log. Whoever did it was skilled, but not quite enough. By leaving a clue behind to let you know it wasn't an accident, they also left something of a digital fingerprint. I would not have noticed it if I hadn't seen something similar in the past."

"Any idea who?"

"Sadly, yes. But I'd rather discuss that in person and not over a comlink, even an encrypted one."

"In that case, we're coming back."

"I'll dig through the code controlling the lift for a similar trace, now I know what to look for. Galdi, out."

I handed the communicator back to Pullar. "We'll have to cut the tour short and save the ice caverns for another day. Arno is rather excited by his find."

"Really? He didn't sound much different."

"That's because you don't know him yet. His moods are subtle but unmistakable. He found something definitive."

— Thirty —

Arno's shaggy head snapped up the moment he spied us entering the bullpen. He nodded toward Pullar's office, eyebrows raised in question. It was his way of telling me we should discuss his findings in private.

"We have ourselves a little problem that transcends Envoy Shovak's murder and Louis Sorne's shenanigans," he said the moment Pullar shut the door behind us. "Do you remember Grint?"

"Sure. Ange and Leoni's investigation." I glanced at Pullar. "Superintendent Angela Rowan and Inspector Leoni Crava, two of my officers. Inspector Grint was one of the Constabulary's bad bargains who attracted the PCB's attention. He vanished aboard a transport by the name *Xenophon*. Officially, the case remains open, but I doubt Grint will ever face justice."

"Didn't Commander Talyn travel to Cimmeria aboard a ship of that name?" He asked.

I nodded. "The very same, Major. Life is full of coincidences. Some of them might even be random. But back to Arno's discovery — though I can probably guess."

"And you'd guess right, Chief. If you'll recall, I dug through Grint's case note repository back then only to find someone had either altered or erased most of the incriminating information without hope of recovery. The folks who did it left a digital fingerprint, maybe because they couldn't remove it or because they wanted to show they could penetrate Constabulary data banks. We never actually figured which."

"And you found the same trace in the lift's programming."

Arno tapped the side of his bulbous nose with a thick index finger. "Precisely."

I fought valiantly to suppress a groan of dismay and failed. Pullar stared at me with incomprehension, and I had a brief debate with myself about how much to say. Full disclosure won out again.

"Have you ever heard of an organization by the name *Sécurité Spéciale*?"

Pullar shook his head. "Can't say I have. What language is that?"

"It's French, for a reason only the SecGen who stood it up knows, and he's not around anymore. I hear he died of a suspiciously terminal illness a few years back. As to what it is, think a human version of the *Tai Kan*, with all the latter's ugliness. It's the SecGen's secret intelligence and security service, answerable only to him. A replacement of sorts for the Special Security Bureau smashed by Admiral Kowalski last century, minus the far-reaching police powers the SSB used to wield. We have those now. They've been around for over a decade, perhaps even longer. The Fleet and Constabulary don't play well with the *Sécurité Spéciale*, something it reciprocates, and our disagreements go beyond typical inter-agency rivalries. For example, the foul bastards corrupted Inspector Grint, who then went on to cause us no end of trouble."

"You're telling me they're here, on my station?" An alarmed expression crossed Pullar's face.

"Yes. And unless they're playing footsie with Sorne, I'd say they're warning me away from the espionage angle. That would mean they're somehow involved with the Shovak murder."

"Have I mentioned how much I hate cases involving the *Sécurité Spéciale*?" Arno asked. "They never finish well for someone. Leoni was lucky to survive the shooting on Merseaux Station."

I was momentarily tempted to call DCC Maras and tell her we were off the case. If the Fleet was playing spy games with the SecGen's goons, they could damn well extract Talyn from this mess by themselves.

But, I knew she would just refer the matter to my actual boss. And the subspace back-and-forth with HQ on Wyvern would end with a terse and none too pleased 'carry on with the investigation.'

"The *Sécurité Spéciale*'s involvement puts a whole new spin on our case," I said instead. "At least we know who sabotaged the lift. Now to find out how and why."

"I think I can answer the how, Chief. My first check of the code controlling your cab shows no traces of hacking. That makes me suspect they did it via a terminal and account that had the right security clearance. Breaking into a protected perimeter always leaves something a knowing pair of eyes can see."

"How sure are you, Inspector?" Pullar asked. "Because your statement means that as the man responsible for Aquilonia's security, I have a problem beyond murder."

"Not a hundred percent, to be sure. The absence of evidence isn't necessarily proof, but I feel pretty confident. It would fit with the rest."

Pullar cursed in a soft tone and said, "I suppose I must consider the possibility someone obtained illegal access to restricted systems. And that might involve Darrien or a person working for him. The resulting political stink could be spectacular."

"Or not," Arno replied with a shrug. "The *Sécurité Spéciale* has a habit of tying up loose ends with extreme prejudice. That's probably what happened to Grint."

"You mean they might kill Dangerous Don or his minions?" Pullar sounded incredulous. "And this organization works for the Secretary General of the Commonwealth?"

"Accidents happen, and people vanish, Major. They're a nasty lot and thoroughly politicized."

"Do you want more time to parse the computer code?" I asked Arno.

"I see no use at this point. We can be fairly confident the *Sécurité Spéciale* did it since they so helpfully left us enough clues."

"You figure they left their mark on purpose?"

Arno grimaced. "I can't say either way. They left no trace in the code itself, at least I couldn't find anything, but that's easier to clean up than a log. Mind you, it's still possible they were sloppy due to time constraints. But if they had access via an authorized account and terminal, I can't see why they wouldn't have been able to leave the log as pristine as the code."

"Perhaps. And although one should never underestimate the opposition, one shouldn't overestimate them either and see intent in mere sloppiness or lack of refinement."

I figured it was time for another talk with Talyn. Besides, Arno should meet her before we tackled the ComCorp folks and Thopok as a duo.

"Is there any way to identify these *Sécurité Spéciale* agents?" Pullar asked.

"No. They could be anyone. The buggers have a talent for infiltrating other organizations, or as with Inspector Grint, corrupting and turning people who are already on the inside. Arno, next chance you get, ask the team investigating Sorne to check for *Sécurité Spéciale* connections. But I doubt he's involved in this particular incident. He's not quite the sort of plutocrat they prefer since his reach is limited to the Rim Sector, but we might as well make sure."

"How is the *Sécurité Spéciale* even legal?" Pullar asked.

"Technically, it shouldn't be, but since the Senate appoints SecGens, there's a lot of quid pro quo between the legislative and executive branches. I'm sure there are enough senators who think an intelligence and security agency independent of the Fleet and Constabulary is a good idea. Political memories are short, and most can't remember the old SSB's scheming during the war. As many historians will tell you, their shenanigans most likely prolonged the conflict by hamstringing the Navy."

Arno grunted. "An agency independent *of*, or in opposition *to* the military and us? Somehow, I'm not surprised they're involved in this, not with a Navy officer sitting in the brig on suspicion of having committed murder, or rather an assassination."

"And on that note, Major, I think it's time Arno meets your involuntary guest."

— Thirty-One —

"Your partner, I presume," Talyn said the moment she saw Arno following me into her cell.

This time her legs weren't tangled in the lotus position and she climbed to her feet in a somewhat graceful manner. She was actually a smidgen taller than I was, but still not big enough to tackle a Shrehari. Not even close.

Arno nodded. "Inspector Galdi. Pleased to make your acquaintance, Commander. I've read the chief's case notes so you may assume I'm up to speed on matters."

That faint, yet somehow mocking smile made a brief appearance. "Glad to hear it, Inspector. Perhaps now that Chief Superintendent Morrow has a backup, I'll be out of here faster."

"We certainly hope to wrap this up soon," I said. "Unfortunately, the situation isn't gaining much clarity. Last night, someone sent me a message via a sabotaged lift car, perhaps to discourage further inquiry into the espionage angle. Among his many skills, Inspector Galdi is an AI forensics expert, and upon analysis, he found that the likely culprit might be *Sécurité Spéciale*."

Talyn's eyebrows shot up, and a low whistle escaped her lips. "Ouch. *Tai Zolh* and *Sécurité Spéciale* in one go is bad news. I'd feel for you, Chief Superintendent, if I weren't the one in police custody."

"Do you think they could be in contact, or even working together?"

"It's conceivable. I don't know what agenda drives the *Sécurité Spéciale*, other than doing the SecGen's bidding. There's nothing illegal about representatives from Commonwealth government agencies meeting with imperial officials, even those from their intelligence or security organizations. After all, the Fleet has regular contacts with the Shrehari military as well on matters that affect both of us, such as anti-piracy efforts and keeping the Protectorate Zone demilitarized. That said, it wouldn't surprise me if the *Sécurité Spéciale* has something to do with Envoy Shovak's death. They're not shy about using violence, much less so than the Navy."

"Could ComCorp be in cahoots with the *Sécurité Spéciale*?" Arno asked.

"Considering their political connections, I'd say it's a possibility, what with the tangle of incestuous dealings between the larger conglomerates and the executive branch. Then, there's the friendship between the family running ComCorp, the Amalis, and our current SecGen. It's a twisted mess for sure, Inspector."

Wonderful. Every step forward took us deeper into a dense fog. A political fog. I was starting to fear we'd soon be wading into a swamp of nepotism and corruption if the stench tickling my nostrils was a sign.

"Why is the Navy's counterintelligence branch not involved in this?" I asked. "We're getting way beyond a mere police matter here, even one for the PCB, and believe me, we've seen a few wacky cases in our time."

"They might already be involved, but Envoy Shovak's murder may not be part of their mission."

"It would be nice of them to speak with us. You know, inter-agency cooperation for the greater good of the Commonwealth."

Talyn chuckled. "If they're here, and they need something from you, they'll reach out. Otherwise..."

"Any words of wisdom, Commander?"

"Wrap this up fast, before they send a warning that might hurt you or your inspector; be ruthless, even with the ComCorp folks. The *Sécurité Spéciale* won't hesitate to do anything in furtherance of their goals and neither should you. And with the Shrehari, act as if you're the biggest *Tai Kan* asshole in existence. Even the *Tai Zolh* tiptoe around their internal security brethren. The *Tai Kan* has been around for a lot longer, and its members know how to make sure the bodies they bury remain buried."

"You want my opinion?" Arno asked once we'd left Talyn's cell.

"If I say no, you'll give it anyway, so why bother asking."

"Talyn's playing games."

"Gee thanks. I think I figured that out after my first time with her. It doesn't mean she's guilty."

"It doesn't mean she's innocent either."

Arno's ability to ignore sarcasm was another useful trait for an internal affairs investigator. We heard more than our fair share from our Constabulary colleagues and either became inured or took early retirement.

He nodded. "Of course, but the real question is why play with the PCB?"

"And you have a theory?" I asked.

"Other than my gut feeling we're being used as pawns in a bloody spy game, not yet."

"Spy game or not, we still have a dead Shrehari and no proof other than circumstantial. It would take a brave or foolish prosecutor to accept Talyn's indictment based on such thin evidence."

After we recovered our weapons at the guard station and left the brig, I remembered something Pullar said earlier. "Our Cimmerian host put forth the idea that Talyn might have an accomplice on Aquilonia. I can see two trained agents tackling a Shrehari, with the accomplice vanishing to leave an unlikely culprit behind."

"Navy spooks angling for the perfect crime?" Arno's chuckle was a rumbling sound rising from deep within his barrel chest. "Mind you, we've seen stranger things."

When we reentered the bullpen, Pullar, framed by his office door, glanced up at us with question marks in his eyes. I pointed at the coffee urn and upon getting a nod of approval, helped myself to another cup before we joined him.

"Did you obtain anything useful from our guest?" He asked.

"A warning that ComCorp and the *Sécurité Spéciale* are frequent bed partners, and that we should be both quick and ruthless to avoid something more deadly than a malfunctioning lift. I can do ruthless in my sleep. Quick is another matter."

"I can believe that," Pullar replied with a faint smile. "What's next?"

"Next, I want Arno to meet Gerri Kazan."

"Should I call the Excelsior and warn her to expect you?"

"Thanks, but no. This time, I'm calling the tune, and that means we show up unexpectedly."

"Just like the Spanish Inquisition," Arno intoned. "As they used to say, nobody expects us and our weapons of fear, surprise, and ruthless efficiency..."

Pullar stared at my wingman for a moment and then glanced at me. "Another one of those obscure and ancient literary references?"

I gave him a sympathetic smile. "Not exactly literary — the quote comes from a humoristic skit. But let's not dwell on it. We don't have time for a lengthy discourse on why that's supposed to be amusing."

"Philistines," Arno rumbled. "I'm merely trying to broaden your narrow police minds with an example of the best pre-diaspora humor."

"Be kind to the Major, even if you show no respect for your boss." I drained my cup and gave him a small nudge, winking at Pullar. "Time to go. We've yet to insult a civilian today, and PCB investigators have a quota to meet."

The Cimmerian shook his head in disbelief, but I could see the ghost of a smile lighting up that sober countenance. Then something caught his eye, and he glanced over our shoulders.

"What is it, Sergeant?"

"Message from the Constabulary on Cimmeria for Inspector Galdi, sir."

Arno turned toward the man standing in the doorway and produced his tablet. "If I link this to your network, can you forward the message?"

"Sure thing, sir. I'll just need your identifier."

A few minutes later, Arno looked up from the device and shook his head with a disconsolate air. "They sent us an answer about Sorne and the Aquilonia Syndicate, and yes, he's a silent member through one of his shell corporations. But you won't like the other news they forwarded, Chief. Haylian's dead."

"What?" My voice went up two octaves.

"DCC Maras put him under house arrest until the Financial Crimes Division completed its dossier on Sorne and he officially retired from the Service. He had the usual tracking implant, of course. According to the Cimmerian Gendarmerie – they took the call and assumed primary jurisdiction — Haylian committed suicide a few hours ago."

"How?"

"The message gave no specifics. Maras assigned a team from the Major Crimes Division to work with the locals on the case."

"At least tell me Financial Crimes have everything they need to charge Sorne and make it stick."

"Sorry, Chief, they don't say, but when I left, Haylian was talking a parsec a minute, so I'm optimistic."

"Was this Haylian fellow the bent cop you arrested before coming here?" Pullar asked. When I nodded, he said, "Perhaps it was a case of Sornecide."

"Pardon?" Both Arno and I stared at him.

"Apparently, people who cross Louis Sorne kill themselves at a higher rate than the general population. Nothing's ever been proven. The bastard has enough influence in political circles to prevent us from investigating. But my friends in homicide figure a lot of them aren't voluntary."

"That puts a different complexion on Sorne's solicitude for your welfare, Chief," Arno said. "If he got to Haylian so quickly..."

"If. I'd rather not borrow trouble just yet." Though I kept my tone light, the news had thrown me for a loop. I abruptly felt more vulnerable than I had in years and wished Sergeant Bonta was here as well, to lend my team added strength and firepower.

"What will you do now?" Pullar asked.

"Find Shovak's killer, Major." I climbed to my feet and pointed at the door. "Time to go annoy ComCorp, Arno."

"Would you like me to assign a few gendarmes as an escort?"

I gave the Cimmerian a grateful smile. "Thanks for the offer, but that won't be necessary just yet. I would, however, appreciate that trace on Burrard's movements, and on any of his people with access to the VIP section."

"Perhaps I should arrest the lot of them," he replied. "If Sorne's coming after you next, I'm willing to bet he'll do it through one or more of his CimmerTek gorillas."

I shook my head. "Too obvious. But don't worry about me, Major. I'll be fine. Until later."

As we headed for the corridor, I said to Arno, "If you've done your research after reading my notes, you'll know Gerri Kazan was my partner when we both worked for the Major Crimes Division. What isn't on file is that we parted under acrimonious circumstances after her behavior almost cost us several cases, and in one instance, had charges thrown out."

"Believe it or not, Chief, there's a PCB file on former Inspector Gerri Kazan, even if your commissioner at the time chose not to pursue disciplinary action. I had a brief scan through it. Would I be correct in thinking your part in her leaving the Constabulary eventually prompted a transfer to the PCB?"

"Probably. It certainly cost me friends in the Flying Squad. When the number of officers willing to work with me dwindled to zero, the boss suggested a lateral transfer might be advisable and sweetened the offer with a promotion to superintendent."

"I see. In that case, we'll assume Sera Kazan will be a hostile witness."

"You enjoy stating the obvious, don't you?"

"Everyone needs a hobby, Chief." We stopped by the lifts, but he didn't touch the call screen. Instead, his perceptive eyes studied mine. "You put on a good show for Pullar back there, but you're more worried about Sorne's intentions than you let on, now that Haylian's dead, am I right?"

"You're right. But I can't do anything about it, so I'll push on with the Shovak investigation. Just promise me that, if out of the blue, I commit suicide or suffer a deadly accident, you'll make sure it's investigated as a murder."

"Promised, Chief. And I'll keep that oath until my dying day."

"Hopefully that day is far in the future for both of us."

— Thirty-Two —

The lift swept us up to the promenade where we merged with foot traffic and headed for the Aquilonia Excelsior. Once there, I forced the reception AI, using my police override, to give me Gerri's room assignment and confirm she was on the premises.

I knew the AI would warn its human manager, who would, in turn, call Gerri. And so it proved. We stepped off the hotel's lift and into the corridor leading to the penthouse suites which, since the hotel was dug into Aquilonia's crust, were only two levels below the lobby.

A door opened, framing my former partner's lithe, elegant form. She stared at us with an expression studiously devoid of emotions, but her crossed arms unconsciously telegraphed annoyance.

"Sera Kazan, this is Inspector Arno Galdi, a Professional Compliance Bureau investigator. We'd like to ask you a few questions. May we enter?"

"I suppose if I don't cooperate, you'll haul me off to the brig for a formal interview." She turned on her heels and reentered her suite. "By all means, come in."

Upon seeing the opulence and luxury of her sitting room, I realized the ComCorp folks weren't staying at the Excelsior just out of loyalty to one of their corporate brands.

Trying to imagine Yan Houko's suite boggled the mind. Though we were many meters below ground level, a display trimmed to resemble a wide porthole covered one wall. It showed a brilliant view of Aquilonia's surface, as it would be seen from the vantage point of Darrien's office, complete with Thule looming over the landscape.

The image seemed almost overwhelming in scale and to my eyes at least, deathly cold. Chalk me up as preferring a lush, living vista, but this one suited my former partner's outward appearance and mood.

She waved at a settee grouping around a low glass table by way of inviting us to sit and took an armchair for her herself, perching on its edge. It was her signal she didn't expect the interview to take long.

"I'm listening, Chief Superintendent. Ask away."

Talyn had advised that I be ruthless. Very well. "Was Envoy Shovak also *Tai Zolh*, or is Thopok the only intelligence officer in the Shrehari delegation?"

I had the pleasure of seeing shock if not dismay in those icy, dark eyes and her carefully fashioned composure began to show a few cracks. Whatever Gerri had expected this wasn't it.

"I beg your pardon, Chief Superintendent?"

"Surely a former investigator such as you can see how Shovak's status has a bearing on his death, especially if he was an imperial officer. I think we can take it for a given that Thopok is *Tai Zolh*. The Shrehari haven't quite figured out how humans read body language or believe we can't pick up cues from their behavior. Losing the war doesn't appear to have taught them to never underestimate our species. Was Shovak, or wasn't he?"

"What in the name of everything that's holy makes you conclude ComCorp is in cahoots with Shrehari intelligence? Has working for the PCB addled your brain?" Her voice remained steady, her tone flat and low-pitched, but we'd been close once upon a time, and I heard the spike of tension loud and clear. That and the words she used instead of merely denying my statement gave me hope that I'd scored a direct hit.

"You seem to have guessed my other question, Sera Kazan. *Why is* ComCorp in contact with Shrehari intelligence?"

"I can't understand why you'd indulge in such baseless conspiracy theories, Chief Superintendent. It doesn't suit you."

"Your presence at trade negotiations indicates that more than import-export matters are up for discussion, and I don't buy the explanation you gave me, so no need to repeat it. Besides, since the Shrehari dictator keeps a tight rein on interstellar trade and the companies that practice it, such as *Quch Mech*, including government agents in their delegation is hardly unexpected."

"I will repeat my explanation nonetheless because it is true. Cross-border trade always has security issues that go beyond those of interest to the military or the police."

"Even when it involves imperial intelligence?" Arno asked, speaking for the first time. A flash of distaste briefly lit up Gerri's eyes.

"Inspector Galdi has a point, Sera Kazan. Certainly, there's nothing illegal about private commercial interests meeting with officials of the imperial government, nor is the presence of *Tai Zolh* officers on Aquilonia our concern. I'm sure the Fleet has its counterintelligence operatives taking care of that particular angle. We're concerned with finding Envoy Shovak's murderer and obtaining enough evidence for a successful prosecution. We have neither right now, but you may hold information that would help. So please tell me, was Shovak a government agent, like Thopok? Or perhaps from another branch of the Shrehari Empire's all-encompassing security apparatus?"

Gerri shrugged, a weary gesture that attempted to show growing exasperation, but I knew her too well. It was her way of hiding emotion.

"Governments often use trade delegations to collect intelligence. It's not beyond the realm of possibility that Shovak or Thopok, or both, work for the Empire on top of their jobs as private sector commercial negotiators. I neither know nor care about such matters. But to assume ComCorp is in contact with the *Tai Zolh* rather than discussing an aboveboard commercial agreement with representatives of an important Shrehari merchant house such as *Quch Mech* is bizarre if not outright grotesque. Take care you don't drift into the realm of actionable libel. You wouldn't enjoy cross-examination by our lawyers. Their bite is worse than that of any barrister you've faced."

There was the Gerri I remembered, always talking too much when she was under stress.

"May I take your rather rambling statement as an admission Envoy Shovak worked for the *Tai Zolh* in some capacity, as does Thopok?"

"You can believe whatever you wish, Chief Superintendent. Now, was slandering my employer the point of your visit? Discussing PCB delusions about spies running amok on Aquilonia might be entertaining, but I have work to do, proper work."

"Slander, Sera Kazan? ComCorp talking to representatives of the Shrehari government is not a criminal matter. But knowing the truth about Shovak and his mission is part of this case because it has a direct bearing on his death."

"Why don't you ask Commander Talyn? She's your culprit. You merely have to firm up your evidence, or did you forget how, Chief Superintendent?"

How did she find out the name and rank of the woman in Major Pullar's brig? The Cimmerian Gendarmerie had done its job and protected the identity of someone not yet charged with a crime.

"You know who the suspect is, Sera Kazan? Interesting. The local authorities haven't released her particulars to the public."

A flash of annoyance crossed her face, and her lips tightened into a white line. My former partner was still sloppy with details.

"I must have heard it somewhere. Few things stay secret on a frontier station such as Aquilonia."

I slowly raised an eyebrow, to let her see I thought she was full of it but didn't bother challenging her explanation.

"Let me summarize, Sera Kazan, you deny knowing about Shovak and Thopok's possible governmental affiliations. You also deny that ComCorp is having anything more than commercial discussions with legitimate representatives of a Shrehari mercantile house by the name *Quch Mech*?"

"I do. And I can't understand from where this *Tai Zolh* nonsense comes. It would certainly be in your and the Constabulary's best interests to avoid spreading such scurrilous rumors. My superiors show little patience with officials who overstep their boundaries. Be warned they have many friendly ears in places of power."

I gave her a frosty smile. "Did you just threaten me, Sera Kazan?"

"It was a statement of fact, Chief Superintendent Morrow, nothing more. I wouldn't dare threaten a senior law enforcement officer."

Her tone and the mocking glint in her eyes said otherwise, and I wondered whether to mention the *Sécurité Spéciale* angle. As that thought crossed my mind, I had the strange notion maybe it was where Gerri ended up after resigning from the Service.

She certainly had a darker side that would fit, the same side that cost her a promising career in the Constabulary. Shame I couldn't bounce the idea off Arno until we were in private, but something told me he would counsel caution.

"However," Gerri continued, "I hope you don't intend to press Ser Houko with this Shrehari intelligence agent nonsense. Corporate vice presidents are much less understanding than I've been and prone to demand the removal of officers from an inquiry — with prejudice."

"I do what I must, as you can understand." Turning to Arno, I asked, "Anything on your mind, Inspector Galdi?"

"No, sir. Nothing that can't wait."

"In that case, thank you, Sera Kazan. We may have other questions for you at a later date."

"The police always have just one more question, Chief Superintendent. It's almost a bloody cliché and not a very imaginative one at that." Gerri sat back in her chair and crossed her legs. "I'm sure you can see yourselves out. And do be careful. One never knows when a technical malfunction might strike on an airless, desolate moon where humans hang on to life by the thinnest of margins."

It took most of my self-control to restrain even the hint of a reaction. "As you might remember, I'm careful to a fault, particularly when it comes to the irritating details that might derail a case."

"Of course, Chief Superintendent. You're a paragon of investigative virtue. Enjoy the rest of your day."

Once back on the promenade, Arno said, "I trust you believed nothing that came out of her mouth, Chief."

"Considering how well I know Gerri, you bet I didn't take her words at face value, not after she let slip Talyn's identity and fired a parting shot about malfunctions..."

"Sloppy, that. It almost felt planted."

"Don't give Gerri too much credit. Sloppiness is what ended her career with the Constabulary."

"Enough to give the game away?" Arno sounded dubious, but then he almost always sounded dubious.

"It would fit the pattern of her life. Do you think she might make a passable *Sécurité Spéciale* operative?"

My wingman came to a sudden and unexpected halt, forcing foot traffic to flow around us. He turned his head toward me, deep-set eyes sparkling with curiosity.

"At first glance, that might seem a tad paranoid, but as you keep reminding your faithful investigators, even paranoids have real enemies. To answer your question — sure, why not? Everything else about this case seems to be ninety degrees off normal." His head swiveled to one side as if he'd seen something from the corner of his eye. “Thopok just entered the Excelsior. Shall we take odds on whether he’s visiting your ex-partner or her boss?”

“My money’s on Gerri.”

“So is mine.”

— Thirty-Three —

"Chief Superintendent Morrow," a cheerful tenor called out from somewhere behind us. We turned in unison to see Montague Hobart emerge from the crowd, a pleasant smile on his angular face.

I made the introductions and watched them shake hands. To my amusement, both men engaged in a silent contest of wills, hands squeezing, eyes locked.

"How's the investigation progressing?" Hobart asked once they'd ended it in a draw — Arno wasn't nearly as soft as he looked. "I just saw Agent Thopok enter the Excelsior, undoubtedly to confer with the ComCorp folks."

"*Agent* Thopok?" I cocked a questioning eyebrow at Hobart and he gave me a grin that was half-sheepish, half-sardonic.

"The more I think about it, the more I'm convinced Thopok's *Tai Zolh*. He gave off unconscious cues of being up to no good if you understand Shrehari body language."

"And you do?" Arno asked, not bothering to disguise his skepticism.

"If you want to conduct business in the Empire and live to tell the tale, you become good at it quickly. There's nothing like misreading a crucial signal to find yourself on the receiving end of a massive and very deadly dagger. They're a touchy species and easily triggered."

My wingman snorted. "Particularly if you're prone to skirting rules and regulations in the first place, no doubt."

Hobart sketched an abbreviated bow. "Just so."

"And based on your in-depth knowledge of everything Shrehari, who do you think killed Envoy Shovak, Ser Hobart?"

"Someone big, strong, and fast, Inspector. My money is on another Shrehari or a Marine Special Operations guy. Or on someone very sneaky and underhanded, a professional assassin who struck before Shovak knew what was happening. We're not speaking of an ordinary human being."

"Are any of these unordinary human beings on Aquilonia?"

Arno wasn't about to let go, and I knew enough to allow him his freedom.

The smuggler's smile broadened. "That, my dear Inspector, is a question to which I have no answer, though it should be clear I'm none of those." He made a sweeping downward gesture with his hands as if to present himself. "You can clearly see that I'm depressingly normal. Although come to think of it, the CimmerTek rent-a-cop, Javan Burrard, has a fairly imposing physique. But he doesn't strike me as the sort to tackle a Shrehari unless the Cimmerian Gendarmerie taught him things they shouldn't while he still wore their uniform."

His disingenuous manner finally made me crack a very restrained smile. Hobart might not seem like a Marine Corps ninja, but he was neither small nor soft.

"I seriously doubt you're depressingly normal, Ser Hobart," I said.

"What you see is what you get, Chief Superintendent. Remember, you have a standing invitation to visit my ship. It covers Inspector Galdi as well. And if you need further Shrehari translated, or wish to hear more about their ancient and mystical society, just put a message to that effect on the comnet. I'll respond within the hour, and no extra honorarium required."

He gave us a mock salute and vanished into the crowd again. We entered the nearest stairwell, which was mercifully empty, and headed down.

"That was an interesting encounter, wasn't it?" Arno said, taking the steps with the slow deliberation of a man who's had his share of spills. "It made me wonder. Is Montague Hobart a scoundrel of the star lanes? Or something entirely different?"

"What makes you say that?"

"When I read your case notes, I thought finding someone who not only speaks Shrehari but is a veritable fount of knowledge about their culture, politics, and intelligence service was convenient."

Arno had a sixth sense about people; the result of years spent dealing with the worst humanity can produce. Not all people and not every time, but often enough to matter. It meant I took his sibylline pronouncements seriously.

"Now I've met Montague Hobart in the flesh," he continued, "I also find him glib and overly interested in the case for a mere civilian."

"He wouldn't be the first. Do you think he's more than he lets on?"

"At this point, I'd say anything is possible, but if you're asking whether Hobart belongs to the *Sécurité*

Spéciale, then my answer would be no. He doesn't give off the right vibe."

"What kind of vibe does he give off?"

Arno stopped hand securely on the railing and smiled over his shoulder. "Pardon me for sounding crude, but it's the one where he'd like to get into your pants, Chief. Which I'd say is merely a cover for something deeper, but that something likely doesn't involve working for the SecGen's lapdogs."

I didn't bother trying to suppress a distinctly indelicate snort. "He's not my type, for one thing."

"Oh? Tall, dark, and roguish isn't your type anymore?"

This time, I laughed outright. "You're stepping onto dangerous grounds, Inspector. But I hear you. I noticed he tries to be charming."

"Who wouldn't? Though of relatively modest rank, you're among the most influential Constabulary officers in the Rim Sector. It makes you someone deserving of a slippery rapscallion's attention, if only for self-preservation."

"Speaking of buttering me up..."

"In my case, I'll freely admit it's for self-preservation. As you may recall, your predecessor didn't have a fraction of your tolerance for eccentricities or humor, so I'll gladly do whatever's necessary to stay in your good graces."

"And keep forcible retirement at bay. But enough about how fabulous your commanding officer is." I shooed him down to the next landing, from where we could reach Pullar's office. "What else does your intuition tell you about Hobart?"

"Don't visit his ship, don't accept invitations to out of the way restaurants and ask yours truly to dig up his background."

"Consider it done."

Upon entering the Gendarmerie station, we found Pullar standing by a projection table, examining what looked suspiciously like a holographic representation of complex circuitry. He waved at us.

"We received the engineering section's analysis of the surveillance sensor that covered the area outside Shovak's suite," he said pointing at the projection. "You'll love what they found, Chief Superintendent."

"Try me."

"Nothing. Or at least nothing physical that is. The unit is in perfect working order."

"Then what..."

Pullar raised a finger to stop Arno. "It is, however, utterly brainless. The programming that turns this hunk of sophisticated electronics into an able spy is missing. Not just corrupted but gone, wiped without a trace."

Arno's eyes lit up as he nodded with slow deliberation. "That makes eminent sense. It's often easier to disable a surveillance module via its software vulnerabilities than to shove a real spanner up its works, leaving the impression it suffered a natural brain failure, electronic dementia, as it were."

Wonderful. Aquilonia Station's systems had dodgier security than a low-rent brothel on Celeste. "That means the hacker would need special access to the network linking the sensor to the rest of Aquilonia's surveillance setup."

Pullar nodded. "Indeed, Chief Superintendent. It, like the other critical networks, is segregated, both logically and physically. I suppose someone could penetrate it with brute force, but as in the case of the lift, it's easier to suborn the weakest link, meaning the human element, someone who has legitimate access."

"Dangerous Don seems to preside over a very leaky sieve, Major."

The Cimmerian gave a helpless shrug. "I can implement the best protocols in the universe, but I have no way of keeping the venal, stupid, or otherwise morally defective from undoing them. The biggest threat has always been the critter occupying the space between the chair and the console."

Arno guffawed. "Truer words have never been spoken. The number of miscreants we nab merely because they forgot to account for the human factor, especially their own lack of intelligence or foresight, would amaze you. Our jobs would be more challenging if most criminals didn't suffer to some extent from the Dunning-Kruger effect."

"How about the other surveillance modules?" I asked before the discussion morphed into a debate about people, especially cops or politicians, who thought themselves smarter than they were.

"Engineering hasn't finished running the full, in-depth scans on those yet, though if someone hacked and lobotomized this one, I'm willing to put money on the rest being in the same state. Once you're inside the security perimeter, the universe is yours to mess with, and if this one received the full treatment, the others would have as well."

Arno grunted, and then said, "Too true. I'll see if our hacker left something."

"I thought you might," Pullar replied, pointing at a nearby desk. "The engineering section has given us a direct link to the module's AI core. It's already set up for you."

I studied the three-dimensional image of the sensor and found myself unable to make heads or tails of its various parts. Seeing my bemused expression, Pullar's composure softened long enough for a rueful smile.

"I'm not learning anything by staring at it, but the engineers assure me the physical components are in perfect working order." He nodded at the urn. "A cup of coffee?"

"Absolutely."

We were staring at the dregs of our second servings fifteen minutes later when Arno swiveled his chair away from the console and stretched his arms.

"There's no point in wasting more time on it. Someone's wiped the code and left no clues I can find. I'll check the other modules once the engineers complete their analysis. Mind you, it doesn't mean there aren't any traces, just that I see nothing. But it would be helpful to find out how the perp or perps breached network security. We might pick up something more instructive."

Pullar nodded, pointing at a larger desk in the far corner of the bullpen. "I already have my best expert, Sergeant Yulich, studying the matter. You're welcome to join him. He's working over there."

A Cimmerian gendarme raised his hand without turning around and waved. Arno glanced at me for permission, in case I had another interview planned.

"Go ahead. We've hit a wall anyway and need new threads to pull on."

With Arno busy, Pullar and I retreated into the latter's office.

"Your interview with Sera Kazan was unproductive, I take it?"

"Not entirely. There are more than mere trade discussions going on between ComCorp and the Shrehari. When I pressed her on the matter, Gerri protested too much. She had a habit, back in her days as a Constabulary officer, of becoming overly talkative under stress or threat and hasn't lost it. The hostility she showed when I mentioned the *Tai Zolh* masked something else. I'm convinced of it. And she knows the name and rank of your prisoner."

Pullar's eyes widened. "Does she now? I wonder how that could be? The only one besides my troops to have seen Commander Talyn is Thopok, and he wouldn't have heard her name spoken in his presence, let alone her rank. And I didn't tell Dangerous Don either."

"Perhaps one of yours has been compromised."

He sighed. "That could well be. Everyone has a price or a weakness. I'm not naïve enough to believe the cops under my command are one hundred percent clean or even able to keep from talking out of school. Besides, with so many of the CimmerTek people being ex-Gendarmerie, letting close-held information slip in front of an old buddy will happen if ethanol's involved. Either way, Sera Kazan has information she shouldn't."

"I also had the notion that Gerri might be *Sécurité Spéciale*. She'd fit right in, I'm sorry to say. And since I've seen her cozy up to Darrien, who appears genuinely impressed by ComCorp, I wouldn't put it past her to have a hand in the lift sabotage. Especially since she warned me to be wary of further technical malfunctions, meaning she knows what happened."

Pullar grimaced. "That bit of news could have easily come from Darrien's office. But what fun. *Sécurité Spéciale* and *Tai Zolh* colluding on Aquilonia Station while Dangerous Don plays his usual brand of politics. My tour of duty here can't end soon enough."

"It would explain why the ComCorp folks are so anxious I charge Talyn as soon as possible. They don't want me digging any deeper into the *Tai Zolh* angle."

"Perhaps."

"You sound skeptical, Major."

A frown creased his forehead. "Part of me thinks this is too fantastical to be true. In my experience, most murders arise from straightforward and basic urges — greed, sex, power, honor. I'd say Ockham's razor still points at an internal Shrehari matter as the most likely cause, and not a conspiracy involving shadowy spy organizations."

"Normally, I would agree, but I know Gerri Kazan, probably better than she knows herself. And I've encountered the *Sécurité Spéciale* before this. It may seem implausible to you, but not to me."

"I suppose you've solved your share of convoluted cases."

"Sure, and most involved one or more of the seven deadly sins rather than sinister motives stemming from evil schemes. But I've investigated the odd crime that would make conspiracy theorists wet their pants, and not always without justification. Most of the time, murder is an act of passion or greed, but sometimes it's an act of politics."

"And Shovak's death?"

"I'm leaning more and more toward politics, whatever those might be. There seems to be precious little passion involved, in spite of the splendid blood spatter redecorating his suite."

"That's what I thought you'd say."

"Don't sound so glum, Major. I've solved nearly every one of my cases since joining the PCB, and I doubt this one will end any differently."

"Yet the exception proves the rule."

My host seemed to have jettisoned his optimism, and somehow I couldn't blame him. Even I didn't feel overly thrilled. Give me corrupt cops or greedy politicians any day of the week, and I'll tear through their guts with gusto. Playing footsie with three intelligence services, not so much.

I felt adrift, stuck in the center of a dreaded triangle. Human organizations who were at each other's throats occupied two of the corners, and an alien species renowned for its martial prowess and its propensity for carrying grudges on an intergenerational basis held the third.

Or I could be wrong, and Shovak's murder had been an act of passion. But the odds were rapidly decreasing. Then there was the matter of Louis Sorne and his CimmerTek henchmen.

"Have your people been able to trace Burrard and company's movements on the night of the murder?"

"Let me check." He scrolled through his messages and nodded. "A preliminary result on Javan. It looks like he's in the clear. We have him entering the Darrien's private quarters just after twenty-one hundred hours and leaving six hours later at around oh-three-hundred."

"That's late for a meeting, considering Aquilonia keeps a standard day and night cycle."

Pullar made a face. "I'm trying hard not to wonder about it. Let's just say Javan is Lisbeth's type, and he's never refused an offer of extracurricular fun."

"Behind Dangerous Don's back? Wouldn't that put a stop to Burrard's ambitions if they're found out?"

The Cimmerian gave me a sad smile and slowly shook his head.

"As I said, I'm trying hard not to think about it, and neither should you." When he saw that I still didn't grasp his meaning, he said, "I'm sure D.D. was home that night."

"Oh. Never mind then. Unless we find fresh evidence on Burrard, I see no need to challenge his alibi."

"Thank you, Chief Superintendent. I feel relieved to hear you say so. Some things are best left unexamined." His eyes darted toward the screen again. "Yulich tells me he and Inspector Galdi have finished."

— Thirty-Four —

"If anyone hacked into the sensor network," Arno announced upon entering Pullar's office, "he or she left no traces that either Sergeant Yulich or I can find, Chief. The operational log is as clean as a plasma conduit, meaning experts tampered with it. There's not a single record of unauthorized access to the network in the days preceding the murder. Yet, one moment the sensors were working, the next their programming vanished as if by magic. This was professional work. Either it wasn't our favorite spooks, or they upped their game and didn't feel the need to leave a signature."

"It would have surprised me to find *Sécurité Spéciale* fingerprints, Arno. What motive would they have to help Shovak's assassin?"

"A falling-out among thieves?" Pullar asked, half facetiously.

I thought about it for a moment and tried to see how the envoy's death might profit the *Sécurité Spéciale* and ComCorp. But I came up with a big fat blank.

"Implausible, but not impossible, Major. One more thread that leads us nowhere."

"Actually, Chief, you may wish to pull on this one and the hack of the lift controls to yank the station's administrator's chain. I'd say the odds that both occurred under cover of legitimate access are pretty high. Breaking into two segregated networks will leave something, and as I said, we saw nothing. If Ser Darrien is willing to play footsie with ComCorp, who knows what he could be bribed or coerced into allowing or covering up?"

"Or perhaps Aquilonia's hiring practices have allowed someone with ill intent to obtain legitimate access." I glanced at Pullar and saw him nod.

"Both you and the inspector have a point," he said. "When you give Dangerous Don a yanking, I'd like to be there, because, CimmerTek notwithstanding, security on this station is my job even if I don't answer to our esteemed chief administrator. Sadly, the actual determination of who gets access to what, let alone who gets hired is beyond my carefully circumscribed responsibilities."

"As long as you don't take my approach to be one the Constabulary necessarily approves."

"What the chief means," Arno interjected, "is she likes to convince witnesses and suspects that her status as the top ranking PCB officer in the sector gives her more power than she really has."

"I believe I've already witnessed that particular method. Shall I set up an appointment?"

"Perhaps I should do the honors if you'll open a link to his office."

Pullar nodded, touched the controls, and waited. And waited. And waited.

"I do believe Lisbeth is cross with me, Chief Superintendent. She usually accepts my calls a lot faster than this."

"Can you tag it as coming from me?"

His fingers brushed the controls. "Done."

Less than twenty seconds later, I had the distinct pleasure of seeing the lovely Lisbeth's querulous features. They hadn't improved since our first encounter.

"What is it, Chief Superintendent?"

"I would like to see Ser Darrien within the next ten minutes."

Her eyes narrowed in distaste at my impertinence. "Impossible. D.D. is a very busy man. I might be able to fit you in sometime tomorrow."

I gave her my iciest glare, something that came naturally to a pale, blue-eyed blond who's seen better days. True, I didn't go on many dates, but bedroom eyes were a hindrance when you were trying to break a suspect's alibi or break into Dangerous Don's schedule.

"You'd better fit me in now. I have evidence of several security breaches in the last few days linked to Envoy Shovak's murder, and they may well involve station personnel. As Aquilonia's chief administrator, he bears responsibly for what happens here. I think it would be in everyone's best interests if we discussed the matter before more severe and potentially life-threatening problems crop up. One dead body is already one too many, wouldn't you agree?"

I had to give Lisbeth props. She held my stare for a good ten seconds without flinching. It felt like we were engaged in an ocular version of the handshake contest men enjoyed inflicting on each other.

"Very well," she finally said. "I'll pull D.D. out of his meeting. He won't be happy. Make sure you're here in ten minutes."

With that, the hologram of her head dissolved. I glanced at Arno. "Do you want to meet the delightful Donul Darrien?"

"He sounds like a peach, but Sergeant Yulich just signaled engineering has given us access to the remaining sensor modules. Maybe our mystery hacker left a trace in one of them. I'd also like to inspect the network controlling the lifts. If we're facing two different factions buggering up the station's systems, perhaps I'll find evidence they've missed or not fully erased. Even the finest pros make mistakes, which is why we're still in business. Please give Ser Darrien my respects."

Pullar and I entered Dangerous Don's domain precisely nine minutes later, to Lisbeth's obvious disappointment. She likely expected us to be tardy, giving her an excuse for a scolding.

"D.D. is quite put out by this you know," she said, not bothering with a greeting or any other social niceties. "And his guests even more so."

If she was expecting an apology, her future held nothing but disappointment.

"Unfortunately, murders have a habit of disrupting the lives of those they touch."

Yes, I could spout platitudes with the worst of them, though I could swear I saw the hint of a smile on Major Pullar's lips.

She ushered us into Darrien's office where we found the chief administrator staring out a porthole at Thule's white orb, arms crossed, and his back to us. I began a slow count in my head, wondering how long he'd wait until acknowledging our presence. I was at twenty when he finally turned around.

Nicely calibrated. Long enough to express displeasure without causing serious offense. He was clearly a pro at the little dominance games so beloved by minor functionaries with an inflated opinion of themselves.

"Lisbeth tells me you found evidence of malfeasance by my personnel in matters affecting security?"

He didn't precisely sneer, but even the minimal courtesy he'd shown me during my last visit was absent. Then, I saw a spark of worry in his eyes, something his arrogant demeanor couldn't entirely hide. It was also plain in the way he kept his arms crossed, either as a subconscious attempt to shield himself or a more conscious pose to prevent any unseemly fidgeting.

"That's not quite what I said, Ser Darrien. I believe my words were that I had evidence of several security breaches in the last two days linked to Envoy Shovak's murder, and they could involve station personnel. I'm here to discuss the matter with you."

"Oh?" An eyebrow crept up as a way to show disdain. It was too theatrical to be anything more than another effort at masking his discomfiture.

When it became clear he intended to stay behind his desk, I headed for the settee group in the far corner and took the seat I'd occupied during my visit the previous day, Pullar in tow. After a few moments, Darrien perched himself on the edge of the chair across from us with an exaggerated sigh of exasperation.

"Say your piece, Chief Superintendent. My agreeing to see you doesn't mean I don't have vital work and important meetings waiting."

"As you no doubt know by now, someone wiped the sensor modules around the crime scene clean of their programming, turning them into expensive but useless adornments. We found no evidence that the saboteurs hacked into the surveillance network, or that someone tampered with its access control log. Our experts found traces of tampering with the lift controls and operational log but no evidence of hacking from the outside. Major Pullar assures me both networks are physically and logically segregated from the rest so any breach would leave traces my inspector could find. He found none. This means there's a high probability the saboteurs gained entry using staff credentials and a terminal with physical links to those networks. That being the case, our saboteurs had help from your staff, or are among your employees. Do you see what I'm getting at, Ser Darrien?"

I held his disdainful stare for a few moments before sticking the metaphorical knife into his soft underbelly.

"If true, it would almost certainly call into question your fitness as chief administrator. I need not tell you what a dim view the Cimmerian government will take of someone risking the lives of those living on Aquilonia due to lax procedures, controls, and hiring policies."

Darrien's pale features hardened, a sure sign he was about to unleash his best stab at blustering.

"You mean to tell me the absence of evidence is evidence in itself? Preposterous. We vet all of our people before hiring them. No one would allow, let alone commit such acts. Now, if that was everything..."

I raised a hand to stop him. "Major Pullar and I intend to investigate these security breaches as they may lead us to Envoy Shovak's murderer."

Darrien jerked his chin at my companion. "He has her in his brig."

"While she could have sabotaged the sensors, she's hardly in a position to tamper with the lift from inside her cell, Ser Darrien."

Dangerous Don shrugged. "Then you have two sets of saboteurs to chase."

"Which would mean you face double the security problems or two different factions have suborned members of your staff. I don't know which will seem worse to your superiors once my report reaches them in a few hours."

That got Darrien's attention. "Surely this is a Constabulary matter, not one for the Cimmerian government."

His reply was Pullar's signal to chime in. "It is also a matter for the Gendarmerie. I'm duty-bound to submit detailed reports on the incidents. These will make their way across from the Minister of Public Safety to the Minister of Interstellar Commerce, the Minister of Transport, and any other minister with jurisdiction over Aquilonia."

"This will no doubt trigger a review of the way in which you manage this station," I added. "And that review can have only one outcome for you."

The fear in his eyes became unmistakable. He evidently thought senior officials wouldn't just brush off warnings that came from both the Constabulary and the Cimmerian Gendarmerie.

Moreover, in light of the bureaucratic struggle between Darrien and the Gendarmerie for control over Aquilonia's security force, he probably figured an outsider like me would carry enough weight to trigger serious questions. I wasn't so sure. Planetary governments didn't always play nice with the Constabulary, let alone its unwanted stepchild, the PCB. But Dangerous Don needn't know.

"However," I continued after letting my words sink in, "I'm sure your complete and entire cooperation with Major Pullar and myself will go a long way in maintaining your reputation as a competent chief administrator. Help us find who allowed unauthorized access to the station's networks, and we'll find the how and why. I prefer my reports to be complete, with the solution identified, and already enacted. Major Pullar feels the same way, and I know your superiors will recognize the merit in you taking decisive action once we brought the matter to your attention."

Why did good old D.D. remind me of a man caught between a plasma cannon and cold vacuum? Someone with his sense of self-preservation should look sly and calculating, but I watched him chew on the inside of his lower lip, as he fought an inner battle.

A prolonged silence, broken only by the ticking of the grandfather clock, descended on us. Then, he shook himself and sighed. Judging by his expression, the decision he'd made didn't please him.

Perhaps someone had previously convinced Darrien to cooperate as little as possible with me, should I do more than merely collect evidence against Talyn. There was no shortage of potential candidates.

"If you give me what your experts have discovered," he said, "I shall make discreet inquiries."

His response sounded a lot like that of a man trying to buy time. But absent a search warrant, which Pullar had requested but not yet received, I couldn't barge my way into the operations section and interrogate the staff willy-nilly.

I inclined my head in a gesture of appreciation. "Thank you, Ser Darrien. I thought you might see sense in helping us with our inquiries. We will send the relevant information to your office as soon as possible."

"Was that all?" He climbed to his feet, eager to see the last of us.

"For the moment."

I nodded at Pullar, and we stood to leave. My last glimpse of Darrien showed a man desperately searching for solutions. Sucking up to ComCorp must have seemed like a way to improve his chances for advancement. But I was tarnishing those hopes with my insistence on uncovering the truth.

After Pullar had ushered me into the lift, he asked, "What do you think, Chief Superintendent?"

"Darrien is an unhappy man. Someone doesn't want him assisting us."

"Yes, that was rather obvious. But who?"

"Houko? Sorne? Your guess is as good as mine. But a senior Constabulary officer almost dying because of sabotage the same week an imperial envoy is murdered doesn't look good. It'll look worse if both incidents are related and stem from laxness in his staff's application of security protocols."

I didn't much care about Darrien's future, though the differences between both incidents bothered me.

"But are they related?" I asked when Pullar remained silent. "The erasure of the sensor AIs feels cleaner, for want of a better word, than the sabotage perpetrated on the lift, which had that *Sécurité Spéciale* signature Arno recognized. I can't reconcile the two instances if we're talking about a single perp, not if we're right about *Tai Zolh* and *Sécurité Spéciale* meeting under the guise of ComCorp's trade mission."

The lift slowed to a halt, and we stepped out.

"Meaning Darrien might have double the trouble, but then, so do we," Pullar replied.

"I know. And we're no further ahead on the murder, even if we're making progress on everything around it. But Darrien will do something helpful now we've put the wind up his backside, and maybe it will trigger events that tell us more."

Which was the best hope I had. Between Gerri, Commander Talyn, and Thopok, I was getting nowhere fast.

Back at the Gendarmerie station, Arno confirmed all he had was more of the same, meaning nothing. What should be there was gone, with zilch to show how it had vanished, let alone who did it.

The entire sensor array in question had been wiped clean by someone who didn't hack into the network, someone who used a legitimate access point. Failing that, it was a hacker so skilled he or she didn't leave a trace. A true professional whose abilities dwarfed even Arno's considerable expertise.

— Thirty-Five —

After lunch, we regrouped in a Gendarmerie conference room graciously set aside for our investigation.

I settled into a chair and slumped back with a sigh. "If you have any suggestions, I'm all ears, and waiting for events to unfold isn't an option."

Arno gave me a knowing grin. "As if I'd forget your inclination to keep moving. But we should wait and see what Darrien turns up. Mind you, we could bully your former partner again. I know you think she might be *Sécurité Spéciale*, which begs the question: what is Kazan doing as a ComCorp executive if she's one of the SecGen's secret minions?"

"She's either there to keep ComCorp in line, or the job's a cover, to hide the *Sécurité Spéciale*'s attempt at connecting with imperial spooks."

He opened his mouth to reply but then held up one hand while the other pulled his tablet from one of his jacket's inner pockets.

"Ah. That was quick. Sector HQ has sent us Montague Hobart's Constabulary file."

"I bet DCC Maras has passed the word that anything we ask for is an automatic priority."

"In that case, may the deity of her choice shower DCC Maras with a thousand blessings," Arno replied in an absent tone as he parsed the information on his tablet's screen.

"I don't think she subscribes to any religion."

"Neither does our rogue of the star lanes. It could be an oversight, but his dossier is remarkably complete." He nodded to himself. "The Navy has detained Hobart's ship on several occasions – suspicion of evading customs and excise duties mainly, but no charges were ever laid. His ship has passed every inspection, and there are no Transportation Act violations on record. Hobart is either less of a rascal than he lets on, or he has a remarkable ability to evade the law."

"If he's clean, then why do *we* have a dossier?"

"It's more a case of the Navy having a dossier, Chief. We received his file from the Fleet as part of our regular data exchange. He's never come to the Constabulary's attention. But it might not be for want of trying."

"Did you consider that perhaps Montague Hobart is one of the many honest beings populating our universe?"

Arno snorted with disdain. "Don't let his magnetism blind you to the fact he could be a highly successful smuggler able to evade arrest. There's something about him that feels subtly wrong and reading his dossier hasn't changed my opinion. Sadly, I can't put my finger on it right now."

"Do you think he's an honest translator?"

"He strikes me as shrewd enough to be so, but it never hurts to check. Did you record the interviews?"

"Yes, but not for use in court. I never let on I was recording."

"If you want, I can send the Shrehari bits to the Criminal Intelligence Division for a fresh translation. If DCC Maras has lit a fire under everyone's backside on Cimmeria, it shouldn't take long." He frowned as he scanned his tablet again. "They've attached a second message to the packet. I wonder what that might be." Then, eyes widening in surprise, he said, "Damn."

"What?"

"It's a confidential 'be on the lookout' notification. Sorne's on the lam."

"Didn't Maras put around the clock surveillance on the bastard?"

"Yes, but he seems to have evaded it, no doubt with help from his friends in the Cimmeria government and law enforcement. It says here Hannah Sorne claims her husband's on a business trip."

"He left without her? Nice guy. Did she say where he went?"

Arno nodded. "Off-world somewhere. But there's no trace of him passing through any commercial spaceport or Valerys Station, let alone arriving on either of Cimmeria's moons. Hence the system-wide BOLO."

"If Sorne's vanished, it means he knows the Financial Crimes Division is about to arrest him. And after Haylian's suicide, or Sornecide as Pullar puts it, this confirms that we have another bent officer in our ranks."

"Aye. Shall I tell Sergeant Bonta to lay the groundwork for another corrupt cop hunt, Chief?"

"Please, but make sure she does it quietly. I don't want to spook whoever Sorne still has inside Sector HQ. He or she will already be twitchy."

He nodded once. "Will do."

"I expect Maras will put every resource she can on Sorne's tail, and if he hired a ship, she wouldn't hesitate to call in the Navy. Sorne can try to run, but we'll eventually get him."

"From your lips to God's ear, Chief. It's a big galaxy, and people like Sorne have hideaways prepared for just such an occasion."

The conference room's main display chimed softly, interrupting my reply. It came to life with Pullar's likeness.

"I just heard from Darrien," he said without preamble.

"That was quick."

"It sure was," Pullar replied in a dry tone. "You were more persuasive than we thought. Dangerous Don says ten of his engineering people have access to both the sensor network and the lift controls, and thus could theoretically sabotage either."

"That doesn't exactly narrow it down," Arno grumbled.

"It doesn't matter, Inspector," Pullar replied. "Because they discovered that the credentials of an engineer with access to both networks were used twice, once shortly before the murder and once immediately before the lift sabotage. The only problem is, said engineer was on furlough at the time and left Aquilonia five days before Shovak's murder."

"A smoking gun," I said. "And no clue who pulled the trigger."

"Convenient, don't you think, Chief Superintendent?"

"Almost egregiously so."

"What's the engineer's name?"

"A Willa Trogo, forty-four, unattached, Cimmerian citizen," Pullar said. "She's worked on Aquilonia for the last three months. This is her first leave. And before you ask, I've reached out to my HQ on Cimmeria. They'll track Sera Trogo and hold her for questioning."

"This brings us back to the question of two separate hackers or one." Arno sat back with a frown. "I think the idea that two different individuals or groups used the same purloined credentials to access separate networks on alternate days beggars belief. The balance of probabilities now definitely points to one intruder for both."

I nodded in agreement. "Yet the lift saboteurs left what we think are digital *Sécurité Spéciale* fingerprints, while the sensor wiper left an uncanny void. If the same saboteur did both why the difference?"

Arno let out a bark of sardonic laughter. "If we knew that, we'd know who did it."

"False flag operation of some sort?" Pullar suggested. "The digital fingerprints are meant to make us believe two groups are in play."

My wingman grimaced. "A possibility, but for the fact they had to know we would eventually find out about Sera Trogo's credentials being used in her absence. The unexplained access and the sabotage could be unrelated. But the likelihood is vanishingly small. Perhaps the fingerprints resulted from haste. The perps would have had plenty of time to sanitize the sensors in preparation for Shovak's assassination. Taking the chief for an unplanned ride, not so much."

I couldn't fault Arno's logic on that point. "So we're back to one perp or group responsible for both instances of sabotage, meaning we've made little headway."

"Aye, though we now have an idea how they did it and perhaps we can even figure out who did it," he replied, "right, Major?"

Pullar's lengthy silence did not bode well.

"Our station engineers are an obstinate lot," the Cimmerian finally said. "They're resistant to heightened security measures within their domain, claiming not without a measure of justification that such an intrusion does nothing worthwhile. Once past the engineering section's checkpoint, you'll find no surveillance sensors."

"Next, you'll tell me no one who isn't supposed to enter engineering passed the checkpoint at the relevant times."

"Precisely, Chief Superintendent." Pullar sounded unhappy. "Someone used Willa Trogo's credentials to access the segregated networks, but not to enter engineering. As far as access control records show, she hasn't passed the checkpoint since going on leave."

"And we do the old one step forward, two steps back dance again," Arno muttered in a disgusted tone. "Except now we face a reverse locked room mystery as well. How about we charge Talyn and let the courts sort out the truth?"

I knew Arno didn't mean it. He had too much professional pride in closing cases with unimpeachable evidence even if the legal system let a perp walk in the interests of expediency. The late Commissioner Haylian was a case in point. But I could understand his sentiment.

"We'll simply work our way through the list of engineering staff present when Willa Trogo's credentials were used. If the sabotage was carried out from inside the engineering section, one of them could well be our perp."

"Which won't be entertaining," Pullar replied. "As I said, they're an obstinate lot and take their cue from the chief engineer, Eoghan Neild. He's an old-time union man with little affection for our sort. Or for the Darriens, but that's a different matter. Eoghan's protective of his realm and people. If you look for the word pigheaded in any dictionary, you'll see his picture. But the bugger is competent, and he'll stand up to D.D. when it concerns important matters, such as keeping Aquilonia's infrastructure in good working order."

"Then I suppose we should start with Ser Neild. Can you set it up, Major?"

— Thirty-Six —

"I was wondering how long it would take the likes of you to darken my doorstep." Eoghan Neild, whose luxuriant beard rivaled Arno's, pointed at a trio of chairs in front of his desk. "Sit. Major Pullar, it's been a while. I wish our policy of noncontact could have continued, but at least you're not an obnoxious prat like Burrard. The man's a real pain in the ass. He thinks he'll be taking your job soon, God forbid."

Neild turned his deep-set blue eyes on me. "You must be the Constabulary bigwig who almost toured the ice caverns without a pressure suit yesterday."

I inclined my head in greeting. "Chief Superintendent Caelin Morrow and this is Inspector Arno Galdi."

The engineer gave Arno a brief but curious glance, then said, "Knowing that idiot Darrien, I'm sure he hasn't apologized for the accident, Chief Superintendent Morrow, so let me do it on behalf of the station. Major Pullar has probably told you Aquilonia's engineers are difficult characters, but we take pride in our work. A lift going haywire and almost killing a guest reflects poorly on my staff and me, and we're sorry it happened."

"I suffered no real harm, Ser Neild, and I can hardly hold you responsible for sabotage."

He met my gaze without shame or hesitation and said in a gruff tone, "The incident happened on my watch. Therefore, I'm responsible. Now, I suppose you're here because of what happened yesterday and the matter of surveillance sensor AIs turned into drooling imbeciles?"

"We are." I nodded. "We understand that a Willa Trogo's credentials were used before each of the incidents, credentials allowing access to both the surveillance and lift networks. But Trogo left Aquilonia on vacation five days before the Shrehari envoy's murder, and her credentials weren't used to enter the engineering section on the days they were used to access the segregated networks."

"You understand correctly, Chief Superintendent. I'm thrilled Dangerous Don's office conveyed the right information for once and with such commendable speed. They usually mess up the simplest things and drag them out, causing no end of chaos. But I suppose that's what happens when you appoint a man with more political connections than relevant education to administer a place such as this."

"You mean Darrien's the sort who has delusions of adequacy?" Arno asked with an innocent air.

Neild guffawed. "Precisely."

When the engineer visibly relaxed, I knew the bearded mafia had been called to order. Arno possessed a knack for saying just the right thing to put witnesses at ease, especially fellow face fur aficionados. With the state of genetic engineering these days, I might be able to grow a beard myself and adopt his techniques, but it just wouldn't be the same.

"I gather," Neild continued, "you're here to ask me how Willa Trogo could have accessed the segregated networks when she wasn't even on Aquilonia. Fact is, I don't know. My folks aren't supposed to let anyone else use their credentials. And Willa, bless her honest heart, wouldn't share access nor would she be able to carry out the sabotage you found in both the lift controls and the surveillance sensors. In other words, I'm not sure how I can help you."

"You certainly know more than you're aware, Ser Neild," Arno said with an engaging smile. "A man of your experience notices many things without realizing. The information's stuck in there," he tapped his forehead with a thick index finger, "waiting for the right question."

"Fair enough," the engineer said after a moment's hesitation. "Ask away."

"How long have you employed Willa Trogo?"

"Three months. The Aquilonia Syndicate recruits on Cimmeria, and that's where they hired Willa as a level three engineer. She came with over ten years' experience and impeccable references."

"You have a copy of her background information, no doubt?" Arno asked.

"Yes, I do. I suppose you'd like to see her file?"

"If you would be so kind."

"And should I refuse on the grounds of privacy, you'll threaten me with a warrant, right?"

"We've no need of a warrant," Arno replied with a sad shrug. "Persons connected to a federalized murder investigation have no privacy rights, in spite of planetary laws."

"I see." Neild reached for a matte screen embedded in his desk and let his fingers dance for a few moments. "There. I've transmitted a copy of Willa's employment record to Major Pullar."

Arno inclined his head. "Thank you. Could you tell us about Sera Trogo's responsibilities?"

"She oversees several vital systems as one of the watchkeepers, including the surveillance net, and the lift controls. We run twenty-four standard hours a day, year-round, and I always have a complement of engineers on duty."

"Eight-hour shifts, I presume?" Arno asked.

"Yes."

"Meaning Sera Trogo is one of three overseeing that particular set of systems."

Neild nodded. "Yes, although my people are cross-trained. Each can work on several other systems."

"Hence ten of your staff with access to both of the networks in question."

"Just so."

"How would you rate Sera Trogo, both professionally and personally?"

The engineer seemed at a momentary loss for words. Then, he said, "She did her job, didn't need much supervision, and didn't mingle with anyone from my department outside work. She had private quarters and mostly stuck to them when she wasn't on duty. I've had no cause for complaint about her work, nor has she shown a spark of genius that would call for a promotion or expanded responsibilities. And that lack of genius means the sabotage you're investigating would have been well beyond her capabilities and those of anyone else here, including me. At least to the extent of leaving no traces."

"In other words," Arno said, "Trogo is an unremarkable employee."

"Most engineers tend toward the unremarkable, Inspector," Neild replied with the hint of a smile.

"We're not only a stubborn lot; we're also mostly introverts with little fashion sense, or so the story goes. All joking aside, I can't see any of my people do what you allege."

Neild sounded sincere enough that I was inclined to believe him.

"And yet, someone using Willa Trogo's credentials, presumably from a secure console within the restricted zone did just that. Can one bypass the checkpoint?"

This time, a whiff of embarrassment softened Neild's stiff countenance. "There is a way, provided a member of the staff who entered the restricted zone via the checkpoint opens one of the emergency exits after disabling the relevant sensors."

"You make it sound as if that's happened before," Arno said.

Neild made a face. "The emergency stairs near the control room offer a short-cut to a commercial area beneath the docks, one used by station inhabitants exclusively. It's a favored place for a quick, inexpensive meal or snack. Taking the stairs considerably cuts down on time and distance. They slash through Aquilonia's labyrinth. I've never been able to catch anyone doing so, but if the rumors are true, duty engineers sometimes sneak out mid-shift for a breather when my deputies or I are elsewhere."

"Covered by their colleagues who temporarily disable the sensors?" My wingman nodded knowingly. "Not an uncommon story. The human factor is always a security system's weakest link. Would you say it's entirely possible someone misusing Willa Trogo's credentials was admitted to the control room via the emergency stairs by an employee on duty — twice?"

The engineer sounded peevish when he said, "Someone used them when she was officially on leave, and that someone *didn't* use them to enter the restricted zone. I'd say there's a good chance, yes. And yes, I'll give you the names of the staff on duty at the relevant times. You have my blessing to interview them."

We didn't need his blessing, but I bowed my head in thanks anyway. Then an unexpected burst of intuition suggested to me that our saboteur didn't access the restricted networks from within the engineering department's secure area.

Someone capable of such refined sabotage could undoubtedly set up a connection through an untraceable node.

Hence the use of Trogo's credentials without a record of her passage through the checkpoint. A remote access scenario didn't require arranging unauthorized entry via the emergency stairs.

As Arno said, the human factor was always the weakest link in any chain of evidence. Why jeopardize an operation as finely tuned as Shovak's murder by involving an engineer who might talk to the wrong people, namely folks such as us?

"Thank you, Ser Neild," Arno said. "We may avail ourselves of your largess in due course."

By his tone, my wingman seemed to have experienced the same epiphany.

"Was that it?" Neild asked. "I'm a busy man. Ensuring Aquilonia remains a livable habitat for sentient beings is no small affair, especially with the management foisted on us by the Syndicate."

I nodded and climbed to my feet, imitated by Arno and Pullar.

"That was all for now. We might have follow-on questions as the investigation progresses. Thank you for your courtesy, Ser Neild."

He made sound halfway between a snort and a laugh. "If I hadn't consented to speak with you, I'd have suffered Major Pullar's harassment night and day."

— Thirty-Seven —

“Why do I get the feeling interviewing the duty engineers has suddenly become a low priority?” Pullar asked once we were aboard the lift.

“Because Arno and I both seem to have concluded the sabotage didn’t occur via one of the engineering workstations,” I replied. “Am I right, Arno?”

“Absolutely, Chief.” My wingman nodded. “It stands to reason. Neild says none of his people are skilled enough to muck up the systems in question and letting whoever used Willa Trogo’s credentials in via the emergency stairwell reeks of amateurishness. Based on what we’ve seen so far, we’re emphatically not dealing with amateurs.”

“Meaning they may have done it via a remote node.” A thoughtful frown creased the Cimmerian’s forehead. “You understand such a scenario makes things even worse for me, right? One should not be able to tunnel into networks reserved for vital infrastructure.”

“Yet, someone did, either through an unauthorized entry into the operations room, or through an illicit connection to the network from somewhere else.”

Pullar opened his mouth to reply, and I quickly said, "We need to concentrate on Willa Trogo. She's become the new focal point of this investigation."

Once more ensconced in Pullar's conference room, the Cimmerian called up Trogo's file. Arno took one look at her image and grunted.

"She shares more than a few points of similarity with Gerri Kazan, Chief. Wouldn't you agree, Major?"

Pullar studied the projection, rubbing his chin, and then nodded slowly. "In a vague way, perhaps. They share a few points of similarity."

I couldn't see much of a likeness myself, beyond generalities — age, build, skin tone, that sort of thing. But then, my mental image of Gerri was years out of date. Our few brief encounters since I arrived hadn't been enough to update it.

"Trogo's been working here for three months," I said as her record scrolled by in reverse chronological order. "Before that, she worked for Universal Exports on Cimmeria."

"I wonder if Universal Exports and ComCorp are connected." Arno's brows pulled together as he consulted the tablet that never left his side. "Indeed. It appears a subsidiary that belongs to a corporation controlled by ComCorp recently bought the company, meaning it's been part of the same zaibatsu for about three months now."

"Considering the size of ComCorp's holdings, especially in this sector — another coincidence?" Pullar asked.

"Two in a row?" Arno glanced up at him. "Find one more, and the chief will suspect enemy action."

"How is that?"

"Once is an accident, twice is coincidence, and three times is enemy action. I believe the quip dates back to the twentieth century and was coined by a chap named Fleming. He did a bit of espionage in his youth before writing novels about it." When he saw Pullar's puzzled expression, Arno pulled a face. "Our chief has a fondness for pre-diaspora fiction. The more lurid, the better."

"That's rich coming from someone whose preference in literature involves mythical beasts and twisted creatures." I scanned the next entry in her employment record. Or rather entries. "She spent ten years moving from one job to another along the Rim before coming home to Cimmeria. Several of the entries in her employment record are suspiciously lacking in detail."

"Not an unusual pattern for engineers. The good ones can make a lifetime's worth of money in only a few years by working on riskier outposts," Arno replied. "See, she lists a nine-month term on Kilia Station, one of the Commonwealth's more nefarious spots."

"Have either of you been there?" Pullar asked.

I nodded. "Once, years ago. The folks running Kilia like to think they're a semi-independent satrapy, but they're quick to call on the Navy or on us when nonhumans threaten their notion of fair trade. Mind you, in my case, it was during the years I worked with the Flying Squad. Kilia's not keen on calling in the Firing Squad when their own security forces show a spot of rot."

It had been during the heady days when Gerri and I were making our bones as sharp, young investigators. The thought gave me a pang of regret at how our lives had diverged.

"Kilia's methods of dealing with internal affairs are rather summary," my wingman said, by way of confirmation. "PCB help not required. And no, I've not graced the place with my presence. Its reputation suffices to keep me at a distance."

"When will we hear from Cimmeria about Trogo?"

Pullar glanced at the time display, then consulted his tablet, more out of reflex than anything else, I suspected.

"I don't know. Perhaps I should have been more precise when I reached out, such as asking them to break down her movements for us while they tracked her. I'll do that now."

We studied Trogo's employment record for a while longer but found no further clues about who she was. Neither could we fathom why her credentials were used on Aquilonia while she was vacationing fifty million kilometers away. Her record also didn't give us any indication she had the skills to carry out both instances of sabotage, once without leaving a trace and the second time, leaving digital markers pointing at the nefarious *Sécurité Spéciale*.

"You mentioned coming up with a third coincidence," Pullar finally said. He touched his controls, lighting up a side display. Three faces appeared. Willa Trogo, Gerri Kazan, and Hera Talyn.

"If there's a hint of resemblance between Kazan and Trogo, how about between Trogo and Talyn?"

"All three seem to have similar phenotypes, I'll grant you that," I replied, studying the women.

Arno glanced at me with a suspicious frown. "What are you thinking, Chief?"

"Something's tickling my subconscious, but I can't quite grasp what that is. Could we trace Talyn,

Kazan, and Trogo's movements, the latter since before the Aquilonia Syndicate hired her?"

"You think they might be connected?" Pullar asked.

"Something's not adding up, Major, but my gut tells me Willa Trogo is the key that will help us unlock the rest of the case."

"I'll put a tracer in motion," he replied.

"So will I," Arno added. "Though I doubt the Fleet will be forthcoming with Commander Talyn's movements if we can't track her via open sources."

"And ComCorp won't cooperate either, I suspect, but let's shake the net and see what pops up."

Pullar glanced at his tablet and then looked up at me. "I think we have our first popup, Chief Superintendent. Cimmeria confirms Willa Trogo passed through Valerys Station arrivals control a week ago and immediately took a shuttle to Howard's Landing. Tracking her movements after she left the spaceport will be more difficult. Cimmeria's privacy laws are relatively strict, compared to many places. But there's no record of her leaving Cimmeria since then."

"Her file's not exactly brimming with known associates or family members we can contact, nor is a permanent home address listed," Arno pointed out. "She doesn't seem to have roots in any community on your planet, Major."

The Cimmerian made a dismissive gesture. "You'd find my background very similar in that respect, Inspector. Many of us have few friendships or family we care to acknowledge. Those with itinerant jobs even less so."

"True," I said. It was something I knew from personal experience since I had few friends and no family. "Neild mentioned she was solitary, but perhaps we could dig through Aquilonia's security database and look for video of anyone socializing with Trogo, someone who might tell us more about her."

"We can," Pullar said. "I'll put one of my gendarmes on it, but it'll take time."

"Thank you."

"And now I suppose I should draft a new protocol whereby station staff credentials are put in suspended animation whenever they leave Aquilonia." He rose with a weary grimace. "As the saying goes, I'm once more closing the airlock after losing atmospheric pressure."

Arno held up a raised index finger. "One question before you leave?"

"Sure."

"Is staff taking a holiday on Cimmeria after only three months normal? I'd have thought someone with Trogo's time on various outposts would be inured to the temptation of spending time and money for a few days of fresh air so soon after taking up a new job."

"It's not unheard of, Inspector, but most people wait until they've been here at least six months — it means more vacation time available."

"Thank you, Major."

With Pullar gone, Arno slumped back in his chair and laced his fingers together over his not inconsiderable midriff.

"You've obviously done the math by now, right Chief? Trogo leaves Aquilonia five days before the murder; both Talyn and Kazan, along with the rest of the ComCorp people, arrive on Aquilonia the day before, leaving a gap of four days. More than enough for a round trip aboard the ferry between Valerys Station and here."

"Meaning Trogo could easily have handed her credentials to someone headed for Aquilonia the moment she reached Valerys."

"Kazan or Talyn, for example."

"Or anyone else who traveled to Aquilonia on the next ferry," I replied. "Since it left twelve hours after Trogo arrived, she had ample time to do so even after landing on Cimmeria, thanks to the hourly shuttle service."

"Alternatively, she could have either lost her credentials before leaving or given them to someone already on Aquilonia," Arno replied.

"That too, and once Major Pullar's gendarmes finish tracing Trogo's movements for the last few weeks, we might be in a better position to see whether that explanation is the more likely one."

"If I were a betting man, I'd wager the handover or theft happened on Valerys. Less risky for Trogo or the thief. The police here can't easily dive into the surveillance database of a station fifty million kilometers away, right?"

I could never argue with Arno's logic. Though he resembled a jolly Doctor Watson, he'd have given Sherlock Holmes a run for his money. And yes, I've read every one of Sir Arthur Conan Doyle's novels over the years. As Arno said, my taste in literature was distinctly pre-diaspora, but not quite as lurid as he made it out to be.

— Thirty-Eight —

Since our multiple lines of inquiry would take the time they needed to produce results, I finally gave in and, after a quiet supper with Arno and Major Pullar, I retreated to my quarters. I immediately dove into a new novel I'd come across in my idle moments perusing twentieth and twenty-first-century literature.

Stepping into the past, albeit a fictional one usually helped me relax and regain perspective on the here and now. The mass of data put at our disposal by sophisticated tools was often overwhelming enough to sever us from the true art of investigation. Technology was an indispensable assistant, but the most successful detectives still solved their cases mainly with logic and the occasional bouts of intuition. And a keen understanding of human weaknesses.

Reading about a time when DNA analysis was still new and computing power a fraction of what we had today always reminded me that in the end, the brain was our most potent tool of all.

Besides, criminals hadn't changed in six hundred years, and those of a nonhuman sort weren't really so different from their human counterparts. Mortal sins were, in no small degree, universal.

I felt pleasingly refreshed the next morning when I met Arno and Pullar for breakfast. Since nothing new had emerged overnight, our host suggested we take advantage of the lull, however brief it might be, and visit the ice caverns beneath Aquilonia.

Rather than use the station's pressure suits, stored on the engineering level, Pullar equipped us with Gendarmerie gear after Arno asked him a pointed question about the safeguards around suit storage and maintenance.

We took one of the regular lifts down to Eoghan Neild's domain and got clearance from Aquilonia operations. Then, we rode the rest of the way in a segregated elevator, now that engineering had physically blocked the older lifts from traveling beneath the artificial gravity envelope.

The abrupt change from the station's one gee to the one-fifth gee of Aquilonia's natural gravity was an unusual sensation, now that I wasn't fighting for my life. It reminded me of the more extreme amusement rides I'd experienced in my youth. But I'll nonetheless confess to a momentary flutter of anxiety during the transition.

A red warning light began to strobe in tandem with a telltale projected on the inside of my suit helmet, showing that our cab was depressurizing under the control of station operations personnel. The strobing stopped along with the lift car, and its doors opened silently, revealing a corridor burned out of the rock by mining lasers.

Light globes, set into the ceiling at regular intervals, came on as we left the cab. Pullar checked our suits one last time, then led us deeper into Aquilonia's subterranean rabbit warren, stopping at regular intervals to make sure sensors linked to the operations center registered our presence.

"This area was dug out during the station's earlier incarnation as a mining operation to support Thule's terraforming efforts, well before the Shrehari invasion," he said. His voice sounded strangely muffled over our short-range suit radios. "The idea to set up something more than a mine on this location didn't occur until they found the massive underground glaciers, remnants of the Cimmeria system's formation billions of years ago."

"Just as ice, hidden away from our original sun, allowed our ancestors to set up the first moon colonies in humanity's home system well before the FTL diaspora," Arno said.

"Though I understand Aquilonia's ice reserves are substantially larger than those of Earth's moon." Pullar stopped in front of a tall, wide armored door with a locking wheel at its center. "As you're about to witness."

"We can't actually appreciate the difference," I said. "Neither of us has ever visited Earth, let alone the first off-planet outposts."

"Thank God," my wingman rumbled. "We have several lifetimes' worth of villainy to investigate out here. There's no need to wallow in the Home World's cesspools."

"Not a fan of our central government, I take it?" Pullar asked.

"Inspector Galdi has seen the worst it can produce, Major. It turns even the most devout believer into a raging cynic."

"And I wasn't much of a believer, to begin with," Arno added. "It made me a natural for the PCB. And don't let the chief fool you. She's as much of a doubter as I am. Her pilgrimage to policing's dark side was a natural progression as well. She just hides it better than most of us."

"Perhaps a spot of natural wonder will offer a temporary antidote. Operations have cleared us to enter." Pullar grasped the locking wheel and turned it counterclockwise. When it could turn no more, he pushed the door with just enough force to make it pivot on well-balanced hinges.

Pullar was right. We stepped out onto a smooth, rocky ledge, like the shore of a petrified sea illuminated only by the ice extraction machinery to our left. The cavern quickly dissolved into an unrelieved darkness beyond the puddle of intense white light, hinting at an underground expanse unheard of on worlds subject to tectonic activity.

Standing there made me feel tiny and vulnerable. And slightly strange from watching massive robotic extractors smashing ice into manageable chunks and tossing them on a continuously moving conveyor belt without a sound. But I fancied I could sense faint vibrations through the soles of my pressure suit.

"This cavern continues for several kilometers, though it becomes impassable after a few hundred meters, and will stay so until ice extraction reaches that point."

Pullar's voice shattered the illusion we were contemplating the edge of infinity.

"Ice covered the ledge we're standing on until a few decades ago. They say there's enough here to generate oxygen, water, and hydrogen for the fusion reactors for at least another two centuries, and this one is merely the largest of the ice caverns in the immediate vicinity. With wastewater recycling improving by the day, new power generation technologies on the horizon, and no projected increase in the permanent population, I daresay we'll be able to stretch it out even further."

"One would almost think you harbored a smidgen of pride for Aquilonia, Major," Arno said. I couldn't see his face but knew a sly smile hid behind his beard.

After a moment of reflection, Pullar replied, "Perhaps not pride, Inspector, but a sense of ownership stemming from my responsibilities for the station's safety."

"A commendable sentiment."

I could not detect the slightest trace of irony in Arno's tone, but the Cimmerian snorted nonetheless.

"There's nothing noble about it. When you live in a closed environment millions of kilometers from the nearest habitable world — and Thule can't support humans yet — you develop an acute appreciation for our precarious situation. It gives you added incentive to make sure no one with ill intent, lack of sense, or both, does anything to imperil lives, my own included."

"Do you often face threats that jeopardize Aquilonia, other than natural ones, I mean?"

"Thankfully, no, Chief Superintendent. Your case, with its two instances of sabotage, is the worst I've seen during my tenure here. We're usually quite good at keeping organized crime and other unsavory activities well away from sensitive areas."

Arno chortled. "But the station's administration has no difficulties giving gangsters the VIP treatment, does it?"

"If you're talking about the Confederacy of the Howling Stars, Inspector, I'll remind you the organization remains unindicted, even though many of its members have and are taking lengthy vacations in the federal penal system. Provided they behave, pay their fees, and don't break Cimmerian law or Aquilonia regulations, Star Wolves are no different from other guests. If you want to discuss troublesome mobsters, several Cimmerian crime families regularly try to establish a presence here, but the free traders who come through Aquilonia aren't the sort to buckle under extortion schemes. In fact, I've had to protect more than one capo-wannabe from a crowd of angry spacers."

"Yet another reason why I don't miss frontier policing," Arno replied. "My time as a constable on insalubrious outposts was enough. How about you, Chief?"

"Frontier policing was never one of my top choices," I replied. "Mostly because I saw no allure in mastering the art of shockstick therapy to calm rowdy roughnecks out for their regular Friday night fun."

"Not to mention that you'd inevitably come across one or two who found the highest setting sexually pleasurable after they'd imbibed enough homemade ethanol. Getting mobbed by drunk, amorous hooligans isn't for the faint of heart. As I stated, I'm glad those days are long past."

"I'm about done here," I said. "How about you, Arno? Is it time to see if fresh information awaits us?"

He didn't answer straight away, eyes still on the mesmerizing spectacle. I could understand his reluctance to leave. But then he nodded.

"I'm good."

— Thirty-Nine —

On our return to the surface, the transition from one-fifth to one full gee was remarkable for the degree by which it dragged not only my body but also my spirits down once more. Thankfully, that brief dip passed by the time we emerged on the Gendarmerie station's level.

After doffing our pressure suits, Arno and I gladly accepted a cup of Pullar's coffee and enjoyed it in silence while we waited for our host to sort through the data captured by our various lines of inquiry.

"Major Pullar is one of the most helpful and pleasant planetary police officers we've dealt with in all our years, isn't he?" Arno said. "Usually, cooperation rarely rises above grudging."

"As I said before, the fact we're taking care of a case on his turf involving not only the Shrehari but one of humanity's biggest commercial empires has something to do with his cooperative spirit. Absent us, he'd be stuck with it and suffering intense pressure from the parties involved without having a PCB investigator's titanium alloy skin."

"True."

Pullar chose that moment to enter the conference room. "What's true?"

"That you're not particularly unhappy at us having assumed responsibility for the Shovak murder investigation," I replied.

He let out a humorless laugh. "I'd be completely out of my depth, so I'm thrilled you took over. You can accuse me of many failings, but I'm no glory hound, and I know when to step back and let others assume the lead."

"I think we should savor the moment, Chief," Arno said. "It's rare to hear someone from another law enforcement organization say those words."

Pullar eyed Arno and then me with suspicion as if he thought we were mocking him. I raised a placating hand.

"The inspector isn't kidding, Major. You're one of the few who's ever expressed joy at our presence. I may have said this before, but we're deeply appreciative of your help."

The Cimmerian grimaced as he took a chair. "I'm afraid my help has been rather ineffective in tracing our persons of interest so far. My colleague on Valerys Station sent us what they have on Talyn, Trogo, and the ComCorp folks. It doesn't tell us anything new."

"Still, we might as well peruse their findings," Arno said. "Sometimes, it's the least remarkable thing that sets a new train of thought in motion."

"I suggest we start with Talyn. She was on Valerys first." Pullar said.

I waved at the primary display. "Sure, since she's also our most important and only suspect."

"This is the recording from arrivals control."

We watched as Commander Talyn, in stylish civilian attire, stepped out of the gangway tube attached to the transport *Xenophon*, a regular fixture on the Rim routes. She passed through arrivals control after the AI accepted her identification and matched it to the routine biometric scan it took.

"I had the ID checked," Pullar said. "The one she presented on arrival here matches the one she used on Valerys in every respect. My colleague confirms she spent approximately twelve hours on the station before boarding the ferry to Aquilonia. She was not seen talking to anyone during her layover."

Brief flashes of Talyn on the station promenade lit up the screen, then we saw a video of her passing through departure control, and that was it.

"Of course, there are gaps in the video record of her movements on Valerys. Since Talyn was not under police investigation during that period, we have nothing more than fragments culled from routine sensor data. The Gendarmerie surveillance net can only account for twenty percent of her time."

"And since *Xenophon* is halfway across the Rim Sector by now, we can't confirm her presence aboard until it docks at the next port of call," Arno said. "That would be Merseaux Station. The local Constabulary regiment will pass our request along to station security in due course, so we'll eventually hear something."

"Next?" I asked Pullar.

"Willa Trogo." He called up a fresh surveillance video. "This is her arriving on Valerys Station six hours after *Xenophon* docked."

Again, the same sort of video capture, this time showing our missing engineer passing through arrivals control without a hitch. The view switched to the hangar bay's departure control after a mere thirty-minute break, showing Trogo headed for the hourly shuttle to Howard's Landing.

"Again, ID and biometrics match those on file here," Pullar said once the display faded to black. "The ComCorp delegation came up to Valerys from Howard's Landing four and a half hours after Trogo's departure, boarding the Aquilonia ferry with less than an hour to spare."

"Meaning their paths would have crossed planetside," Arno pointed out.

I nodded. "She could have contacted both Talyn and Kazan in passing. Any chances of getting surveillance recordings from the Howard's Landing spaceport for the relevant time frame, Major?"

"I've requested them. And now for Gerri Kazan." The display lit up again. "Same story as before. The IDs and biometrics taken by Valerys for the ComCorp delegation during arrival and departure match those on record here. Based on timing, they went straight from the shuttle hangar to the ferry dock."

I watched my former partner, her colleagues and her boss pass through the control gates twice, and then the display darkened again.

"Exit Willa Trogo, minus her credentials. Eighteen hours later, Hera Talyn and Gerri Kazan show up on Aquilonia. One is an avowed intelligence officer; the other is a security executive who might also belong to the *Sécurité Spéciale*. Shame we found no video of Trogo interacting with either."

"There's still the spaceport," Pullar said, though the dubious glint in his eyes told me he held no hope of spying on an incriminating rendezvous.

"And there's whatever your folks can cull from the Aquilonia security net showing Trogo's movements in the weeks before her departure. It might tell us something more useful," I replied. "How's that coming along?"

"Reasonably well, Sergeant Yulich tells me. We should see a digest of her last week on Aquilonia later today."

One of Pullar's watch commanders, a lieutenant, stuck his head into the conference room.

"Begging your pardon, sirs, but station ops just advised us that a Shrehari naval transport dropped out of FTL ninety minutes ago. It's headed here to retrieve the trade mission and Envoy Shovak's remains and is scheduled to arrive in twenty hours."

I groaned inwardly. Now I would have to make good on my threat to detain the delegation until I completed my investigation. That wouldn't do any good to human-imperial relations. But unless the transport brought full diplomatic credentials for Thopok and his guards or without a direct order from Wyvern to let them leave, I still had a little freedom of movement.

"We also received a notification from HQ, sirs. The Howard's Landing Police Department believes Willa Trogo died in a traffic accident forty-eight hours ago. Her death remains unconfirmed, pending analysis of what little they found once the fire was put under control, but the evidence points to Trogo as the victim."

I took a moment to digest the lieutenant's statement, then glanced at Arno, expecting to see consternation in his eyes. Instead, he gave me a sly glance, and I realized the news didn't surprise me as much as it should have. My expression must have mirrored my wingman's because he gave me a knowing nod.

"Convenient," Pullar said. "If a third time is enemy action, what do you call the fourth coincidence in a row, Chief Superintendent?"

"*Maskirovka* — an act of deception intended to confuse us. Except this might be our first evidence of overreach by whoever orchestrated Shovak's assassination. I'd have thought it better if Trogo just vanished, with no one to report her missing for weeks."

"Then there's the Shrehari ship," Arno said with a thoughtful air. "Am I the only one who doesn't understand why a Shrehari *naval* vessel is on its way? I thought the trade delegation was purely mercantile, and not officially representing the imperial government. Or does the Shrehari Deep Space Fleet offer transportation to their private sector?"

"Maybe it's a sign Chief Superintendent Morrow is right," Pullar replied. "And either Shovak, or Thopok, or both are imperial officers. Perhaps Shovak's assassination convinced our Shrehari friends the time to be coy has passed. Let's just hope the transport's captain doesn't intend to allow shore leave. I'd rather not deal with the problems that would cause. The buggers might behave, considering the discipline their navy enforces, but I can't say the same for other folks. It takes only one drunk spacer hurling a mortal insult across the bar for the knives to come out. And most drunks don't appreciate the fine line between rough kibitzing and words impugning a Shrehari's honor."

Arno chuckled. "Now there speaks the voice of experience."

"Sadly. One of the many things I won't miss once my tour here ends." Pullar's communicator buzzed. He glanced at it and said, "Sergeant Yulich has finished putting together the first compilation of Willa Trogo's movements on Aquilonia."

— Forty —

"This digest starts five days before Trogo's departure," Sergeant Yulich said as he lit up the conference room's primary display.

We observed snippets of an ordinary life, the sort lived by a human working in a habitat on an airless moon. Glimpses of Trogo enjoying the promenade were interspersed with sequences showing her window shopping, entering food establishments, and moving between her work area and the living quarters set aside for unattached station personnel.

As we neared the end of the recording and approached the hour of Willa Trogo's departure, something caught my eye.

"Is that Montague Hobart?"

Arno dipped his shaggy head. "It is. They seem rather chummy if you ask me."

We saw Hobart and Trogo sharing a small table by the front window of the Aquilonia Arms where Pullar had taken me on my first day here. They seemed lost in an intimate discussion, heads almost touching.

"Interesting. This is the first time we catch her with Hobart."

"But they know each other," Arno replied. "That's not a first date. Far from it. We'll find them exchanging sweet nothings on earlier videos."

"Interesting development. I doubt it's a coincidence. Hobart's role in our case has always seemed overly convenient." I turned to our host. "Major, would it be possible to have Sergeant Yulich focus on recordings of Hobart and Trogo together since she arrived on Aquilonia? He's the only one, so far, who seems to have a personal connection with her and with our investigation."

Pullar glanced at his sergeant who said, "Immediately."

"And could we also pull up everything the Gendarmerie and station operations know about him?"

"Of course."

Both gendarmes left us to wait in silence. I caught my fingers dancing on the tabletop and then saw Arno's quizzical stare.

"What's bugging you, Chief?"

"I'm getting that annoying impression someone's trying to play us for fools, manipulating us. The question is who?"

"Not that I disagree, but why do you think we're being manipulated?"

"The same reason I figured the late Commissioner Haylian's weakness was between his legs. Gut instinct. Unfortunately, it isn't giving me a hint as to the motives and identity of these schemers."

After three decades as a cop, I'd learned to trust my gut when it came to bagging bad guys — although it didn't do me much good with personal matters, but that was neither here nor there. And the moment I saw Hobart and Trogo hunched together so intimately, the feeling I always get when I've found a vital clue overwhelmed me.

"Delving into Haylian's sexual proclivities gave us the leverage we needed, Chief, so I'd say we can't go wrong by using your hunch as one of our working theories."

"Our list of suspects isn't exactly short. The *Sécurité Spéciale* has played us before — the Grint affair most prominently. But then, the Fleet plays its own games without letting us know we might stumble across an operation in progress. That's happened often enough in recent times as well. ComCorp, by dint of being the largest mercantile conglomerate in the Commonwealth, plays politics like an off-duty cop plays cards. And the Shrehari? That's a question for a xenoethnographer, not a PCB investigator."

"Why can't it be all four, Chief?"

"Trying to make my day even more surreal, Arno?" I gave him a crooked grin.

Of course, he was probably correct, and we'd stumbled into a multidimensional game of interstellar chess. But why? Why us, the PCB? I must have voiced my thoughts without realizing because Arno answered.

"Why us, Chief? Simple. We're the patsies whose verdict will be final. What we report will become the official story. We're supposed to be the most honest cops in the galaxy. The ones who can't be bought and have nothing to lose because we have no careers outside the PCB."

"So we find the real answer and bust this nonsense wide open, politics, Fleet, *Sécurité Spéciale*, and ComCorp be damned."

Arno chuckled. "That's what I like about you, Chief. Your eternal hope of striking a blow for truth and honesty in a universe built on the stories we tell each other so we can sleep at night."

"Everyone needs a hobby."

"Or in your case, a hobbyhorse."

Pullar's return saved me from a reply. "Yulich has narrowed his search to Hobart and Trogo appearing together on surveillance recordings, and I've queued up what Aquilonia knows about Ser Hobart."

The image of a grounded FTL-capable starship linked to a docking arm filled the primary display. Thule hung low over the rocky, cold horizon.

"His ship, *Harpy*," Pullar said. "We're seeing a live feed from the landing strip. The vessel is registered and certified."

"Looks like a large FTL yacht," I said. "A well-armed one, if those blisters on its hull conceal gun ports and the keel protrusions hide missile launchers."

"They do. Hobart makes no bones about his ship's ordnance. His weaponry is strictly legal, even the missiles he carries."

"His business dealings must be lucrative," Arno remarked. "Most small traders can barely afford a pair of pop guns and prefer to let their speed be the best defense. This one has guns, missiles, *and* hyperdrive nacelles big enough for a small corvette. Either Hobart is swimming in cash, or he has generous backers."

"We wouldn't know, Inspector. He pays the docking and transaction fees that keep Aquilonia profitable. Otherwise, any income declared, or undeclared doesn't concern the Gendarmerie. *Harpy*'s a single-hander, meaning no crew members we could question."

"What about his movements?" I asked. "It seems as if he comes and goes on a whim."

"Erratic." Pullar called up an extract from the harbormaster's log.

"A week here, a few days there," Arno said. "But it probably doesn't mean much."

Something tickled my instincts, and I took a closer look at the dates. "Am I dreaming or did *Harpy* first land here only three months ago?"

"The records are complete, Chief Superintendent," Pullar replied. "If station operations have no record of *Harpy* older than three months, the ship won't have landed here any earlier."

"And we have coincidence number five." Arno's eyes narrowed as he studied the shipping list. "You said four is *Maskirovka*, Chief. What would this one be?"

"An invitation to interview Ser Montague Hobart. But not just now. I'd like more evidence of him with Willa Trogo."

"What shall we do while the excellent Sergeant Yulich works his magic?" My wingman asked.

I glanced at the time and immediately felt my stomach giving birth to a growl of hunger. It was loud enough to hear, embarrassingly so.

"Eat. Figure out how we can annoy the ComCorp folks a bit more and see what might escape unwary lips."

"Make a plan to goad the Shrehari again," Arno added, "and ask Thopok why his navy is giving them a ride back home."

"Only after a substantial meal." I stood. "Major, care to dine on the Fleet's cred again?"

Pullar shook his head. "As much as I'd like to, and as much as I enjoy taking part in your investigation,

I have administrative work piling up. But I appreciate the invitation. I will, however, put tabs on Montague Hobart so we can haul him in for questioning the moment you ask."

"Much appreciated, Major. And we'll put a tracer on *Harpy* after lunch."

"I'll do that right now, Chief," Arno said, "if the Major can give me access to his secure communications channels again, I'll reach out to Sector HQ."

The Cimmerian touched his tablet and nodded at a terminal by the door. "Use that one."

My wingman busied himself for a few minutes. Then, he climbed to his feet and said, "One last thought. Has anyone considered asking when the meeting date between ComCorp and the Shrehari was set?"

"No, but let me guess. It'll have been a little over three months ago."

A slow smile parted Arno's beard. "That's what I think. Willa Trogo started working for the Aquilonia engineering section three months ago. Montague Hobart showed up here for the first time three months ago or at least his ship *Harpy* did. The two obviously knew each other."

"Why don't I give Gerri a call and find out?" As I turned to Pullar, he shook his head.

"No need, Chief Superintendent. I can find out when Aquilonia received notice of Shovak's visit. Dangerous Don likes to have these things announced well in advance. It's one of his few useful habits."

He touched his tablet's screen, waited for a few moments, humming almost inaudibly, then nodded to himself with satisfaction.

"ComCorp made the arrangements almost exactly fourteen weeks ago."

"And there's your third time again, Chief, except it's the sixth coincidence in a row." Arno patted his ample midriff. "Now we've established that, shall we go eat something before one of us faints from hunger?"

— Forty-One —

I took Arno to the Excelsior Court, in part to give him a taste of luxury on the Navy's expense account, but mostly because I was hoping to see the ComCorp people, something he figured out almost immediately.

"Are you eager to irritate your former partner and provoke a few unguarded, possibly incriminating words, Chief?" He asked as we strolled along the promenade, following the stately flow of foot traffic.

"Sure. Gerri's temper played a large part in her downfall back then. Why not try it again?"

The maître d' sat us at a table that allowed me to see the lobby and anyone entering the restaurant. He then handed us leather-bound menus and waved one of the service staff to our table.

"Enjoy your meal." He bowed and left us with a thin middle-aged woman whose attempt to hide old Star Wolf ink wasn't entirely successful. Confederacy of the Howling Stars members didn't just get VIP treatment on Aquilonia — they also found employment in one of its swankiest eateries. It shouldn't have surprised me, considering free ports were strange places where almost anything could happen. We ordered drinks — ale for Arno and tea for me, then scanned the offerings.

"Pricey," he said. "Way more than our normal meal allowance covers."

"The Fleet's paying and I doubt their bean counters will care enough to scream for reimbursement."

"Provided we pull the Navy's butt out of the fire, Chief. If we come up with a result they don't like, I figure they'll send a regiment of heavily armed auditors to hunt us down."

A sigh escaped my lips unbidden. "I see I'm not the only one who thinks we're being herded into a specific direction and expected to come up with a particular conclusion."

He nodded. "We've been given a role in some sort of spy game."

"And the role is providing the alibi. Or an alibi."

"I'd say we will *become* the alibi, and preferably before that Shrehari ship appears overhead." He nodded at the transparent ceiling. "We won't be able to prevent Thopok and company from leaving if they force the issue. Major Pullar's ability to back up our bluster has its limits. His superiors won't want the Cimmerian Gendarmerie involved with an interstellar incident, now that we've picked up the radioactive meteorite that fell into his lap."

"Speaking of radioactive..." I jerked my chin toward the lobby. "The ComCorp folks and Thopok just stepped out of the lift. They don't look particularly happy."

Arno, unconcerned about being noticed, turned in his seat and examined the cluster of humans surrounding the taller alien.

"Your ex-partner just saw you, Chief. Pardon me while I scramble away from what will shortly be incoming fire."

"Cheerful bugger, aren't you?"

"Voted cheeriest in the PCB. Or at least that's what they say in the canteen when they think I'm not listening."

"They're referring to the bugger part, Arno."

"So am I."

Gerri stalked up to our table, in much the same way as the last time I graced the Excelsior Court with my presence while the maître d' led the others to a secluded alcove.

"There's something disturbing about public servants living large at the taxpayer's expense," she said. "One time, I can understand, but this is ridiculous. Perhaps Ser Houko needs to discuss clientele filtering with the Excelsior's management."

"As in no cops allowed?" I asked in the arch tone of voice I knew she hated. "Is that everything you wished to convey, Sera Kazan?"

"No. I also wanted to let you know you're on the verge of getting an FTL missile up the backside for failing to charge the sole possible suspect in this lamentable matter and thereby wasting everyone's time."

"Oh? Do tell."

"My superiors have informed the Chief Constable of your lackadaisical attitude in dealing with the assassination of a Shrehari dignitary, something that has the potential to imperil relations between the Empire and the Commonwealth. Wyvern will tell you soon enough to charge Talyn and wrap it up. Oh, and the Shrehari delegation will leave on the ship coming to fetch them, no matter what you might believe. Gullible people may credit you with enough power to stop them, but I know you're bluffing."

I held her gaze for a few silent seconds, then asked in a soft tone, "Which superiors would that be, Gerri? The ComCorp lot or your *Sécurité Spéciale* bosses?"

Anyone other than I might have missed the subtle tightening of the skin around her eyes, but a sudden flash of concern behind those clear orbs gave me all the answers I wanted.

When she didn't reply, I said, "Perhaps we should look more closely at what's really going on here, beyond Shovak's death. You seem keen on getting both Thopok and me out of the way as fast as possible, to the point of wanting someone charged based on circumstantial evidence. And you never told me how you knew the identity of the suspect in Major Pullar's custody. That's something we should also investigate. Don't you think so, Inspector Galdi?"

"Definitely, Chief. Maybe Sera Kazan can stop by the police station later this afternoon for an interview."

Gerri glared at Arno for a few seconds before turning her angry eyes back on me. "You've been warned, Chief Superintendent. Sort this out within the next twenty hours, or prepare for orders sending you to a new duty station, something even less pleasant than the PCB. I hear the Constabulary intends to establish a detachment on Andoth. Living at the bottom of a ten-kilometer chasm should suit a rat like you."

We watched her walk away in silence while Arno grimaced. "Now there's a woman who's a bit spooked, pun intended."

"Yes, but is she, and by extension the *Sécurité Spéciale*, involved in Envoy Shovak's murder?"

"My gut instinct says no," he replied with a thoughtful mien. "Someone capable of turning an entire section of the surveillance suite into so much mindless junk without leaving the slightest hint of a trace can easily plant *Sécurité Spéciale* markers in the lift control programming. I think we were meant to realize the SecGen's minions are in play."

"Spy games. And we're the damned alibi," I replied, repeating Arno's earlier comment. "The question is why?"

"Once we figure that out, we'll know who and how, Chief."

"Agreed. Let's have Major Pullar reel in our helpful friend Montague Hobart for a chat."

I pulled out my borrowed Gendarmerie communicator and tapped out a brief message. His reply came almost immediately. Hobart would be waiting for us in an interview room by the time we finished our lunch.

When the server returned with our drinks, I found my appetite missing in action and settled for a chef's salad made with greens from Aquilonia's hydroponic gardens.

Arno, true to his appetite, went for the extravagantly priced steak platter, featuring meat from the best Cimmerian beef, shipped across millions of kilometers aboard a starship. If the Navy unleashed its auditors on us, this meal would become exhibit number one in the prosecution for gross mismanagement of government funds.

Funnily enough, I didn't care.

— Forty-Two —

“Hobart came willingly,” Pullar said when we checked in with him. “My desk sergeant says he acted as if it was an invitation to tea and cake rather than a police interview with the Constabulary’s much-feared Firing Squad.”

“Cheeky bastard,” Arno grumbled. “Entirely too much so for honesty.”

“No arguments from me, Inspector, though his parents might have been married to each other,” the Cimmerian replied, deadpan. “His sort always seems too much of something for honesty. We’ve not heard back about his ship, however.”

“That shouldn’t be an issue for now,” I replied. “I doubt it plays a central role in this affair.”

“We could always search *Harpy*,” Arno suggested.

“Without a warrant?” I asked. “What’s our probable cause?”

My wingman gave me a tolerant smile, the sort I get from my investigators when I have what they like to call a senior officer’s moment.

“I seem to recall Major Pullar telling us he has greater latitude in applying police powers here than he might on Cimmeria. Perhaps he feels some irregularity with Ser Hobart’s shipping license merits a safety inspection. Provided we don't expect to find evidence we might need in court..."

"I'm beginning to think nothing of this will ever end up before a judge and jury," I said, interrupting Arno.

He dipped his shaggy head in agreement. "More than likely."

I turned to our host. "Could you secure Ser Hobart's ship, please, Major? I think we'll search it after our interview. No one's allowed aboard until further notice."

"Of course, Chief Superintendent."

Hobart was waiting patiently in interview room number one, seated on a hard chair, arms crossed, and an almost meditative expression on his face. I had a momentary flash of Commander Talyn displaying the same dispassionate tolerance. We watched him on the video monitor for nearly a minute before entering.

As soon as he saw me, a broad smile replaced his contemplative mien. "Chief Superintendent. We must stop meeting like this. Folks will talk."

Arno and I each took a chair across the table from him without replying.

"Ser Hobart," I started, "thank you for accepting Major Pullar's invitation to this interview."

"Ser Hobart?" He parroted. "How chillingly formal. Monty does me just fine."

"But not me. We want to ask you a few questions related to our investigation of Envoy Shovak's murder."

"I'm not sure how I can help, but ask away." That easy smile never wavered, nor did the aura of nonchalant self-confidence.

I placed my tablet in the middle of the table and called up the missing engineer's picture.

"Who is this?"

"I'm sure you've already identified the lady, Chief Superintendent."

"Humor me."

"Willa Trogo, of course."

"And how do you know her?"

"How does someone like me befriend others? By offering them a cup of coffee or a drink, then letting them discover how much fun I can be. Surely you must have noticed when we had lunch the other day."

"Cut back on the smartassery, son," Arno growled, "and answer the chief properly."

Hobart arched an eyebrow at him. "I guess we found out who the bad cop is today. Or at least the cranky one. Please keep in mind I'm here voluntarily to help the Constabulary with its inquiries."

"Then tell us how you came to know Willa Trogo," I said, keeping my tone reasonable and even.

"I met her in the Aquilonia Arms — a pub favored by the locals, as you might have heard — a few months ago."

"Define a few months," Arno said.

Hobart's smile vanished, and his gaze shifted toward the ceiling, as if in thought.

"Three, I guess, give or take a week." His eyes met mine again. "It was during my first layover here with *Harpy*, and I wanted to celebrate a successful passage. Willa was at the bar by herself, nursing a gin and tonic. I offered to buy her a fresh one, made with real gin, imported from Earth, not the local swill distilled beneath the reactor core and flavored with rat droppings. She had just arrived from Cimmeria and was friendless."

"Was that your first visit to Aquilonia?"

He shook his head. "No. I used to come here a few years ago when I still had my previous ship."

"Why the absence? I'd have thought a free port such as this would be a favored spot for an import-export specialist."

A self-deprecating shrug accompanied a grin that was half-guilty, half-sly. "A falling-out with an important client kept me at a distance, for my own safety, you understand, Chief Superintendent. Said client no longer operates on Aquilonia, or anywhere else for that matter, if the rumors are true. It meant I could safely make this place a base of operations once again."

"With a new ship."

"Yes, with a new ship. I acquired it not long after my abrupt departure from Aquilonia. My falling-out with the aforementioned client left me with funds to recycle."

"Launder, you mean."

"I prefer the term recycle. It sounds much more socially conscious even if it is feel-good bunkum at best."

Arno said, "I'll make a note to let the Financial Crimes Division know about Ser Hobart's recycling efforts. There may be an award in it for him — handed out at an appropriate ceremony in a penal colony on Parth."

"Please, Inspector Galdi," the smuggler replied with mock dismay. "It was a little off-the-books trading, not a federal crime."

"We'll see about that," my wingman grumbled. "I will also have the Transportation Safety Agency do a follow-up on his ships, both old and new."

"Excellent idea, Inspector." I gave Hobart my full attention once more. "Back to Willa Trogo. You met her on your first day here after an extended absence. How long had she been on Aquilonia when you first encountered her?"

He made a dismissive gesture. "I don't know. A week, perhaps two."

"How did your relationship progress after that first gin and tonic?"

"Slowly. We didn't jump into bed right away if that's what you're thinking."

"When did you?"

"During my second layover with *Harpy*. Willa and I had a great time spending my profits, and I treated her to a night at the Excelsior. The rest, as they say, happened behind closed doors, since a gentleman never tells."

Arno's snort of derision was loud enough to wake the dead — on Cimmeria. But my wingman didn't back down under Hobart's scornful glare.

"In a murder investigation," Arno said, "what happens behind closed doors becomes part of the official record, gentlemen included."

"As you wish." Hobart glanced at his fingernails. "Willa found our night very enjoyable. Enough to ensure have a warm bed or a bed warmer, as the case may be, every time I touched port. *Harpy* has a nice stateroom, lest you think I cheapened out on her after that first time."

"Did your relationship progress beyond casual sex? Or was she simply the one in *this* port?" Arno asked in a gruff voice.

"I'm not one to bed them and leave them, Inspector. We had wonderful times together outside the boudoir."

"And what is it a scoundrel such as you had in common with a mousy, middle-aged engineer? I'd have pegged you as one who prefers the sort of entertainer working in the gaudier promenade establishments."

"What would you know about my preferences, Inspector? I happen to find Willa rather endearingly cute and exceedingly well-informed in many fields, able to hold up her end of any conversation." An exasperated expression creased his brow. "May I ask what this is supposed to be in aid of, considering neither Willa nor I had anything to do with your murdered bonehead?"

"Keep humoring us, Ser Hobart," I said. "The point will become apparent. Are you aware of Willa Trogo's recent movements?"

"Certainly. She's on Cimmeria, visiting with family. It's her first leave since arriving on Aquilonia."

"You're close, yet she went on leave without you?"

"I have unavoidable business dealings to sort out, Chief Superintendent. Besides, we're good friends, but we're not attached at the hip thanks to an antiquated idea of relationships. Again, why this line of inquiry?"

"Would it surprise you to know Trogo's credentials were used to access restricted systems after she left Aquilonia?"

"Yes, it would. Willa's not so careless as to share them with anyone."

"Not even you?" Arno gave him a skeptical scowl.

"Heavens, Inspector. What would I do with her credentials? If she were working in Aquilonia's finance department, I might be interested. But engineering? I can keep my ship in good enough condition, but that's mostly out of sheer familiarity. And for the third time, how does this concern your murder investigation?"

"We believe whoever used her credentials helped the perpetrator, Ser Hobart," I replied. "And since it happened after Sera Trogo's departure, we can be reasonably confident she wasn't directly involved.

But it's a near certainty she either gave her credentials to someone else or was careless with them."

"Really?" Hobart sat back with an air of disbelief. "I'm sure once you speak with Willa, you'll discover she's neither venal nor careless."

"That, I fear, might be impossible," Arno said in a somber voice. "The Howard's Landing Police Department has reason to believe Willa Trogo perished in a traffic accident shortly after her arrival on Cimmeria."

"What?" Hobart half rose from his chair. "You're joking. What do you mean have reason to believe?"

"The accident caused a conflagration hot enough to destroy any human tissues. Thus, identification can never be certain, but evidence points to Sera Trogo as the victim. No one has seen her or heard from her since she exited the Howard's Landing spaceport."

"That's impossible." Hobart shook his head, dismay twisting his face. "Do you suspect..."

"The Cimmerian authorities are investigating her death," I said. "You'll have to ask them what they suspect."

"Did Trogo have any other close friends on Aquilonia?" Arno asked.

"Not that I'm aware. Willa is — was solitary and content with her own company, perhaps even a tad anti-social. Unless I was in port. I suppose I could have served as her emotional release, something she required only every so often."

"And you don't know how or why her credentials were used to access restricted networks during her absence?"

"Not a clue, Inspector. Perhaps if you told me which networks, I might be able to help."

"As you said earlier, you're not an engineer, so I doubt it." Arno's dismissive, almost contemptuous tone was designed to get a rise out of Hobart. It failed. He merely shrugged and turned his eyes on me again.

"What do you know about Sera Trogo's past?" I asked.

He exhaled noisily, his face sagging with sadness. When he spoke, it was in a mournful tone. "Not much. We were concerned with the present. I didn't discuss my checkered career, and she didn't regale me with anything more than a few amusing stories about her pilgrimage through the Rim's less savory outposts. She was an itinerant engineer, just as I'm an itinerant trader. We talked about the wonders of the universe. We also discussed music, the older, the better, debated literature, politics, and amused ourselves with people watching. You'd be amazed at the assortment one encounters in a place such as this. Every example of humanity's variety eventually passes through Aquilonia. It's the nature of a free port."

"Did she mention anything out of the ordinary to you, or seem in an unusual mood the last time you met, right before her departure? You were sharing a window-side table in the Aquilonia Arms, I believe."

"No. The prospect of breathing real air and feeling real gravity after three months under Eoghan Neild's gimlet eye excited Willa."

"One would think that after a decade spent moving from one artificial habitat to another, she wouldn't find three months here a hardship."

"Our perspectives change as we age, Chief Superintendent. The taste for adventure fades in favor of one more heavily weighted toward comfort and security." He sighed. "All I can tell you is that she looked forward to a brief vacation on Cimmeria. Was there anything else, or can I go hoist a quiet gin and tonic in memory of a good friend?"

I glanced at Arno, who gave me a minute shake of the head.

"It'll be all for now, Ser Hobart, but please don't leave Aquilonia without my permission. We may have further questions for you."

"You're holding me here? But I have a business to run."

"Another day or two won't harm your affairs," Arno replied. "You'll make it up by pushing your hyperdrives harder or squeezing a higher payment from your next mark — pardon me, I mean client. Leave without the chief's say-so, and the Navy won't be as lenient as before."

Hobart nodded once. "Understood, Inspector."

"Oh," I added, rising to my feet, "we'll be going over your ship from stem to stern with Major Pullar's folks. We don't need you for that, but I suggest you give us access if you don't want airlocks and such damaged."

"You intend to search *Harpy*? On what grounds? I've done nothing wrong."

"I'm sure Major Pullar has found enough grounds while we were talking, Ser Hobart. You've not had a permanent notation in the Constabulary's files up to now, though for reasons we don't understand, the Navy likes to keep you in mind. Continued cooperation will make sure matters stay as they are."

The smuggler raised his hands in surrender. "Very well. You'll have my full cooperation if only to ensure the station's finest don't mar *Harpy*'s finish. She's no longer under warranty. I'll gladly give you a full tour."

Arno and I stood. “Thank you. Please wait here for us. We won’t be but a few minutes, and then we’ll head for the docks together.”

— Forty-Three —

When we were in the corridor, I asked my wingman, "What do you think?"

"Starting from the premise of no coincidences in a murder investigation, much less a case potentially involving three separate intelligence agencies, I'd say Montague Hobart is a good liar and a decent actor. His reaction to the news of Willa Trogo's demise was right on point. Perhaps a little too much on point, but that may be my natural distrust of humanity showing."

"Perhaps we should have asked him about his movements on the night of Envoy Shovak's assassination."

Arno nodded. "Perhaps, and had we done so, he would have presented us with an alibi he could neither fully prove and we couldn't entirely disprove. Have you decided Hobart is more than just a helpful member of the public?"

"I suppose so. Let's see what alibi he can offer."

When my wingman and I sat once more across from Hobart, he gazed at us with an expectant air.

"Back so soon? Did you forget something?"

"Where were you on the evening of Envoy Shovak's murder?"

A faint smile creased his mischievous features. "And we've finally come to it, Chief Superintendent. In what way have I suddenly joined the list of potential witnesses to the crime if not that of suspects?"

"You need to ask, Ser Hobart? Surely a man with your appreciation of law enforcement can draw a line through the various events surrounding this case and end up with us sitting here, contemplating my question."

"I'm ruing the day I volunteered to serve as your interpreter."

I gave him a cold smile. "That was rather convenient, wasn't it? Since we've found a connection between you and our case via the late Willa Trogo, I have to wonder whether good luck placed you in my path, or whether someone contrived it."

"Come now, Chief Superintendent. How would I maneuver my way into your investigation based on linguistic ability? I don't know you, or your inspector, nor did I know beforehand you weren't conversant in Shrehari and needed an interpreter."

A mocking lilt had crept into his voice, something I found strangely irksome.

"How would you like to give us an overview of your whereabouts on the evening in question, Ser Hobart?" Arno asked in his grumpy cop tone.

"Should I call my solicitor?"

"We've not cautioned you yet, and you're free to refuse us an answer. But if you do so, we will caution you, and make this interview part of the formal record."

The smuggler raised his shoulders in a gesture of pure indifference. "I was at the Aquilonia Arms until just short of twenty-four-hundred hours, station time. Then I returned to my ship and went to sleep. The regular barflies will confirm my presence at the Arms. And I'm sure Major Pullar's surveillance network tracked my movements to the docks and noted I didn't step off *Harpy* until after oh-eight-hundred the next morning, something my ship's log will confirm."

As Arno had predicted, an alibi we couldn't entirely disprove. I gave my wingman a glance, and he nodded before tapping on his tablet's screen.

"We'll know about your movements to and from the docks momentarily, Ser Hobart," I replied.

"Provided the relevant sensors aren't broken. Lax maintenance seems to be a curse in these parts."

I could have sworn I saw a faint hint of mockery in his deep brown eyes. Was he toying with us?

"But seriously, Chief Superintendent," he continued. "If you believe I have something to do with Envoy Shovak's death, you're grasping at hydrogen atoms in a vacuum. I've had enough dealings with the Shrehari to develop a healthy respect for their fighting prowess. Granted, I'm not a small man by human standards, but still nowhere strong enough to face one of them with a mere blade. And I have no motive to involve myself in such a deed. I'd rather keep my freedom to visit the Empire. There will always be profit in cross-border trade, especially now that the *Kho'sahra* is tightening his grip on legal channels and funneling everything through his favorites, such as *Quch Mech*."

"Why is he tightening his grip?" I asked.

"Control, Chief Superintendent. The current dictator isn't as comfortable on his throne as he might wish. By controlling trade with the Commonwealth, he keeps a tighter leash on the mercantile class, and through them, the nobles who finance commercial ventures. Those would be the nobles who also provide most of the officers for their military and security forces. It wouldn't shock me to see restrictions that favor a handful of politically safe Shrehari and human corporations to the exclusion of others."

Arno and I exchanged curious glances. Why the sudden tangent? Was Hobart attempting to tell us something? Or was this meant as a diversion?

"Are you saying the *Kho'sahra* considers *Quch Mech*, Shovak's employer, and ComCorp politically safe?"

"Sure — they're both on Aquilonia, the sector's leading free port, talking trade without an army of bureaucrats hovering over them, aren't they? I'd say they're also considered politically safe by the SecGen's office. When the Commonwealth's largest zaibatsu glances at the Empire with avarice in its heart, the executive branch pays attention. It's no secret ComCorp has friends in high office on Earth, even the highest one, if you believe the rumors."

"You know what a zaibatsu is, Ser Hobart?" Arno asked. "I didn't think the term was in general use outside the Constabulary."

"Sure, it's an old Japanese term for politically influential family-owned industrial and financial conglomerates. I must have picked it up somewhere in my travels."

I recalled that Talyn had also used the term, but it hadn't struck me as unusual, probably because I assumed it was part of Navy lingo. Now, I had to wonder.

"And what would this discourse on Shrehari politics have to do with Shovak's death, Ser Hobart?"

"I don't know, Chief Superintendent. Perhaps everything, perhaps nothing."

"Meaning?"

"Perhaps Shovak died to disrupt whatever *Quch Mech*, and by extension, the *Kho'sahra*, are cooking up with ComCorp and its political allies. Or maybe Thopok killed him in a fit of Shrehari pique. Or perhaps a bit of both. The Shrehari psyche is hard to fathom at the best of times."

"Why are you suddenly being so helpful, Ser Hobart?" Arno asked in a tone oozing with incredulity. My wingman had a lock on over-the-top disbelief when interviewing suspects.

"Since you seem intent on shoving me into the frame, I thought I'd share my hard-won knowledge to explain why I couldn't possibly be involved. Mind you, I'm not in a position to explain how I came by said information, but if you check it with your criminal intelligence folks, they'll confirm what I said."

"You're not really a tax avoiding import-export specialist, are you?" I asked.

He gave me a winning smile. "I most certainly am. But like many of my kind, I also freelance for anyone who buys information, no questions asked and is willing to line my pockets with money. Traders can go places and see things without arousing suspicion."

Arno nodded with a grunt. "Anyone, in your case means the Navy. That explains why you've never been charged, even though you've been stopped and searched many times."

Hobart sketched a mock salute at us. "Exactly. I'm something of an unofficial expert on our Shrehari neighbors, or at least on Shrehari matters that aren't widely known outside the Empire. The Navy pays well for such information, especially when it's obtained without involving their own agents. And now I'm sharing it with you at no cost as a gesture of goodwill and cooperation."

"Were you here this time to meet with Commander Talyn and share the latest results of your xenoethnological studies?" I asked.

"Commander Talyn?" He shook his head. "No idea who that is. I don't usually meet buyers where we can be seen. The exchange of money for data happens mostly in interstellar space, during a stop and search by the Navy. When the Navy is buying, of course. Other clients, other methods."

I expected him to ask whether Talyn was the suspect in Pullar's custody. But he showed no curiosity at hearing the name, no reaction whatsoever, in fact. That in itself raised my suspicions.

"You mentioned that you wished to tour *Harpy*," he said. "Shall we do so now?"

— Forty-Four —

Hobart's ship was a nice, trim little free trader. Over-engined and over-gunned, as Arno remarked, but the visit gave us no new clues, let alone fresh evidence.

After releasing the smuggler and returning to the conference room, Arno, Major Pullar, and I sat through Yulich's latest extracts. They proved to be informative if puzzling.

We caught Hobart crossing paths with both Talyn and Gerri Kazan in the twelve hours before Shovak's death. Our sole suspect and the smuggler showed no signs of knowing each other. But he and Gerri briefly spoke on the promenade a few hours before the reception in Shovak's quarters.

"We'll need to interview Hobart again," Arno said in a resigned tone.

I nodded. "After we ask Gerri about her connection with him. Did we find evidence of Hobart returning to his ship in the hour before Shovak's death?"

"We do," Yulich replied, calling up a brief video of the smuggler entering his assigned docking arm at five minutes after midnight. "He doesn't appear again until oh-eight-hundred."

"Could he have left the docks unseen?"

Pullar shook his head. “Not unless he knows about the hidden maintenance tunnels and has the right codes to access them, something I would consider unlikely. His alibi seems good.”

“More’s the pity,” Arno muttered.

“Is it possible to spoof the sensors?” I asked.

Pullar glanced at his sergeant, who said, “An expert can fool just about any surveillance system, sir, but I checked the sensor units and the network records, and they show no evidence of tampering. Everything is working as it should. Nor is there any record of someone accessing the maintenance tunnels during the relevant timeframe.”

“Whoever wiped the sensors near Shovak’s quarters and screwed with the lift controls could have messed with anything else on Aquilonia and left no traces,” Arno remarked. “And filched one of your closely held codes.”

“Sure, and if that’s the case, we may never know.”

Yet the truth was out there. We had most of the pieces: Trogo’s supposed death; the ever helpful Hobart and his convenient alibi; Talyn claiming innocence, never mind not having the size or strength to kill a Shrehari; and a three-sided spy game on top of everything else.

They were connected. I could feel linkages just beyond the reach of my conscious mind. My subconscious was processing clues that hadn’t registered yet, things I’d seen, heard, or read in the last few days, perhaps even in the last few hours. Something...

“Run that sequence with Hobart and Talyn crossing paths again, Sergeant,” I said, suddenly sure my answer lay in what we weren’t supposed to see.

A view of the promenade reappeared on the wall-sized display, showing a steady parade of humans and nonhumans, most walking with purpose but a few merely idling. Telemetry data in the bottom right corner gave date, time, and location.

"Can you give us the full, three-dimensional rendering?"

Yulich nodded. "I'll have to project it onto the table, sir, and that means a reduced scale."

"It doesn't matter. I want to see full body imaging of Talyn and Hobart."

"What's up, Chief?" Arno had evidently sensed my mood change.

"Watch our two friends from the moment they enter each other's line of sight," I replied. "Watch their entire bodies. Move around the table and watch them from every angle."

"Why?" Pullar seemed genuinely puzzled.

"Best do what the chief wants," Arno said. "When she gets like this, it often means we're on the verge of a breakthrough."

I turned to Yulich. "Run it, Sergeant."

While the sequence played, I walked around the table, staring intently at the miniature rendition of a sparsely populated promenade at twenty-hundred hours on the day of the cocktail party in Envoy Shovak's quarters. Five hours before his death. Pullar and Arno imitated me while Yulich frowned in puzzlement.

"Play it again from the beginning," I said when the first run-through ended.

It took three repetitions before I finally spotted what my subconscious had noted the first time.

"Freeze the playback, Sergeant." The three men turned their eyes on me when the holographic figures stopped moving while they were less than two meters apart, almost facing each other. “Did either of you detect anything unusual about Talyn and Hobart?”

Pullar shook his head. “No. They seem to be acting like perfect strangers.”

“You know, I don’t think that’s correct,” Arno said, his brow puckering. He kept his eyes on the projection and said, “Can you zoom in please, Sergeant? Double the scale if you would.”

The answer sat on the tip of my tongue, eager to erupt into words. But I needed to hear someone else point out the same thing I’d seen, if only to prove it wasn’t wishful thinking on my part.

My wingman grunted as he leaned over to place his shaggy head straight into the hologram, eyes at the height of Hobart’s foreshortened face. “They’re not looking at each other straight on, but slightly downward, near waist level. A tad unusual, I’d say.”

I mentally urged Arno to make the next connection and prove I was right. When he didn’t notice what I’d seen, I asked Yulich to set the projection in motion again, but this time at a third of the speed.

“Aha!” Arno straightened his back. “I believe the chief saw a brief burst of dancing fingers as Hobart and Talyn neared each other. Play the entire sequence again, please Sergeant, but keep it at one-third speed, and zoom in on Hobart’s hands.”

Yes. Blessings on the deities that had given me a sharp investigative mind like Arno Galdi’s.

Yulich played it once, focused on Hobart, then again, focused on Talyn. The conclusion became so inescapable that even Pullar understood what we saw. Fingers that were still when their owners entered the sensor’s pickup range became almost frantic for a few seconds as Talyn and Hobart passed each other.

"They were communicating in sign language," Pullar said in what was almost a whisper of awe. "Hobart was lying. He knows Talyn."

I nodded. "Precisely, Major. Which makes me doubt he's a mere smuggler who occasionally sells intelligence to the Navy."

"Yet since we saw him speak with Gerri Kazan, they may also know each other. And you suspect her of being *Sécurité Spéciale*."

Arno made a sour face. "He could be a double agent. If he's a real freelancer, he'll be playing every angle that brings the slightest chance of profit."

"Definitely," Pullar said. "The slick bugger has always struck me as devious."

"Aye. Who do we interrogate first, Chief? Talyn, Hobart, or your former partner?"

I hesitated. Had the key to unlock this case shifted once more? This time from Hobart to Talyn? Or to Gerri? And why did Willa Trogo's face just swim past my mind's eye?

"Sergeant Yulich, could you pull up the surveillance video clips of Hobart and Willa Trogo you compiled earlier, please?"

"Sure thing, sir."

I stood and wandered over to a work board dominating one wall. It was a model in wide use by most police forces, the Constabulary included, and it didn't take me long to draw a schematic summarizing the facts we knew to date, though Pullar helped bring up visuals.

"Three women." I pointed at Talyn, Trogo, and Gerri's pictures in turn. "Same general phenotype, age, and build. Even their facial bone structures seem remarkably similar, now that I think about it. One openly identified as Naval Intelligence, one corporate security but suspected of being *Sécurité Spéciale*, and one who disappeared. The latter left behind credentials that allowed a murderer to commit the deed and a saboteur to warn me away. Montague Hobart, a self-avowed smuggler, knows them. He has no law enforcement records but has connections with the Navy, which arraigns him often but releases him without charges. Is he the sole common point, or are the three women somehow known to each other directly as well?"

"Talyn and Kazan could be acquainted," Arno said, "if the latter works for an organization at odds with the Navy. Trogo? Nothing in her record shows links with security or intelligence agencies, but a decade working on outposts along the Rim, some of dubious legality, might have brought her into contact with the dark side."

"Trogo's record, indeed. One that claims years spent far away from the Cimmerian system, followed by a return home to work for a company now belonging to our favorite zaibatsu. And then, suddenly, she changes jobs again and comes to Aquilonia just in time for delicate negotiations involving Shrehari who might be intelligence operatives. We know almost nothing about her life, other than what's on her employment record. It makes you wonder, doesn't it? And now she's vanished. Oh, the Howard's Landing Police Department thinks she perished without leaving a trace in a conflagration powerful enough to carbonize any organic matter. Doesn't that seem almost too convenient? What if Trogo never existed?"

The major stared at me, incomprehension writ large in his eyes, but Arno's luxuriant beard quivered with a sudden burst of excitement.

"Of course," he said. "Someone created Willa Trogo from whole cloth to infiltrate Aquilonia's engineering section with the express purpose of accessing secure networks. The job done, she's no longer needed, and returns to the oblivion whence she came."

With another piece of the puzzle in place, I tapped the work board. "What would you say if I told you one of these two played the part of Willa Trogo, gentlemen. I doubt we'll come across a new, as yet unknown player on Aquilonia at this stage of the game."

Arno grinned. "I'd say you were on to something. A shame we've not yet traced Kazan or Talyn's movements further back than the day of their arrival on Valerys."

"We saw Commander Talyn arriving on Valerys Station aboard the transport *Xenophon*, whose previous stop was Nabhka, six light years away," Pullar said. "Talyn could hardly play Trogo if she wasn't in this system at the same time."

"True." I smiled at our host. "But only if it was indeed Talyn who stepped off *Xenophon* and not someone disguised as her."

"Perhaps." He sounded dubious. "Yet if either Talyn or Kazan played Trogo for three months, I'd say it's more likely to have been the latter. Ockham's razor, Chief Superintendent. We *know* she didn't arrive on Valerys aboard a starship coming from another system a few hours earlier."

"The biggest stumbling block remains motive, Chief. If Gerri Kazan played Trogo, what's her motive in facilitating the assassination, considering her employer was about to engage in highly profitable trade negotiations with Shovak? If Hobart wasn't feeding us horse manure earlier about the SecGen's interest in controlling trade with the Empire, and she really is *Sécurité Spéciale*, she would have even less motive."

"Agreed, Arno." I turned to Yulich. "Did you line up the relevant video sequences, Sergeant?"

"Yes, sir."

"Play them in reverse chronological order, please, starting with the bit taken of them in the Aquilonia Arms. Zoom in on Hobart and Trogo's hands."

I saw understanding dawn in the eyes of both Cimmerians. My wingman gave me a sardonic smile, proof he'd made the same leap of logic I had.

— Forty-Five —

"I see a lot of touching, but no finger dances like the ones we observed when Hobart passed Talyn on the promenade," Pullar said after we watched Hobart and Trogo's last meeting in the Aquilonia Arms.

"Is it just me, or does none of it look like what you'd expect between two people in love, or at least in lust?" I asked. "Those caresses aren't anything of the sort, are they?" I turned to Yulich. "Could you please zoom in on their hands and reduce the speed to one-third, Sergeant?"

"Sure thing, sir."

"Aha." Arno nodded with vigorous satisfaction. "Finger dances of a different variety. They're talking."

"What are the odds of Hobart interacting with two different people using sign language, in the space of what? Seventy-two hours, give or take?" I asked the room at large. "His last contact with Trogo and his first, albeit hidden contact with Talyn?"

"Are you saying this confirms Talyn and Trogo are the same person?" Pullar's tone remained one of cautious skepticism. "Then how do we explain Talyn passing through arrivals control on Valerys Station while Trogo's ferry from Aquilonia was still inbound?"

"Simple. The Talyn we have in your cells isn't the one that stepped off *Xenophon* three days before Shovak's murder."

"And what about the Trogo that passed through Howard's Landing after taking the shuttle from Valerys? We know she didn't turn around and board the next shuttle up, along with the ComCorp folks. And a later one would have made her miss the ferry's return to Aquilonia."

"Perhaps the Talyn who arrived on *Xenophon* became the Trogo tagged by Howard's Landing arrivals control," Arno suggested. "While the Trogo that arrived on the Aquilonia ship turned into the Talyn you now hold."

"Pardon my doubt, Chief Superintendent, but doesn't that sound incredibly convoluted? Wouldn't it be simpler if Trogo turned herself into Gerri Kazan at the spaceport before joining the ComCorp delegation?"

"Perhaps that's what we're meant to think, Major."

Pullar had a point. If Trogo was Talyn, then we had at least one more person involved, the woman who vanished on Cimmeria. She undeniably existed.

And if my former partner had been the one moonlighting as an engineer on Aquilonia, it didn't call for more players. Yet I couldn't help but feel the Navy had a higher motive for Shovak's assassination than the *Sécurité Spéciale* — if that was Gerri's real employer — let alone ComCorp.

"Run the sequence showing Hobart and Kazan again, Sergeant."

He did.

"No finger work," Arno said once we'd watched it in slow motion. "But it'll be damn near impossible to read their lips. They're using the old troublemaker's trick of vocalizing with minimal lip movement. That adds weight to your suspicion Kazan isn't just a corporate executive, Chief."

"Let's find out how far back the touch-talking between Hobart and Trogo goes. Run the remaining sequences, please, Sergeant."

Interestingly enough, we saw only one other instance, shortly after the two supposedly first met, but encountered three more manifestations of dancing fingers. What were the odds that two people, ostensibly unknown to each other before they met three months ago, could speak in sign and touch languages that took time to perfect?

When I voiced the thought, Arno said, "The odds aren't *that* bad, Chief. Tactile codes aren't restricted to secretive government agencies. Organized crime syndicates, like our Howler friends, have their own versions, and you can develop only so many offshoots of the universal sign language before they resemble each other. Both Trogo and Hobart would have rubbed elbows with Confederacy members or others of their ilk on the Rim."

Pullar's communicator pinged unexpectedly. He glanced at it and then frowned. "Chief Superintendent, we've just received a message directly from Wyvern addressed to you. It's from Deputy Chief Constable Hammett. Isn't he your boss?"

"He is indeed the Commander-in-Chief of the Firing Squad," Arno said. "And when he reaches out across the light years to commune with us, it's never good news."

"If you want to hear it in private, feel free to use my office. I'll have it piped to my terminal."

I already had an idea of what the message would say and shook my head. "No need. Run it on the side display, please, Major. You and Arno should hear this."

The sergeant sprang to his feet and dipped his angular head. "If you have no objection, I'll take the occasion to refresh myself and leave you to it."

After he'd left, I gave Pullar a knowing smile. "Sergeant Yulich is a perceptive man. He cleared out before I had to ask."

"He's actually wasted here," the major replied. "But he has a young family back on Cimmeria, and the extra pay we earn during a tour on Aquilonia is a welcome bonus. He'll be returning home with an efficiency report that should get him promoted to staff sergeant and assigned where he can use his skills to good effect. Now, about your message... Are you sure you want me to witness it?"

"It may be our case, but it's still your territory, Major."

A grim chuckle escaped his lips. "If only your colleagues were as diplomatic as you are. I've dealt with investigators from your Organized Crime Division, and they seem to believe we Cimmerian Gendarmes are no better than mushrooms."

"I beg your pardon?"

"Kept in the dark and fed organic waste."

That sounded like the hotshot detectives of Organized Crime all right. They disliked sharing information because they believed anyone, even fellow members of the Constabulary, could be taking bribes from the bad guys. Which was ironic because the Organized Crime Division accounted for a plurality of my corruption cases.

"I've queued the message," he continued. "Whenever you want."

"Play it."

Deputy Chief Constable Maximilian Hammett's pinched face came into focus. I'd last met him in person when he appointed me to head the Rim Sector's PCB detachment a few years earlier, and he looked unchanged beneath that brush of iron-gray hair.

Hammett was one of those men who could pass for any age between fifty and ninety. And I had the sneaking suspicion his disapproving schoolmaster's appearance dated back to well before he joined the ranks of the Firing Squad.

"Chief Superintendent Morrow," he began, in a low raspy voice that always seemed at odds with his severe demeanor, "as you know, I hate to interfere with ongoing investigations. It creates the sort of mess that jeopardizes a successful prosecution. However, circumstances compel me to issue orders which you will obey without question. I'm sure your handling of this case is beyond reproach. But, you have been generating enough turmoil to bring unwelcome attention from the Secretary General's office, attention that might cause the Chief Constable to feel the PCB is overstepping its bounds. That could entail unfortunate consequences. Therefore, you will release the remains of Envoy Shovak and the surviving members of the Shrehari delegation into the custody of their compatriots when the imperial transport arrives on Aquilonia. You will also endeavor to give the captain of the Shrehari vessel a report on your investigation. It would be preferable if said report identifies Envoy Shovak's assassin. Finally, you will refrain from interviewing members of the ComCorp delegation as of now. I expect to receive an acknowledgment of these orders by return subspace message soonest. Hammett, out."

"I guess Ser Houko has the right connections, or at least his boss does," Arno said in a quiet tone after we had digested my commanding officer's message in silence. "A shame this didn't come in after we asked Sera Kazan about her connection with Montague Hobart."

When my wingman saw a mischievous smile twisting my lips, he sighed. "I fear we're about to witness an act of gross insubordination — again."

"Perhaps not gross," I said. "Has your communications officer logged his receipt of the message, Major?"

"No." He shook his head. "Not knowing how you wanted your correspondence handled, I've ordered messages shunted to a quarantined folder until you told us what to do."

"In that case, we will wait until after our interview with Gerri Kazan to log receipt of DCC Hammett's message."

Arno grunted. "Thereby violating the spirit of his orders via a most underhanded subterfuge. If we weren't the PCB, we'd surely open ourselves to an investigation by it. But, you're the chief, Chief. Dare I hope you intend to speak with Sera Kazan this afternoon, so as not to drag out your act of rebellion?"

"You may dare. I wanted to tackle Talyn first since we have her at hand, but needs must."

To say I was entirely comfortable fudging DCC Hammett's orders would have been a lie. He may have seemed like a middle-aged schoolmaster, but there was nothing academic about his ruthlessness, honed by decades of experience.

In private circles, Hammett was known as the Constabulary's Conscience, and that wasn't always meant as a compliment. But I couldn't believe he was entirely happy with his orders either.

We were intended as the final line of resistance against political interference and every time we retreated in the face of pressure, we lost a little of our aura as the last incorruptibles. But Hammett probably expected me to take a few liberties with his orders. He wasn't one to micromanage across several dozen light years. Still, I'd never know, and I wasn't about to ask.

"Major, can your folks track down Gerri Kazan for me?"

"Certainly."

"And you're welcome to join us for this interview."

"Thanks, but it's best I don't, just in case I'm asked about your movements after your DCC's message arrived." He gave me a shy grin. "Plausible deniability, right?"

— Forty-Six —

“What do you want now?” Gerri asked the moment she saw us standing in front of her room’s open door. “Hasn’t Wyvern told you to lay off the harassment yet?”

“Apparently not, since we’re here. You might remember that I never disobey orders.” My tone was so sweet it caused her eyes to harden with suspicion. “We need answers about your connection to a man named Montague Hobart. We’ve seen a video sequence of you speaking to him on the promenade a few hours after your arrival.”

Gerri gave me an exaggerated sigh, the sort she used to mask anxiety rather than express irritation. Though that might have changed since I last worked with her.

She stepped aside and invited us in with a lazy wave of the hand. Once we were in her suite’s lobby, she leaned against a wall, crossed her arms, and glared at me, apparently unwilling to let us go any further. Since the door to her sitting room was shut, I wondered whether she had a visitor we weren’t meant to see. Or was she being inhospitable on principle?

"So I spoke with a random individual on the promenade. What of it? Is he a wanted criminal? Am I suspected of aiding and abetting?"

"We couldn't overhear your conversation, but that's not unexpected with the ambient noise. What struck us as strange was the fact we couldn't read your lips either. Both of you vocalized with as little lip movement as possible. It's not something one does when meeting a random stranger in a crowded place, so it attracted our attention. Who is Montague Hobart to you, Sera Kazan?"

"I fail to understand how that pertains to your investigation, Chief Superintendent. Unless this man is a suspect, I am not obliged to discuss my dealings with him."

"As a matter of fact, he is a suspect."

I had the satisfaction of seeing a reaction, faint as it was, when her jaw muscles jumped. Although I had no qualms about stretching the truth when questioning witnesses, I realized it wasn't actually a lie. Hobart was slowly slipping into the frame.

"His dealings with you are part of my investigation," I said. "What is your connection to Montague Hobart? Keep in mind we'll be asking him the same question once we're done with you."

She chewed on my words for a few moments, then said, "If you believe Hobart might be involved in Shovak's assassination, then surely you know by now he's an information broker and not just a smuggler. His forays into the Empire and other hard to reach places give him a unique opportunity to collect data useful for commercial operations. As the ComCorp security executive for the Rim Division, I run our in-house intelligence collection and analysis team. We obtain most of our material from freelancers such as Hobart."

"For a price."

She nodded. "For a steep price."

"How long have you been buying information from Hobart?"

"A year, perhaps longer. I don't deal with sources directly. My staff does that."

"Was this your first encounter with Hobart?"

"It was. He intercepted me on the promenade, using the recognition code we'd given him when he first approached us to sell information."

"What did he want?"

"To introduce himself and tell me he'd come upon intelligence about Shrehari trade we might find interesting enough for a bonus on top of the usual."

"And your reply was?"

"I told him to contact his normal handler since I don't deal with sources directly."

"How did he react?"

"He thanked me, and we each went our own way." Gerri held my gaze long enough to convince me she was telling the truth. "I hope that's it, Chief Superintendent, and I sincerely hope I never see your face again."

"It is. Thank you for your cooperation, Sera Kazan. Enjoy the rest of your stay on Aquilonia."

The door opened at her touch and Arno, who was closest, stepped into the corridor. But I stopped on the threshold and snapped my fingers as if I'd just remembered something. I turned to face Gerri.

"Just one more question, Sera Kazan. Who is Willa Trogo?"

This time, she showed no sign of recognition, not even a twitch. Knowing Gerri, it was the only proof I needed that she hadn't impersonated our mysterious engineer. The name meant nothing to her.

"I have no idea, Chief Superintendent."

"Somehow, I didn't think so."

Once on the promenade, I asked, "Did Gerri have a visitor in her sitting room? Someone she didn't want us to see? Or was she being a bitch on general principles?"

"Easy enough to figure out, Chief. Why don't we find an innocuous observation post and keep watch on the Excelsior's front door?"

I pointed at a café across the promenade. "Fancy a cup of something? My treat."

We took a window table and placed our order, which materialized within moments. After taking an appreciative sip of a coffee confection that seemed more sugar than caffeine, Arno said, "You've come to one or more conclusions, Chief. I can feel it."

"Why? Am I surrounded by an aura visible only to my loyal, hardworking team?"

"Pretty much."

"Gerri didn't impersonate Willa Trogo. She didn't react at the name, and trust me, Gerri isn't that good at hiding her emotions."

"So we're left with Talyn, is that it?"

"Yes. There's something else, however. That chance meeting between Hobart and Gerri on the promenade the day before Shovak's death — I'm sure it wasn't by accident. I'd give odds on Hobart setting it up solely to provide evidence he and Gerri are connected."

"You mean he did it to manipulate whoever might investigate Shovak's murder? To implicate Kazan in some fashion?"

"That's what it seems like. Then there's the matter of Hobart not being a long-standing ComCorp contractor, and Gerri having never met him before that day. Anyone could feed information to her staff for the last year under the guise of Montague Hobart. You know, the more I think of our so-called evidence, the more I'd say someone contrived this entire case."

Arno took another sip and stared at me with an accusatory gleam in his eyes. "What is growing in your fertile brain, Chief?"

"An idea I want to develop further before we speak with Talyn again."

In reality, it didn't need much developing, but I wanted time to make myself comfortable with the notion. Someone was maneuvering us toward a given conclusion, making us play our part in a game of empires, a spy game, to offer an alibi, and send a message. I knew who and even how. What I didn't have yet was the motive, but a few educated guesses were slowly taking shape.

And the idea someone was manipulating us for political gain really stuck in my craw. There was a reason why damn near everyone considered PCB investigation results as the most reliable in all of law enforcement.

We might not always bring our culprit to justice, but when we did, no one could gainsay us. I had the feeling this would be one of those times when we wouldn't make an arrest but still had to present a conclusion that no one could question, be it on Earth, Wyvern, or Shrehari Prime.

I was about to take a bite of my pastry when two humans emerged from the Excelsior's lift and crossed the lobby. The moment they stepped through the doors, I knew who Gerri's hidden visitor was. Javan Burrard.

"Well, well," Arno said. "What's this then? Sera Kazan and Pullar's favorite gorilla out for a stroll."

"Do you remember how to tail a suspect?" I took one last sip of my tea and stood.

"Sure, but Aquilonia isn't the sort of place where you can stay invisible, as that CimmerTek prat found out — remember, the one who passed on Sorne's message the other day."

"I want to know where they're headed. And if they spot us, so what?"

We left the café in time to see Burrard, who towered over most people on the promenade, lead Gerri down the ramp leading to the docking ring.

"Why is your ex-partner talking to CimmerTek, let alone accompanying their Aquilonia GM to the docks?" Arno asked.

"Gerri is in charge of corporate security in this sector and works out of ComCorp's Cimmeria offices. Why wouldn't she have business links with one of the largest private security firms in this star system?"

"The mind boggles, Chief. Remember who owns a big chunk of CimmerTek. If she's what we think beneath that polished veneer..."

"Mind-boggling indeed."

We hurried after them and reached the docking ring only to watch Burrard usher Gerri through an unmarked opening at the base of docking arm fourteen. A door shut behind them and became part of the wall, undetectable to the casual eye.

"One of Pullar's coded entrances, no doubt," Arno said. "Like the one Hobart might have taken to hide his leaving *Harpy*."

I tapped the communicator Pullar had loaned me, and a voice replied almost instantly.

"This is Control. How can I help you, Chief Superintendent?"

"Is a ship using docking arm fourteen?"

"Wait one, sir." Half a minute passed before the duty gendarme spoke again. "The FTL yacht *Ambergris*. She landed thirty minutes ago."

"Where from and what ownership?"

"She came straight from Cimmeria and is registered to the Deep Space Foundation."

Arno and I glanced at each other. The Deep Space Foundation was one of Sorne's creations, a not-for-profit organization he used to launder ill-gotten gains and advance his political agenda.

Arno whispered, "Could it be?"

"Why would Louis Sorne come to Aquilonia? If he has access to a starship, he might as well head for a place we can't find him once Maras orders his arrest."

My wingman made a dubious face. "Maybe he's on a legitimate business trip just as Hannah Sorne claimed and not running away. He *is* a member of the Aquilonia Syndicate."

Just what I needed — the infamous Louis Sorne, soon to be under indictment for a long list of crimes, getting mixed up in my murder investigation.

"Or he intends to change ships," I replied. "We'd eventually have traced his foundation's yacht. Let's give Sector HQ a call and tell them he might be here. We can't do anything more, even if Sorne's aboard that ship. Maybe we'll get lucky, and Maras will issue a warrant based on flight risk."

Arresting a man who pimped out his spouse to turn a cop would give me great pleasure, but his sort wasn't part of our remit. Unless, of course, Maras ordered me to step in and make the collar.

"I fear you'd enjoy that too much for your own good, Chief," Arno replied.

"Probably." I gave the entrance to the docking arm one last glance before we returned to the promenade and a lift to the Gendarmerie station.

The duty sergeant intercepted us when we entered. "Sirs, the major asked to see you the moment you returned. He's in his office."

We found Pullar behind his desk, wearing the face of a man brimming with bad news.

"Your sergeant said you wanted to speak to us?"

"Yes." He waved at the empty chairs. "Please sit. We have a problem, Chief Superintendent."

"Oh?"

"Montague Hobart has gone missing."

"You mean a dummy in operations let him lift off without my permission?"

Pullar shook his head. "No. *Harpy*'s still sitting in her berth, untouched since our inspection. I've had my patrols on the lookout so we can bring him back here for another interview, but no one can find the blasted bugger. He was last seen taking a lift in the warehouse section. Since then, nothing. His communicator's vanished from the net, and he hasn't appeared on any surveillance sensor."

"Aquilonia's a big place," Arno said. "Anyone with a mind to hide won't lack for choice."

"True," I replied grimacing, "but why did he go into hiding, and why now?"

"Perhaps it wasn't voluntary," Pullar offered. "A man of his ilk must not lack for enemies, especially if he's known to pass along secrets. Aquilonia plays host to all sorts as you might have noticed."

I didn't bother restraining the sigh that offered itself up for a sacrificial exhalation. "Then I suppose our next step is Talyn again. And before I forget, Major, please log DCC Hammett's message as received at this hour. If you can point me toward a communications station, I'll prepare an acknowledgment for the next subspace packet headed in the right direction. There's no point in delaying. At this juncture, I doubt the ComCorp folks can tell me anything I can't find through other means."

Besides, I didn't much care to run across Gerri again, either. She exuded an even darker aura than before, one that matched her mood whenever I confronted her. And presuming she was a member of the *Sécurité Spéciale*, then the less contact, the better.

If unknown forces had pulled Arno and me into an undercover battle between the SecGen's underlings and the Fleet, we could quickly become collateral damage, since the outcome of our investigation would be sure to displease someone immensely.

And because we couldn't play favorites, the evidence would have to fall where it did, as would the consequences. Honesty comes with its perils, something every PCB investigator learns to accept as part of the job.

"I'll tell Sector HQ about the Deep Space Foundation yacht *Ambergris*," Arno said.

"Why?" Pullar asked.

"Louis Sorne evaded the surveillance DCC Maras put on him," I replied. "His wife says he's off-world on a business trip and as it happens, Sorne is the man behind the Deep Space Foundation."

"You mean he's here? On Aquilonia?" A brief spark of alarm lit up Pullar's eyes.

"Possibly. We followed your favorite rent-a-cop and my ex-partner to the yacht's docking arm. Burrard seems to have the code for the maintenance tunnel door."

Pullar stunned us with a string of choice cuss words I didn't think a man of his solemn mien even had in his vocabulary.

"Time to change the locks?" Arno suggested.

"And put eyes on docking arm fourteen," he said. "If Louis Sorne is aboard *Ambergris*, I'm sure you'd like to find out, especially if he's here to take a ship headed for parts unknown."

"Much appreciated, Major."

He waved away my thanks. "Professional courtesy. But answer me this. I'm not surprised about Javan meeting folks aboard the yacht, considering he works for one of Sorne's companies. Why did Gerri Kazan go with him? Do you think Sorne's in on whatever ComCorp and the Shrehari are doing? I recall you saying he wasn't the right sort of plutocrat for this *Sécurité Spéciale*."

"Perhaps I underestimated Sorne's reach, but I doubt it. His coming here likely has nothing to do with Shovak's mission or murder." I gave Arno a glance. "Let's send those messages and have another chat with Talyn. We can speculate about Sorne afterward."

— Forty-Seven —

Merely watching a serene, meditative Commander Talyn on the brig's security monitor triggered a surge of bilious irritation somewhere south of my breastbone. I knew it was in reaction to my conclusions about her role in this mess and to the part I was about to play by submitting a case report that wouldn't reflect the unvarnished truth.

Give me a venal commissioner or a shifty warrant officer any day. Heck, I'd even take a politician addicted to a dozen unspeakable vices. Unwillingly to be sure, but the PCB doesn't let me choose my cases. And I'd never run out of them because humans never learned from Lord Acton's dictum about power and corruption.

Sadly, even ninety-nine point nine percent of my own colleagues wouldn't recognize Acton from a cactus plant. And that's why my unit would stay in business until our current civilization collapsed. I fancied we cops did our bit to push that time a little further into the future, but experience had taught me little good came from noble acts.

"Shall we?"

"It's your show, Chief. I'm not sure I can contribute much beyond record keeping, and I suspect said records might not see the light of day anyhow if your instincts are on the mark. And they usually are."

"I may have mentioned this before but you're a cheerful bugger, aren't you?"

"I try. Although I mostly fail at cheer, I still try."

"And no one appreciates that more than I do, Arno." I patted his arm and gave him a sad smile.

He scratched his beard absently as if lost in contemplation, but then he nodded. "True. Your tolerance and forbearance make this job almost bearable. Good cop, grumpy cop?"

"Only if we want to make her wonder about the Constabulary's collective sanity. Role-playing games won't impress her."

Talyn's eyes fluttered open, and her gaze turned to the video pickup above the cell's door.

"Why do I feel like she's waiting for us?" Arno asked.

"Probably because Talyn has calculated that we've reached the beginning of the end and is expecting our appearance at any time."

Arno snorted. "Are you saying she's prescient, Chief?"

"No. Of course not. I'm saying Talyn's controlled this game from the beginning, with Hobart's help. And since we'll never see the slick bastard again, we can make him fit the bill quite nicely."

"Should I ask which bill he fits, Chief? Or would that ruin my last bit of belief in humanity?"

"It would, though I'm surprised you have any left."

"So am I. But this case hasn't exactly helped me regain a positive outlook on our species."

"Perhaps we should offer our services to the Empire. The *Tai Kan* might be looking for fresh blood and new ideas."

"Heaven forbid. I gather you're not acquainted with Shrehari cuisine." He patted his ample stomach. "A human could positively starve while he watches them scarf down live critters of indeterminate origin."

"As humanity has done throughout the ages. What do you think raw oysters are? Dead?"

"Next you'll tell me they're no good as an aphrodisiac."

"No idea. I've never had to worry about it."

Arno gave me a suspicious look from of the corner of his eyes, but he wisely held his peace.

A sardonic smile greeted us as we entered the cell. "Did you finally figure out I'm not responsible for Shovak's death, Chief Superintendent?"

I took the single chair facing her and crossed my legs while my wingman leaned against the far wall. With as much nonchalance as I could muster, I asked, "How about I tell you a story, Commander, and you let me know if you've heard it before?"

Talyn waved a hand to indicate the confines of her forced accommodations. "As you can see, I'm a captive audience."

"Several months ago, a plan was put in motion to set up a secret link between the Commonwealth SecGen and the Shrehari *Kho'sahra* using the *Sécurité Spéciale* under ComCorp and the *Tai Zolh* under *Quch Mech* cover. Does that story ring a bell?"

I thought I saw Talyn's lips twitch, but it could have been an optical illusion.

"Naval Intelligence," I continued, "never a friend of the *Sécurité Spéciale* or a fan of our government's top executive, heard of the matter, and devised a plan to disrupt what would be a sensitive first meeting. The Shrehari place great value in face-to-face negotiations, to assess a potential ally's sense of honor. Therefore, if intelligence could make the human delegation seem weak and untrustworthy, dishonorable even, then the *Kho'sahra* would back away from whatever our SecGen was planning. How am I doing so far?"

"Sounds like it would make an interesting plot for a spy novel."

"An agent, taking on the identity of one Willa Trogo, started working for Aquilonia's engineering section three months ago, shortly after the first arrangements were made for the meeting between ComCorp and *Quch Mech.* She came with an extensive, but false background that allowed her to access systems vital for Naval Intelligence's plans. In reality, Willa Trogo never existed other than as a false identity."

I paused to gage Talyn's reaction before continuing – but in vain. Her expression of amused interest didn't waver.

"Trogo socialized with a smuggler who had a sideline as an information broker working for the highest bidder, ComCorp and the Navy included. The smuggler who called himself Montague Hobart, showed up on Aquilonia at around the same time as Trogo, though he claimed a long-standing acquaintance with this place, something difficult to prove or disprove. Hours before Trogo returned to Cimmeria for a holiday, she was seen conversing with Hobart using a touch version of sign language. A few days after Trogo's departure, you showed up. You never met with Hobart and claimed no knowledge of him, just as he claimed not knowing you. Yet we have a video of you and him communicating in sign language while passing each other on the promenade a few hours before Shovak's assassination. Still with me so far, Commander?"

"A fascinating story, Chief Superintendent. I can't wait to see the live-action rendering they'll make of your novel. I wonder who will play the role of Caelin Morrow?"

"Trogo conveniently vanished on Cimmeria. The police think she perished in an accident so violent, it left no organic residue for analysis. But I'm sure the woman who played Hera Talyn passing through Valerys Station arrivals control after stepping off *Xenophon* and then became Willa Trogo while you resumed your normal identity to return here, is alive and well. Still drawing a blank?"

Her lips seemed to twitch again, and I could almost believe I saw a brief spark in her dark eyes. "Who knew PCB investigators had such a rich imagination?"

"We also have a knack for putting together disparate facts and coming up with enough evidence to support an indictment. Although to round out this story, I'm still a bit short in certain areas, such as how you and Montague Hobart managed Shovak's assassination."

"Why not ask your smuggler?"

"Because he conveniently vanished earlier today. His ship still sits on the apron, but there's no trace of the man anywhere. You wouldn't perchance know where he might hide?"

"Not a clue."

"And what is your relationship with him?"

"Hobart is an information broker, a freelancer who the Navy sometimes pays for data he collects deep within the Empire."

"Was he your reason to visit Aquilonia?"

"No. Meeting him was a mere coincidence."

"Why is it I don't believe a word you're saying, Commander?"

She gave me a weary shrug. "PCB investigators are well known for their skepticism, so I'd say you're running true to form. What is your favorite dictum again? Trust no one?"

"Let me finish my tale. Somehow, you and Hobart killed Shovak, or was it Hobart alone? He has more of the size and strength you lack. For now, I'll assume he was the main actor in the murder, then vanished while you stayed at the scene of the crime and had yourself arrested. Why? So we would take over the investigation. If Shovak's assassins had merely vanished, the murder might well have remained a Gendarmerie matter. And the *Sécurité Spéciale* or ComCorp might have pressured Major Pullar or his superiors to investigate in a manner that wouldn't cause an irreparable rift with the Shrehari."

I paused to assess her reaction again, but she kept gazing at me with dispassionate eyes.

"But with you found at the scene, it gave the Navy enough cause to ask that the Constabulary take over at once. You no doubt hoped DCC Maras would give the case to the one unit known for its ability to resist outside influence. Perhaps my and Inspector Galdi's mere presence has given the Shrehari enough reason to back away from striking a deal with the SecGen. Better yet, if they knew the Fleet was involved in Shovak's death — and escaped any consequences under the very nose of the PCB — it would definitely make them reconsider the notion of trusting our government. I doubt they understand the SecGen has no control over the day-to-day operations of the military, since our Grand Admiral reports to the Senate, our equivalent to their council of nobles.

From my readings, that sort of situation would be intolerable for the *Kho'sahra*. And if perchance they discovered our unique constitutional arrangements, they would think the SecGen was contemptibly weak."

"Still fascinating, Chief Superintendent. I hadn't realized the Constabulary was well-versed in both Shrehari politics and cloak and dagger stories."

Her aura of detached irony was getting tiresome. I shook my head with an irritated exhalation.

"We can tell when someone tries to use us as patsies, Commander. Perhaps not right away, but eventually. I daresay this wasn't the first time the Fleet has manipulated us to cover dark deeds. It was merely a first for Inspector Galdi and me. What I don't know yet is exactly how you carried out the assassination, the reasons behind the covert rapprochement between Commonwealth and Empire, and the result you expect from me. While it's true we don't always collar our perp, I still have to satisfy my superiors as well as the Shrehari and Commonwealth governments. And apparently to please Naval Intelligence, I must do it in a way that leaves both the Shrehari and the *Sécurité Spéciale* staring at each other with mortal suspicion. Would you care to shed light on the matter? I wouldn't want your carefully crafted plot to result in a big fat goose egg."

Talyn unfolded her legs and stretched. "Were you aware the *Sécurité Spéciale* also used Montague Hobart as a freelancer? Or did Gerri Kazan tell you she knew him through the ComCorp business intelligence section?"

"I see you're cognizant of Gerri's affiliations." No surprise there.

"I know her, and she knows me. We try to stay abreast of the competition's order of battle. Kazan is the *Sécurité Spéciale*'s woman inside ComCorp — with the full knowledge of the company's senior management. The relationships between the SecGen's office, his private security agency, and the largest zaibatsus like ComCorp are terribly incestuous."

I should have known Gerri lied. Once you slipped into the habit of dissembling, it became hard to quit.

"Care to tell me what role I'm supposed to play? You know, help out a fellow member of the uniformed services?"

I realized my tone was becoming somewhat testy, and at this point, I didn't care if Talyn noticed my growing impatience. But the disappointed expression that briefly crossed her face was enough to jog my brain cells just a little more.

I'd hit the right notes with my tale of espionage and murder, but she expected me to form my own conclusions. And the moment I came to that realization, I also understood why.

It was the only way I could present a credible case report and still consider myself one of the last incorruptibles. Otherwise, Talyn risked me breaking Naval Intelligence's plot wide open on a matter of principle.

"If Montague Hobart was one of your freelancers," I said, meeting Talyn's eyes, "would you perchance know of any difficulties he might have experienced with Shrehari officials, be they governmental or mercantile? The sort of challenges that might see him run afoul of someone like Envoy Shovak?"

And there it was — a faint, almost imperceptible nod of approval.

"On several occasions, though he didn't care to share details with us," she replied. "He may even have tried to broker information for the *Tai Zolh*, which might have put him in contact with Shovak or Thopok, or with any of their colleagues at some point. The Shrehari experience as much difficulties spying on us as we do spying on them, which makes freelancers valuable sources to the *Tai Zolh* and the Navy alike."

"So you're saying Shovak and Thopok belong to imperial intelligence?"

She nodded. "They do."

"And if Hobart had met Shovak on a previous occasion, the envoy might have admitted him into his suite. They could have quarreled, with deadly results, especially if Hobart carried something like a needler that might knock out a full-grown Shrehari and leave his neck exposed for the slaughter."

That earned me another minute nod of approval. The devil was, it probably unfolded almost precisely in that manner or near enough to make no difference. But Hobart was no freelancer. He had to be a Fleet operative, someone who spent a long time undercover posing as a neer-do-well. Whatever the SecGen and the *Kho'sahra* were contemplating, it had to be significant if Hobart compromised what was likely a very complex and long-serving cover identity to stop it.

"It seems you've found your murderer and a motive, Chief Superintendent." Talyn's tone was soft, if emotionless.

Yes, I had my assassin all right, and his accomplice sitting in front of me, but the motive was bogus. Even the killer's identity was false, but as I told Arno before we entered, he fit the bill.

I had to wonder how much of what occurred since I arrived on Aquilonia was contrived and how much was happenstance. Yet now that the Navy had maneuvered me, and by inference the PCB into accepting a man called Montague Hobart as the guilty party, my options were limited. I could stubbornly continue, with little chance of finding more palatable results. Or I could put out a warrant for Hobart's arrest, even though I realized he, or at least his identity, had joined Willa Trogo's persona wherever old covers go to die.

"When will you release me?" Talyn asked.

I examined her for a few moments with the mocking expression she seemed to favor. "I'd like to say until Montague Hobart sits in the cell next door, but I doubt we'll ever see him again. Major Pullar will set you free once I've announced the findings of my investigation. It might not be politic for you to swan around Aquilonia while the Shrehari and the ComCorp folks are still here. There's such a thing as rubbing the opposition's nose in it, right?"

Talyn nodded. "Very perceptive of you."

I stood, feeling physically and emotionally drained. "If you'll forgive me, Commander, I must put out an all-points bulletin for Ser Hobart's arrest on a murder charge."

— Forty-Eight —

"I can't believe you're about to go through with that cockamamie story, Chief," Arno said once we were alone in the conference room.

His thunderous expression told me I had to let him vent before we faced the Gendarmerie. He understood where I was going and why, but had a burning need to speak his piece, if only to assuage his conscience.

"It has more holes than a colander," he continued. "How will you explain the instances of system sabotage, for one thing?"

"You know it was sabotage, and I know it was sabotage, but what concrete proof do we have? None. Everything is circumstantial, explainable by maintenance glitches. Our evidence is the absence of evidence."

I sighed — something that was rapidly becoming a bad habit. Senior officers shouldn't sigh in front of their subordinates.

"Look, Arno, the fact is, we're stuck supporting the Navy's black ops. Considering the parties involved, it's probably the least objectionable alternative. They spent a lot of time and effort preparing, so I doubt the motive's a trivial matter. We may never find out.

Yes, I think Talyn had a bigger role in the actual assassination than she's prepared to admit, though Hobart is the most logical culprit. I'm sure if we'd been able to conduct an autopsy, we'd have discovered evidence showing a needler firing drugged or poisoned projectiles incapacitated Shovak. And once immobilized, even someone Talyn's size would have been able to strike the mortal blow and redecorate the suite in purple blood."

My wingman's disgruntlement was evident, and I knew he was chewing on his growing anger by the way his beard moved. "And we'll just let Talyn walk away from this?"

"We will. I don't like it any more than you do, but we have no choice unless we want to shine a public light on the espionage angle. I'm sure the Chief Constable won't consider that as being for the good of the Service. It might make his relationship with the Grand Admiral trickier than it needs to be, especially in the face of Earth politicking."

"You realize we'll never find Hobart."

"Of course. The operation was designed to leave us with a likely culprit, possibly even the actual culprit while discrediting the *Sécurité Spéciale* and its masters in the executive branch."

"And how do we discredit those buggers?"

"By describing Hobart as he presented himself to us — a freelancer selling information to the highest bidder, including corporations and government agencies with access to the most powerful political offices. It should suffice for the Navy's purposes."

This time, Arno exhaled noisily. It sounded so earnest I had to smile. "That's why I never accepted promotion, Chief. I'm not sure I could convince myself fudging facts for the greater good had no bearing on the PCB's integrity. It's something best left to those of you with oak leaves around your pips."

"Don't think I enjoy doing it, Arno. But since I'm literally being forced to choose between Gerri and Commander Talyn, I'll go against the corrupt devil I know, and pray the Naval Intelligence assassins I'm covering for are on the side of angels."

"From your lips to God's ear. And the attempt on your life?"

"A false flag operation designed to put the *Sécurité Spéciale* bug in our ears. I doubt I was ever in any real danger. Evidently, the Navy hoped we'd find incriminating traces when we examined the code and the log. I've always suspected Naval Intelligence was involved with Grint's disappearance, based on something Ange Rowan said back then, so it stands to reason."

"Meaning they wanted us to find out about the *Tai Zolh* playing footsie with the SecGen's myrmidons?"

"Precisely. The Navy was counting on our deciding we'd do the Commonwealth a favor by supporting their operation, however unwittingly."

"Bastards."

"That they can be. But not all of them, and not all the time. Right now, the Constabulary is able to keep a reasonably honorable neutrality in the various power struggles being fought *sub rosa*. But I doubt we'll be able to stay nonaligned forever."

"Alas."

"That being the case, we're honor-bound to remember Grand Admiral Kowalski created the Constabulary after she had the Special Security Bureau wiped out, while the *Sécurité Spéciale* is a try at reviving the SSB. Since we're the legitimate descendants of the Fleet's former Criminal Investigation Branch and blood is thicker than water,

I'd say supporting our cousins in the Armed Services is the right thing to do. It's really the only thing to do, in spite of the bad taste it'll leave."

A dark chuckle rumbled up from Arno's barrel chest. "And to think you were accusing me of lacking cheer. Your summation of our situation is the saddest thing I've heard in a while."

"What's the trope in those epic novels you enjoy? Evil is moving across the land; the forces of the Dark One are growing in number?"

"Aye. It sure is if we're stuck giving Naval Intelligence assassins official cover, for the good of the Commonwealth – or at least the good as it's understood at Fleet HQ."

"Which is more palatable than the way it's understood on Earth."

"And that's the pity of it." He sighed again. "Weren't you supposed to put out an arrest warrant for Montague Hobart?"

"I was, but there's no hurry. The Fleet agent who wore Monty's face is someone else by now. That warrant will never be executed, nor will he."

But I still had to do it. And so, with Major Pullar's help, we issued two bulletins, one system-wide through the Gendarmerie and the other Commonwealth-wide through the Constabulary, for Hobart's arrest on suspicion of killing the Shrehari Shovak. It was our point of no return because it made the story official. If Pullar had any qualms or reservations, he was careful to keep them unvoiced.

That evening, I allowed myself a stiff gin and tonic in the Aquilonia Arms, a reward for ostensibly solving Shovak's murder. It would be the only reward I'd reap under the circumstances.

Sharing the real story with DCC Hammett, let alone DCC Maras would be inadvisable for reasons of plausible deniability. I hated lying to my superiors, which meant I'd have to finesse the truth just enough so my conscience suffered only a minor flesh wound.

With our departure imminent, I wished I could splurge on a final supper in the Excelsior Court on the Navy's cred, considering they owed me big time. But that would put me at risk of stumbling across Gerri, who by now would know we had fingered one of her informants as Shovak's killer. I didn't doubt she would face consequences, not least to her *Sécurité Spéciale* career, and probably hated me more than ever.

"I wonder," Arno said, staring into his half-empty beer mug, "if we'll hear of an accident deep in Aquilonia's bowels claiming Hobart's life as he tried to escape arrest. A repeat of Willa Trogo's supposed fate, as it were."

"That might be gilding the lily," I replied after swallowing a healthy slug of my drink. "Two deaths with no identifiable remains? I doubt we'll ever come across the name Montague Hobart again. He's become an unperson. A fugitive who'll never be apprehended. A permanent cold case."

"Have another gee and tee, Chief. You're about to become maudlin." He climbed to his feet and made a hand signal at the bartender, then he dropped back into the hard chair. "What will happen to *Harpy*?"

I placed my hand against my forehead and hummed tunelessly, then said. "My vision of the future shows Navy personnel disguised as creditors taking her away."

"Ah, yes, that would explain why an oversized space yacht is so well armed."

The second drink didn't help ease my conscience, and I left Arno to sample the pub's extensive selection of ales while I took a long, solitary stroll around Aquilonia to reflect. Part of me wondered whether betraying the PCB's ethos, even for the best of reasons, meant we were now on the same slope to tragedy that had claimed Gerri Kazan's career and integrity.

Lost in thought, I wandered down to the docks, my feet moving of their own volition to escape the crowded promenade. As I neared docking arm fourteen, something sharp stung my right cheek. Then darkness overtook me, and I fell into a black hole.

— Forty-Nine —

The thunder of a thousand starships lifting at once echoed through my skull, leaving me with dented brain matter. A snake of nausea wormed its way up my gut, threatening to block my throat and choke me to death. I didn't usually react that badly to needlers, which meant the sonofabitch who knocked me out used the nastiest load possible. That would cost him.

I cautiously opened my eyes, and a stab of light sent a second wave of starships into my mind's sky, with predictable results. Acid burned a path up my esophagus, forcing me to swallow convulsively as I tried to raise my head.

Although tears blurred my vision, I saw a wood-paneled ceiling overhead, rich and dark, with a silver inlay in the shape of a stylized galaxy, the logo of the Deep Space Foundation. I was aboard the Foundation's ship, *Ambergris*. Sorne's ship.

"She's awake," a resonant basso announced somewhere beyond my peripheral vision, a voice filled with malicious glee, "and sick enough to wish for a quick and merciful death. But she'll live — for now."

My arms were bound at the wrists and my legs at the ankles, and I could tell my shoulder holster was empty. My back sensed cold, hard metal decking beneath a thin carpet that smelled of shampoo.

A shadow blocked the overhead light, and Javan Burrard said, "She doesn't look like she'll puke, sir."

"Then by all means," a much older, dryer voice replied, "have her sit in the chair. A condemned woman should enjoy a modicum of comfort."

I tried to speak, but no words came out, another side effect of the needler load, presumably fired by Burrard. I briefly wondered if this was how Shovak felt in the moments before his death, or whether he never saw the knife coming.

Burrard effortlessly picked me off the floor and dropped me into a deep, well-padded armchair, facing the man with the dry voice.

Baggy eyes above sagging jowls examined me with the coldness usually reserved for roadkill. Thin lips set in a disapproving arc reinforced the impression. Louis Sorne's face seemed ravaged by the evil in his soul, but I knew it was merely age and lack of vanity. He was old enough to remember the Shrehari occupation. Rumors even said his collaborating with them laid the groundwork of his fortune and political power.

"Condemned?" I asked in a broken voice that didn't rise above a whisper. "Sornecide like Haylian?"

Malevolent laughter shook Sorne's jowls, though it never reached those watchful eyes.

"Scurrilous terminology, Chief Superintendent Morrow. I'm not responsible for people choosing to end their own lives."

"Why am I here?"

"I wanted to meet the woman whose misplaced zeal brought so much attention to my affairs, the one who thought it would be appropriate to record my wife enjoying herself in private. What is this universe coming to when senior police officers turn into amateur pornographers?"

"Assault and abduction of a police officer," I rasped. "It'll cost you an added five years on Parth, Sorne."

Another cruel laugh echoed off the saloon's paneled walls, and this time, with the headache and nausea retreating, I felt a chill run down my spine. It turned my previously heaving guts to ice.

"I sincerely doubt that, Chief Superintendent. The Constabulary is about to learn it has bitten off more than it can handle. Haylian is no longer in a position to testify, and soon, you won't be either. That leaves me room to sue the Constabulary for a long list of wrongs. It'll be interesting to see my lawyers turn your inability to solve the Shrehari envoy's murder into a general condemnation of your competence and integrity. I'd say the much vaunted Professional Compliance Bureau is about to face the cost of its hubris. And I'm not even counting the price my friends from the Honorable Commonwealth Trading Corporation will make you pay."

"Is that why Gerri Kazan visited you earlier today? To enlist your help in having me die of Sornecide before I could discover the truth about ComCorp's machinations on behalf of the *Sécurité Spéciale*? Criminals helping each other? You take care of me, and she makes sure you become a most favored person in her circle, one currently beyond your reach?"

Sorne shook his head and tut-tutted. "Again with derogatory words, Chief Superintendent. My interests happen to align with ComCorp's, and we're inclined to do each other a few favors. That's how friendships work in my universe, something you vulgar cops obviously can't grasp since you keep persisting with unwarranted persecution. And when it comes to the question of your continued existence, we are in complete agreement."

As his words sank in, the drumming of my heartbeat in my ears became overwhelming. But the throbs swept aside the last dregs of needler sickness, leaving me with the chilling realization I had only one card to play. Yet I knew it wouldn't be enough. At least I was able to keep my composure, a small and temporary victory in the face of Sorne's malevolence.

"A shame that your gorilla Burrard waited too long," I replied. "He should have abducted me this morning because I solved Shovak's murder a few hours ago. I've issued an arrest warrant for the culprit, and formally recorded the evidence on ComCorp's dealings with the Shrehari for the case report, which is already on its way to Wyvern via subspace. Even if you kill me — pardon, arrange for my suicide — neither Kazan nor her superiors will emerge from this unscathed. The indictment against you will go ahead, justice will be served, and you will spend the rest of your life in custody. If you're lucky, you might be exiled to Desolation Island."

"Your belief in what you call justice is so touchingly naïve, Chief Superintendent. People like me don't subject themselves to it — we make it serve us. Shame you've already submitted your report, but I'm sure ComCorp can deal with the fallout, especially since you'll no longer be there to defend your conclusions." His eyes turned to Burrard. "Inform Kazan about this development."

"Yes, sir. If I can make a suggestion. Why don't we grab Morrow's inspector as well and terminate them together?" The CimmerTek man asked. "With both rats gone, I'm sure ComCorp can make her case report vanish."

"And how do we explain two dead PCB investigators?" Sorne asked in a flat tone.

"A decompression accident. They were snooping in *Ambergris'* docking arm, looking for you, and it had a catastrophic airlock failure. I can set it up so that Pullar and his gendarmes won't find any traces of sabotage."

"Hmm." Sorne tilted his head to one side and gazed at me with narrowed eyes. "I suppose we can survive the resulting Gendarmerie and Transportation Safety Board investigations. I know people in both who owe me a favor."

For the first time since coming to, I looked for a timepiece to see how long I was out and caught sight of Sorne's antique wristwatch as he rubbed his chin. An hour. Not nearly long enough for Arno to wonder where I was and ask Pullar to track me. I glanced at my left breast pocket, searching for signs of the Gendarmerie communicator, but in vain.

"Your device vanished from the net right after I shot you," Burrard said. "No one knows where you are and no one can find you. I brought you here via the maintenance tunnel."

I gave him what I hoped was a contemptuous stare. "Underestimating both Inspector Galdi and Major Pullar is a fatal mistake. There's a reason you never made it past master sergeant in the Gendarmerie and Pullar became a major."

His face tightened at the implied insult, and the corner of his upper lip curled back in a sneer.

Sorne raised a wrinkled hand. "Enough. On second thought, ComCorp will have to deal with their difficulties as best they can. Inspector Galdi won't join his commanding officer — for now. I'd rather not take the risk of waiting until we have him before dispatching Morrow."

Burrard inclined his head in acknowledgment. "As you wish, sir."

"Honor among thieves?" I asked in as scornful a manner as I could.

"I'll be holding up my end of the bargain. Too bad the timing is off." Sorne pointed at the door. "Get going, Burrard. I've had enough of Chief Superintendent Morrow's impolite behavior."

"You know you'll be suspect number one, Burrard," I said to his retreating back. "My inspector has orders to investigate my death as a murder committed at Sorne's behest. And he knows you're in contact with the evil bastard."

"I'm afraid that insult will cost you," Sorne said.

"How? By having me commit suicide twice?"

His lips twisted into a spiteful smile. "You'll see."

The lump of ice in my gut turned sour, and nausea welled up again.

— Fifty —

Burrard returned moments later trailed by the man who'd given me Sorne's message when I first arrived on Aquilonia, Ward Loriot.

"Everything is ready, sir," he said. "They'll find her body in the maintenance tunnel, electrocuted in an attempt to reach your ship undetected."

"Oh dear." Sorne shook his head. "Another display of your incompetence and lack of judgment. My lawyers will love it. There's just one more thing I'd like you to do beforehand, provided you can make sure her body burns to a crisp so as not to leave traces."

"What's that, sir?"

"Enjoy her as your spoils of war." He turned his dead eyes on me again. "Call me a bastard, eh? Even your imminent demise won't spare you one last humiliation. No one insults Louis Sorne and escapes unscathed."

Burrard accepted the order with an impassive nod, his expression carved from stone. But Loriot's hungry leer sparked a surge of terror I hadn't experienced since shortly before Marines rescued me from a long-ago undercover operation that had spun out of control.

"Here or in the tunnel?" Loriot asked.

"Not aboard my ship," Sorne replied in a dismissive tone. "I'm not inclined to be a spectator."

"That's not what I heard," I said, feeling reckless bravado momentarily overcome my fear. "You let Haylian fuck your wife provided you could watch every thrust and listen to every groan. There's no pervert like an old pervert."

Sorne raised his eyebrows in disgust and said to Burrard, "Make sure she suffers."

When they lifted me from the chair, I spat in Sorne's face and had the satisfaction of seeing his stunned reaction as my spittle ran down his cheek. Then the CimmerTek goons dragged me out of the saloon and to *Ambergris*' main airlock. I yelled and struggled as best I could but in vain.

Panic reared its ugly head, and the urge to plead for my life became overwhelming. But before I lost what little dignity I had left, Burrard slapped a muzzle patch over my mouth.

He caught Loriot's eye and jerked his chin at the main hatch. "Check the sensors spoofs and open the maintenance tunnel. I can handle the little rat by myself."

As soon as Loriot released me, I put my remaining strength into one last effort, but Burrard merely tightened his grip on my right arm until I thought I would faint from the pain. He heard my whimper through the muzzle and laughed.

"You're not going anywhere, Morrow. Mister Sorne always gets what he wants, and he wants you to die in agony. You should have charged the Navy bitch sitting in Pullar's brig and left Aquilonia while you had a chance."

Loriot stuck his head through the hatch and leered at me again. “We’re good, boss. Let’s go have fun.”

My guts turned to water while a gibbering voice in my head prayed to a God that I’d tossed aside shortly after the Pacifican State Security Police kidnapped and murdered my family.

Burrard half-shoved half-dragged me through the airlock and into docking arm fourteen, where Loriot waited beside a dark, human-sized rectangle cut into one wall — a normally hidden entrance to the maintenance tunnel. His expression, as he watched me approach seemed almost exactly like that of a hungry Cimmerian pseudo-wolf, one of the planet’s apex predators. I suddenly experienced an overwhelming need to void my bladder.

Then, Burrard shoved me through the opening and up against a rough concrete wall. Loriot closed the door panel behind us and giggled.

“Party time.”

Burrard ripped off the muzzle, released my arm, and stepped away, his expression as stony as ever. Loriot took his place and pressed himself against me, right hand reaching for my crotch. His fetid breath washed over me as he leaned in for a kiss, and I turned my face away, retching loudly.

“That’s not nice,” he said. “Tell you what, show me a good time, and I’ll make sure it doesn’t hurt too much. It’s your last chance to get off before you die.”

I wanted to spit in his smirking face but discovered I’d run out of saliva. Then, without warning, his eyes rolled back, and he collapsed at my feet like a sack of wet noodles. Burrard joined him on the dirty floor a second later.

“Are you all right, Chief Superintendent?” A voice asked from the shadows.

I tried to answer but couldn't manage anything more than a partial sob.

When he stepped into view, I read genuine concern on a face I had never seen before. He placed a steadying hand on my shoulder and reached for the wrist restraints. They fell away at his touch. He then crouched and removed the shackles holding my ankles together.

"Who are you?" I finally uttered in a strangled voice. "And why are you here?"

"Let's say I'm the friend of a friend and leave it at that. As to why I'm here, on my way to my ship I saw Burrard shoot you and take you into the maintenance tunnel. Naturally, I followed, but by the time I reached this end of the docking arm, he'd already taken you aboard Sorne's ship."

"Why not call Pullar?"

"The moment Sorne saw a bunch of gendarmes entering this docking arm, he would have lifted off, and you'd have vanished for good. I figured that whatever he wanted done to you wouldn't happen aboard his ship, for fear of leaving traces that your forensics experts could find. That meant Burrard and his sidekick would take you into the maintenance tunnel again."

"They meant me to die from accidental electrocution in here after they raped me." I began to shiver, not from cold but from delayed shock, and my rescuer wrapped his arms around me.

"That will not happen now. You're safe."

"What about Sorne, Burrard, and Loriot?"

"I'll leave that up to you. The CimmerTek goons will sleep for a few hours. That's plenty of time to lead Pullar back here and take them into custody. As for Sorne, you'll figure something out. He'll not leave

Ambergris and will lift off without hindrance the moment he realizes his revenge scheme failed. No one on Aquilonia will dare keep him grounded, not even on your say-so."

He released me, knelt beside Burrard and rifled through his pockets, producing, in quick succession my own needler and the borrowed communicator. Once I'd returned the one to its holster and the other to my breast pocket, he pointed toward the station end of the tunnel. "I'll take you to the entrance, then I have to go. My ship is leaving very shortly, and I can't afford to miss it."

I followed him on unsteady legs until we reached the door. He tapped its control screen with dancing fingers, and it slid aside with a mechanical sigh. After sticking his head out to check for more CimmerTek gorillas, he stepped through and motioned me to follow. The door shut behind us, turning the wall into a smooth, unbroken surface again.

"Take care, Caelin." Then he gave me an outrageous wink and said, "Monty sends his regards."

Before his final words registered and I could react, he walked away with an energetic stride and entered the next docking arm. I felt a slow smile pull up the corners of my lips. So that's why he knew my first name and could follow my trail.

Fifteen minutes later, Pullar and his gendarmes dragged Burrard and Loriot out of the maintenance tunnel and carted them off to the brig. But as my rescuer had predicted, Sorne's ship lifted off before we could disable the airlock release and keep him grounded.

Arno, predictably, was furious and ready to give Burrard a dose of old-fashioned retribution, but after

I pointed out he and Loriot would be in pain when they woke up, he relented. I had seen the way the gendarmes had handled both unconscious men, and it would be a miracle if they didn't suffer from a few broken bones on top of painful bruising.

Pullar asked me for a formal statement so he could charge them the moment they came out of their needler-induced coma. Arno took a copy for DCC Maras, after pointing out the abduction, assault, and attempted murder of a Constabulary officer was a federal crime and beyond Cimmerian jurisdiction.

I also swore out a warrant for Louis Sorne's arrest on charges of abduction and conspiracy to commit murder. It joined my statement in a special subspace packet addressed to both the Director General of the Cimmerian Gendarmerie and DCC Maras. The latter wouldn't like me short-circuiting the Financial Crimes Division's investigation without her permission, but the sooner we arrested Sorne, the better.

He'd fight it of course and do his best to discredit me. I knew Maras would have my back, as would Hammett, but I was better off preparing myself for the shit storm to end all shit storms. The only bright spot was that Sorne couldn't risk anything happening to me after this because he'd be our prime suspect. Still, I'd have to watch my back.

With Burrard in custody, Pullar unilaterally suspended CimmerTek's authorization to act as private security on Aquilonia and ordered them to turn in their weapons. Predictably, his actions drew an immediate reaction from Darrien.

Arno and I were in the room when Pullar told Dangerous Don to commit an impossible act of self-fornication. And he did so with the sort of pleasure my wingman derives from a bottle of fine ale. Darrien's complaint to Gendarmerie HQ would arrive well after my statement and Sorne's arrest warrant and would receive the consideration it deserved. I suspected Darrien's tenure as chief administrator was about to end anyway, considering Lisbeth's involvement with Burrard.

Once the whirlwind of activity died away, Arno asked about my rescuer.

"As I stated, he didn't give a name, nor did I recognize him. He said he was a friend of a friend. That's it."

"Whoever he is," Pullar said, "if he boarded the ship that was docked at arm fifteen, he's long gone, so we can't do much more than go through the passenger manifest."

"I doubt we'll find any familiar names or faces," I replied. "He certainly didn't look like anyone I'd ever met."

Arno gave me a suspicious stare. "The Chief knows more than she's letting on, Major. And there's the matter of her savior knowing the code to open docking arm maintenance tunnels. That should limit the possibilities. But I recognize the stubborn look in her eyes, so we'd better drop the matter. For now."

I took a sip of coffee and smiled. "Wise decision."

"Do you intend to speak with either Burrard or Loriot?" My wingman asked. "And see if one of them wants to turn state's evidence?"

After considering the question, I nodded. "We have to. Hammett and Maras will ask, but there's no way either of them will accept."

"Fear of Sornecide," Pullar said. "Can't say I'd blame them. The moment they wake up?"

I glanced at Arno, then said, "That would probably be best. Get them while they still feel the aftereffects."

"I've asked the custody sergeant to warn me when one of them stirs."

That moment happened while we were enjoying our second cup of coffee, and I soon found myself sitting across the interview table from a manacled, battered, and still groggy Javan Burrard. He refused to speak other than acknowledge the charges Pullar laid. When I offered him leniency in return for testifying against Sorne, he merely stared at me. It was like talking to a block of granite. When I pointed out he faced twenty years in a penal colony, Burrard's only reaction was a dismissive shrug.

Ward Loriot, on the other hand, couldn't stop twitching the moment he saw me. His demeanor betrayed a deep fear of retribution, and he refused to meet my gaze. Loriot was in worse shape than his boss, but he too declined to speak after hearing the charges against him, even though the added count of sexual assault meant he faced thirty years to Burrard's twenty.

Having done our due diligence, Arno and I retreated to our rooms. Although I was dead tired from my misadventure, I still had my report on the Shovak murder to write. The Shrehari transport was landing in a few hours, and as per DCC Hammett's orders, I had to present a copy to its captain.

— Fifty-One —

The next morning, I returned to the Gendarmerie station so I could avail myself of its secure communications facilities and file my report. It had taken me most of the night to write it in a way that should satisfy DCC Hammett, the Shrehari, and Naval Intelligence. Whether it satisfied the Commonwealth government was the least of my concerns.

Hammett, with his background and his keen understanding of political realities, would likely figure out at least part of the truth, though I doubted the Shrehari could. The cultural differences between our species were broad enough. Add in the particularities of a police force that had never entirely forgotten its military origins, and you have jargon even average humans would find challenging, let alone nonhumans.

"Commander Talyn would like a word," the desk sergeant said when he spotted me. "We've released her from custody, but she won't leave until she's seen you. We've put her in the conference room."

I found a snappily dressed Talyn taking her ease, reading from a small tablet, a travel bag at her feet. She glanced up the moment I entered.

"Chief Superintendent. It's kind of you to see me." That faint, ironic smile still fluttered on her lips. "I understand you had a close brush with death yesterday. If so, I'm glad to see you alive and well. I have a last favor to ask, and one to offer in exchange."

"What would that be?"

Talyn gave the ceiling a significant look and then nodded when I pulled the scrambler from my pocket. I activated it and sat across from her.

"I have orders to take *Harpy* home. As you may have surmised, she's a naval vessel, albeit an undercover, unacknowledged Fleet unit. We can't leave her here unsupervised. We were hoping Monty could escape aboard her, but he seems to have felt it would be imprudent. And since I haven't heard of an arrest, I'm sure he's left Aquilonia by now. Which leaves me."

I briefly debated whether to tell her about Hobart's role in freeing me from Sorne's henchmen, but then figured she would hear about it when she returned home. Instead, I said, "A spy who can fly a starship. I'm impressed."

"Don't be. It takes many skills to stay alive in this universe. Besides, I've piloted that particular ship before. The favor I want to ask is get me to the docks unseen and have station operations let me lift with no awkward questions. I'd rather the *Sécurité Spéciale* lose track of me. They'll have figured things out by now, meaning I've become a target. Remember, Gerri Kazan knows who and what I am."

"And the favor you offer?"

"When we're aboard, where I know we can't be overheard, I'll satisfy much, perhaps even most of your curiosity." She cocked an elegant eyebrow at me. "What do you say, Chief Superintendent?"

"You'll reveal secrets about an operation that never happened? I find it hard to believe."

"When I was read into the mission, I objected at leaving the PCB entirely in the dark. Your attempt to stay neutral in the ongoing power struggle between various factions inside the Commonwealth government won't last. And the Constabulary's natural place is along with the Fleet. We're two sides of the same coin."

"Funnily enough, that's what I told Inspector Galdi yesterday. We still carry the DNA of your defunct Criminal Investigation Branch."

She smiled, and for the first time, it felt genuine rather than contrived to manipulate me in some fashion. "Great minds thinking alike. I believe it's important you understand what you helped carry out and why, even if it's never officially recorded in the case file. We will need Constabulary support again someday, perhaps sooner than you think, and the PCB is almost the last organization where we can still count on honesty being the defining quality of its members."

"Flattery will get you nowhere, Commander. And drafting the case report has strained my idea of personal integrity, thank you very much."

"But does the offer of an explanation help me reach *Harpy* undetected by the opposition? After hearing me out, you might feel better about stretching the truth."

"I doubt it, but getting that damned ship out of the way will leave one less headache for us." I climbed to my feet. "Is now convenient?"

She inclined her head, unfazed by the sarcasm that replaced my usual stoicism in the face of circumstances I could no longer influence. "Now would be excellent."

"In that case, let me figure something out with Major Pullar's help. Since I've wrapped up my case, he owns a hundred percent of Aquilonia's policing once again. We've become mere guests, and ones I'm sure he'll be glad to see leave."

"Then he shouldn't object to my slipping away with *Harpy* unnoticed. One less problem for him as well."

Ten minutes later, after passing through emergency corridors and up escape stairs, one of Pullar's sergeants led us to the airlock at the far end of the docking arm via a maintenance tunnel. It was a twin to the one where I had come close to dying the previous day, and I shivered as we passed a spot identical to the one where Loriot tried to assault me.

She handled the ship's airlock controls with suspicious ease and headed unerringly for the bridge with a steady, if not entirely an impatient stride. For a moment I wondered whether she intended to kidnap me because I knew, or suspected too much. But after taking a seat at the controls and rousing *Harpy* from her slumber, she turned her chair around and gestured toward one of the unoccupied bridge stations.

"You might as well make yourself comfortable, Chief Superintendent. It'll be a few minutes before she spools up in preparation for liftoff, and we have things to discuss."

When she noticed my hesitation, Talyn smiled. "I don't intend to take you with me if that's a concern. I've successfully completed my mission, and what remains is leaving the stage with the audience none the wiser, I hope. Except for you, that is. You occupy a unique position as head of the Rim Sector PCB detachment. One that's been and hopefully will continue to be instrumental in preventing certain factions from sowing chaos. And believe me, it's the sort of chaos that will inevitably trigger the collapse of democracy and the rise of empire."

"That sounds a tad dramatic, Commander." I tried to make light of her words although I realized she was speaking in all seriousness.

"Doesn't it, though? But sadly I'm not exaggerating. This has been churning for decades. The people making up these factions are essentially attempting to reverse what our ancestors achieved at the cost of a billion lives during the last Migration War. They call themselves the Coalition, and it's an apt term since they're a collection of power-hungry, greedy sociopaths."

"They sound like nice folks. I think I met one of them last night, an evil bastard called Louis Sorne."

"Sorne? He's more of a hanger-on trying to join the inner circle. Your former partner, however, is one of their foot soldiers, one of many who've abandoned their oath to the constitution in return for a promise of wealth and power. If I had a taste for drama, I'd say the only things standing between our current republic, maddeningly flawed as it is, and a jackbooted, tyrannical human empire ruled by this Coalition are the Fleet and the Constabulary. But it's not that easy, or that clean. Neither is immune to corruption or outside influence as you well know. We fight where we can, with what we have, and achieve small victories, such as landing the covert operations equivalent of a kinetic strike from orbit on this latest scheme — with your help."

She paused to study my reaction, then nodded with apparent satisfaction.

"I see you're not particularly surprised by my words."

I wasn't. Many of us, especially in the PCB, sensed dark forces working to undo almost two centuries of uneven peace between the various interests ruling the fifty-odd self-governing human star systems. Not to mention the countless colonies and outposts they had spawned since the last murderous civil war. It had been fought over system rights, and the terms of the war's cessation included carefully circumscribed federal powers.

The central government on Earth had been deprived of even more authority when the Fleet, under Grand Admiral Kowalski, declared itself subject solely to the Commonwealth legislature. And that meant the sovereign human systems acting as one, rather than an executive under Secretaries General always looking for ways to increase their influence to the detriment of the self-governing star systems.

"I suppose I've come across various Coalition players in recent years, Commander, without necessarily connecting them to a single movement. The *Sécurité Spéciale*, corrupt zaibatsus, and Earth-First politicians aren't unknown to the PCB, and I've long suspected they were linked in some way."

"I'm glad to hear you say that. The Rim has become one of the Coalitions major focal points because they see potential in using restive colonies, the porous border with the Shrehari Empire and various criminal organizations to advance their cause. We — Naval Intelligence — can't counter every one of their moves every time. Lord knows my regular partner and I spend most of our lives gumming up Coalition schemes only to find more of them. It's akin to a low-level cold civil war at this point, but I'm not sure how long that will last before things turn hot. Had we failed to disrupt this latest scheme, we would have found ourselves one step closer to the brink."

Hearing her put words to the uneasy feelings many of my colleagues and I had experienced for years was further depressing my already damp spirits.

"And what was that scheme?"

"Nothing less than repudiating the clauses of our peace treaty with the Shrehari that created the Protectorate Zone. Both the *Kho'sahra* and our SecGen, the latter on behalf of human commercial interests, have been casting covetous eyes on the Protectorate Zone's unclaimed star systems. And on those whose native sentient species are too weak or primitive to resist annexation. But under the settlement, neither government may operate within the defined sphere, to remove a potential cause for fresh hostilities due to competing claims. We caught wind of the first feelers put out by the *Kho'sahra* and decided on a counterstrike designed to make him genuinely distrustful of human intentions. But I fear imperial and human interests are already violating the spirit if not the text of the treaty. So we may have a clash someday anyway, and woe betides the sentients caught in the middle."

"Now you told me the motive for Shovak's assassination, I think I can guess the rest, Commander."

Talyn's ironic smile returned, and she said, "I'm sure you can. The tale you told yesterday came close to the mark. But let me lay it out for you anyway, so we have no misunderstandings."

Her tone irked me though she was not condescending. But after spending most of the night sorting through my thoughts while I drafted a case report satisfactory to all concerned, I figured I'd earned my personal moment of truth. Nonetheless, I clenched my teeth and said, "Then please do so."

"You were entirely correct in assuming that several months ago, we uncovered the plan to organize a meeting between ComCorp and representatives of a Shrehari mercantile house wholly owned and controlled by the *Kho'sahra*. It was clear from the beginning that the commercial aspect was a cover for discussions between Shrehari intelligence and the SecGen's Praetorian Guard. I'm sure you understand I can't discuss how we came by that information. Under the identity of Willa Trogo, and helped by a fellow Naval Intelligence officer calling himself Montague Hobart, I joined Aquilonia's engineering department. It allowed me to lay the groundwork for our counterstrike. We designed the operation as a crime that would go unpunished and thus send a strong warning to the Shrehari that their human counterparts were dishonorable and untrustworthy."

"I thought your partner was gallivanting across the galaxy."

"He is. I wasn't lying when I said he was on a quest of his own. Which is just as well since he doesn't have the skills to corrupt AI systems while the man who played Hobart does."

"And you had help from a third operative who played Talyn arriving on Valerys."

When she nodded agreeably, I continued.

"The Talyn playing Willa Trogo, meaning you, then joined her doppelgänger and swapped identities. The third agent ensured we would trace your alter ego to the surface before she vanished. Meanwhile, Talyn, newly arrived in the Cimmeria system, couldn't be held responsible for the sabotage done with the help of Trogo's credentials."

"Nicely deduced, Chief Superintendent."

"I assume you prepared an undetectable remote access node while you were still Trogo, to allow yourself and your accomplice a backdoor into various systems. And when the Shrehari arrived, you and Hobart set the assassination in motion. Surveillance sensors recorded Hobart going aboard *Harpy* an hour before Shovak's death. That gave him an alibi, and no one in her right mind would believe someone of your size and strength able to kill a large, powerful Shrehari male with his own warrior's knife."

Her lips twitched with a faint smile. "Precisely."

"Hobart must have slipped out of the docks via a hidden maintenance tunnel, then used his knowledge of Shrehari to enter Shovak's quarters after the sensors stopped recording, and immobilized him with a needler. He knew the Shrehari wouldn't allow us to examine the body and find puncture wounds, thanks to their taboos. Then he killed Shovak with his own blade, to throw everyone off the scent. You and Hobart must have crossed paths in the stairwell where he told you he'd done the deed so station security could find you standing over the body, but in no ways be taken as a serious suspect."

Talyn gave me a minute shake of the head. "Not quite, Chief Superintendent. While the man who played Montague Hobart is one of ours, he's not a designated assassin. I am. I gave Shovak the killing stroke."

Her tone was so business-like, so matter of fact, that I felt a frisson run down my spine. I knew the Fleet had its dirty tricks people, but the woman sitting in front of me was something else altogether.

A soft chuckle filled the silence that followed her admission of guilt. "Don't worry. I'm not sizing you up as my next victim. We only kill when necessary and eliminating Shovak was essential. He was a top-level *Tai Zolh* officer with an extensive list of assassinations to his credit. Thopok is more of the same. The *Kho'sahra* will miss Shovak, but the rest of the galaxy won't. I'm speaking the naked truth, so you understand the gravity of our covert cold war, and why it was necessary to manipulate the PCB into supporting our scheme."

"Montague Hobart did a fine job steering me toward the conclusions you wanted. What if I hadn't looked for a Shrehari interpreter?"

She made a dismissive hand gesture. "He'd have found another way to approach you and make himself useful."

"I guess he's the one who triggered the lift sabotage, so we would find evidence of *Sécurité Spéciale* involvement, leading us to look more closely at the ComCorp delegation."

"That too. Monty had full access to the remote node I prepared and is almost as good at compromising AIs as I am. It's something Naval Intelligence teaches those of us with the right aptitude. You were never in real danger, but we had to plant the idea Shovak's death was more than just a simple murder."

Surprisingly, Talyn's revelations didn't trigger another outburst of resentment on my part. I felt nothing more than resignation at being forced to accept my role in the Navy's latest black op.

Though Arno and I would know our reputation for incorruptibility had been tarnished, no one else would see the blemish on our shining armor. And now that Talyn had confronted me with the facts, it was hard to dispute the necessity of her actions.

Besides, we've been known to let more than one corrupt cop or politico slip into anonymous retirement in the past, because a prosecution would not have served the interests of the legal system, justice be damned.

"And his contacting Gerri was another push in the right direction."

"Yes. We knew you'd eventually zero in on Hobart, Trogo, and Kazan, and use Major Pullar's surveillance system to gather video evidence of our activities. So Monty and I seeded the record with enough clues to orient you and your inspector."

"You're that good at predicting someone else's moves? I find it hard to believe."

I didn't bother hiding my incredulity. Something about her unassailable self-confidence was tiresome.

"Within general parameters, yes. We studied your record beforehand, Chief Superintendent, to get a sense of your methods and way of thinking. Then we planned several contingencies, enough to cover most possibilities and still steer your investigation in the direction we wanted. However, and this isn't idle flattery by any means, we didn't expect you to figure things out quite so quickly, hence Monty's abrupt departure. And before you ask, he's not hiding aboard *Harpy*. Have Major Pullar scan her for life signs if you like."

"I know he's not here, or anywhere else on Aquilonia. But please pass on my deepest appreciation for his help when you see him again."

"Oh?" She tilted her head to one side in question. "Why?"

"You can ask Monty, or whatever his real name is when you see him."

"I will pass it on. And with that, I've told you everything I can about the operation. It's important you understand not only what but why." A soft chime echoed through the small starship's bridge. "*Harpy*'s AI is telling me we're ready to lift."

"Your AI doesn't speak?"

Talyn groaned with resigned amusement. "It does, but it's forbidden to do so in my presence. A while back, my regular partner and I used this ship on a mission. Before our departure, he had the engineers who refurbished her set the AI to speak in my voice, then locked out any attempt at changing it."

"Really? A black ops spook with a juvenile sense of humor?"

"He's one in a billion, Chief Superintendent. His idea of fun can be rather unsophisticated, but I wouldn't change him for anything."

I caught a hint of wistfulness in her voice and wondered how someone able to murder a sentient being in such cold blood and with so much premeditation could also show normal human emotions. But since I would find no easy answers to that question, I climbed to my feet.

"Since you don't intend to kidnap or otherwise silence me, I'll leave you to vanish while I wrap up the last few loose ends of *your* spy games, Commander."

"Believe me, Chief Superintendent, the Navy appreciates your part in this. A letter of commendation will probably land on DCC Hammett's desk in the next few weeks, signed by the Chief of Naval Intelligence."

"For the good it'll do my bruised conscience. But please take this message back to your superiors. Never manipulate the PCB into doing your dirty work again. The next time we will blow the lid off your operation, no matter what it is."

"*Fiat justitia, et pereat mundus*? Let justice be done, though the world perish? A noble, if self-destructive sentiment. I don't doubt you might feel the impulse to do so, but I'm also sure you won't. You've seen too much of the darkness that lurks even in the most hallowed places to believe justice can ever be an absolute."

Though I didn't want to admit it, even to myself, she was right. Big words and noble sentiments meant little when reality bit you in the ass with a vengeance. I swallowed an exasperated retort.

"Listen, Commander, if the Navy wants our help – ask. We can keep our mouths shut. Heck, we can even suggest better ways of doing things. My folks and I might not be intelligence agents, but we're damned good cops, something you lot aren't. If we're to be on the same side when this covert cold war heats up, then we should act like it. You should act like it."

"Duly noted. I will pass your message verbatim to my commanding officer, and for the record, I agree with you. If my regular sidekick had been part of this mission, I'm sure he would have disregarded orders and talked to you on the sly. He's not what you would call a conventional operative, wedded to the unwritten rules of intelligence operations. He's more of a practical man who clings to a notion of honor that seems almost anachronistic in this age of deceit."

"Then perhaps you should learn from him."

She surprised me with a delighted laugh. "People who don't enjoy my partner's style have accused me of becoming too much like him, so I guess it's a work in progress. Once again, thank you, Chief Superintendent. I expect our paths will cross again someday. And when that happens, I promise I will do my utmost to make sure we won't use the Constabulary as a patsy but bring you in as a full-fledged partner."

— Fifty-Two —

I watched *Harpy* lift from behind a thick porthole at the base of the docking arm, not so much to make sure Talyn actually left Aquilonia, but as a way to procrastinate.

Tying up loose ends was a job I usually left to my juniors, but this time, I couldn't avoid doing most of it. After Talyn's departure, I invited myself into Dangerous Don's office and let him know Lisbeth and he were now on our roster of people to watch.

Then, I gave Thopok a copy of my case report. Yes, my orders were to hand it to the Shrehari transport's commanding officer. But I figured it would help widen the breach between the *Tai Zolh* and Gerri's lot, as the Fleet intended, if I let Thopok see my conclusions before he left.

And apparently, it did. After meeting the Shrehari captain at the station end of a controlled-access docking arm, I waited for Thopok and company to pass through with Shovak's remains. They came escorted by Gerri, who gave me a glare so venomous it would have felled a king cobra.

"I can't begin to understand what you think you achieved," she muttered between clenched teeth as we watched the imperial officers walk away. "But there will be consequences for your part in disrupting the negotiation of a profitable trade arrangement. Blaming a man who conveniently vanished for Shovak's death instead of charging the obvious suspect in your custody gave humanity a black mark. These sentients have a highly developed sense of honor, and you've offended it by perpetrating the next best thing to a cover-up. Mark my words, you will pay."

"Possibly," I replied, pleased I could keep my tone light and without the slightest hint of concern. "But many sentients in the Protectorate will keep their freedom a little longer. That also counts for something."

I ignored the involuntary gasp that escaped her lips.

"Yes," I said, "I'm aware of what you were up to, Gerri. And since Montague Hobart, the suspect who so conveniently vanished, also has ties to ComCorp and the *Sécurité Spéciale*, I daresay we might both face tough questions. At least I'll be able to answer them with a clean conscience. You, on the other hand, seem to have lost what little scruples you possessed when you resigned from the Constabulary. Making a deal with Louis Sorne to have his henchmen rape and murder me? Really, Gerri? That's low even for you."

"You can't prove it, and any accusations you make will be treated as libelous. But understand this, Caelin — it isn't over. Not even close. You don't understand who you're fucking with."

"Considering what occurred here in the last week, I'd say neither do you. And as for proof? It will come in due course. The moment Sorne lands, he'll find himself in police custody, and then the dickering starts. I doubt he'll protect you if he can negotiate a deal. He's not the sort who sees loyalty as a virtue."

Gerri smirked at me. "Sorne won't spend more than thirty minutes in jail, honey. He has connections you can only dream of."

"We'll see. Don't make any vacation plans, in case I show up with a warrant for your arrest." Out of sheer devilment, I blew her a kiss. "Until the next time, *honey*."

I turned and walked away without a backward glance. Gerri might have been sufficiently angry to shoot me in the back, but not enough to lose her sense of proportion. No matter her many faults, she remained a survivor.

A glance at the time showed our ferry back to Valerys was leaving soon, and after watching the Shrehari ship lift from a nearby porthole, I joined Arno at the Gendarmerie station. He had spent the last hour guarding our luggage and kibitzing with Sergeant Yulich while drinking Pullar's excellent coffee.

"I was just telling my friend here that we could use a man of his talents in our information analysis section, Chief."

"Why?" I poured myself a mug. "Has Sergeant Yulich offended a large enough swath of the Gendarmerie to contemplate life as a member of the Firing Squad?"

Yulich's vigorous headshake was almost comical to behold. "No, sir. I'm happy serving Cimmeria in this manner, but I appreciate the offer."

"Our loss." Arno drained his mug. "Major Pullar asked that we drop in on him before leaving. How was Dangerous Don?"

"Shaky. It wouldn't surprise me if he's suffered the sharp edge of Gerri's tongue. She certainly unleashed it on me, or at least she tried. I told him to pack and book a cabin on the ferry. By now DCC Maras will have reached out to her contacts in the Cimmerian government with a suggestion they force the Syndicate to replace Aquilonia's management forthwith."

"Few people will weep at his departure."

"It's a given that the good major won't."

"Cleverly deduced," Pullar said as he emerged from his office. "If your investigation results in D.D. leaving, then you'll have done us a favor that transcends solving a mere murder."

"Provided his replacement is cut from a better cloth," Arno replied, climbing to his feet.

"True. But after this, maybe the Aquilonia Syndicate will take more care in choosing a chief administrator."

I held out my hand. "Major, it's been a pleasure. We couldn't have done it without you and your gendarmes. Your director general will receive a letter of appreciation signed by DCC Maras thanking the Gendarmerie for its assistance."

Pullar made a dismissive gesture. "Some of us still believe in professional courtesy. Besides, watching you and Inspector Galdi at work has been educational."

"Then perhaps the letter of appreciation will help you secure a pre-retirement posting to your hometown."

A shy smile lit up his face. "In which case, I'll owe you my thanks."

"And on that note," Arno said, "it's time to go; otherwise, the ferry will leave without us."

We made our goodbyes and reached the docks with only a few minutes to spare. For reasons best left unexplored, the ComCorp delegation had opted to take the next one. That suited me fine. Spending eighteen hours in a tin can with Wildcat Gerri wouldn't have made the trip more congenial.

Once ensconced in our first class cabins — the last courtesy of a grateful Navy — and with my jammer at full strength, I told Arno the whole sad story. As it turned out, he'd already guessed a lot of it.

"I trust you warned Talyn against trying something like that again, Chief?" He asked when I fell silent.

"In so many words. Not that it'll make a difference. Our brothers and sisters in Naval Intelligence will do whatever they consider necessary to preserve the Commonwealth."

"I suppose someone needs the freedom to fight dirty when faced with an even more contemptible enemy."

"Perhaps, but I'd be happier if they didn't involve the one organization that can still boast of being the straightest of straight arrows. Once we lose that distinction, we lose the answer to the age-old question of who will watch the watchers. And when that happens, we'll find ourselves on a slippery slope with nothing but grief at the bottom."

The idea was depressing, but I had learned to avoid dwelling on matters I couldn't influence, let alone change. An inability to let go invariably ended with an unhappy and early retirement if it didn't end with the barrel of a blaster under the chin.

"By the way, Chief, while I was waiting for you, I dug into Aquilonia's database for a tidbit that both of us missed. A small matter that's been bugging me since we first came across Talyn's alter ego."

"Oh?"

"It's related to that chap Fleming, whose novels you so enjoy."

"And what of him? You've always disdained that sort of literature."

"I may have read one or two of his stories, merely to see what the attraction was, you understand. I predict you're about to hate yourself, Chief. Do you recall the cover name he gave an organization known as Military Intelligence Six in those spy stories?"

He smiled at me expectantly while I rifled through my ever-growing fund of trivia. That smile became a rumbling chuckle when he saw the light go on in my eyes.

"Universal Exports."

Arno nodded. "Universal Exports, indeed. The company that supposedly employed Willa Trogo before her move to Aquilonia. Talyn's people must have the same taste in pre-diaspora literature as you do, Chief. And a rather perverse sense of humor. The tricky buggers left us a hint. We just didn't understand it at the time. I guess Talyn wasn't lying when she said they studied you in great detail."

"Why would they plant something that obvious, I wonder? It seems like a rather silly thing to do."

"Perhaps to help lead us down the garden path, except we didn't need it to find our own way."

"Thankfully. It's gratifying to see we can still detect unaided by our friendly neighborhood spooks. And on that note, did we hear back from Sector HQ?"

"Aye." He nodded. "Sergeant Bonta has come up with a few viable candidates for Sorne's other source within the Financial Crimes Division. We can start on them as soon as we land."

"Any news about the man himself?"

"Sorne? Yes. Maras has asked the Navy to intercept his yacht and escort it to Valerys where a squad of her detectives will be waiting to cuff him."

"Gerri thinks he'll weasel out of it."

Arno gave me a sympathetic grimace. "Perhaps. With Burrard and Loriot taking an oath of silence, it's his word against yours. I doubt forensics will find traces of your presence aboard *Ambergris* and even if they do, Sorne can claim you were there of your own free will and left unmolested."

"Thanks for managing my expectations."

"Much as I'd like to see the bastard hang alongside your ex-partner for what they did yesterday, it's better to let the financial investigation take its course. The resulting indictment will be backed by evidence Sorne can't refute so easily."

"And knowing Gerri, she'll screw up somewhere along the line and get her comeuppance." An involuntary groan escaped me. "What I wouldn't give for a simple corruption case."

"I can help you there, Chief. Along with the update on Sorne, DCC Maras' office sent us a complaint against an inspector in the Technical Services Division. According to his commanding officer, the man has a nonstandard interpretation of the inventory disposal rules, possibly fed by an uncontrollable urge to splurge on loose companions."

"It sounds delightfully banal and even a bit sordid, but after the last few days, I'll take it."

Anything to scrub away the lingering shame I felt after submitting a report that stretched the truth even if it was for the greater good.

Arno emitted a sound resembling the dying breath of a drowning wildebeest. "Our bent inspector hardly requires your high-priced intellect, Chief. I can handle him with one of the sergeants. That'll leave you free to ferret out Sorne's other mole."

"Humor me, Arno. I need to cleanse my palate with something that doesn't involve dirty politics or malevolent tycoons. Besides, it shouldn't take much time. I'll let Bonta lead the mole investigation for a while longer. It'll look good on her record when I present her name to the inspector's promotion board. She's due within the next year or so."

"You'll hear no arguments from me on that point. Very well, the bent inspector it is. But don't forget you still have a unit to run."

"Are you saying you'd like to see me drown in administrivia like every other chief superintendent in the Constabulary? Fat chance of that happening."

"The administrivia won't go away just because you ignore it, Chief."

That's how much Arno knew. Over the years, I had mastered the art of dodging useless protocols and procedures.

"Actually, it does," I replied. "You have no idea how much is so unimportant that most folks don't bother me about it more than twice before giving up."

This time, Arno laughed. "That's because no one wants to annoy the sector's Firing Squad CO to the point where they might end up in her crosshairs."

"Running the PCB detachment should come with a few compensations, so I'll take whatever my lofty status gives me, even if it's exaggerated."

"Oh no, Chief. You've earned your lofty status, and that means our next suspect won't know what hit him the moment he sees you sitting across the interview room table. It should be a pleasure to watch."

About the Author

Eric Thomson is the pen name of a retired Canadian soldier with thirty-one years of service, both in the Regular Army and the Army Reserve. He spent his Regular Army career in the Infantry and his Reserve service in the Armoured Corps.

Eric has been a voracious reader of science fiction, military fiction, and history all his life. Several years ago, he put fingers to keyboard and started writing his own military sci-fi, with a definite space opera slant, using many of his own experiences as a soldier for inspiration.

When he's not writing fiction, Eric indulges in his other passions: photography, hiking, and scuba diving, all of which he shares with his wife.

Join Eric Thomson at
http://www.thomsonfiction.ca/
Where you'll find news about upcoming books and more information about the universe in which his heroes fight for humanity's survival.

Read his blog at:
https://ericthomsonblog.wordpress.com

If you enjoyed this book, please consider leaving a review with your favorite online retailer to help others discover it.

Also by Eric Thomson

Siobhan Dunmoore

No Honor in Death (Siobhan Dunmoore Book 1)
The Path of Duty (Siobhan Dunmoore Book 2)
Like Stars in Heaven (Siobhan Dunmoore Book 3)
Victory's Bright Dawn (Siobhan Dunmoore Book 4)
Without Mercy (Siobhan Dunmoore Book 5)
When the Guns Roar (Siobhan Dunmoore Book 6)

Decker's War

Death Comes But Once (Decker's War Book 1)
Cold Comfort (Decker's War Book 2)
Fatal Blade (Decker's War Book 3)
Howling Stars (Decker's War Book 4)
Black Sword (Decker's War Book 5)
No Remorse (Decker's War Book 6)
Hard Strike (Decker's War Book 7)

Commonwealth Constabulary Casefiles

The Warrior's Knife

Ashes of Empire

Imperial Sunset (Ashes of Empire #1)
Imperial Twilight (Ashes of Empire #2)
Imperial Night (Ashes of Empire #3)

Ghost Squadron

We Dare (Ghost Squadron #1)

Made in the USA
Monee, IL
21 April 2021

66431774R00223